We Came From Away

THAT SUMMER ON "THE ROCK"

PATRICIA J. PARSONS

MOONLIGHT PRESS | TORONTO

ISBN   978-1-998358-01-4

For information or permissions:

Visit www.moonlightpresstoronto.com

Or email moonlightpressinfo@gmail.com

For my mom, Gwen, who turned 101 years old this year.

If you cannot get rid of the family skeleton, you might as well make it dance.

~ George Bernard Shaw

There is no such thing as fun for the whole family.

~ Jerry Seinfeld

RELATIVELY SPEAKING

When your mother asks, "Do you want a piece of advice?" it's a mere formality. It doesn't matter if you answer yes or no. You're going to get it anyway.
~ Erma Bombeck

Mrs. Thomas Houlihan
St. John's, Newfoundland

Dear Family (by which I refer to Maureen & Frederick and your various offspring: Erica, Phillip, Eliza, and Emma. I'm copying this to Lucy.):

As you're all aware (or at the very least, I expect you to be aware), I'll be turning the corner to 100 years old on August 1 of this year, by the grace of the Almighty. No congratulations necessary for merely having hung on this long, but by Jeezus, I did it, and you'll all come to see me. In addition to the celebration (which I know will be well planned by the only one of my descendants with a good enough head on her shoulders, dear Lucy), there'll be a family meeting. You'll all be there, minus any of the later descendants. No need for those great-grandchildren to be reminding me of my age, mind you.

Of course, as I have made abundantly clear over the years, I have been sorely disappointed by the behaviour of my family and even more disappointed about how little you all know of your home. You've turned into the worst kind of come-from-aways there is. You're Newfoundlanders who've forgotten who knit them. So, you will all fly into Deer Lake on the west coast, and you will make your way to me in St. John's as a group.

It's all arranged (and paid for — I know Frederick will be wanting to know this, skinflint that he is). You all will be taken together on a one-week tour of the island. I have a friend, who will be your tour guide. You'll meet him at the airport in Deer Lake, and then he'll show you what needs to be seen. I expect every last one of you to partake, and by God, you'll make an effort to appreciate it.

My travel agent, Angela, God bless her, has all your contact details. She will be calling each and every one of you within the week so that she can give you the details. She will report back to me.

I WILL NOT TAKE NO FOR AN ANSWER. DO YOU HEAR ME? So, mark the date.

I will see you all in St. John's on August 1. I trust you all remember where I live.

Sincerely,

Nora Houlihan

(Your mother or grandmother, as the case may be—in case you've forgotten)

PS Lucy suggested I include a map here in case you lot have forgotten where Newfoundland is.

ONE

Erica

IT HAD BEEN A LONG DAY—LONGER THAN MOST FRIDAYS. I had spent the entire day sitting in meetings listening to everyone, from the new intern to my producer, Samantha, who also happened to be my best friend, pitching story ideas. Should I choose to consider these ideas, they would form much of the content for upcoming episodes of *The Pulse*, the weekly prime-time news magazine show I anchored. When the discussion began to coalesce around the topic of women's place in the family, my eyes started to glaze over.

I'd always felt just mildly uncomfortable with the fact that "the pulse" to which the program's name referred was the pulse of women. You know, things like women's place in society, women's place in politics, and now obnoxiously, women's place in their families. In my view, women's place was wherever they wanted it to be and whatever they wanted it to be. So, when Samantha (Sam) pounced on the idea and suggested we do a series on this objectionable topic, I gagged and told everyone I'd think about it.

I was still thinking about it an hour later when the studio's shiny black Suburban, chauffeured by the dapper, white-haired Kevin, who was eighty-five if he was a day, drove me through the rainy downtown streets. As he did every day, Kevin was driving me home—one of the perks of being a television personality with her own show.

The discussion about women and families started me thinking about my own family—not my little nuclear family consisting of my husband, Andrew, and my thirteen-going-on-thirty-five-year old daughter, Madelaine—Maddie. I was thinking about my extended family and realized the main reason I didn't want to touch the topic of families was that my relationship with my extended family was fraught. Then my thoughts strayed to something I'd read more than twenty years ago, Douglas Coupland's novel, *All Families Are Psychotic*. I remember him writing, "All families are psychotic. Everybody has basically the same family — it's just reconfigured slightly differently from one to the next." And I wasn't at all sure I wanted to do a series of television stories on the madness of family life for women or anyone else for that matter.

As I watched the city streets pass by through the rivulets of raindrops as they scurried down the glass, I couldn't help but begin to wonder about the individual lives of the people hurrying along outside, umbrellas held high. Did any of those women, frantically rushing home from work, ever think about their place in the world or even their families? I figured they did not. I figured they just got on with their lives, and all of us erudite pundits be damned. I sighed again as the car pulled up in front of my house.

"Home again, home again, Ms. Flanagan," Kevin said as he did every time we pulled up in front of my house every weekday afternoon. "Need me to get the umbrella out for you?" Kevin had turned as best he could and looked at me with those eyes that begged me to say no. So, I did.

"Thanks, Kevin, but I think I can manage. I won't melt."

Kevin smiled. "Have a good weekend, Ms. Flanagan. See you bright and early on Monday." I'm sure he was relieved he didn't have to get out of the car to help me in the rain.

"You will, Kevin. And can you please call me Erica?" I'd been asking him this for six months.

"Nope. Not going to happen, Ms. Flanagan." He smiled broadly, then turned back toward the windshield as I disembarked.

As I stepped over the threshold of my house and closed the door behind me, I exhaled and then breathed in the inviting aroma of something delicious coming from the kitchen. Andrew was cooking tonight. I dropped my bulging tote bag on the floor and shook off my raincoat before hanging it in the closet, hoping he was making his famous meatloaf that I'd been promised when I left this morning. I also hoped he had a bottle of pinot noir breathing. I was so looking forward to a drink.

"Hey, Erica, honey. You home?" As Andrew's voice floated out of the kitchen, my eyes fluttered toward the pile of mail on the hall table. There, on the top, were three copies of the new book with Andrew's handsome face peering out from the cover. It was here! *Well*, I thought, *that means we're celebrating*. I smiled as I thought about something even better than a glass of pinot. We'd be popping a cork.

I picked up the book and felt a jolt of excitement for my wonderfully talented husband, who had been working on his memoir for over two years, and here it was. Andrew's career as a highly regarded television news anchor was the basis for this story—from his early beginnings as a foreign correspondent to his days in the anchor chair for the nightly national news from which he'd retired several years earlier. He'd retired early, wanting to get out while he was still at the top of his game. As much as I'd thought he'd regret leaving early, I now realized he had been right. He'd moved forward to a new phase of his life, and I could not have been prouder.

"Hey, I see you've seen the book," Andrew said as he emerged from the kitchen, wiping his hands on the silly apron that he loved to wear to tease me. It was white with a red ruffle, and the word "Wife" embroidered in red across it. I had never been much of a cook myself, although, over the past two years, I'd made great strides—and a lot of messes into the bargain. The apron was his way of teasing me about his superior culinary prowess.

"We're celebrating," he said as he enveloped me in a bear hug. "Or maybe we're drowning our sorrows."

"What?" I said, breaking away.

Andrew nodded toward the pile of mail under the books. "I take it you haven't looked at the mail yet."

I had no idea what he was talking about. In point of fact, we received very little snail mail these days, so I never expected anything remotely interesting and certainly not anything that would cause me to want to drown my sorrows. Yes, well, I've learned that we should never get too comfortable with our lives.

Andrew picked up the books, revealing an unassuming-looking envelope underneath. He lifted it and handed it to me. It was flimsy, as if it might contain a single page rather than all the material that was so often stuffed into those mailers we received from charities. The address was typewritten on a label that had been stuck onto the envelope. It was addressed to *"Mrs. Andrew Taylor (AKA Ms. Erica Flanagan)."*

I started to feel the hairs on the back of my neck prickle just a little as I forced myself to look at the return address. There was only one person in the world who insisted on calling me Mrs. Andrew Taylor. Nora Houlihan. My grandmother.

"Dear god, Andrew, what do you suppose Gran is sending me a letter for?"

"No idea, hon, but whenever any family member apart from your mother or brother contacts you, it's not usually good news—although I can't remember the last time someone in your extended family did contact you. Anyway, I suppose the silver lining is that if Nora sent it, then she isn't dead, at least."

Not much of a silver lining, I thought wickedly. I mentally swatted myself up the side of the head for even thinking that. She was, after all, my grandmother. Still, as I considered that eventuality, I realized that news of Nora's death would probably not bring too many tears to too many of her offspring, my mother in particular. It's not so much that I didn't love and appreciate my grandmother— as long as she lived in Newfoundland, and I lived in Toronto—but my mother was a different story. Toronto had never seemed far enough away for her. I suppose Mom loved her mother, but for my entire life, I'd observed that they had never seemed to get along very well. I never knew why. But why on earth would Nora be writing to me?

"Aren't you going to open it?" Andrew said. "I have wine and champagne waiting in the kitchen. And something stronger if the news warrants it. I cannot wait to hear what it says." He was smiling cheekily as he left me alone with my family correspondence. We had been married for two decades, and my darling husband was well aware of my convoluted family dynamic.

I wandered into the living room and sat down on the sofa. After staring at the envelope for a few moments, I slid a finger under the envelope's flap and tore it open. I unfolded the single sheet and shook it out flat. "Dear Family…" it began, then specifically listed who was meant by the vague term "family." I quickly scanned the five or six paragraphs, and by the time I'd reached the PS at the end, I was even more confused. It sounded like my grandmother was summoning us to her birthday—although summoning might be too tame a word. Demanding our presence, perhaps? Before I had a chance to read it again, the phone on the side table rang. I didn't need to have caller ID to know that it would be my mother, one of the few people who used our landline. And it occurred to me that she must have opened her copy of the letter.

"Have you read it yet? The letter?" Mom was breathless, as if she might be having a panic attack, and this was a woman who panicked at nothing—or almost nothing. "From your grandmother?" I could hear a sharp intake of breath.

If there was one word that no one would ever associate with my accomplished mother, it was deferential—except in dire circumstances. A missive from her mother would be one of those dire circumstances. For my entire life, there had always been only one person before whom Dr. Maureen Flanagan, Professor Emeritus of Philosophy, and widely published academic, crumbled. That person was Nora Jane Houlihan. Gran made her crazy.

"Hi, Mom. Yes, I got the letter and have only just opened it." I skimmed the letter once more. "It's about her birthday. I guess she wants us all there, but I'm not really getting the reason for the summons."

"Yes," Mom said, "she does want us there. But it's about so much more."

"Yeah, I see she expects us to take some kind of a tour of the island. I do think that's a bit odd."

"Erica, for such a smart woman, sometimes you can be positively dense. Read between the lines," Mom said.

I tried to read more into the letter than was printed on the page. Still, all I saw was what I might have expected from a woman who was turning one hundred years old and was—and had always been—an overbearing busybody whose personal mantra had never changed. *I may not always be right. But I'm never wrong.* Yes, she said that on every occasion where anyone might have questioned her and to anyone she thought might need to be reminded.

"Well," I said, trying to find a way to be diplomatic yet knowing that Mom was overly sensitive to her mother's demands—not unlike I was with her, I must point out, "I suppose going to Newfoundland to celebrate her centenary isn't the worst idea ever. Weren't you planning to go anyway?"

I could hear Mom sighing on the other end of the telephone. "Oh, Erica. It's not a clear-cut yes or no proposition. You never spent a lot of time with your grandmother when you were growing up. You only had to endure summer vacations and Christmases. If you had a mother like Nora, you'd better understand my position."

I kept my mouth shut. Mom wasn't *exactly* like her mother, but as the saying goes, the apple doesn't fall far from the tree.

"Well, Erica, were *you* planning to go?" Mom said. "Hadn't you mentioned something about taking Maddie for a visit?"

She had me there. Andrew and I had talked about the possibility of making it a family summer vacation. Maddie had mentioned she'd like to visit her great-grandmother because she hadn't seen her since our visit to Newfoundland about five years earlier. Before that time, Gran—Nora—used to come to Toronto every Christmas, so Maddie saw her every year at least. Those annual pilgrimages Nora made to the Big Smoke (or that den of iniquity as she liked to call Toronto) changed ten years earlier, the year Nora turned ninety, which was part of the reason we'd felt obliged to take Maddie to "The Rock" to see her great-grandmother.

Although so much time had passed, I was still a bit rankled by that last Christmas visit, where the great Nora Houlihan got herself into a tiff with Mom over the settings on Mom's thermostats that December. Gran thought Mom kept her house too cold and that her thermostat readings were inaccurate in any case. Mom attempted to change them all, but Gran found one she had missed. To hear Mom tell it (I wasn't there, so this is hearsay), she lost her shit, after which Gran vowed never to return.

Given that Gran had spent every single Christmas for all the years that she came to Toronto complaining about the city (too big, too crowded, too many Christmas lights, not enough fish on the menus, too many people speaking foreign languages, too many restaurant servers whose accents she couldn't understand, and the list went on *ad nauseum*), this should not have come as a surprise. To tell you the truth, no one except Maddie was disappointed that Nora Houlihan had ever after spent Christmas at home in Newfoundland. Of course, I suppose that since Nora turned ninety that year, and her complaints about flying, in general, were legion, she probably planned to cease her festive season visits anyway. She was like that.

I told Mom that I had considered the possibility of a trip east since it was such a momentous birthday.

"Erica, did you actually read this letter? This letter is not an invitation. This letter is a demand, not unlike those demands made by, oh, let's see, Don Corleone in *The Godfather*."

Dear god, Mom was invoking Mafia-esque imagery to describe her own mother. Things were getting dire. As I reviewed the letter once more, I saw she had a point.

"And do you see her header? Mrs. Thomas Houlihan—as if Father hasn't been dead for decades."

I ignored this last statement since I had never understood Mom's relationship with either her mother, now about to turn one hundred or her father, who had died when I was about thirteen. I looked at the letter again and could see that she might not be the only one with a problem here.

"Dear god, Mom," I said, seeing the salutation once again. "Eliza is on that list. I don't know if I can go if she's going to be there." There are people in this world I find tedious, and then there are those who are so insufferable that just being around them is enough to make me lose the will to live. Eliza Houlihan Cohen, my cousin, was one of them. She and I had barely exchanged a word since a falling out we'd had during that summer vacation the year before Grandad died. Yet, I'd heard chapter and verse about her perfect life.

"As annoying as Eliza is, she's not nearly as disagreeable as your grandmother can be when she wants to, and especially when she doesn't get her own way."

That wasn't my experience, but I wasn't going to argue the point with Mom. "And what's this about copying Lucy?" Lucy was Eliza's youngest sister, another cousin. "Why is she being copied? Why isn't this missive for Lucy, too?"

"Lucy is the least of my concerns, Erica, but if you kept in better contact with your extended family," (was this the pot calling the kettle black?), "you'd remember that Lucy moved back to St. John's and sees her grandmother regularly, or so I'm told by Frederick." Fred was Mom's only sibling, her younger brother. "I don't suppose your grandmother thinks Lucy needs any reprogramming regarding her roots. In any case, Lucy probably had a hand in writing the letter."

I seemed to remember Mom mentioning this situation a Christmas or two ago. She was right about me not keeping in close contact with my extended family. I found my little nuclear family, plus Mom and my brother Phillip, who had escaped his roots by settling in Montreal, to be enough relatives to keep tabs on. So, the news about Lucy's move from her home in Halifax to Newfoundland hadn't made much of an impression on me.

"Anyway, Mom," I said, getting back to the issue at hand, "what do you suppose this tour is all about?" I shivered as I recalled, once again, the line about psychotic families.

"I suspect it's your grandmother's way of showing all of us what we're missing by not living in god's country, as she likes to say. Note that she thinks we're all the worst kind of CFAs."

"So, are we going?"

"Do we have a choice?"

~

The following day, when my cell phone rang as I sat going over a document Sam had slipped me on the way out the studio door the day before, I wasn't surprised at the caller ID this time, either. I had known it was only a matter of time before the next country was heard from.

"Hello, Phillip," I said. "I was wondering how long it would take you to call. I take it you've finally read your mail unless it takes longer for a letter to get from Newfoundland to Montreal than to Toronto."

"Darling, sister, how I've missed your slight sarcasm since you started on that new show. What happened to the bitch everyone loved to hate?" My dear brother was, of course, referring to my previous employment, from which I'd been forced to take a sabbatical for what the studio brass referred to as an "unacceptable on-air utterance." Phillip had called me after that infamous on-air debacle, laughing his head off. I distinctly remembered his words at the time. "Ah, Erica, your bitch wings have been clipped." How right he was.

"How's Marcus?" I said, changing the subject.

Phillip and Marcus had been together since the day they met in a first-year English class at McGill University in Montreal. Phillip had chosen McGill to study fine arts, and Marcus had fled his homophobic Texan family the moment he had the chance. Marcus had worked his way through undergrad and his MBA and now owned half of Montreal, to hear him tell it. His holdings included the ancient building in *Vieux-Montréal*—old Montreal—that housed Phillip's ground-floor art gallery and their two-story apartment above. It was to die for with its exposed stone walls, massively high ceilings and wide-plank floors that gleamed under the cleverly placed light fixtures. They had now been together for over thirty years, having both recently celebrated their fiftieth birthdays.

"Marcus is as vain and self-centred as he has ever been, and I love him more than ever," Phillip said, as he always did. "But I didn't call to talk about Marcus. You know why I called. I presume you've already talked to Mom. What's her take on this strange request?"

"Her take on it is that it's not a request. She says it's a dictum."

"Oh, no, Erica. No. I'm not going to spend my summer vacation submitting to a demand from a woman who, when informed that her grandson is gay, said she takes a dim view of these things."

I rolled my eyes. It had been years now since Irish Catholic Nora Houlihan had the bad manners to diss her grandson. Phillip still hadn't completely gotten over it, and I can't say that I blamed him. Gran was unrepentant about just about everything she ever said. She's never wrong, remember?

"She's turning a hundred, Phillip," I said. "We should celebrate this milestone with our own flesh and blood." Now, who was I trying to convince? I could feel my own words pointed squarely at myself.

"Don't give me that line, Erica. How often has Gran told you your hair is the wrong colour and you could afford to lose a few pounds?"

He had a point, but we were all grown-ups now. Why was I being so accommodating about this idea of going to Newfoundland this summer? Just yesterday, I had been so sure I would do everything in my power to avoid it—at least I would avoid the proposed cross-island trip if not the actual birthday itself. However, I could feel the tiny pricking of my journalistic curiosity kicking in. For an as yet unclear reason, Gran wanted us to see the island of Newfoundland. Gran talked about a family meeting—mysterious indeed. I wondered what I was missing.

Phillip and I talked about the situation for a few more minutes, and in the end, he said he'd think about it.

"Don't think too long," I said. "It seems that Gran's travel agent will be calling at any moment. Why don't we just do it and consider this an adventure like we used to have when we were kids on summer holiday?"

"An adventure, eh? *Si tu le dis,*" he said.

"Yes, I do say so." I laughed. It was going to be an interesting summer.

~

The following week was so busy I hardly had a chance to give my family situation another thought. Sam and I usually had a late lunch on Fridays after she told the crew that it was a wrap for the week, letting everyone off early if it had been a good one. The week before, we'd had to cancel it since we all had to work late. We often grabbed a quick bite at a diner across the street from the studio, but since we'd missed our lunch the week before, we decided to splurge and go to a restaurant called Jump, a hotspot in the Financial District. We always loved to eyeball all the suits from the vantage point of our more artistic pursuit—media.

"So, tell me more about this summer trip," Sam said, sipping her wine as we waited for our Bay Street Poke Bowls.

I had told Sam about Gran's missive and that I'd decided to play along despite my misgivings. "I suppose one of the biggest turn-offs for me about the whole thing is that my cousin Eliza will probably be there."

"You never mentioned any Eliza. What's wrong with her?"

I rolled my eyes. "You have to meet this woman to believe her. You'd think she owned the world."

"Sounds like your grandmother."

I laughed. "I suppose Eliza does have some of Gran's characteristics, but I'd avoid telling her that. It's just that she's let her success go to her head." I sipped my wine. "You might have heard of her. She's Eliza Cohen, the cookbook author from New York."

"Eliza Cohen is your cousin? Why did you never say anything about it? We must have her on the show!"

I think I might have growled. "Your reaction is precisely why I never told you. Eliza is perhaps the most insufferable person I've ever met. Ever since she moved to New York, became an American citizen, married her rich Jewish husband and converted, she has this huge chip on her shoulder. Anyway, I've disliked her ever since we were kids when our obligatory summer visits to see Gran in Newfoundland overlapped."

"Where did her rich husband come by his richness?" Sam said.

"His family owns Bluestone Pharma, that obnoxiously big generic drug company."

"Wow, Ricky, aren't they the ones who were accused of price fixing a few years back?" Sam was one of the few people who was allowed to call me Ricky. "And I seem to remember a more recent incident involving a whistleblower."

"That and a few other ethically questionable things over the years. Yeah. That's Jake's family business."

"Well, Ricky," she said, sitting back and peering closely at me, "it sounds like you're going to have a fascinating summer vacation, my friend."

Fascinating wasn't precisely the word I'd choose, but I was willing to go with it—for the moment.

TWO

Eliza

THINGS WERE NOT GOING WELL. I madly tapped away at the keyboard, hoping the right words would magically appear on the screen when what I really wanted to do was smash the screen and have a big drink of scotch. My neck was hurting, my eyes were crossing, and I was distracted by the sound of rain pounding on the window behind me. I hated to be distracted or otherwise disturbed when I was on a deadline. I turned toward the window where the April rain drummed unrelentingly against the glass like an insistent percussion orchestra, persistent and irritating. I reached for my earphones.

"Knock, knock."

I put the earphones back on my desk and slid my reading glasses down my nose where they perched precariously, the glittery chain that I kept them on dangling on either side of my neck. I then looked up to see who was interrupting me when I'd explicitly told everyone I was not to be interrupted for a full three hours. It was Mary-Lou, my assistant—or PA, as she liked to call herself.

"What the hell is it?" I said. "Can't you see I'm trying to work?"

"I'm sorry to disturb you, Eliza, and I know you asked me not to, but I have a woman on the telephone who says you will be expecting her call. I told her she should call back, but she said she was under strict instructions to speak with you today. She is very insistent and will not take no for an answer." Whenever I was irritated—as I was at that moment—Mary-Lou's habit of dropping her "Rs" and pronouncing call, "caul," made the hairs on the back of my neck stand on end like they did when I heard chalk grating across a chalkboard. It was the same sound my mother-in-law made. Why couldn't anyone from Brooklyn say "call" like the rest of the English-speaking world?

I slid my readers back up and peered at my giant desk calendar, where I made notes about things like phone appointments. Yes, I had a digital calendar, but this one was always at hand, and frankly, I preferred it.

"I see nothing about any expected phone call. Find out who this person is, and I'll decide if I'm prepared to take the time to talk to her." The very thought of someone calling me and telling me she would not take no for an answer was almost enough for me to refuse to speak to her entirely. I got a lot of odd calls from people who thought that the person who wrote the cookbook they're using in their kitchens would be a friend. I most assuredly was no one's friend.

Mary-Lou didn't budge. She and I had been working together for almost twenty years, ever since the success of my first cookbook. After that, I'd needed an assistant as my cooking empire grew with more cookbooks, a line of cookware and dishes and more invitations to share my vast food knowledge than I could handle. Mary-Lou even did some recipe testing for me, a situation that was clear by the pounds she'd gained since our first days together. Whenever I offered her the rest of this chocolate cake or that pan of lasagna to take home with her, she never refused. What puzzled me now was that she knew me well enough to know that if I wasn't prepared to talk to someone, then she should just handle it herself. This time, she did not.

"Mary-Lou, what the hell is it? Why can't you just deal with it as usual?"

Mary-Lou, who was the only person who worked for me who wasn't frightened of me (I'd always considered this to be one of my best managerial skills—to be able to evoke fear in my employees), stood in the doorway, her arms crossed, tapping a foot. "This person says her name is Angela, and she is calling on behalf of Nora

Houlihan. She says it is with regard to the letter you received last week."

"Letter? What damn letter? I didn't get any letter, and who is…" I trailed off as it hit me. Nora Houlihan was my grandmother. I hadn't seen her in what? However long it had been, it was probably not long enough. My first thought was to wonder if she could possibly still be alive. I should know if my grandmother is alive or not, you say? Well, sue me. She was a cranky old woman, as I recalled. Then I thought for a moment and remembered something my father had said when he called me to wish me a Happy Hanukkah in December (god bless his Irish Catholic soul). It was something about Gran's age. Oh, yes, she was still alive and turning one hundred years old this summer. Can anyone actually be that old?

"Mary-Lou, where is this letter, and who is this Angela person?" I had no recollection of any Angela in our family. I had two sisters—Lucy and Emma—and a cousin, Phillip. And the less said about his bitch of a sister, my cousin Erica, the better. But there was no Angela.

Mary-Lou was still standing there with her arms folded. "First, I put all your mail from last week where I always put it." She pointed over my shoulder. "It's probably in that pile on the credenza behind you—the pile you do not seem to have touched yet. Second, Angela—who, by the way, is still on hold—says she's a travel agent."

This situation was getting more peculiar by the moment, and none of this nonsense was helping me to reach that deadline my agent had told my publisher I'd meet.

I pushed my chair back from the desk and spun it around. The pile on the credenza under the window was daunting, as usual. I got a lot of fan mail, and these foodies didn't seem to have grasped the concept of email yet. I looked back at Mary-Lou. "A little help, please."

Mary-Lou trundled over and quickly rifled through the pile.

"What are we looking for?" I said.

"A return address, Eliza. You remember those little lines of print in the upper left-hand corner of envelopes? A return address will tell us who sent it." She lifted a plain envelope triumphantly. "Bingo!"

Mary-Lou passed the envelope to me after peering at the return address herself. "Weren't you a Houlihan before you were a Cohen?" she said.

"You know perfectly well I was," I said, grabbing the envelope from her fingers. "I left that name behind when I left my Canadian roots behind." Even saying the word "Canadian" made me wince a little. I'd now been an American—specifically, a New Yorker—for so many years that I had even forgotten I still had a Canadian passport. Dual citizenship, they called it, although it did me little good. I visited my father once a year. Facetime was as good as a visit in between times.

Mary-Lou was still standing there as I stared at the envelope. I could feel her leaning in. "You can go now, Mary-Lou," I said finally.

She shrugged and turned. "What should I tell this Angela person?"

I had no idea what to say to this Angela person yet. "Tell her to call back in an hour." I wasn't sure why I even said that, but there was something about receiving an unexpected letter from an extended family member I thought should have died by now that put me off my usual decisiveness. Mary-Lou finally left me alone in the office.

I held the envelope gingerly in my hand as if it might burn me if I held it too securely. The air suddenly felt heavy, like a weighted blanket settling on my shoulders. I stared at the letter that was addressed—oddly, if you must know—to "Mrs. Jacob Cohen (aka Ms. Eliza Houlihan Cohen)." My grandmother knew perfectly well that I never used the name "Mrs. Jacob Cohen," but that was only one thing we'd argued about on the occasions when I was visiting my father, and he insisted we call her. I hadn't seen her in the flesh more than two or three times in two decades and not at all in the past five years.

My heart began pounding in my chest—an unwelcome sign of the free-floating anxiety to which I'd become prone in recent years. Despite the unsettling feeling of apprehension, I also felt unusually intense curiosity. Why would my grandmother be sending me a letter out of the blue?

I traced my fingers over the envelope, still hesitating to open it. Memories of past conflicts floated through my mind from those summers when my father and mother had insisted that we should spend our precious holiday time in Newfoundland with his parents and then just Gran after Grandad died. *Damn*, I thought, *why is it like time has stood still, and I'm still that annoyed child?* I was always annoyed about one thing or another, an affliction I'd been working on for years with my therapist. Perhaps I needed a new one. I'd always found Calista—Dr. Calista Geller, the therapist recommended by my sister-in-law, Allegra, whose neuroses ought to have made her an expert at finding therapists—a tad underwhelming. I took a deep breath to steady my nerves, wishing my office was like the offices people had on television—wishing it had a bar so I could pour myself a stiff glass of scotch. I could almost feel the weight of the letter pressing into me.

I slowly and carefully tore open the envelope. Unfolding the letter, I began to read what appeared to be carefully penned words. I wondered if Gran had actually written it herself, but by the time I got to the end of the letter, it was clear that my insufferable sister, Lucy, had probably done the honours. I read it again, not entirely understanding what Nora was saying. It sounded like a demand to attend some sort of family reunion, two words that stabbed fear more deeply into my heart than anything else I could think of at that moment.

I was still sitting, staring at the page in front of me on my desk, when Mary-Lou returned.

"Knock, knock, Eliza. She's on the line again."

"What? Who's on the line?" I must have been in an altered state of consciousness, a situation not unexpected when the Houlihan clan was involved.

"Angela? The travel agent? You told me to ask her to call back in an hour. Well, she's on the line."

"Has it been an hour?" I was momentarily dazed and confused, a state that I disliked intensely. I shook my head as if I could loosen the cobwebs and looked down at the light blinking on my phone. "Okay, Mary-Lou. I'll look after it." I looked at my watch. "You might as well go home."

Mary-Lou beamed. It was not often her slave driver of a boss suggested she knock off fifteen minutes early. I picked up the phone. "Eliza Cohen," I said.

"Mrs. Cohen," the voice said, "it's a pleasure. I have two of your cookbooks and love them to bits. But that's not why I'm calling, as you know." Her light, almost Irish lilt that was the townie accent among people I'd known in my father's hometown brought back a flood of memories of hilly streets, fog over the harbour and the smell of the ocean.

"I'm not entirely sure that I do know why you're calling," I said.

"Well, dear, I'll just bring you up to speed," Angela said. She then began what sounded like a script, telling me that Nora, my grandmother, had bought airline tickets for her two children and their children and had arranged a seven-day tour of the island of Newfoundland, starting on the west coast and ending on the east coast in the city of St. John's. "The great culmination," Angela said, "will be the party to celebrate one hundred years of a great woman."

I winced at that. I would never have thought of Nora as a great woman, but then, I hadn't known her in recent years. Perhaps she'd changed.

"Well, I don't think I'll be able to attend," I said. I was planning to put an end to this as soon as possible. "No, I'm certain I have a commitment at that time."

"Oh, my love, I don't think you understand," Angela said. "I don't believe there is a choice in the matter here. Your gran says I'm not to take no for an answer and that you'd all be there as directed."

As directed? *No one directs Eliza Cohen*, I thought.

"Eliza?" The voice came from outside my office, down the hall. "You still in your office?"

It was Jake, my husband. My offices were on the main floor of our Upper West Side Manhattan brownstone, just down the hall from our spacious, custom-fitted kitchen, where I did much of my recipe testing for my cookbooks.

Jake appeared in the doorway, still wearing his suit jacket, his tie loosened, holding a piece of the cake he obviously found on the kitchen counter from an experiment earlier in the day. I bit my tongue to keep from telling him that he might want to step away from the cake if he wanted to lose a bit of that middle that hung over his very expensive alligator belt. However, I was still holding the telephone receiver with Angela still on the line, so I thought better of it. I waved it at him so he could see I was busy. He shrugged and left the doorway.

"Sorry for the interruption, Angela, is it? You were saying?"

"I was saying that your gran says you'll all be there. I'm just calling to check the email address so I can send along your airline ticket and to remind you that it's just for you — no husbands, partners, spouses, or other assorted hangers-on to quote your grandmother." Angela laughed and then recited the email address she had for me. I must have grunted something that sounded to Angela to be an acknowledgement of both the edict and the accuracy of the email address because seconds later, my email pinged. She'd sent it. I was still a bit stunned by it all.

"I've sent it on to you," Angela said. "Can you just check that it has all the right information? You coming from the US and all, it needs to be perfect."

I clicked on the email, and it opened. There in front of me was a ticket on an Air Canada flight from New York to Halifax, Nova Scotia, with a six-hour stopover and then a connection to Deer Lake,

Newfoundland. The ends of the earth. I felt dizzy. Deer Lake? Dear god, it was worse than I thought. Not even St. John's. My eyes scanned the document.

"This is unacceptable," I said as the absurdity of the situation began to come into focus. I was shaking my head, although I was not sure what good that was doing since she couldn't see me.

"What's unacceptable about it? Your grandmother's paying for everything."

I smirked. *As if money is the problem*, I thought.

"No, Angela. Money is not the problem. There are several problems, and none of them have anything to do with money. First, it's an economy-class ticket. I haven't flown economy for two decades, and I don't plan to start now. That is definitely unacceptable, impossible, objectionable. Choose one. And second, I'm not spending six hours sitting alone in the Halifax airport for anyone."

"Oh, Mrs. Cohen, you are such a card," Angela said. Was she laughing? "Haven't flown economy in decades. That's a good one. No, Nora specifically told me to tell you that she thought it would do you good to plant yourself with the rest of the masses. Your gran does know her grandchildren well." What on earth was she talking about? Gran didn't know me at all. Angela continued droning on in my ear. "And as for the six-hour layover alone, well, you'll not be alone. Your father and your sister Emma will be joining you. Isn't that just wonderful how it all worked out? We've put them on the same flight as you to Deer Lake. And," she stopped for a moment as if checking on something, "your grandmother has asked me to be sure you all could sit together on the way to Deer Lake. I have him on the aisle and Emma in the middle seat right next to you at the window. You'll have a lovely view of the scenery as you land on the west coast. Nora says you've never been there. It's just grand, you know. She said you and your dad and your sister would love to get a chance to catch up."

It just got worse. Spending time in an airport departure lounge with my father and younger sister could only be made worse by then being imprisoned beside them in a window seat in economy for the better part of two hours. Then there was the "tour." I had no idea what that was all about. Before I could get to any more of my objections, Angela told me it was late there in Newfoundland, and she would be going. Then she hung up, leaving me to stare at a computer screen as if I were staring into my future. It wasn't pretty.

When I told Jake about the letter later at dinner (brisket with all the trimmings that his mother, Esther, the family matriarch, had sent her driver Kyle over with earlier in the day), his response was, "Family is family. You should go." Then he turned his attention back to the noodle kugel, which he always inhaled.

~

My father and I had always had a complicated relationship. I had a complicated relationship with everyone in my family, for that matter. The oldest of three girls, I had always felt the weight of being the eldest sister. From my earliest years, I always felt my parents' expectations fell most heavily on me. They relied on me to help out with Lucy, who was three years younger than I am, and Emma, who was eight years my junior. Then there were their expectations about how I should do in school and everything else. I always had to be the best. The only good thing in all those expectations was that I was smarter and more ambitious than either of my sisters, so I was almost always able to achieve what my parents required of me. But that accomplishment came at the expense of my relationship with my sisters, especially Lucy.

Over the years, throughout our childhoods and into our teenage years, I could feel a growing resentment toward them. I was always expected to succeed, and when I did, my parents acted as if it were simply what was expected of me. When Emma or Lucy succeeded even at half measures, they were praised and rewarded.

I remember asking my mother about this once, angrily, it has to be said. My mother was a high-strung woman who jumped at the slightest provocation. I was sixteen years old and had just watched both her and my father praise Lucy for getting a "B" on her algebra test when they would accept nothing less than an "A" from me. All she said to me was, "Eliza Houlihan, you know perfectly well that Lucy struggles with her schoolwork. We only expect that each of our daughters lives up to the gifts that the good lord has bestowed on them. You should be grateful for your gifts."

I happened to know that by the time Lucy was thirteen, it was clear her particular gifts were not of the academic variety. Unbeknownst to my parents, she spent most of her time sneaking around school with any boy who looked kindly in her direction. I also knew that Lucy sneaked lipstick into her school bag and put it on at school. I knew this because although she was three years younger than I was, we were in the same school—a Catholic high school—when I was a senior. I wondered what my mother would have thought of that.

My mother was a pious woman, but even her steadfast devotion to the Catholic church (just imagine her horror when her eldest daughter told her she was converting to Judaism) did nothing to prevent the breast cancer that ate away at her until she died at the age of seventy, leaving my father to fend for himself for these past five years. I had thought my mother's death would have softened my father (and I had secretly hoped he might meet someone new), but he seemed to have hardened. He had only recently retired after over forty-five years of medical practice—he was a well-loved family physician—and every time we spoke, he seemed more and more introverted. Since I lived so far away, I usually asked him if he'd seen Emma lately.

Emma, my youngest sister, lived closest to Dad. He was in the city of Halifax, almost due north of where I lived in New York, and Emma, an artist if you can believe that my parents were happy with that decision, lived in a small coastal village called Chester, Nova Scotia, less than an hour's drive from Dad's house. I guess she made the trek into the city once or twice a month, so there was that. Now, it seemed we would all be required to spend ten or so days in forced conviviality.

The following morning, I was considering these family dynamics when I recalled reading *Anna Karenina* many years ago. I hated the book, but the first line was seared into my brain. "Happy families are all alike; every unhappy family is unhappy in its own way." It was a motto that should have been stamped on our family crest. As I meditated on this, my cell phone rang. It was, unsurprisingly, given the letter from Nora, my father.

"Hello, Dad," I said. "How are you?"

"Fine, fine, Eliza. Or, at least, I was until I read the letter I received from your grandmother last week. I presume you have read yours?" Before I could say anything, he continued. "I do not know quite what to make of it. I did tentatively plan to visit Mother around her significant birthday, but forcing all of us to participate in what I can only assume will be one of her stunts is a bit beyond the pale. Don't you agree?" I did agree, but he wouldn't let me speak. "Of course, I will be going, but I know you're busy." Did I detect a bit of whining coming on? My father had a habit of avoiding issues straight on and weaselling around situations until someone else moved the conversation in the right direction. I think this was one of the reasons we had such a complicated relationship. I had always been too direct, and he had always been too convoluted in his approach to his daughters—me in particular. I think he was a bit frightened of me.

"Of course I'm busy, Dad," I said. "But Jake thinks I should go. Family is family is his motto." It was a motto that drove me increasingly insane as he constantly deferred to his parents, particularly his mother. Whatever she wanted was what he wanted, regardless of what I wanted. I was in last place.

"Eliza, that would be wonderful, just wonderful. It's been too long since my girls were all together."

Was that wistfulness I heard in his voice? I suppose it was since he used to include Mom in "my girls." In any case, I'd never really thought Dad cared much about having "his girls" all together. When Mom died, all I remember him saying was that we girls sent her to an early grave. I didn't doubt that he blamed us for her breast cancer. After all, we were the ones who drove her to drink, or so he said more than once. And didn't drinking contribute to breast cancer? Ergo, we caused Mom to die early of breast cancer. Did I mention I never saw my mother without a glass of something in her hand? Anyway, I guess that was water under the bridge.

"And she's paying for it all, you know," he said finally.

What was it about the Houlihan's who seemed to think that if they didn't have to pay for something, it was a good thing? It wasn't that my father, the retired doctor, couldn't afford to travel. He certainly could unless he had some half-baked idea that he should leave his grandchildren an inheritance. Isabel—Izzy—my daughter, certainly wouldn't need it, and Lucy's brats would never appreciate it. My father had never been what you'd call generous with his money or his affection, although we'd never wanted for anything.

I suddenly felt cornered by my father, who seemed to think it would be a good idea and my husband, who believed that family was family. Every time I thought about Jake and how he was encouraging me to go away, the more I remembered his secretary arriving at our door on that Saturday in February with a birthday gift for him. What was that all about?

THREE

Erica

OUR SEASON ON *THE PULSE* WAS WINDING DOWN. We had only two more episodes before our summer hiatus, but we'd already been considering topics for the new season. Sam had pitched the idea of a series on modern families. And thinking of family just made me cringe at the thought of all the emails I'd received from Angela since the day when Mom and I discussed my grandmother's upcoming one-hundredth birthday.

First, there were the airline tickets. Those arrived via email the same day I spoke with Angela on the phone. I sighed, thinking how circuitous it all was. Evidently, on instructions from Gran, Angela had booked the tickets in such a way that we had to make a connection in Montreal despite the fact that we could have easily taken a non-stop flight. Gran had made this decision so that Phillip could join us. Of course, it would have been much more pleasant to fly non-stop from Toronto, and I happened to know Phillip preferred to fly alone, but it seemed that Nora wanted to make this something of a trial for her children and grandchildren. And Mom seemed especially irritated by the whole thing.

She hadn't been herself since she received the letter. Since then, she called me almost daily, which was something she had never done. I usually spoke with her when I called her once a week. Her calls often rambled on about the upcoming trip—or tribulation, as she liked to say. She wondered what the accommodation would be like, what she should wear at every juncture, what we would eat, how much we should or should not drink, why Nora was planning a "family meeting." It was frankly exhausting. On one particularly fraught day, Mom even asked me if I thought Armageddon might be upon us. I think I rolled my eyes at that, but a part of me thought she might be on to something.

After the airline tickets arrived, we had to wade through the rest of the emails. They gave us chapter and verse on where we should assemble when we arrived at the airport (were we all arriving at the same time?), who we should be looking for (wasn't the guide going to be holding a sign?), what the travel itinerary would look like for the touring week (without, I might add, any hint about accommodation) and oddly, how large (or small) our luggage should be. This last one made me wonder what kind of vehicle we would be in for the so-called tour.

The luggage requirements were as follows: one small carry-on suitcase and one smaller handbag. I didn't think that boded well for luxurious transportation. This thought almost made me giggle when I thought about Eliza, who I knew would expect only the very best. Then there was the email with wardrobe suggestions. When we received that one, I immediately called my mother so that she could find guidance for at least one of her many questions. She just said, "If my mother thinks this is what I should wear, then I have to move in the opposite direction." Oh, this was going to be fun.

Finally, summer was upon us. School was out, and Maddie was scheduled for dance camp and photography camp while I was away. Andrew was working on a new book. This one was on the history of journalism in Canada. In spite of my background as a journalist (oh, yes, I had an actual degree in journalism and a decade of experience as a front-line correspondent), I found the topic dry. He, on the other hand, found it fascinating, and from time to time, as we sat with a drink in hand in the evening, he regaled me with fascinating (not) tales from the Canadian media landscape. Kill me now or pour me or another drink was all I could think. I loved my husband to bits, but I didn't care that the first newspapers in the country emerged in the late eighteenth century. The problem with this, though, was that it meant the history was long, and I was destined to learn more about it as his book progressed. Oh, well, I was nothing if not a supportive wife. A ten-day trip to "The Rock" was looking more appealing as it approached.

A couple of days before Mom and I were to fly to Newfoundland, I finally stood at the door of my walk-in closet and wondered out loud, "What on earth will I wear in Newfoundland?" I had read that email and thought Mom have a point about her mother.

I hadn't realized Maddie was behind me. "Well, Mom," she said, "you might want to consider the weather."

I turned to look at my brilliant daughter. "Now, why didn't I think of that?"

Maddie was holding her iPad (Maddie always seemed to be holding one technological device or another) and tapping on it. "Where did you say you were going on this tour?"

I reminded her of the itinerary, and after moaning again about not being able to go, she said, "The Great Northern Peninsula? I think it might be chilly there."

"In July?" I said, peering at my summer clothes that were front and centre in my closet at this time of year.

"Well, it says here the average daily temperature in St. Anthony is seventeen degrees Celsius, and it goes down to eight at night. You might want to take a few jackets and sweaters."

This was going to be harder than I thought. St. Anthony would be the farthest north we were supposed to go, but even the rest of the Great Northern Peninsula was up there.

"What about St. John's these days?" I said, considering my sweater choices. Although I'd spent some summer vacation time in St. John's, I wondered if global warming might have altered the summer weather.

"Twenty in the daytime," Maddie said, tapping away as she sat down on my bed. "But that's just the average. It could be colder."

"Or hotter," I said, thinking about what kind of attire might be appropriate for a grandmother's one-hundredth birthday party.

In the end, I opted for jeans, sweaters, a packable puffer jacket, some T-shirts and two possible outfits for the party—I still couldn't make up my mind.

"Hey, Mom, did you read this?" Maddie was now looking at the printout I'd made of the emails. If I was going to spend time with my extended family, I wasn't going to get this wrong.

"I think I read everything, Maddie. What grabbed your attention?"

"Two words, Mom. Hiking boots."

"What?" I said, turning toward Maddie and grabbing the page from her hands. "Where does it say that?"

Maddie pointed out the offending line. Hiking boots? I didn't own anything remotely resembling hiking boots. I sighed. "I don't know what kind of tour this is supposed to be, but I suppose I should take a pair of sneakers I can walk in, right?"

Maddie's eyebrows raised. She looked so much like her father when she did that.

~

Early morning flights were something I avoided at all costs—at least when I was in control of the itinerary. My teeth were already on edge when Mom arrived at my front door in the back seat of an airport limousine at four-thirty the following morning. Mom had insisted we needed to be at the airport two hours before our seven am flight. I had thought one hour would be enough, given that I assumed we were flying with carry-on luggage only. Mom had other ideas.

"I'm not dragging a slightly oversized piece of carry-on luggage on a plane and heaving it over my head like some stingy Scrooge. It's bad enough that we have to fly economy. I plan to take only my handbag on the flight. I will be checking a bag," she had said when we were planning our departure time.

So, I had dragged myself out of bed at three-forty-five and had managed to shower and dress just in time to be at the front door to see the limo pull up in the dark.

Needless to say, we arrived early and managed to finesse the security line with our trusted traveller cards. However, it hadn't really been necessary since there were so few people in the airport at five o'clock in the morning.

Once we found ourselves a couple of seats near a window in the departure lounge—Mom liked to be able to see her aircraft—I settled myself down to get used to waiting. Did I mention that our flight to Montreal arrived twenty minutes after eight am, but our onward flight to Newfoundland did not leave until one-thirty pm? No, perhaps I didn't. Five hours at Pierre Elliott Trudeau Airport in Montreal were too much to have to think about in advance. I hoped Phillip would arrive early to relieve some of the monotony and that everything was on time.

When we were finally airborne, Mom patted my hand and said, "Catch that little flight attendant, will you, darling? I want a drink."

I looked at Mom, incredulous. "Mom, It's seven-thirty in the morning."

She shrugged. "It's nine o'clock in Newfoundland."

Oh, that made it so much better. So, this was the kind of vacation it was going to be.

~

By eleven am, we had already been in Montreal for two and a half hours. Mom and I were sitting in The Ice Bar—where everything was white and sparkly—near Gate 47 with a bottle of Prosecco and a cheese platter between us on the table. I had decided Mom had the better approach to this trip—eat and drink and get through it.

It was almost noon when Mom poured the last of the bubbles, and my phone pinged. It was a text from Phillip.

"*At the gate,*" it read. "*Where the heck RU?*"

I quickly texted him our location, and he was there within five minutes.

Phillip looked good. He was wearing a pair of narrow, faded blue jeans that looked expensive with a pristine white T-shirt and a taupe-coloured linen jacket that was expensively wrinkled. On his feet, he was wearing the only kind of shoes I ever saw on him in the summer—taupe suede Louis Vuitton driving shoes. As I looked at them, I started laughing as I thought about the email containing the words "hiking boots."

"Hello to you, too, sis. What's so funny?" Phillip said as he embraced Mom.

"I'm thinking about those shoes you're wearing and the email that said we needed hiking boots."

Phillip looked down at his feet. He shrugged. "You know I don't do hiking boots, Erica. If we need them, I'll sit that one out."

"Good luck with that," Mom said sotto voce.

"I heard that, Mom," Phillip said, sliding in beside me on the bench seat. "What gives with this trip anyway? Not that I'm complaining about the chance to spend some quality time with my sister and my mom. But what about all the rest of the sordidly assorted extended family group?"

"Phillip, that's not a very nice thing to say about your relatives." Mom was trying to get that stern look on her face that we used to see when we were kids, but it was coming off as more like a zombie grimace. She hiccupped.

"I've heard you say worse," I said wryly as I sipped the last of my Prosecco.

Phillip turned to me. "I see that your dear cousin-friend, Eliza, has also been summoned." I made a face at him—I may have childishly stuck out my tongue—and he started laughing. "I think the last time I saw that face was the summer you two seemed to have started to loathe the sight of one another. I never figured out why."

He hadn't figured out why, and I had no intention of telling him. "Teenage girl things," I said.

"What time is it?" Mom said, checking her watch.

Phillip drew back his cuff, revealing what looked like a new Cartier watch. Before he could tell us the time, or I could ask him if Marcus had given it to him, Mom said, "For the love of god, Phillip, don't let your grandmother see that watch." My mother knew an expensive watch when she saw one.

"What?"

"You know how she feels about people she thinks have money."

"I'm not sure I do, Mom. What're you talking about?" Phillip said. Even at age fifty, he was still pouting like he used to when he was a kid, and Mom had caught him doing something she'd told him not to. I also happened to know that he was baiting her. He certainly did know what she meant.

"I think the word disdain covers her feelings quite well," Mom said. She looked like she was sucking on a lemon. "Contempt comes a close second, followed by disapproval." She looked at her watch again. "It's almost time to board. Let's go." She got up, picked up her purse and coat and headed in the direction of our gate.

Phillip and I hurried to keep up.

"Erica," Phillip said as we spied the morass of humanity waiting to board the plane for Deer Lake, "are we going to have any fun on this trip?"

"If you and I have anything to say about it, we certainly will." As we reached the gate, I looked around at the crowd. "Dear god, Phillip, why do you suppose all these people are going to Deer Lake, Newfoundland?"

"Maybe they all have a pestiferous grandmother turning a hundred." He smirked boyishly.

Pestiferous? Is that even a word? I'd have to look it up. Anyway, I realized we were both regressing into our childhood personas. We were going to have some fun if it killed us.

FOUR

Eliza

SOMEWHERE ALONG THE LINE, my editor had been possessed by a demon. That is the only way I could describe it. At some point after the wild success of my second cookbook, *A Schmear on a Bagel: Jewish Cooking for Everyone Else*, wherein I introduced the tasty basics of Jewish cooking to the Jewish-curious and everyone else who loves a good nosh, Margot Talbot, my non-Jewish editor had a brain wave—at least that's what she called it. I considered it more like a break from reality as in a psychotic episode. What else could you call it if your editor, who by all accounts has loved the two bestsellers one of her authors has produced, tells that author to take the next book in a different direction? What was wrong with the direction we were going?

I had taken Julia Child's view of cooking. She had once said that the only real stumbling block to producing something fantastic in the kitchen is fear of failure. "In cooking, you've got to have a what-the-hell attitude," she said. I had taken that view, and my two books had encouraged my readers to do the same. I had—I thought successfully—melded life as a recovering Catholic with my more recent decades as part of the Jewish community on both occasions and shared my well-tested recipes and tips. Now Margot, in her wisdom, had a new idea. She wanted narrative. What the hell is narrative in a cookbook?

When I asked her this very question (mind you, she told me this after I had signed the contract for my next book), she smiled across her cluttered desk. Helen Becker, my agent, and I were sitting in the middle of Margot's chaotic office with its piles of books on the floor and the stacks of files everywhere (had she not learned the joys of going digital?). The disarray was sucking all the air from the room. I had now been acquainted with Margot for the better part of a decade, and I found her to be an incredibly detailed editor with whom I had generally enjoyed working, despite our occasional arguments about the placement of a comma in recipe instructions. Now, she sat there, running a hand through her wild red hair, hunching toward us as if she were telling us she'd discovered the secret of the universe. Her hair was always a source of vexation for me since its colour resembled my own natural colour. When I turned twenty-one, I'd put a quick end to the red curls with an every-four-weeks, eyewaterinlgy expensive colourist who did wonders covering the red. And her assistant did wonders with shilling for companies that made those hair straightener gadgets. Over the years, the technology had improved to the point where not a single person I knew even realized I had curly hair—with the possible exception of Jake. We had gotten caught without an umbrella one day early in our relationship, and he'd had the bad taste to opine thus, "You have curls! I love curls!" I have always believed that only men of distressing taste appreciate the promise of a bohemian free spirit suggested by wild hair. Anyway, I digress. I was talking about Margot's new fixation on "narrative."

"Narrative, Eliza, hun, narrative is the ticket." Margot always called everyone "hun," a throwback to her early life in England, I guess, when it was probably a term of endearment in her world. It was just one more thing that made the hairs on the back of my neck stand on end.

"And what, precisely, would you mean by narrative, Margot?" I said as I sat there with my hands clasped firmly on my lap, tightening their grip by the second. I could smell the problem that was coming.

"Of course, you know what narrative is, Eliza, hun."

There it was again. "Well, Margot, if I knew, it's highly likely that I might not have asked you. Perhaps we should define the term just so that we have a shared understanding. I would not want to go off to create something in error." My neck was bristling with rising indignation.

"Yes, yes, of course," Margot said, leaning in again. Now she, along with her mess, was sucking what was left of the air from the room. "I'm talking about stories."

"Stories? I'm not really understanding this. I don't write stories. I discover, test and perfect recipes, then write cookbooks. I'm a cookbook author."

"Yes, yes, of course," Margot said, sitting back and waving her hand around as if to swat away my displeasure that I was sure she was beginning to perceive. "But everyone these days is looking for stories. Adding stories to cookbooks is the way of the future. It will bring in a whole new demographic to the cookbook target market. It's bloody brilliant, don't you think?"

I did not think it was brilliant then, and months later, as I sat in my office struggling with the concept of "story" in a cookbook, I was even less convinced. My recipes told the stories as far as I was concerned, and that was the end of it. Margot disagreed and sent the first section of my new book back to me with the admonition, "You're not getting it, Eliza. But you will." I was not convinced that I would.

I thought I'd trick her, so I decided to try using AI to write about the raptures of cooking and send that on to her. We'd see how that worked out. Of course, I edited it, but here's what I came up with.

You must listen to the sizzle and crackle of ingredients meeting heat, whether in a pan or the oven, as they create an enticing symphony that promises culinary delight. Those are the sounds you will come to know as well as you know the sounds of your children's breathing. You will recognize each one and what it means. The transformation of raw elements into a symphony of colours, textures, and aromas is nothing short of magical and is yours for the taking. The alchemy of cooking is an art form, and the kitchen, a canvas where flavours are painted with precision and passion.

I then dared to send the new draft, including the computer-generated material, to Margot. Here is what she said. "Now you're getting it! Now, you're onto something. Now we're cooking!" Ha-ha. Was that supposed to be funny? Was she serious? I found it humourless in the extreme if you must know. I never did tell her that it was written mainly by a computer, and I was somewhat offended by the idea that what she was asking me to do—me, a talented cookbook writer—was done better by a non-human. It was mortifying. And yet, I had a contract, so I persisted. Without the benefit of AI—thus the problem I was having.

So, when that Angela person, the travel agent from Newfoundland, called, I was in no headspace to even contemplate going on a frivolous trip to visit my obnoxious grandmother, whether for a milestone birthday or not. However, as I mentioned, my husband thought it was essential that I appear at such a family gathering. My mother-in-law, Esther, was also so inclined, an opinion she elaborated on *ad nauseam* one Friday evening when Jake had the bad manners to mention my family matters to her. She even had the nerve to tell me that I should be grateful that I still had a grandmother, and I should be ashamed that I saw her so infrequently. She had then asked me when was the last time I'd seen my father. That was the point when I believe I might have suddenly, and quite unexpectedly, developed gastric upset and had to leave, thus cutting the evening short. So, Jake called me a cab. On the bright side, if I went to Newfoundland for ten days, I could skip at least one and perhaps even two Shabbat dinners at the in-laws where we were expected to appear every Friday evening. It wasn't the Shabbat I wanted to skip since I enjoyed the ritual and its promise of peace in the home. It was the people. Dear god, the people I was required to spend it with. Were there no families one would wish to inhabit? Out of the frying pan and into the fire, as they say. That was all I seemed to have accomplished by moving from the Houlihan clan to the Cohen.

~

After the first telephone call from Angela and the appearance of airline tickets in my email inbox, the instructional emails kept coming. Each one was more unnerving than the one before.

There were who, what, where and when instructional emails, but there never was one that answered the all-important question: why? Why was my grandmother summoning us? Why was she summoning only her children and grandchildren? Surely, a party of this magnitude warranted the complete line of descendants. Perhaps I'd been part of Jake's family for too long because this was how they approached celebrations. Every cousin, no matter how far removed, was invited and, I might add, happily attended even the most mundane of family gatherings. If there wasn't a momentous occasion to celebrate, such as a Bat Mitzvah or Bar Mitzvah, then Esther would cheerfully come up with another reason. Whereas this kind of random family togetherness was a Cohen thing, it most certainly wasn't a Houlihan thing—at least not in my experience. Then there was the tour.

Why were we all required to participate in this tour? Then, I was especially baffled and annoyed by two specific emails: the email detailing the luggage requirements (far too small for a ten-day trip, in my view) and the one detailing the tour itinerary. The latter was infuriating, mainly because, although it provided a mapped touring route, there was no mention of accommodation. Was this a deliberate oversight? I decided to ask.

As the time for the trip approached, I emailed Angela to ask her if she could provide specific information on the hotels where we'd be staying. (I wanted to look each of them up online to determine their suitability.) Her response was less than helpful.

"Such a card you are," the email said. "Nora was specific that we should stay loose on the accommodation. Gordie will know where to take you."

I had gleaned from the previous email exhaustive details on where to assemble at the airport and who would be meeting us. I had also learned that our tour guide's name was Gordie, a personal selection of Nora's, no doubt. However, all the communication to date had also left me still in the dark as to what I should wear while on tour.

I considered tours Jake and I had done in recent years. We had toured Spain and Portugal, Turkey, Ireland and the south of France. I was having difficulty determining which of these would most closely resemble a tour in Newfoundland.

I eliminated Spain and Portugal because of the weather. Newfoundland, at least according to my father's recollections of his home province, was cold all year round. I remembered him saying that summer arrived on July 10 at noon and left at four pm the same day. I had never really considered what this meant, but it was now going to be a guiding principle. As a child on vacation in the summer in Newfoundland, I don't suppose I'd paid much attention to what I was wearing, and my only memory was of the weather vacillating between rain, fog and sun. Whether I'd worn a sweater or a jacket seemed to elude me.

I then eliminated Turkey for the same reason. The south of France had possibilities as a guideline. I remembered that the French islands of St. Pierre and Miquelon were just off the coast of Newfoundland, so surely some of the French *je ne sais quoi* sensibility permeated the culture. An elevated casualness would seem appropriate, and then I remembered our tour of Ireland.

I knew that Newfoundland had strong ties to Ireland through its ancestors. Indeed, Ireland was the ancestral home of the Houlihan family, who made their way to Newfoundland sometime during the potato famine in the middle of the nineteenth century. So, I sensibly concluded that my experience in Ireland might help.

When Jake and I were in Dublin, we'd stayed at the Shelbourne, the most prestigious and best-reviewed hotel in the city. It was exquisite. Then we went on to stay at the Hayfield Manor in Cork, The Killarney Park Hotel in Killarney, and finally, the eight-hundred-year-old Ashford Castle, the jewel in the crown. I remembered sitting in the stunning Prince of Wales bar in a plush chair beside the vast fireplace, feeling like the lady of the manor in a warm cocoon of dark, polished wood and money. I remembered sipping my scotch—Lagavulin Distillers Edition Islay Single Malt if memory served—and thinking that I could live there, but only if I were willing to give up the many advantages of a big city. In the end, I concluded that this tour in Newfoundland would be like the Ireland tour, so I would pack accordingly.

In the three weeks leading up to the day I was scheduled to fly to Halifax to meet my father and my sister Emma, I had told Jake three times I'd changed my mind. I wasn't going to go. Each time, he'd taken on the look of a deer in the headlights. He must have been looking forward to a bit of alone time in the house. Then, each time, he'd told me that I would regret it if I didn't go, that I'd have only one chance to say happy birthday to my centenarian grandmother, and then reminded me that I actually liked my younger sister, Emma, and wouldn't it be nice to see her? I hadn't thought about that. Yes, despite our eight-year age difference, Emma and I were actually friends as well as sisters at one time. That was before we went our separate ways.

~

The morning of the flight finally arrived. Three days earlier, when Jake was visiting his mother, he must have mentioned the exact time of my departure because Esther insisted on sending her car to drive me to the airport. I suppose she wanted to be assured I went—or perhaps it was Jake's idea all along. I have no idea. I only knew that on the appointed day, I found myself sitting behind Kyle, Esther's driver, glumly staring out the window at the rain that was pelting down. The skies had opened the night before, waking me up as the sound of the rain lashing against the bedroom window reminded me of childhood summers in Halifax when it often rained for days at a time—or so it seemed to me in my memories.

Kyle had been outside our door at nine-thirty am on the dot. I would have preferred to leave an hour later since the drive to Newark was usually less than forty minutes, but Esther had called early that morning to inform me that since it was raining, Kyle would come an hour earlier. It seemed I had no say in the matter. Over the twenty-five years of being a member of this matriarch's family, I had discovered, through unpleasant experience, that it was easier to go along with Esther than to fight her. I remembered the first time I'd given in to her without a fight. Jake's father, Marty—high-powered businessman by day, toadying husband by night—had leaned over to me at the dinner table and said, "Well, done, my dear. I've always found that the best approach when dealing with Esther. May I offer you a dinner roll?" And that was how I'd played it ever since. At least thinking about how miserable it would be to have to wait an extra hour in the lovely (not) international departure lounge at Newark overshadowed the misery of considering what the next ten days would be like. I'd had nightmares about that for weeks.

As it turned out, the rain did nothing to delay the traffic. In fact, Kyle managed to deposit me at the departures door in thirty-five minutes flat. I thanked him for the drive and dragged my carry-on bag toward security. Given my state of mind, it seemed inevitable that I would be the one selected for a random pat-down, an experience I always found humiliating. Wasn't it enough they could see our underwear via the machines we had to walk through with our hands in the air? I suppose not.

I trudged through the departure area en route to my gate. Despite the early hour, I thought it might be nice to have a glass (or two) of wine to get me through this experience, but there were no bars to be seen. In my view, the international departure area in Terminal A is fairly dismal. It's as if no one wants the Canadians. I suppose they might have a point.

I found a seat, popped in my EarPods and listened to an audiobook. I was halfway through a novel called *Elinor Oliphant is Completely Fine*, which I had heard was inexplicably being adapted for the screen. It was supposedly funny, but I must say I didn't find the character humorous in the least. I found her inordinately sad, yet I persisted in listening. My EarPods were so good at blocking out the sound that it seemed I missed the boarding announcement, and it wasn't until everyone around me began to gather their belongings and surge toward the gate that I realized I should join them.

As I approached the desk, one of the gate agents walked over and said, "Ma'am, you'll have to gate-check that bag."

I looked at her as if she might be a daft child. "Why ever would I do that?"

"Because it's over our size limit for cabin baggage." The agent then helpfully pointed to the sign and baggage sizer.

I looked at my bag and sighed. Could this get any worse? I handed it over and took my baggage tag.

Once settled into my very narrow economy aisle seat, and everyone had managed to push and thrust and otherwise maneuver their own apparently not oversized carry-on luggage into every space imaginable (the best argument I know for flying business class), I closed my eyes and began a breathing exercise. My therapist, Calista, was a big believer in therapeutic breathing. I had never found it very useful, but this occasion seemed to call for it.

"Ma'am." Then, a poke on the shoulder. "Ma'am, I'm sorry to bother you, but we were wondering if you might consider changing seats."

I opened my eyes and looked up into the face of a pretty but tired-looking young woman with a baby on her hip.

"I wonder if you might change seats with me so I can sit with my husband." She nodded toward the young man sitting beside me in the centre seat and then back toward the baby.

My first thought was to tell her that I was settled and that I was sorry, but I was staying put. But I sighed and looked at the longing on her face and relented. I surprised myself by thinking how much easier it would be for her if she could give the baby to her husband to hold once in a while through the flight. After a complicated dance of moving carry-on bags, I found myself ten rows farther back in the plane in a window seat, wedged in beside a rather large man wearing a plaid shirt and a baseball cap—brand new as far as I could tell—that said New York Yankees. And the misery deepened. I sighed yet again and stared out the window.

As we taxied to the end of the runway and prepared to take off, the large man grabbed my hand. "Sorry, ma'am," he said. He must have been a Canadian—always sorry for something. "I'm not usually like this—only when I fly. May I?" He looked down at where his hand was firmly clamped on my hand. I had little choice but to nod.

Once we were airborne, he removed his hand and turned to me as best he could, given that he was wedged between the armrests. "Thanks so much. I'm Brian, by the way. Buy you a beer?" He held out his hand for me to shake.

"Eliza," I said. "And if you make it wine, you're on." Who was I to refuse a drink from a stranger? I was on vacation. And damned if I was going to spend the entire time being miserable.

As that thought crossed my mind, I realized that I had a choice here. I could either spend the next ten days wallowing in misery, or I could get with the program and see if I couldn't salvage something. Perhaps agreeing to a glass of wine with a man whom I'd just helped over his fear of flying might be an excellent way to begin.

Two hours and three glasses of wine later, Brian and I were the best of friends. Well, he'd told me all about his family just outside Corner Brook (which happened to be the first stop on my upcoming, largely unknown tour), his job in Calgary with an oil company (he was a geological engineer who had graduated from university in St. John's where my grandmother lived), his brother and sister who owned a restaurant in Gander (another stop on my tour) and his dog, Dory, a Labrador Retriever who was being cared for by a friend back in Calgary while he visited his family for a few weeks. He had flown from Calgary via New York so he could meet some friends and attend a baseball game—hence the new hat. The Calgary friends had stayed in New York for a few days while he carried on to Newfoundland for a visit via Halifax.

"Hate having to stop in Halifax on the way, but what can you do? Deer Lake's not so easy to get to from New York, eh?" Brian laughed, sipping his third beer while munching on a large (now almost empty) bag of cashews. I had declined his offer of cashews. He turned to me. "You visiting Halifax?"

I never like to share much with people I don't know. Truthfully, I probably don't like to share much with people I *do* know, but I was well into my third glass of wine when we got on this subject.

I told him that I lived in New York and my final destination today was also Deer Lake, and I was going to visit my grandmother, who was turning one hundred. Why on earth did I tell him that? Of course, it was the wine talking. In any case, that was all he needed to know to set him off on a monologue about how long-lived his family members were. He also gave me tips on what to eat, all of which seemed to involve cod in one form or another. My memory of cod was from summers visiting Nora, who was a lover of everything cod-related, and all I seemed to remember were bones, something I detested about seafood. I suppose it's why adding a Gefilte fish recipe to my Jewish cookbooks was something I'd avoided resolutely. Like the cod Gran served to us when we were kids, it was supposed to be de-boned, but I'd never met a Gefilte fish or a codfish that was, indeed, boneless.

As we neared Halifax, Brian, who evidently flew home to Newfoundland from Calgary via Halifax often, so he was more than familiar with the route, began to get excited. According to Brian, all he usually got to see from the air when he approached Halifax were trees surrounding the airport—or fog, to hear him tell it. Today, the approach was from a different direction.

"Don't often approach the airport this way," he said, leaning into my space. As I mentioned, he was rather a large young man. "Can't lie," he continued, "I'm like a little kid when I get to see a city from the air. Here," he said, thrusting his phone at me. "Could you get a few photos for me?"

I wasn't any more interested in taking photos of Halifax from the air than I had ever been in taking any from the ground when I lived there or when I visited my parents over the years. But I took his phone from him and did as he asked. He was delighted.

As we waited for the hordes in front of us to deplane, Brian turned to me and said, "Eliza, it's been a right hoot to have someone as cultured as you to talk to. Don't meet too many cultured people on planes these days."

Indeed.

~

By the time I finally got off the plane and made my way through Canadian immigration—this was the only situation in which I dusted off my Canadian passport to make immigration lines easier—I had less than an hour to make my connection. When I arrived at the departure gate, I looked around at the sea of passengers, dully awaiting the boarding announcement. I didn't see Dad or Emma in the crowd.

The pre-boarding announcements had just begun when I saw them sauntering toward the gate. Both of them were smiling and seemed to be sharing a joke.

"There you are," I said as they approached.

"Hello to you, too, Eliza," Dad said, opening his arms to embrace me. This was new.

"Eliza!" Emma shrieked as her carry-on bags thudded to the ground. She sounded just like she always had.

Emma, as I mentioned, is eight years my junior, but even now, at forty-two years old, will forever be my baby sister. As strained as our relationship may have become from time to time when we disagreed (about almost everything), I still considered Emma to be my favourite sister. Lucy was (and is) an entirely different thing.

After extricating myself from my father's unexpected physical contact, I turned to Emma, who also threw her arms around me. "It's good to see you, sis," I said.

"Good to see me? It's awesome to see you!" Emma shrieked again, kissing me soundly on the cheek. "It's been way too long."

She then stood back. "Let me see that New York outfit," she said as she appraised me.

I was wearing my usual travel uniform—black Ralph Lauren stretch jeans, a black Gucci T-shirt, black boots (I know it was summer—so sue me, it's who I am) and a black, ultra-lightweight cashmere wrap.

"You know she's not dead," Dad said, apropos of nothing I could fathom.

Emma elbowed Dad in the ribs. "You're so funny, Dad," she said. Emma seemed to have a better grasp of Dad's sense of humour than I did. Then she looked at what must have been a blank expression on my face. "Dead? Funeral? Eliza, you must know that you look like you're on your way to a funeral."

I looked down at my chic outfit. "I always wear black when I fly," I said defensively. I looked at Emma.

She was wearing her own uniform—one I'd seen in various iterations over the years. Today, Emma's wardrobe consisted of a pair of what I could only describe as balloon pants in what looked to me to be an African print, a coral-coloured T-shirt of questionable provenance (it might well have been from the Canadian version of Goodwill), and a short, white sweater. She was wearing (horror of horrors) Birkenstock sandals. Thank god she wasn't wearing socks, but I knew full well that if the weather in Newfoundland turned cold, the wool socks would emerge. I had been the unfortunate witness to that particular sartorial faux pas on more than one occasion. Emma looked every bit the artist she considered herself to be, from the top of her curly red hair (yes, she and I would have shared that trait if not for my expensive hair habits) to the tips of her toenails that she had painted a fetching shade that I can only describe as glitter bile.

All in all, Emma's colour choices were reminiscent of her artwork, about which I was confident we'd have plenty of conversations over the next ten days since it was her favourite subject—after Tobias, her live-in boyfriend of some years. The last I heard of Tobias, a wannabe actor, was that he was tending a bar at a pub in the village where they lived on the south shore of the province of Nova Scotia. This was another subject I was sure I'd hear more about as the trip progressed. *No point in broaching that subject too soon*, I thought.

In recent years, on the infrequent occasions when I saw my little sister, I had always marvelled at the fact that she seemed years younger than her actual age. If I didn't know better, I would have pegged her at thirty at the most. And we all know the sad state of maturity of the twenty-first-century thirty-year-old. Emma seemed to have managed to maintain that ebullient youngest sister schtick she'd had going for her entire life.

"Girls," Dad said, "the reunion can continue on board. I believe they're calling our zone." We had always been "girls" to my father, and I was sure we always would be.

"Finally," I said. I hadn't had much experience of being among the last to be called to board a plane in recent decades.

The three of us joined the morass of cattle that the gate agents were trying to herd onto the plane while at the same time dealing with the throng of people still waiting at the desk. Listening to the griping as we passed by them on our way to board, I concluded that they were all attempting to get standby seats on a full aircraft. I knew it was full because of the more-than-sufficient number of announcements a gate agent had already made on the subject. I couldn't believe the number of people who were willingly going to Deer Lake, Newfoundland. Was there a convention of some sort? I finally reached the gate, showed my identification and boarding pass and followed Dad onboard.

While we were still standing in the aisle, Emma said, "Eliza, I'll sit at the window, and you can take the middle seat so you can talk to both of us. You hardly ever get to talk to us." I could see Dad's raised eyebrow. That could only mean that he intended to sleep his way to Newfoundland.

"That's okay," I said. "I'd prefer the aisle."

Dad turned to look at me. "Not happening, Eliza. You know my legs are a lot longer than yours. I'm on the aisle."

Foiled again, I thought. I sighed loudly, causing Dad to say, "I heard that, Eliza. It didn't work when you were twelve, and it's not going to work now."

So, I settled into the middle seat for the hour-and-a-half flight. The best-laid plans and all that.

I started to relax when we left the gate only two minutes after our scheduled time and taxied out to the runway. That was the moment when the plane stopped dead for a full five minutes before the captain came on the intercom.

"Ladies and gentlemen, sorry about this little delay. We've got a light on here that we need to have checked before we can get underway. Just sit back, and we'll let you know how it's going." He then repeated it in French as that low-level collective sigh emanated from the full load of passengers. It seemed that my short trip in the middle seat was going to be longer than I anticipated. I could feel my jaw tightening. I think the way airline pilots seemed so laissez-faire about these things was what got to me the most about such delays on airplanes. He sounded like he didn't have a care in the world while I sat at the back of the plane with gut-churning annoyance beginning to simmer as I considered the possibility I might be imprisoned in this metal tube for longer than the expected time.

"Damn it," Emma said. "I'm excited to get going. I wonder how long it will take."

She was excited. I was at least happy for her, if not for myself.

I looked at my watch and started timing. I know I should have just let it go, but I couldn't. I hated nothing more than I hated delayed flights. Dad was already asleep. I had often been amazed at how easily he could fall asleep. My mother used to say that he had learned it as an intern many years ago when catching sleep whenever and wherever was imperative for full functioning on long on-call shifts. He had then perfected it over his years of being on-call for obstetrics. In addition to his family practice, Dad had delivered thousands of babies.

When the plane finally jerked into motion, almost an hour had elapsed, and I was nearly fit to be tied. My earlier wine had worn off, and I was stone-cold sober. I desperately needed another glass of wine or something stronger. We were finally airborne, and a flight attendant eventually got to us to ask if we would like to purchase anything. I had never been so happy to offer my credit card to anyone since my first foray into the Louis Vuitton store on Fifth Avenue to buy my first LV tote bag. I hoped my liver was up to this trip. I could feel daily alcohol coming on. Who was I kidding? In recent months, it had become a way of life. I poured my wine from the little bottle into the plastic cup. *Newfoundland, here I come*, I thought. *And god help me. Mazel Tov.*

WELCOME TO "THE ROCK"

Fun Facts About Newfoundland

- *St. John's is closer to Milan, Italy, than Vancouver, BC on Canada's west coast. (4,614 kilometres versus 5, 022 kilometres)*
- *Almost everyone pronounces Newfoundland wrong. (Noo'-fuhn-land)*
- *The busiest airport in the world used to be in Newfoundland. (YQX Gander)*
- *Newfoundland has its own time zone. (No one else shares it.)*
- *The first Europeans landed not in the Caribbean (take that, Christopher Columbus) but in Newfoundland. Vikings, anyone?*
- *The island of Newfoundland is the sixteenth largest island in the world and is bigger than Ireland. 111,390 square kilometres (43,010 sq mi) versus 84,421 square kilometres (32,595 square miles)*

FIVE

Eliza

THE PLANE BEGAN ITS DESCENT THROUGH THE LIGHT CLOUDS. Emma was staring out the window, her phone in hand. "Oh, Eliza! Just look at that scenery! I want to paint it."

Emma wanted to paint everything she saw. She'd been that way since we were kids. I loosened my seatbelt so I could lean over to see what Emma was talking about. All I could see were what appeared to be miles and miles of green. The verdant fields and forests stretched out in a patchwork of shades of emerald and olive. Weaving through the green were ribbons and patches of blue—lakes and rivers that looked like veins and arteries coursing through the earth. I thought I could almost see a shimmer from a lake as we passed over. I had no idea the island of Newfoundland looked anything like this. I had no memory of ever seeing anything like it when we'd visited Gran for our summer holidays back in the day. The one thing I knew for sure was that I was a long way from New York. The plane pulled up near the terminal.

"Have we stopped already?" I said, looking across Emma out the window to the stretch of asphalt tarmac. "Why are we stopping? Surely, there can't be another plane at our gate. We're an hour late." I couldn't imagine there were so many flights into Deer Lake that this could be a problem. And yet, I could hear seatbelts snapping open and people beginning to unfold themselves from their seats as if we had come to a full and complete stop, as the flight attendants like to say.

Dad, who had woken up just as the wheels hit the runway, peeked across. "You're not in New York, Eliza. We *are* at the gate."

Emma looked out the window and back to me. "Yes, we are. I can see them just pulling the staircase up to the plane now."

I was trying to remember the last time I'd landed in any airport anywhere in the world where I didn't exit the plane into a jetway. I was having a difficult time remembering anything more recent than an ill-fated trip to Antigua many years ago when Jake and I attended a reunion for his business school class. The less said about the pompous asses I was forced to spend a week with, the better. To say that the airport was Dickensian would be an understatement.

When everyone ahead of us had finally lifted their oversized carry-on bags from the bins and headed up the aisle trailing neck pillows, puffer jackets, hiking boots (hiking boots? Dear god, they really had hiking boots) and backpacks, we finally followed behind. As I passed over the threshold of the plane, I immediately crashed into an unknown substance. *Yes,* I thought, *I seem to have a memory of this from years ago.* I breathed in for a brief second before I started down the metal steps. *Yes, I know what it is. Fresh air.* I coughed. Dear god, had it been that long since I'd breathed in fresh air? I wasn't sure I was ready for this—on so many levels.

We entered the small terminal through a corridor that led directly to the baggage carousels, except they weren't carousels. They were conveyor belts. I was the only one of the three of us with a checked bag. We stepped away from the door, and Dad said, "I have everything here, girls." He dug into the breast pocket of the light grey blazer he was wearing and pulled out several sheets of paper he had stapled together. I knew he'd have the itinerary and all the instructions at the ready. I was about to ask why he didn't simply keep them on his phone, but I decided that perhaps this was an excellent time to start practicing not saying everything that came into my mind.

Emma was looking around excitedly. "This is so quaint," she said, smiling at everyone around. "Oh, look, there's a local shop. I'm going to go over to see if they have any local artists' work."

I grabbed her arm before she could get away. "Emma, we don't have time. Our driver is here somewhere in the crowd." She pouted but didn't make any further moves. Just then, I spotted my small suitcase on the conveyor belt and wove my way through the excited crowd to retrieve it. *Dear god*, I thought, *what are they all so excited about?*

"It says here we should be looking for someone called Gordie O'Brien," Dad was saying to Emma as I returned. He was peering at his notes.

"Dad, we have no idea what this Gordie O'Brien looks like. Surely, he must be holding a sign with our name on it. Professional drivers always look for their passengers," I said. I did, however, wonder what kind of individual might constitute a professional driver to Nora Houlihan.

We had moved across the wide corridor to get out of the way of the stampeding crowd of well-wishers who had come to greet the arriving passengers. Driving to the airport to meet people must have been a thing here. In New York, if you had friends coming, you didn't get in a car and drive to JFK or LaGuardia (and certainly not Newark). You let them fend for themselves at the taxi stand outside arrivals and greeted them with open arms when they finally made their way into Manhattan.

The three of us were now leaning against the wall, Dad with his pages, Emma and I with our phones out. I glanced up and saw a white-haired man wearing a plaid shirt under what appeared to be a fishing vest (the kind with all the pockets for whatever it is fishing people take to fish) leaning against a pillar on the far side of the corridor. He had his arms crossed and seemed to be staring at us. He was smiling or perhaps smirking. When he caught my eye, he began to stroll toward us. When he was standing in front of Dad, he reached out his hand to him and said, "Hey, Doc, I'm Gordie O'Brien. Welcome back to the Rock."

~

Fifteen minutes later, Gordie had us sitting at a table in a donut concession, with a large cup of coffee in front of each of us. As he placed a cardboard box full of donuts in the middle of the table he said, "Didn't know what you'd all like, so I bought a couple of different ones."

Emma peered into the box as he rattled off the names—and, peculiarly, the calorie counts. "These ones are the classics that might run you between one-ninety and two-hundred sixty calories." Then he pointed to four icing-sugar-covered confections. "These are those fancier classic ones. You'll remember this kind, Doc," he said to Dad. "But that added sugar and jam in the middle can run them up to four-hundred-fifty calories." Then he proudly lifted an odd-looking mound dotted with what appeared to be apple slices. "This, ladies and gentleman, is the crème de la crème of donuts. I give you four hundred calories of mind-bending deliciousness—the apple fritter." That was the point where he lifted it to his lips, took a huge bite and then sat back with a look of rapturous delight on his face.

Emma stared at him, fascinated. "Oh, that looks wonderful," she said. "I might try one." Before she touched it, she sat back, frowning. "But what are they fried in, Gordie?"

"Fried in? What are they fried in?" He wiped his mouth with a tiny paper napkin. "I'm not sure I've ever known. Doesn't matter, though. They're delicious."

Emma shook her head and took on a look of grave concern. "Oh, Gordie, but it does so matter. If they're fried in any kind of animal fat, I can't eat them."

Gordie looked confused. "Why not?"

"Oh, Gordie," Emma said earnestly, "I'm vegan." That statement popped almost everyone's bubble every time it was uttered by anyone, especially someone as earnest about it as I knew Emma was. It has been ever thus since she announced to all of us via email ten years earlier that she had embraced a new lifestyle. At the time, I thought she was going to tell us she was a lesbian. I would have found that much easier to digest—if you'll pardon the pun.

Gordie just looked at her and said, "My ducky, you're going to have a hell of a trip, then, is all I can say." Then he laughed. Emma frowned.

Through all this conversation, Dad was silent. He was sipping his coffee, staring off in the distance for a bit and then back at Gordie. Dad hadn't said a word when Gordie had quickly herded us not to a waiting vehicle but to this donut shop in the airport, muttering something about having to wait.

"Gordie," Dad said at last, "please tell me again why we're waiting and how you knew who we were."

"Well, that last question is easy. Nora gave me chapter and verse on every one of you, so I knew who you were the minute you set foot outside that aircraft." I shuddered at the thought of what Gran might have thought to be critical information about each of us. He continued. "As for why we're here enjoying a restful donut and coffee, that's because we're waiting for the rest of your family. So," he said, looking at me, "there's your silver lining to your delay. We only have to wait another forty-five minutes. If you'd been on time, we'd have had to wait two hours."

I might have uttered something about the shit-show of having had the delay on top of the cattle-herding that is modern air travel as I entered the terminal. He may have overheard.

Then Dad stared at Gordie. "Have we met before? You look familiar."

Gordie picked up his paper coffee cup and sipped before answering. "Don't think so, Doc. I'm sure I'd have remembered you." Then he kind of winked at me. What was that supposed to mean?

"So, Gordie," I said, "what kinds of things did Nora tell you about us?"

"Oh, she always tells me how proud she is of Dr. Fred here," Gordie said, pointing to Dad.

I was puzzled by this. "Gran always tells you? Do you know her well? I thought you were the guide she'd hired to take us on this tour."

"Guilty on both counts. I've been happy to count Nora Houlihan among my friends for years. She and Douglas—god rest his soul— and my parents—god rest their souls—were the best of friends. And

I am, indeed, the person who will be taking you on a custom tour of the island."

Dad seemed to be stuck back on what he'd said about Nora's comments. "So, my mother told you she was proud of me?"

"Proud as a peacock. Tells everyone about her son, the doctor. She's a proud mom, no doubt about it."

"Did she tell you she was proud of her granddaughters?" Emma said.

"I don't think proud quite covers it," Gordie said.

No, I was sure that it didn't quite cover it.

"Did she tell you I'm an artist?" Emma said, taking out her phone, no doubt, to show him some of her work.

"She did, Emma. She did." He peered at the tiny screen and didn't comment. He was smarter than I'd taken him for.

I thought I'd make him squirm a bit more. "And what did Gran tell you about her American granddaughter who writes cookbooks? The Jewish one?"

Gordie smiled and ran his fingers through his still-thick hair. I guessed his age to be about seventy-five or even a well-preserved eighty. "I do believe the words traitorous Yank may have crossed her lips," he said, smiling.

Of course they did, I thought. I suppose there was some truth in them, at least.

Anyway, we waited. We were waiting for the next Air Canada flight from Montreal, so I quickly rechecked the arrivals on my phone. At least it was on time.

SIX

Erica

THE FLIGHT FROM MONTREAL WAS UNEVENTFUL except for the bickering Phillip and I seemed to have fallen into as if we were still ten and thirteen years old. First, there was the bickering about who should have to sit in the centre seat. Of course, Phillip's argument about his six-foot height meant that he won that one. Once we were airborne, that particular decision left me squished between Mom at the window and Phillip on the aisle as I poured myself some wine from the tiny bottle into the plastic cup. I loathed drinking wine from plastic cups, but you do what you have to do in dire circumstances. These circumstances qualified. Then we bickered about who should take the last almond from the bag we were sharing, and about Phillip's (and Mom's) decision to check a bag.

"Didn't you get that memo? The one about the permitted size of our luggage?" I said tetchily. I was pouting because I had wanted to take a larger bag, too, and check it like Mom did. Mom and I shared a dislike for that scramble for bin space, especially in economy, and I, too, preferred not to have to drag a heavy carry-on bag. I, too, liked to be relatively unencumbered when I arrived at my assigned seat, not caring at all if there would be space for my stuff. But unlike my dear brother and mother, I had followed the luggage restrictions set by Gran and did not check my small suitcase. So, by the time I got to sit in my airplane seat, I was already hot, sweaty, and annoyed from having to stuff my suitcase in the overhead bin, and I was sitting with my large handbag under my feet for the duration.

"Well, if it is that important to you, why didn't you just check your bag when I checked mine? We did check in together, if you'll recall." Mom sounded just a tad exasperated.

"I cannot tell you how long I spent planning my wardrobe and packing my liquids for carry-on, it just seemed ridiculous to check it," I said.

Mom shrugged. "Then it was your choice, Erica."

I chose to ignore her perfectly logical conclusion and turned to Phillip. "Anyway, Phillip, just how many clothes do you really think you'll need for ten days in a place where dressing up means clean jeans and a new baseball cap? You're not in Montreal." I said.

"Erica, you might want to put a cork in that attitude about Newfoundland. You know nothing about it. It's not like that," Mom said. She sounded more defensive about her home than I had expected or ever heard her before, given that she had fled at the first available opportunity half a century ago and complained bitterly every time she made a trip back. And I felt rightly chastised. I hadn't had that feeling since I was a kid, and it did make me feel the tiniest bit chagrined. I would have to watch my tongue on this trip.

As Phillip and I continued our good-natured bickering, Mom seemed to have fallen into an altered state and spent most of the flight gazing out the window. As we neared our destination, I was sure I could feel her clench her muscles as she sat beside me.

"You know, kids," she said finally, still staring out the window, "I've never been here before."

Phillip and I looked at one another, each of us frowning in incomprehension.

"What do you mean, Mom?" Phillip said. "How can you never have been here before?"

Mom turned to look at us. "I mean that I have never been on this coast of the island in my entire life." She glanced out the window again. "I spent my entire childhood on the East Coast in the city other than the time spent at our cottage out on the bay. But this…" She seemed at a loss for words. "This is something else entirely."

I leaned across her to see if I could figure out what she was talking about. Then I shoved my phone into her hand. "Take some pictures, Mom," I said.

Mom took my phone and started clicking. She gave it back to me just before the wheels hit the tarmac. Phillip and I leaned our heads together and looked at the series of shots she'd taken. As I scrolled through shot after shot of trees and fields, lakes and rivers, it was as if we were looking at paintings. It was as if a watercolourist had painted a tableau for a storybook, splashing greens and blues and mixing in just enough water to feather out the edges and add a line of glittering silver grey as tiny rivers ran through, connecting the blues of the lakes. It was not at all like the Newfoundland I remembered from previous flights to Newfoundland. It had been a while, but I seemed to remember a lot of ocean and rocks on approach to the airport in St. John's. This was like a different world.

The plane finally came to a halt in the middle of the tarmac.

"Ha," Phillip said, peering across both Mom and me out the window. "An outside staircase. It has to be if we're stopping this far from the terminal. I love them. They always make me think I'm somewhere exotic."

"I think maybe we are, dear brother, if by exotic, you mean strange, unusual, or alien," I said as I readied myself to pull and tug my carry-on, which was firmly stuck in the overhead bin. Mom glared at me but said nothing.

We finally made our way to the front of the plane and stepped out from the airplane door. I was momentarily confused. Were we not in Newfoundland? Maddie and I had spent some time discussing the expected weather at this time of year and clothing selections that might be best suited to the climate. My memory of summer vacations with Gran involved a lot of light sweaters and jackets, especially for after sundown. And this trip was taking us much farther north. So, I had filled every corner of my carry-on suitcase with long-sleeved shirts, a second sweater (I was wearing one) and a rain jacket. There may even have been a scarf and a pair of gloves, but I wasn't admitting to that as I breathed in my first breath of air. What I felt as I stepped down the stairs onto the asphalt below bore no resemblance to those predictions.

"Mom," I said as we walked toward the terminal. "It's so hot." I tried to shrug off my sweater, but between my massive carry-on bag and my handbag (that probably exceeded the airline regulation size by some measure), I could not. I was sweating more than I had been after stashing luggage at the start of the flight.

Mom didn't turn as she made her way toward the low building. She was staring straight ahead. "I suppose it is," she said distractedly. "I think we might all have to consider changing our expectations about this trip. You know what I have always told you kids, Erica."

"Mom, you've told us a lot of things." Phillip was desperately trying to keep up. Despite his long legs, he was having difficulty since Mom was practically running, with me at her heels, and it was oppressively warm for people dressed like they were headed—where *did* we think we were headed? I was beginning to wonder if we had any idea where we were at all.

Mom stopped so abruptly just before we walked into the door of the terminal that I crashed into her back. She turned to us. "I always said, if you want to make god laugh, tell her your plans." She turned back and hurried straight ahead into the crowd within, and I could hear her saying, "And she's certainly laughing now."

~

The baggage conveyor belts were just inside the building. As we made our way toward them to find Phillip's and Mom's suitcases, Mom said she'd nip to the ladies' room and see if she could find our driver along the way. I stood in the crowd, looking around at all the people with their hiking equipment and remembered I'd read that this was the gateway to Gros Morne National Park, a planned stop on our way north to see the Vikings. After our mother-daughter discussion about my travel wardrobe, Maddie did the research for me and insisted that I buy a pair of hiking sneakers, if not hiking boots. I had reluctantly made a trip to one of the local camping and hiking megastores where I'd felt very much outside my comfort zone. Indeed, the very idea of hiking and camping made me itch. I was a city girl. But now that I saw how everyone else seemed to be prepared for such activities, I was feeling pleased with myself for my foresight (or Maddie's foresight). My pleased feeling lasted mere seconds. As I gazed around, I saw a familiar face. Our eyes locked. It was my cousin Eliza. *Shit*, I thought, *why does Eliza Bloody Cohen have to be the first person I see on Newfoundland soil?* I do have to admit, she looked just as peeved as I felt.

I busied myself helping Phillip to identify his suitcase. I should not have been concerned that he'd have difficulty finding it or that anyone else would mistake it for theirs. Among all the backpacks, hockey equipment bags (god, those were huge), black suitcases and more black suitcases, his was the only Louis Vuitton Monogram suitcase among them. I rolled my eyes as he lifted it off the conveyor belt. No one else even noticed.

When I looked up, I saw Mom striding determinedly toward us with a tall, white-haired man trailing behind her. His thick, wavy hair and knowing half-smile made me immediately think he was likely to be a character. He was a handsome man in a rugged kind of way, probably Mom's age or close to it, although his stride matched Mom's, and no one would ever have thought she was seventy-nine. He was wearing one of those fishing vests with multiple pockets, and as he caught my eye, I got the feeling he was getting a kick out of following Mom as she resolutely made her way toward us like a mamma sheep gathering her lambs. At least he didn't have a bell.

No, really, I had already noticed a guide in the arrivals area wearing a bright blue vest, holding one of those old-fashioned school bells in his hand. When I first noticed him, I wondered what the bell was all about, so I had amused myself while we waited for Phillip's and Mom's luggage by watching what he was doing. As I observed him, I was dumbfounded to see that he was using it to round up a group of guests who I could only guess were about to embark on a bus tour. But the thing that truly amazed me was that each time he rang it (oh, yes, he rang it and more than once), they would follow him like Pavlov's dogs. I wondered how long it would be before one of the guests grabbed the bell, whacked the guide over the head with it, and shoved it "where the sun don't shine."

"Do you suppose that's our guide?" Phillip said over my shoulder as we wound our way out of the crowd to meet Mom and her man. Before I could make a bitchy remark about who else he thought it might be, he pivoted and said, "Oh, wait, Erica. Isn't that Uncle Fred? And could that be Emma? God, she's a bit pasty, isn't she? I would have thought she'd be an outdoorsy type, living in that oceanside village in Nova Scotia." Then he hurried over to greet his long-lost cousins, who were now trailing behind Mom and the guide. The Pied Piper had nothing on my mother.

As Eliza sidled up beside me, I noted her all-black outfit. She looked a bit like the New York version of the Wicked Witch of the West, but I chose to keep my mouth shut this time. I could not remember when I'd last laid eyes on her. She looked older (that made me inexplicably happy) with her too-dark hair and her reading glasses dangling from her neck on a sparkly chain festooned with faux diamonds—or perhaps they were real?

She came up beside me and leaned in for the double air kiss. "Erica, how long has it been?" Did I detect a modicum of condescension? One thing I'd always observed about cousin Eliza was that she was consistent—consistently patronizing with a soupçon of superiority.

"Eliza," I said, biting my tongue to prevent me from adding, not long enough. "You look chic, as usual."

"What I look is warm, and how I feel is cranky," she said, fanning herself with what looked like a tourism brochure. So, what else is new? I thought but purposefully refrained from speaking. Then she glanced at me as if she might be appraising an opponent in a boxing ring. "I haven't been able to catch your show on television since Canadian content isn't really our thing in New York or the rest of

America, for that matter, as I'm sure you're aware, but I hear good things."

I doubted that very much, but at least Eliza got to get in her first dig about the superiority of all things American. There are no more obnoxious citizens in any country than those who have adopted it.

"I hear your last cookbook was a success," I said by way of making safe conversation.

"You heard that, did you?" Eliza said, with that touch of arrogance she had down to a science.

Perhaps it hadn't been the best topic for safe conversation. If she asked me whether I had bought it and tried out any recipes, I would be in trouble. If I recalled correctly, it was something about Jewish cooking for people like me—culinarily challenged and not at all Jewish.

Before we had a chance to come to blows on any number of other seemingly innocuous subjects, Mom intervened.

"We're going to the car," she said, but it was more of a command than a statement. "This is Gordie O'Brien, and he's our guide," she was trying to say to Phillip and me, but Phillip and Emma seemed to be involved in an animated conversation. I could not imagine what they had in common.

We finally all trailed behind Mom and Gordie as we made our way out of the terminal into a wall of heat that was more reminiscent of disembarking in, say, Barbados than the northeast reaches of Canada. We followed Gordie across the parking lot to the waiting vehicle.

"Was it too much to expect that he'd pull the damn thing up to the curb?" Eliza was saying, trailing a black wrap that, if I didn't miss my guess, was cashmere, a tad too warm for these temperatures.

"So, Gordie," Phillip was saying now that he'd caught up to our guide. "*Pourquoi fait-il si chaud ici*?" He was met with stony silence. "Sorry, forgot where I was. Why the hell is it so hot here? We were expecting more temperate weather." Phillip often liked to feign forgetting he wasn't in Montreal.

"Having a heat wave," Gordie said as we approached what appeared to be an overgrown SUV. A man of few words, or so it seemed.

I could see a tiny trickle of sweat making its way down Eliza's forehead, threatening to ruin her impeccable eye makeup. *That won't be pretty*, I thought while silently cheering on the rivulet.

"I hope there's AC in that thing," Eliza said under her breath, then more loudly, "Please tell me our accommodation is air-conditioned, Mr. O'Brien."

"It is, ma'am," he said as he clicked his car key, and it chirped to life. I was sure I heard him add "tonight," but I thought better of asking him to repeat it. Eliza was peevish enough as it was.

"Hey, this is quite the cool vehicle," Phillip said as we all approached. I had no idea Phillip would find anything larger or less sleek than the BMW he and Marcus drove when they weren't Ubering around Montreal cool or even of any interest at all. Phillip had never been what you would call a "car man."

"Precisely what kind of vehicle is this thing?" Eliza said. Were her nostrils flaring?

"This, my love," Gordie said, extending his arm in a flourish across the sparkling thing, "is a brand spanking new Ford Transit Passenger Wagon. Seats fifteen without luggage and all of us with your small cases." He then pointedly looked at the suitcase, which was now sitting beside Phillip, and raised an eyebrow.

"It is a truck, Mr. O'Brien," Eliza said as she mopped her forehead with the end of her cashmere wrap. "But if it is air-conditioned, I don't care."

"I'll have that air-con blasting asap," he said. "And Ms. Eliza, we're going to get to know one another real well this week, so please call me Gordie." Eliza scowled.

Phillip dug me in the ribs. "You know what this reminds me of, Erica?"

I had no earthly idea. What could such a truck-like vehicle (which looked more like a bus to me) remind my fastidious art-gallerist brother of?

"Remember those DVDs you had for Maddie that I used to love to watch with her when she was little?"

Phillip hadn't visited us often, but when he did, he was the very best uncle any kid could hope to have. He had spent hours with little Maddie, and I suddenly remembered the DVDs he was talking about.

"Oh, my god," I said when it struck me. "*The Magic School Bus*!" Phillip nodded. "So, that makes us Ms. Frizzle's adventurers."

The Magic School Bus was a children's television show that had aired for about four years in the 1990s, but it had a much longer life after it was reissued on DVD. A whole new generation of kids got hooked on science by watching the inimitable Ms. Frizzle, everybody's favourite science teacher, as she packed her pupils into her magic bus and took them off on adventures. That bus could blast off into space and go into orbit, fly across continents, dive beneath the ocean waves, and reduce itself in size to such minuscule proportions that it could take those kids anywhere that there was a science lesson to be learned—perhaps even Newfoundland. We—grownups and kids alike—had all loved it.

"Too bad Gordie doesn't look like Ms. Frizzle," Phillip said.

"If you squint?" I said, and we both laughed.

A few minutes later, we were all finally settled into our seats without too much argument about who would sit where. Mom was riding shotgun but only after winning the argument with her brother, Uncle Fred, and rest of us just took any seat available. We were ready. We figured it would be a short ride to the hotel, so where everyone sat mattered very little.

"We've got about forty-five minutes, give or take, to our hotel in Corner Brook," Gordie said as he turned on the ignition and the AC started blasting.

"Corner Brook!" Eliza said. "That seems like a long distance and in the opposite direction of where we're going, I might add. I did check the maps before coming on this little junket. Why aren't we staying in Deer Lake tonight?"

"Lovely lady," Gordie said, "I don't suppose there are many places in this fair village where a splendid woman as yourself would want to stay."

That put Eliza in her place quickly, as far as I could see. She didn't say another word.

Gordie turned slightly in his seat. "Seatbelts everyone!"

Phillip and I looked at one another and broke up laughing.

"What's so funny?" Mom said.

"You have to know Ms. Frizzle," I managed to say. Then I turned to Phillip. "'Take chances, make mistakes, get messy.'" In addition to "seatbelts everyone," it was what Ms. Frizzle always said to her pupils as they embarked on a new adventure.

Phillip smiled broadly, and I could see the mischievous little boy he used to be lurking behind those sparkling eyes. "Let's do it, sis!"

And we were off.

SEVEN

Eliza

HOW COULD I NOT HAVE KNOWN it was going to be hot in this godforsaken place? Everything was against me. I was going to have to seriously consider firing Mary-Lou when I got home. It was her job to investigate these things for me. As I sat in the third row of that miserable truck pulling out onto a highway in the middle of nowhere, all I could think about was that I didn't deserve this level of misery. I had no idea how I was supposed to find the inner courage to endure this road trip, not to mention the people. I was only too aware that these were members of my extended family, and perhaps that made it even worse. I'd had enough already, and we hadn't even reached our first hotel. I wanted nothing more than to sit in the bathtub (I was hoping it would be a deep, jetted one) with a room service drink while sampling the hotel bath products.

I tuned out all the noise around me and leaned against the window as we made our way to the town of Corner Brook, Newfoundland. Gordie was droning on about the town being something he called "purpose-built." How could a town be purpose-built, I wondered. I didn't have to wonder long.

"Town wouldn't be here if it hadn't been for the pulp and paper company. Yes, back in 1923, they needed some place for workers to live, and that's what got it started," Gordie was saying. "They built it on purpose."

It seemed my father, an original Newfoundlander himself, didn't know any more about this place than any of the rest of us, so he was peppering Gordie with questions. Gordie was only too happy to answer. Would they never shut up?

Finally, Gordie announced that we'd arrived. He turned into a short, curving driveway leading to a parking lot forming the front yard, so to speak, of a quaint Tudor-style building. Our accommodation for the night, it seemed. I looked at the building.

It was constructed of dark timber beams, accented by whitewashed plaster, and I had to grudgingly admit that it did exude a kind of timeless elegance and historic charm — at least from a distance. As I disentangled myself from the vehicle and my various family members, I breathed in the scent of what I seemed to remember freshly cut grass smelled like. I was feeling slightly more relaxed as we each took our suitcases and approached the front porch that had looked so inviting from a distance.

As I got closer, I thought I could see some peeling paint, and as I stepped onto the first step, it sagged just slightly, forcing me to grab the railing. It seemed that quaintness had its price.

As we walked into the lobby, Gordie began filling us in on the inn's history. "The place is a hundred years old," he said. As I looked around at the lobby, my first thought was that I hoped Nora was in better shape for her one hundred years. This place hadn't seen any renovation or possibly even a paintbrush in that entire century. My nose began to twitch.

The lobby was dark with wood-beamed coffered ceilings from which hung porcelain chandeliers. The wallpaper that went up the walls to about the three-quarter mark, where it stopped at a dark wood rail, was an indistinguishable floral print with peeling edges between the strips. It did, indeed, look one hundred years old. Then there were the carpets and the drapes.

The wood floors were covered in places by dark red patterned rugs, and the heavy reddish draperies had long fringes and tassels. The lobby was finished by dark leather wingback chairs and a wood-panelled reception desk next to a wooden staircase that reached straight up in front of us. Oh yes, and there was a six-foot poster board on a stand in one corner of the space.

"Come From Away," it said. As I peered more closely, I realized it was an advertisement for a production of the Broadway musical of the same name. I watched as Emma noticed it and went over.

"Take my photo, would you, Phillip?" she said as she posed beside it. "Ooh, I've been wanting to see this musical."

Erica walked over beside her and looked at the poster. "I saw it in Toronto when it debuted. It was one of the best musicals Andrew and I saw in several years." Then she turned to me. "Did you like it when you saw it on Broadway?"

"I haven't actually seen it," I said. "I didn't think it would be for me."

"You really missed out, then, Eliza," Phillip said as he clicked photos of Emma. "It was a terrific story, and the music was so fun. Marcus and I saw it a couple of trips ago in New York."

"I'm not even sure I know what it's about," I said. "Jacob and I prefer the ballet." That wasn't entirely true. I preferred the ballet, but Jake liked musicals. Frankly, the ballet patrons were more my kind of people, generally possessing better manners. In my experience, there was far less rattling of candy wrappers and whispering at the ballet. In fact, I remembered that Jake had asked me if I'd like to see it since it was evidently about Newfoundland. I had demurred.

"Oh, you are such a snob," Emma said as she took her phone back from Phillip. "It's about the week after 9/11 when Gander — one of the places we're visiting — hosted planeloads of displaced travellers whose flights were all diverted from New York that day. They were stuck here, and the Newfoundlanders opened their lives to their guests." She turned and tapped her finger on the poster. "Come from away? Get it? Like Gran said in her letter. We're all come-from-aways. CFAs?"

I rolled my eyes. Who cared?

Emma turned to Gordie. "Is there any chance we might be able to get tickets to it when we're in Gander?"

Gordie smiled. "Funny you should ask, love. As it happens, I have a buddy who knows some people, and I can get tickets for everyone if you like."

Of course, he knew someone. I supposed this would be the way the trip would unfold. Did everyone in Newfoundland know everyone else? I sighed. Emma looked like a delighted child—or perhaps a demented one if you remembered she was over forty.

"Let's all go!" Emma said. "It could be a great family outing."

Wasn't this whole trip a family outing? I wasn't sure I needed anything extra and said so.

Erica said, "Geezus, Eliza, can't you get into the spirit?" She turned to Gordie. "Well, I've seen it before, but I'm in. I'd love to see it on Newfoundland soil."

"Tickets for everyone, then?" Gordie said as he stood at the reception desk, checking the lot of us in.

Even I had to agree—but reluctantly. I guess I was destined to have the whole experience. I just knew I'd be drawing a line at kissing the cod—some kind of dreadful local ritual I'd read about.

Gordie passed out the keys, and I gratefully made my way to the tiny elevator behind the staircase, dragging my little suitcase behind me. I could hardly wait to get out of these clothes and chill for the evening with room service. As I passed by the reception desk, I said to the largeish woman with a broad face and toothy smile, who seemed to be very friendly with our guide, "Is the room service menu in our rooms?"

She suddenly looked startled. "Room service?" she said, shaking her head. "No, my ducky, it is not. We're a wee place and have no such thing, but our dining room is charming. Lovely menu, too, I might add."

I clutched at my cashmere wrap that was now festooning my shoulders. If I'd been wearing pearls, I would have clutched them, too. Dear god, it only got worse. I didn't know the half of it.

"Listen up, everyone," I could hear Gordie saying. "Before you all rush off to freshen up, I just wanted to tell you that we'll meet up in the dining room in," he checked his watch, "exactly half an hour.

We'll have a gay old time with a drink or two," he winked at Aunt Maureen who was sitting on a sofa facing the reception desk, "a great scoff and a wee bit of planning for the days ahead."

I wondered how Aunt Maureen was handling all this family time. I'd always liked Dad's sister (I could forgive her for being Erica's mother) and vowed I'd try to spend some time with her during this trip. I'd always admired her—moving away on her own and getting a PhD at a time when women didn't do that sort of thing. I hated to admit it, but I had often felt that I respected Maureen more than my own mother. Yes, I was that kind of daughter.

"A gay old time?" Phillip said, raising an eyebrow.

"Pardon my manners," Gordie said, hanging his head in mock contrition. "I'm just an old guy, and you know what I mean."

Phillip smiled. "I'm just pulling your leg. But you might want to avoid that in future."

"Will do, sir," Gordie said. "Now, are we all settled?"

"Just one question, Gordie," Emma said. "What is a scoff?"

He laughed. "You'll find out soon enough, my love, soon enough." He stared at Emma and seemed to be laughing harder.

I was afraid that I *did* know what it meant.

~

When I finally managed to make the enormous brass key to my room work in the lock (hadn't they heard of key cards around here?), I opened the door to find myself in a dark space with brown wall-to-wall carpets, gold wallpaper and dark wood everywhere. At least, as Gordie had promised, the air conditioning was working well.

I immediately peeled off my black clothes and threw myself on the bed to enjoy a few moments of cool air before figuring out if, at least, I might be able to have a nice bath later. When I finally ventured into the bathroom, all I found was a vintage pedestal sink, a toilet and a small, plain bathtub with oddly short sides. There would be no luxuriating in a tub with jets this evening. That much was clear.

I checked my watch and saw that I had only ten minutes more to fluff myself up and dress unless I wanted to incur the wrath of our tour guide. I was the queen of the quick makeup fix anyway, so I got up, slapped some water and a few products on my face, grabbed a wrinkle-free travel dress I had rolled up in the corner of my tiny suitcase (yes, it was black) and slid it on. The long sleeves wouldn't even be a problem, given the AC that I was now enjoying.

I took the stairs down, and it was only five minutes past the expected time when I arrived at the double French doors that led from the lobby into the dining room. It was called The Carriage Room. There wasn't a carriage in sight, but I could see my travel mates already seated at a huge round table inside. It seemed I was the last to arrive. I took a deep breath and opened the door.

EIGHT

Erica

I WASN'T SURE WHAT I'D BEEN EXPECTING, but our first night's accommodation didn't seem to fit the bill—in a good way. I had set my expectations fairly low after I'd done some intelligence gathering with Maddie in the days leading up to the trip.

"Mom," Maddie had said as she clicked through websites, "I don't think they have any actual hotels in that area." She was referring to the Great Northern Peninsula because I knew very well there were hotels in Newfoundland and nice ones—just not here.

So, to find myself in a charming vintage hotel was a treat. Yes, I had noticed the peeling paint and the dingy carpets in the lobby, but none of that mattered. I had an idea for a story about families for the show and something else in my head. I wasn't sure yet what it was, but I could feel my old journalistic curiosity beginning to bubble to the surface. There had been a time in my professional life when I'd had an insatiable desire to unearth stories—to discover what lay beneath the veneer of everyday existence. In recent years, though, I'd become a "personality" rather than a journalist. Perhaps I had a hidden desire to reconnect with who I used to be. Maybe this trip would be the catalyst. But that was a consideration for another time. I was on a deadline here and now. I had half an hour.

I settled quickly into my room because I wanted to call Andrew and Maddie before dinner, and I didn't have much time if I also wanted to throw some water in my face.

"How are things on The Rock?" Andrew said when he answered. I told him about the flight and about Gordie. "How's your mom doing?"

"You know, I'm not sure. She's been unusually quiet. I guess there's a lot for her to think about. We'll see how it goes."

Then I spoke with Maddie, who wanted to be filled in on every detail. I told her I'd start sending photos tomorrow. "What about video clips?" she said.

I knew she would want content for her TikTok channel, so I'd have to be judicious with what I sent to her. She was a creative video clip editor even at her young age. Kids these days were amazing.

Before I went down to dinner, I texted Sam. "Got a few ideas for the show," I wrote. "And other things maybe. Will call you in the next few days to discuss. E." I got a thumbs-up back from her. Now, it was time to join the fray once again.

When I arrived in the dining room, Gordie was already holding court at a large round table in the middle of the room under its beamed dome. Phillip and Emma were once again deep in conversation while Mom and Uncle Fred listened to Gordie. Eliza was nowhere to be seen. *Typical,* I thought. I was, however, delighted to see that Mom was more animated now. I hoped she was going to enjoy this trip as much as she possibly could. When you're knocking on the door of eighty, it's so important to live each day to the fullest, don't you think? Well, perhaps it's important at any age, but the older you get, the more significant it seems to be — at least in my view.

I walked toward them past several tables where people seemed to be enjoying their dinners, judging by the way they were heads down, not talking to one another. I took the empty seat beside Phillip, leaving one empty seat next to Gordie for Eliza. Of course, that meant we would be sitting side by side, but there were no other options.

"Gordie was just telling us about tomorrow's plans," Mom said as I sat down.

Gordie poured me a glass of wine from the open bottle on the table. I had to stifle a snicker when I noted it was a bottle of Lindemann's Bin 65 Chardonnay, something I hadn't had since Andrew and I were first married over twenty years before—before we became those insufferable wine snobs who chose their wines based on some wine critic's snotty rating and drank only from the right shaped crystal glass. This was not, in anyone's world, a chardonnay glass, and it certainly wasn't crystal. I hadn't had a glass of wine from one of those little round diner glasses in years. However, I had promised myself (and Phillip) that I'd throw caution to the wind and go with the flow. Lindemann's it was. I took a sip and was transported back in time. But what surprised me the most was how much I liked it.

"We're off on the Viking Trail bright and early," Gordie said as Emma and Phillip ended their tête-a-tête to pay attention to the itinerary. "About an hour's drive will get us to Gros Morne National Park. You're in for a treat tomorrow. Hope you all have your hiking boots."

That was the moment Eliza appeared. "Did I hear someone say hiking boots?" she said as she slid into the seat next to me like a slithery snake. Okay, so I needed to get off Eliza's case, but in my defence, I only thought those things. I again refrained from saying anything. I was gunning for a medal.

Gordie half stood with his hand on the back of Eliza's chair as she slid in. "We've got about a couple of kilometres hike in and back out from Western Brook Pond. I suppose if all you have is sneakers, that'll have to do."

I happened to know that Eliza was a sneaker person, but only when it meant tennis sneakers with whites to play at her club in Manhattan. She'd mentioned it enough times five years ago.

"Well, that's for tomorrow," Gordie said, lifting his menu and turning to Emma. "Now, let's get at that scoff." And the light seemed to dawn on Emma's face.

The menu was not unexpected as far as I was concerned. There was seafood, seafood and more fish. Sprinkled in were chicken, a bit of pork belly, and, oddly for this time of year, I thought, a roast turkey dinner. That sounded divine since turkey only made it onto our household menu at Thanksgiving and Christmas. I thought I might skip the appetizer. Gordie had other ideas.

"Ladies and gents," he said, "a trip such as this one can't start well without a feed of cod tongues to begin. It whets the appetite, as it were, for all that follows after."

I was sure I heard Eliza retch. She seemed to recompose herself quickly and said, "What precisely are cod tongues, if I may ask? I was unaware that fish had tongues."

"Well, lovely lady, strictly speaking, I suppose, if I'm being completely honest, you do have a point. There are no real tongues like ours—we all know fish can't talk, don't we?" His eyes sparkled. "But there is a piece of flesh at the base of a cod's throat that we call the tongue. A bit of flour and salt and pepper, then fried up in pork fat with a few scrunchions, and you'll think you've died and gone to heaven."

"Scrunchions?" Eliza asked as she reached into her handbag for her bejewelled reading glasses, a notebook and a pen.

"Delightful, crispy pieces of fried pork fat, my dear," Gordie said, practically smacking his lips.

Eliza made a note as I heard what sounded distinctly like quiet gagging—the dry heaves, perhaps—from Emma, who was just on the other side of Phillip.

"Mr. O'Brien—Gordie," Emma began, "as I mentioned to you at the donut shop, I'm vegan."

I snorted as quietly as I could and looked across at my mother, who was looking confused. Phillip dug me in the ribs and joined me in the snorting. Before we knew it, we were both laughing.

"What's so funny?" Emma said earnestly.

"You say it like you're a member of some kind of religious sect," I said.

"Erica, I'll have you know that veganism has a long history."

"I'm sure it does," Phillip said with his head turned fully toward me so that she couldn't hear. "So does meat-eating."

"You're only flippant because you know we have the moral high ground," Emma said. "So, I'll not be partaking in anything animal-related, no matter how authentically Newfoundland it is."

"The rarefied air of the higher moral ground must interfere with sanity," Phillip whispered, which started me snorting again.

"More for us, then," Gordie said, taking it all in stride.

"Emma, dear," Mom said from across the table, "how long have you been vegan?"

"Ten years, Aunt Maureen."

"That explains her pallor," I whispered to Phillip.

"Ah, the creature of moral superiority and kale-infused righteousness," Phillip said out loud this time. "I suppose you're about to wax poetic about the environmental benefits of your chosen lifestyle while scoffing down a kale salad with quinoa on the side."

I had no idea Phillip was so anti-veganism. I'd have to ask him about that later, but he was on a roll, and I was enjoying this.

"I'll have you know, there are statistics backing up the vegan lifestyle as the only way for planetary survival while at the same time ensuring the death of the commodification of animals," Emma said.

She sounded like someone rattling off a memorized catechism at Sunday school.

"Well, I didn't expect anyone to embark on a moral discourse, Emma dear," Mom said. Did I mention that Mom used to be a philosophy professor—with a specialty in ethics? No? Well, Emma had come to the wrong table if she thought she was going to make a moral argument that a philosopher and a bunch of hedonists would buy.

"I will eat nothing that has ever had a face," Emma said like a petulant schoolgirl.

"What about shrimp? Lobster? No face there as far as I can figure out." I couldn't help myself. Emma shook her head. I shrugged. "I'll try the cod tongues, and then I'll have the turkey dinner," I said.

Everyone except Emma agreed to the cod tongues, along with orders of lemon dill salmon and stuffed chicken. Gordie ordered creamed spinach cod, but that seemed a step too far too soon for the rest of us. Since there were no vegan entrees on the menu at all, Emma ordered French onion soup (no cheese and no slice of toasted baguette. Dear god, French onion soup without cheese and bread was just a bowl of wilted onions) and a Caesar salad—no bacon, no anchovies, no parmesan cheese and no Caesar dressing—since it's made with egg yolk. As far as I'm concerned, a Caesar salad without bacon, anchovies, parmesan cheese or Caesar dressing is just a bowl of lettuce. I wasn't sure why she didn't just ask someone to kill her now. She wasn't going to have any fun.

When the cod tongues arrived in advance of our main meals, we all tried them. Mom and Uncle Fred had both experienced them as kids—Mom liked them, Fred, not so much. Phillip loved them, and I thought the consistency was something I might not repeat. Eliza pronounced them interesting and made notes in her little red notebook. I wondered what she was writing.

Gordie had arranged for us all to sample his favourite Newfoundland dessert.

As the two servers arrived with steaming bowls on large platters, Gordie announced, "Now we've had quite a time this evening getting to know one another, but we're not quite through. I'm after chatting to the pastry chef here earlier, and she's made us proud again. Ladies and gents, may I present a sample of my favourite Newfoundland dessert. I give you Blueberry Duff with a large measure of rum and caramel sauce." Then he stared right through Emma. "My love, surely you can eat a bit of dessert, can't you?"

Emma looked like she was sucking on a lemon. "Does it have dairy in it?"

"If by dairy you mean the milk and butter and eggs that stand as culinary cornerstones to every good dessert ever made, then the answer is yes, my dear." Then he turned to the server who was just about to place a steaming bowl of what smelled to me to be an aroma just this side of heaven and said, "Alice love, better not put that in front of her lest she be tempted into the iniquity that is the heavenly hedonism of tantalized tastebuds."

I had to hold my hand over my face to stifle a giggle. Phillip didn't even bother. He erupted, which got the rest of the table going. Mom even cracked a smile.

"Ah, you are a testament to the power of conviction, my dear," Gordie said to Emma. "But mark this. We shall have you this week as a reminder that in a world full of choices, it is still possible to avoid opening oneself to experiences." Then he looked around at the rest of us as he sat down. "*Bon appetit!*"

I raised the first spoonful of the caramel-sauce-covered blueberry studded cake-like pudding to my mouth and swooned. The hell with the diet this week. I almost felt sorry for Emma as she sat there toying with her bowl of raisins and bananas—the only thing the servers could find for her. *God love them*, I thought, *at least they're trying.*

"Well, I know I'm stogged," Gordie said as he wiped the last morsel of rum caramel sauce from his chin. "Breakfast at eight, then."

I just assumed that stogged meant full. I was stogged, too.

ALONG THE SHORE & UP THE POND

Iris's Steamed Blueberry Pudding – a.k.a. Newfoundland Blueberry Duff

- 2 ½ cups flour
- 3/4 cup sugar
- 2 tsp baking powder
- 1 to 1 ½ cups blueberries
- 1/3 cup melted butter
- ¾ cup milk
- 1 tsp vanilla extract

1. Whisk the flour, sugar and baking powder together.
2. Add the blueberries and toss to distribute them in the flour mixture.
3. Mix the melted butter, milk and vanilla extract together and add all at once to the wet ingredients.
4. Mix all together with a wooden spoon just until a soft dough is formed.
5. Press the dough into a cotton pudding bag that you have soaked and wrung out. Push the dough to the bottom of the bag, leaving a space at the top for it to expand.
6. Tie the bag closed with a piece of butcher string.
7. Put a rack or upside-down plate into the bottom of a large pot and fill it with water just to the top of the rack or plate.
8. Lay the bag on the rack or plate. It's okay if it dips in the water a bit, but it should not be submerged, or it will be a boiled pudding!
9. Boil gently for approximately one and a half hours (more if you need it, but you probably won't), checking occasionally to ensure the water has not boiled dry. Add more as necessary.
10. Remove from the pudding bag carefully, slice and serve with a caramel rum sauce or whipped topping if you're lazy.

NINE

Eliza

I HADN'T EXPECTED TO SLEEP THAT WELL. My neighbourhood on the Upper West Side of Manhattan wasn't exactly suburban quiet, but it wasn't Times Square either. But the quiet here was almost absolute. We were in the middle of a town, but I didn't hear a single shouting voice, a single siren or a single car horn honking in the distance. At first, lying there in the silence had seemed strange, but then I began to relax. *So, this is what small-town life must feel like*, I thought. Then, I started thinking about dinner.

As much as I'd been hoping for a solitary evening with a glass of wine in my room, I hadn't hated dinner. I hadn't even hated the company—with the possible exception of that smug Erica with her national television job and her Toronto I-live-in-the-centre-of-the-universe attitude. I was the one who lived in the centre of the universe. New York was more than a step above anything this country had to offer. I had lived in the US long enough to recognize Canada's foibles—one of which Erica embodied in her smugness. They have no idea. Then I thought about Emma. Poor Emma.

I had been aware for some time that Tobias, the live-in boyfriend—her partner, to hear her tell it—was less a partner than he was the ranking member of the household. Whenever Dad and I chatted those two or three times a year (to my credit, I did visit him once a year), he always mentioned how he worried about Emma. At first, it had primarily been about her choice of careers—or lack of career from Dad's point of view. It was a view I shared. Being an artist anywhere in the world these days, even in cities where opportunities for connection and mentoring abounded, was an almost impossible way to make a living. Trying to do so in a small village on the coast of nowhere was beyond insane. Yet, Emma, egged on by Tobias, persisted. Then there was this veganism.

Although I'd seen Emma a few times over the past years, I didn't remember it being such a religious-like commitment for her. I recalled a time when Emma loved nothing more than a juicy hamburger topped with cheese and bacon if memory served, and chocolate cake for dessert, not raisins and bananas in a bowl. I wondered if her piety and devotion to the gods of veganism were genuine or influenced by an outside force. As I drifted off into sleep, my last thought was about something Gordie said. Something about in a world full of choices, it is still possible to avoid opening oneself to experiences. I knew a thing or two about that.

~

When I awoke the following morning, I was disoriented. I'd had only a couple of glasses of that oddly tasty cheap wine, but I felt hung over. As I pushed back the duvet, I realized it wasn't a hangover I was feeling. It seemed to be more of a sense of disconnection. I'd set the alarm on the ancient clock radio for seven, thinking an hour would be enough time for me to get ready, but I could see that it was only five-forty-five. It seemed I was awake with the sun.

I walked across the small room and opened the curtains to the bright sun rising, casting shadows across the parking lot under the trees. I picked up my phone and clicked to see if there were any messages from Jake or Mary-Lou. I'd left it on silent throughout the night because I'd wanted a full night's sleep. There were no messages, but of course, it was an hour and a half earlier in New York. I'd forgotten. Then I clicked on the weather.

Dear god, I thought, *another hot day ahead. How is this possible?* The app told me the expected high would be twenty-eight degrees Celsius. At first, I couldn't remember what that meant. Then I noticed it was also in Fahrenheit in smaller letters. It was going to be eighty-two degrees. In Newfoundland! I wondered if it might be possible to buy a few lighter clothes, but it occurred to me that this probably wouldn't last. I'd be wearing my jacket before the week was out. Of that, I was certain. At least I was getting a bit of "summer" vacation.

I decided to get dressed and take a walk since it wasn't that hot yet. I showered (in the bathtub—had these people never heard of stand-up showers?) and dressed for a fitness walk—an outfit that included my tennis shoes. I slipped quietly out my door so as not to disturb anyone around and made my way downstairs and through the lobby. There was no one at the desk, so I was able to slide out without having to chat with anyone—an activity I'd noticed seemed high on everyone's list of things to do around here. Chatting has never been my thing.

The morning felt new, light. And I started to feel the same. I noticed a sign that said something about a pond, so I headed in that direction. Just behind the inn was a dirt path leading down into a meadow, and at the bottom was a pond, complete with swans and ducks. I could hear gentle quacking coming from behind a stand of bull-rushes and a distant birdsong. It was enchanting. I smiled. I have no idea why I smiled. The swans in the lake in the middle of Central Park never had that effect on me. Even as recently as two weeks earlier, Jake and I had taken a walk through the park. After all, it was a mere two blocks from our front door, yet it was something we rarely did. We'd walked silently past the swans— together and yet miles apart. I remembered being deep in thought about how I'd approach the new book because it wasn't working as well as I'd hoped. Jake had his EarPods in, listening to his latest favourite motivational speaker. I happened to know it was someone called Dan Hardy, and I also happened to know that Jake had been channelling this Dan person when, just days before, he had quoted him as saying, "Track every action that relates to the area of your life you want to improve." I'd thought long and hard about that one, wondering if he had considered applying the philosophy to our marriage. But I digress.

I started to walk around this lake, every step feeling a bit more invigorated as if the atmosphere was seeping into my veins. I could almost hear Mother Nature breathing, something I couldn't ever remember experiencing.

"Hey, Eliza," came a voice over my shoulder. "*Bon jour!*"

It was Phillip, of course. I turned to find my cousin decked out in expensive looking running clothes, including a pair of running shoes that I happened to know retailed for close to five hundred dollars. I'm sure my eyebrows raised slightly. I figured he must be a serious runner to be able to justify that expense. I noticed his cheeks were rosy and his hair not quite as perfect as it usually was, so I deduced he was at the end of a run. He must have been up even earlier than I was.

"Good morning, Phillip. I didn't know you were a runner."

"Ten kilometres every day, three seasons out of the year. Montreal winters, though—I do a treadmill. How about you? You out for a run?"

I told him I was just strolling. Phillip decided to join me.

"Phillip, I noticed you and Emma deep in conversation yesterday. I hadn't realized you two had much in common—a Maritime village girl and you a cosmopolitan kind of guy."

"If you're wondering what we talked about," he said, "she's anxious to have her art represented by a gallery. And since I'm a gallery owner, well, you can see where that conversation was heading."

"Have you seen her work?"

Phillip nodded. "She had some photos on her phone." I waited, but Phillip didn't elaborate. "Well? What did you think?" As much as I thought Emma was a birdbrain for pursuing her "art," she was still my little sister, and I wished her well. "Did she show you her sculptures as well as her paintings?"

"Yes, she did," he said. "Interesting."

Interesting. So noncommittal. It was my personal favourite word for describing things that I didn't have any idea how to put into words how I really felt. I wondered if he was the same.

Phillip lifted the front of his T-shirt as if to smell himself. "Wow, I really need a shower," he said. "Nice to chat. See you at breakfast." He sprinted away back up the hill toward the inn.

I continued strolling, now thinking about Emma's art. I had seen it in the flesh, as it were, only once. When Mom died five years ago, I spent an entire week in the Halifax area with Dad, helping him with the estate issues as much as I could. He had run a medical practice for decades, but his administrative tasks had been looked after by his staff. He was hopeless when it came to paperwork. After the funeral, Jake and I had rented a car and driven down along what is known as the South Shore to where Emma and Tobias lived and worked.

They lived in the middle of a village called Chester, presumably named after the town of the same name in England. It was a small, seaside village whose population swelled each summer as wealthy Americans and increasingly Canadians from the rest of the country (presumably Toronto or thereabouts) flocked to their oceanside "cottages." These so-called cottages were mostly massive, clapboard-covered Cape Cod-style houses with wrap-around porches and vast lawns. Emma and Tobias, however, did not live in one of these houses.

At the time (and I had no reason to suppose anything much had changed), they were renting a two-story, cedar-shingled house in the middle of the village (not on the water), the square footage of which could have fit into my kitchen. Despite the lack of space, Emma still managed to have what she called her atelier—aspirational if nothing else. What she really had was a living room whose walls were covered from the ceiling almost to the floor with her paintings. And let us not forget her sculptures, although I would love to be able to do so. Once I had seen them, there was no way to unsee them, despite trying very hard.

I checked my watch and decided it was probably time to turn around and head back if I wanted to be on time for breakfast. I was still considering Emma's artwork, though, and how Phillip must have felt when he saw it. He was a cosmopolitan kind of individual with connections to some of the most coveted contemporary artists in the world. I knew this because I'd done my updated online research on all members of my extended family before I boarded that plane—only the day before, but it seemed like a lifetime ago. Surely, he was as alarmed by Emma's belief in her talent as I had been. I should think his clients might be a tad more sophisticated than those who might collect the style of art Emma produced.

Admittedly, her work was reminiscent of another Maritime artist. A woman named Maude Lewis was now something of a celebrity despite her artwork resembling what might have happened if Dr. Seuss and Frida Kahlo had birthed a surrealist baby. Her brightly coloured paintings looked to me like they'd been painted by a four-year-old, devoid as they are of both perspective and shadows and yet, they have become something of a phenomenon. They call it folk art. I call it atrocious. And my little sister's artwork was of that variety.

Emma painted everything from the cat next door to the lighthouse at the end of the point. Every one of them was rendered in primary colours—oils on Masonite—with the brush strokes of a demented toddler. But it was her sculptures that alarmed me the most and made me concerned for her mental health.

Emma worked with *papier mâché*, that horrendously messy stuff where you coat strips of newsprint with a flour and water mixture, then mould it onto a frame which, after drying, is painted. The results are usually something between quaint and grotesque. As far as I could tell, her brightly painted cats and lizards approached grotesquely hideous. Why anyone would do this is beyond me. But perhaps even more beyond me is why anyone would expect someone to buy one and put it anywhere their sane friends might see it.

That was the final thought on my mind as I walked into the lobby, and Emma breezed by me in the general direction of the dining room. I reflexively checked my watch.

"Oh, hi, Eliza. Just on my way for an early cup of tea before breakfast. See you soon!"

Emma was wearing a breezy dress that swept her calves. It was in a faded cornflower-blue print cinched at the waist by a rope belt. My first thought was that she was unsuitably dressed for "hiking," whatever that turned out to amount to, but who was I to talk? Then I noticed her feet. She was wearing a large pair of what appeared to be hiking shoes in red and green fabric and sturdy white soles. I hoped my tennis shoes would fit the bill.

When I finally dressed and arrived in the dining room, it seemed that everyone had eaten on their own schedules, and only Aunt Maureen and Dad were left at the table. Gordie waved to me as he passed me on his way out. "Nine on the dot, Ms. Eliza," he said, saluting.

I sat down and pulled the menu toward me. We exchanged good mornings and that kind of small talk I detested so much. How are you? Did you sleep well? Nice day—blah, blah, blah. I usually ate high-fibre cereal with a cup of coffee and four ounces of vegetable juice in the morning, but today felt different. Today, I felt like pancakes—with maple syrup and blueberry sauce, which the server brought to me in double quick time.

"Eliza, darling," Aunt Maureen said, sipping her coffee. Her face was slightly obscured by the steam that rose from the cup that she had just poured from a carafe on the table. "Tell me. How is Jacob?"

I inhaled another piece of the extraordinary pancakes and said, "Marvellous, as usual, Maureen."

"I heard his family's company was embroiled in another lawsuit. Must be tough on business," Dad said. Did I detect a touch of schadenfreude?

Jake had always said that my father, the doctor, had an abhorrence of drug companies. Dad considered big pharmaceutical companies to be repugnant bottom-feeders behind a smokescreen of compassion. He had opined that on more than one occasion since I'd been married to Jake—and his family. It was difficult to disagree with Dad's stance since most of the issues he had with Big Pharma appeared to me to be accurate, but I had always considered it better if I stayed out of the drug company chatter.

"Jake never talks much about legal issues or how they might affect business. There's always someone who thinks a drug company is to blame for something."

"Probably because it's true," Dad said.

This was not a topic I wanted to pursue on a day that had started so well for me. I also had no desire to talk any further about my family. I turned to Aunt Maureen, who was finishing her coffee, but before I could say anything, she excused herself and said she'd see us "on the bus."

"So, Eliza, Jake is marvellous, is he? Why do I detect a modicum of discontent there, then? Trouble in paradise?" Dad said.

I hated that my father seemed to know me so well, even after all these years and all the distance I'd deliberately put between myself and my family. And if there was any trouble in paradise, I certainly didn't want anyone in my family to know about it.

"I think we're going to be late if we don't get going," I said.

"I've never felt like I know my daughters very well," Dad said, "but there is one thing I know about my oldest. You, my dear daughter, are a master of deflection." He got up from his chair and put his napkin on the table. "And you never change. See you in a bit, Eliza."

~

The truck was waiting out front when I arrived at the bottom of the steps with my luggage in hand. Before I could get to the open door, however, I had to break through a throng of people who seemed to be waiting for someone to organize them. I noticed lots of silver and white hair tucked under ball caps and those hideous brimmed hats made from nylon fabric that are so ubiquitous among the older tourist crowd. Do people not realize how undignified they look wearing those hats when they're not embarking on an African safari? And why is it that women of a certain age who travel in packs always seem to wear those hideous wide capri pants? You know the ones. They are always ill-fitting and fall at that most unflattering place, either mid-calf or just above. I had often wondered if women reach a certain age and descend into a deep pit of sartorial blindness.

Just then, I was startled by the loud clanging of what sounded suspiciously like an old-fashioned school handbell immediately behind me. I glanced behind and saw that I was indeed correct. A weasel-faced man in a bright blue vest was ringing it. Dear god, what had the world come to when people had to be herded like children—or even cattle?

When I reached the truck, Gordie was standing there in hiking boots and hiking shorts (I deduced this from the excessive number of pockets hanging off them everywhere it seemed), his thick, curly white hair neatly combed this morning. He was holding the door for me. I peeked inside and realized I was the last to arrive—again. I'd have to make more of an effort.

As I settled myself in the third row beside Emma, I found myself thinking that it had been an odd eighteen hours—possibly among the strangest of my life.

Gordie then swung himself in behind the wheel.

"Seatbelts everyone!" Erica and Phillip chanted together. What the hell had gotten into them?

TEN

Erica

I HAD SLEPT SURPRISINGLY WELL in the dark little room. It was decorated in so much brown that, at one point, I began to think I was sleeping inside a chocolate bar. Or maybe I dreamed it—I can't be sure. When I woke up in the morning, I remembered that I used to have strangely vivid dreams back in the days when I drank cheap wine, and last night's chardonnay fit the bill. It seemed to have transported me back to a time in my life when my only responsibilities were to myself and my employer. Those were the days when I travelled light—a "go bag" was always just an arms-length away. That was when I was working as a stringer for several Canadian and American news networks, even before I was a regular foreign correspondent—and long before marriage, motherhood and a mortgage. I rarely thought about those days any longer since my life had evolved to the point where my days were full. But I had recently begun to wonder if I had stopped evolving. That couldn't be a good thing when you were only in your early fifties. Anyway, the sun was well up when my alarm went off.

I jumped out of bed, quickly showered and had breakfast in the dining room as the rest of my entourage came and went. I was spared any encounter with Eliza while I settled myself into the bus (truck, perhaps?), wedged in beside Phillip. I watched Eliza as she emerged onto the hotel's front porch into the middle of a gaggle of older tourists. Presumably, they were waiting for their tour guide to lead them to the enormous tour bus that was parked just past the hotel building. I wondered why they all didn't just walk over, but maybe there was a group rule or something.

As I peered out the window, I recognized several of them as people who had been on our flight and others who had been milling about the baggage conveyor belt at the airport the day before. They were the unfortunate souls who seemed to be trapped on tour by that guide with his insufferable school bell. And, just as I thought of him, he appeared behind Eliza. And if you're wondering, yes, he started ringing the bell. I snorted so hard that the coffee I'd been quietly sipping from the take-out cup Gordie poured for me in the lobby came out my nose.

Phillip, who had been peacefully listening to something through noise-cancelling earbuds, hauled one out and said, "What's wrong with you, Erica?"

While mopping coffee drips from my T-shirt—which thankfully was black—I gestured toward Eliza, who was still standing there with a horrified expression on her face. Together, we watched as she turned slightly, and I was fully expecting her to whack him with that huge, black, nylon Prada tote bag that seemed to be glued to the crook of her elbow. She didn't, and I was sorely disappointed.

Gordie helped her clamber in behind us and closed the door. As soon as he had slid into his seat, I nudged Phillip in the ribs.

"Seatbelts, everyone!" we crooned in unison, then cracked up.

Mom turned from her front-row perch and frowned. "What's gotten into you two? You're acting like incorrigible children." She looked just like she had all those years ago when she and Dad sat in front with the two of us in the back seat on summer vacations, driving from Toronto to the ferry in Sydney, Nova Scotia, to sail across to Newfoundland to visit Gran.

Phillip must have thought so, too because that started us laughing again, and we began singing *The Wheels on the Bus*. Before we knew what was happening, Gordie was putting the bus in gear and singing along. Emma, who was directly behind me next to her father, also started singing. I don't think Uncle Fred knew the words, and Eliza was—well, she was Eliza. She continued to try to find a place to stow her tote bag and ignored us. *Well, we'll just see how long she holds out*, I thought wickedly. *We'll just see.*

~

"We've got about an hour and three-quarters to our first destination," Gordie said as he merged onto the Trans-Canada highway heading north. I used the word merge, but it was more of a nudge. There wasn't much traffic, if any. "We'll retrace our route to Deer Lake, then head on north toward Gros Morne. Everyone heard of Gros Morne?"

Of course, we'd all heard about it. But I was sure Gordie was supposed to give us further information—probably on Gran's orders.

"Over four hundred and eighty million years in the making and over eighteen hundred square kilometres of spectacular scenery, the park is. You won't find anything like it anywhere in the world," he said. "By the way, Ms. Eliza, that's just under seven hundred square miles for those of you who are metrically challenged." He then went on to talk about hiking and boating and rock climbing. Today's destination was a place called Western Brook Pond that, according to our tour guide, was a land-locked fjord. I'd never heard of such a thing.

"One thing I've learned in my lifetime," Gordie said, "is something Mark Twain once said. 'Travel is fatal to prejudice, bigotry and narrow-mindedness.' I guess Nora had a thought or two about that."

"Maybe that's Gran's problem," Phillip muttered so that only I could hear. "A bit more getting off the island might have helped with all that narrow-mindedness."

I knew Phillip had a point, but as he had done, I said nothing that anyone else could hear. The less said about our grandmother's narrow-mindedness, the better. We'd arrive on her doorstep soon enough.

I settled in to take some video clips of the scenery as we drove along. I was struck by the vast emptiness of kilometre after kilometre of tree-lined highway past multiple lakes that dotted the scenery. And yet, somehow, I knew it was only empty of civilization—no people, no high-rises, no traffic. It wasn't empty at all. It was sublime.

It was closing in on ten o'clock when we pulled into a parking lot. Gordie directed us to the toilets (rule number one of road-tripping: never pass up the opportunity to visit a toilet), then told us we'd gather and hike the three kilometres into the fjord.

"Aren't fjords on the ocean?" Phillip said. "I don't see any ocean." He swivelled his head.

"Did you have your earphones in when Gordie was talking?" Mom said. "He said it was land-locked, although I have no idea how there could be such a thing."

We joined the group and, en masse, trekked along a wide, well-kept walking path across what appeared to be a bog toward where Gordie said we'd board a boat. Emma caught up to Phillip and me, her light skirt blowing in the breeze.

"Did he say boat?" she said, anxiety dripping from her voice.

"He did. Why?" Phillip said. I could almost hear the rest of what he wanted to say: is boating non-vegan? But neither of us did.

"I get deathly seasick," she said. "Does anyone have any Gravol or anything else? I don't think I'll be able to go with you, and I know Gran will be so disappointed."

Phillip pulled Emma to the side of the path while Mom, Gordie and Uncle Fred carried on ahead, not noticing anything. I took Eliza, who was again bringing up the rear, by the arm, and we fell in line behind our respective parents, leaving Phillip with Emma. Eliza looked at me like I had two heads, quickly shook me off, and kept walking. I glanced back at Phillip and Emma, who were now bringing up the rear. She'd be okay now. Phillip had her back.

When we arrived at what appeared to be a lake, there was a small café (with more washrooms) and a waiting boat. It was a two-deck touring boat with an enclosed main deck and an open-top deck. The crew members all wore bright red polos that matched the paint colour of the boat, and they acted like they thought they had the best jobs in the world. Maybe they did.

"Best day I've seen on the water in years," the young man with the neatly trimmed beard said as we boarded. "Best kind."

Once we'd found seats and were settled on the top deck, I leaned forward to whisper in Emma's ear. "You going to be okay?"

"Phillip says I'll be fine," she said.

The crew cast off, and we began gliding over the water toward the cliffs ahead. Before long, we were slowly advancing between soaring mountains while the ripples on the water coruscated like gems. Diamonds on the water, I liked to say. It was mesmerizing.

By the time we reached what felt like an entrance to a different realm between two sky-scraping mountains majestically towering above us, I could feel my slackened jaw dropping to my chest. I had no idea this existed in the world—in my world. I suddenly felt a tear forming in the corner of my eye behind my sunglasses, and my breath caught in my chest. I remembered the last time I'd had this kind of experience.

Andrew and I were in Florence and on a tour of the Academia Gallery. We rounded a corner from a hallway into an exhibition hall, and I found myself staring up at Michelangelo's David. I was overcome with the majesty of what was in front of me. And just like Michelangelo had carved David with care and genius, it now felt like Mother Nature had done the same here. Is this where Mother Nature lived? I had to shake myself to get back to the present moment.

For the next hour, we glided over the lake—pond as it was called in Newfoundland. We listened to the crew tell us about how glaciers had carved out the fjord and how, at one time, it had been a fjord that reached the sea until a new mountain range erupted to land-lock it. We heard them talk about how it had taken billions of years for this to occur, and I was struck by how unimportant one single life can be in the face of time. Then, as we turned and made our way back toward the dock, there was one more surreal treat. The crew members were a Newfoundland band.

Rory, he said his name was as he took to the microphone he'd just set up. Rory then grabbed a guitar out of a case while Sean, the other crew member, retrieved the spoons from his pocket. Then they began. As I listened to them singing something about black rum having a hold on them, I noticed that Emma was slowly rocking her head back and forth to the music. She turned around, and I caught a dreamy kind of expression on her face. Phillip dug me in the ribs with his elbow.

"See," he said, "no seasickness there."

I looked at Emma again and thought, *Oh, oh*.

ELEVEN

Eliza

THREE KILOMETRES. Why did the car park have to be three kilometres from the pond? My tennis shoes were going to be ruined. As I trudged ever onward, I reconsidered the wisdom of bringing my tote bag with me. But when Gordie suggested I leave it behind in the truck, I suddenly felt the hairs on my neck rising, and I was determined to do what I wanted. Sometimes, more than ever lately, my initial reactions were proving to be deadly. Perhaps I needed to learn not to react so quickly. Nevertheless, I had made my decision, and I prided myself in living with my choices. I sighed just thinking about that.

As I brought up the rear behind my various and sundry family members, at one point, Erica took me by the arm, an uncharacteristic gesture if ever I felt one. I immediately shrugged it off and then found myself thinking perhaps I shouldn't have. I had never been someone to second guess herself, and I didn't like the feeling it gave me.

When we finally reached our destination and boarded the boat, I sat at the rail with Dad and Emma in the row beside me and Erica, Phillip and Maureen behind. Gordie seemed to be making the rounds.

I remembered how seasick Emma used to get when we were kids on the odd occasion when Dad would take us out on a friend's sailboat. When I asked her if she thought she'd be okay, she smiled and told me not to worry. She even patted my hand and thanked me for caring. It was odd behaviour if I ever saw it.

The "pond" was curiously captivating. Nature had never been my thing, so this trip was making me feel a bit like a square peg in a round hole. I was a city girl from the top of my expensive haircut to the tips of my Louboutin-clad toes (although not clad as such today). When crew member Rory told us to scan the top of one of the mountains to see the reclining giant, my first reaction was to roll my eyes and consider them all daft. Then, I found myself peering as hard as I could.

Gordie noticed me and walked over, handing me an enormous pair of binoculars. I held them up and looked again.

"Can you see it now?" he said.

I was convinced they were all crazy until the moment when the face in the mountain came into view, and I felt a shiver creep down my spine. There he was—a sleeping giant. There was no doubt about it any longer, and I sensed a strong force pulling me into a vortex of feeling. I wished I had someone to tell. For the first time in my life, I felt utterly alone, even among this group of family members and the rest of the gaggle of tourists.

When the boat ride came to an end, and we'd hiked the three kilometres back to the truck, Gordie informed us we were having a "boxed lunch." I seemed to recall a vague memory of Gran saying something similar to us when we were kids heading out with Gran and Grandad on a road trip in their dusty Ford Country Squire station wagon—the one with the fake wood on the sides.

We climbed back into our seats, and Gordie passed out boxes. They were, indeed, lunches—sandwiches, granola bars and bottles of water. I was so hungry that I even ate the granola bar that was, no doubt, loaded with additives that rarely touched my lips. I noticed Emma smiling dreamily as she removed the meat and cheese from her sandwich, leaving her with a mustard sandwich. But she didn't seem to mind.

According to Gordie, we were continuing to head north, and in another two or more hours—more depending on how long we stopped at the places he had in mind—we'd reach our destination for the night, some place called Plum Point. I sat back and watched the world go by.

~

We stopped twice along the way for photo ops and took a side trip down into what looked to me like an abandoned fishing village. According to Gordie, it only looked that way because lobster season had been over for a few weeks, but it would come to life again.

As I strolled by myself along the shoreline of the tiny village, I stopped to stare out to sea. I could hear mournful calls of seagulls, a sound I remembered from Gran's cottage in a place called Topsail. When I turned, I could see the rest of my family members, Dad included, walking through and around a maze of lobster traps stacked almost six feet high. Draped over them were what appeared to be fishing ropes, also drying, with their attached colourful buoys that presumably allowed the fishermen to find their own lobster pots. I wondered if the bright red and yellow stripes (that were well-faded) signified a specific owner. In any case, the traps themselves and the colourful buoys seemed to have mesmerized my family members, who were snapping photos as if they were touring the Palace of Versailles. I took my phone from my pocket and snapped one of all of them—from a distance.

As we all scrambled back into the truck, Gordie said, "One more stop on the way." He put the truck in gear and turned back onto the highway. We drove along the shore for a while, then took a turn that seemed to me to be west. I heard Dad ask Gordie where we were going.

"Headed out to Port au Choix to the lighthouse. Hoping to show you people a few caribou since we haven't had any luck with the moose sightings." Did I hear Phillip snicker at Gordie's pronunciation of the French place name? Even I had to look it up on the map on my phone to figure out what "port-a-shwa" meant.

Well, at least we had something to be grateful for. I'd heard that moose on the roads in this part of the world could be deadly—and not to the moose.

As we drove out along what Gordie explained was a peninsula, the fog began gathering. By the time we arrived at our destination, the lighthouse was almost entirely obscured, giving the place an atmospheric quality that begged for animals to emerge from the shadows.

"I love fog!" Emma said. And she should know about fog. She had been living in fog central for years, known to others as the south shore of the province of Nova Scotia.

The moment we stopped, Emma shot out of the side door with her camera in her hand. Gordie was shouting after her to be careful because he'd spotted several caribou that seemed to be a family and a lone buck. I looked over to where Gordie was pointing.

There, on the top of a rise, was a magnificent buck. And directly in front of him, a mere ten yards away, were two fools with cameras. One of them was lying on his belly on the ground, pointing his enormous lens directly at the animal. At the same time, the other one held his equally enormous camera and lens aimed straight at the caribou's face.

I could see the animal begin to move forward and back, pawing his ground. Gordie was waving his arms to try to get the attention of the imbecilic photographers who clearly didn't have the same knowledge of Newfoundland's flora and fauna as Gordie did. Finally, in an effort to avoid mayhem, Gordie started honking his horn. That got the attention of the photographers—and the caribou, who was now looking at Gordie. When the animal began moving, Gordie started yelling. "Back in the truck, Emma! Back in the truck!"

Emma climbed in and closed the door as the animal nosed up to the front of the truck and sidled along where Gordie had the window half down. Gordie reached into a bag on the floor under Mom's legs and retrieved a carrot.

"Here you go, buddy. Sorry to have disturbed you."

I had noticed that Gordie had a habit of treating all flora and fauna on the island as if they were all sentient beings. Who was I to judge? Maybe they were.

By the time we pulled into the parking lot at our accommodation for the night (two nights, to be exact), I was feeling exhausted.

Gordie suggested we disembark and gather our things while he went inside to register our clan. While we were waiting, I took the time to register where in the world we were supposed to be staying.

The sign out front said, "Ocean Point Motel." Not hotel, mind you, not even inn—that word that could be at least promising. It was *motel*—with an M. I don't know about you, but the word motel conjures a series of pictures in my mind, and none of them is the slightest bit appealing. For anyone who ever stayed in a motel with their parents on a road trip (I had), there was the picture of the family crammed into one small room with a tiny bathroom consisting of a sink, toilet and questionably clean bathtub with a fraying shower curtain. There may have even been a vibrating bed involved—the kind that would shake for a quarter. Of course, then there was the Bates Motel. Who could forget the shower scene in that Alfred Hitchcock movie?

The Ocean Point Motel looked to be a single-story building where the doors to the rooms opened directly out into the parking lot. Outside each room was one of those ubiquitous basket chairs, except now they were plastic in myriad primary colours. I remembered sitting in them as a child and getting up with the indentations of the slats on my bare legs.

We all then moved in the same direction that Gordie had gone, presumably into the lobby. As I stepped inside, I would have to say that the word lobby might be a bit grand and more than a bit overstated to describe what we were now experiencing. It was like a tiny storefront with two hideous upholstered wingback chairs and a table like the ones at church basement bazaars. On the table were brochures about everything from the ferry to Labrador, which evidently sailed from a pier very close by to rock climbing in the national park. The reception "desk" looked like the place where they brought prisoners when someone came to visit. I only know this from watching television—evidently far too much. Gordie was leaning on the counter, his head up against the glass, chatting amiably with the receptionist.

The motel may have looked from the front as if it were a single story, but now I could see steps down to a lower level and a ramp that seemed to go up to another one. Beside the reception desk was an enclave with shelves holding drinks, snacks, and an array of T-shirts and sweatshirts, all of which seemed to be adorned with Newfoundland flags and sayings. I shivered in spite of the heat. The heat—I had just noticed how hot it was in the lobby. I began to get a sense of foreboding.

Gordie finally saluted the receptionist and then turned to the rest of us, who were waiting like little lemmings to be led off the cliff.

"Well, everyone, I have good news and bad news and perhaps even two bits of bad news. I'm going with the worst news first. You may have noted the excessive heat in the lobby." Gordie looked at me, presumably because I had started fanning myself with a brochure I picked up from the table. "Well, sorry to say that's the way it is. I may have neglected to mention that Ocean Point has no AC—not that they ever really need it. It's usually ten degrees colder this time of year. Anyway, the other bad news, which, if you look at it a different way, could be good news, is that there's a bus tour on board today, meaning we all have to double up."

"Double up? As in share rooms?" I said, hardly able to think. I was still back on his first bad news—no air conditioning.

"I do, indeed, ma'am," he said. He cleared his throat. "And I suppose now might be a good time to remind you that you'll all be sharing rooms for the rest of the trip. Angela might not have been as clear as she might have."

"Oh, Eliza, sharing a room with your sister can't be construed as bad news, can it?" Aunt Maureen said.

"I suppose not," I said, looking at Emma, who was sitting in one of the two hideous chairs upholstered in faded floral print. I only hoped she wasn't picking up bed bugs as she sat. The dreamy half-smile on her face said, "I don't care about anything." What in the world had come over her?

"And the good news, Gordie?" Aunt Maureen said, sounding more optimistic than I felt.

"Ah, that's the great part. All the rooms overlook the water." Gordie smiled and handed out our keys. Yes, they were actual brass keys again. "And a bit more good news—there are fans in each room."

I rolled my eyes. I could not help myself.

"Dinner in the dining room at six," he said. "Don't be late. There's a treat in store."

"Is there a bar?" Phillip said.

Gordie smiled from ear to ear. "Sure is, my boy. Right through there." He pointed to a door just past the reception booth.

"Good stuff, my man," Phillip said. "Good stuff." Then he looked around. "Anyone care to join me? I'm buying. Half an hour."

~

Emma and I managed to find our room up the ramp I'd seen earlier, and yes, it was facing the water—which you could see if you looked past the enormous tour bus parked behind outside the door to another building that took up the rear. I could see a line of brightly coloured Adirondack chairs facing the view and briefly wondered if I might be able to catch a breeze out there. I was going to have a great deal of difficulty sleeping in this heat.

The room was just what I would have expected of a motel— wooden headboards on twin beds, quilted bedspreads festooned with faded pink and blue flowers and drapes that matched. There was, indeed, a fan in the corner. Suddenly, I had a brain wave. I had seen an ice machine along the corridor. We'd get some ice and point the airflow over it. That should do it. I plugged in the fan and turned it on. It started chugging, and for the briefest of moments, I thought it was going to die. I held my breath. But it perked up and started spinning. I breathed out. I sat on the side of the bed, exhausted from the thought of two nights here.

"I'm going to meet everyone in the bar," Emma said. "You coming?"

I told her I'd be along momentarily and continued to sit there on the side of the bed after she left, wondering if I could turn over the mattress to check for bedbugs. I sighed. That just seemed like too much trouble. Suddenly, my quiet was shattered by the loud ringing of my phone.

I leaned over to where my tote bag sat on the other side of the bed and retrieved my phone from its depths. It was Jake.

"You have to come home!"

"Hello to you, too, Jake. What the hell are you going on about?"

"Where have you been? Why weren't you answering your phone?"

"Calm down, Jake. I was touring. Service is spotty. You remember where I am, don't you?" I suspected he was simply having trouble dealing with the household on his own. We did have help. He could just ask our housekeeper to do some extra cooking.

"Eliza," he said, "I mean it. You have to come home. Now." I could hear his rapid breathing.

"Unless someone died, Jake, I'm not coming. And maybe not even then, depending on who it is. You're the one who told me I should come. Family is family. Remember?"

"This is an emergency. I can't cope by myself."

I was getting exasperated. "Are you going to tell me what precipitated this meltdown?"

"It's Izzy," he said. "She's here."

"Here as in our home?"

"That's what I said, isn't it?"

I felt a heavy blanket of anxiety begin to descend on my shoulders. There was no way I was going home now.

TWELVE

Erica

MOM AND I WERE SHARING A ROOM, and Phillip was bunking in with Uncle Fred. As we dragged our small suitcases along the faded corridor carpeting, I could feel the heat closing in around us.

"Dear heavens," Mom said. "I don't suppose anyone around here is used to this kind of weather."

"Did you see Eliza's face, Mom? I thought she was going to explode when Gordie told us there was no air conditioning. It's almost worth the heat just to see her like that."

"She can be amusing," Mom said, "although she is not the only one among us who likes her creature comforts."

Of course, Mom was right. We were all a bit spoiled. Then we opened the door of our room, and a wall of heat hit us squarely in the face.

"Dear god, Erica, open a window, will you?" Mom said as she fanned herself with a brochure she'd picked up in the lobby. I had seen Eliza with one and now wished I had one as well. "This is going to be challenging."

We settled our things, and I asked Mom if she was going to join us in the bar. "I'll be along, but you go ahead, Erica. Phillip will be waiting, and the two of you can cook up some more childishness."

I was happy to see she said it with a smile.

When I arrived at the bar, Phillip was already there. Emma was standing beside a pool table, holding a pool cue in her hand and giggling at her father, a strange situation if ever I saw one. Uncle Fred had never been known for his wit.

I slid into a tall wooden bar chair beside Phillip, and he ordered us both rum and coke. It wasn't my drink of choice, but it went with the territory.

When the older woman who was tending the bar placed the ice-filled glass in front of me, I lifted it, holding it against my temple for a moment to try to cool down a bit. "So, Phillip, what did you give Emma to help her seasickness?"

Before he could answer, Eliza swept into the bar, saw us sitting there and said to the bartender, "I'll have what they're having—but a double." There seemed to be trouble in paradise.

Eliza had always taken great pains to make sure everyone around her noted her perfect life. Her perfect house, her perfect clothes, her perfect husband, her perfect—I seemed to have forgotten to ask. "Eliza, how is Izzy? You haven't mentioned her. Isn't she in medical school?"

Isabel was Eliza's twenty-something daughter—I couldn't remember her exact age. She had gone to the best kindergarten, the best primary school, the best private girls' school, and Harvard undergrad. The last I'd heard, she had a scholarship to attend medical school at Columbia or Johns Hopkins. Gaggingly impressive. And Eliza had always made sure we all knew. Perhaps I'd forgotten to ask about her because I didn't want to hear any more about the perfection of the American way of life.

Eliza lifted her glass and downed it. She didn't even bother with the straw. She turned to the bartender and asked for another one. "The same," she said, then turned to me. "Izzy? I suppose Izzy is as she has always been."

I shrugged and figured we were moving on to other topics. Eliza wasn't finished.

"Izzy has arrived home. Jake just called me."

"That's wonderful," I said. "She must be on a school break."

"I wish," Eliza said so softly that I almost missed it.

"What's up, Eliza?" Phillip said. "You seem a bit off. Is it the heat?"

"That too," she said, downing her second double rum and coke. I wanted to suggest she slow down, but this was getting good.

Eliza ordered a third drink. "Let me tell you about Isabel Rebecca Cohen, daddy's princess, grama's darling, and her mother's nightmare."

I was shocked. Nightmare? As far as all of us knew, Isabel Cohen was the apple of her mother's eye.

Then the floodgates opened, and slightly drunken Eliza Houlihan Cohen told us about her daughter. According to the story, as she told it, Izzy had become something of a rebel when she was in high school, always getting into trouble to the point where she had come close to being kicked out of her exclusive school for a variety of transgressions, including underage drinking and smoking. Jake and his family were able to assuage the school's administration, though, with a sizable donation. It seemed money could accomplish a lot, but perhaps not everything.

"Izzy was always the top of her class, though," Eliza said. "That made Jake very happy, but I could see the rising anger in her. I suppose all daughters have difficulties with their mothers. I know I did." I kept my mouth shut because, up until then, I hadn't had any problems with Maddie. Perhaps they were yet to come, but I hoped not. She continued. "All that money. Her father and grandmother gave her everything. I wanted to be on board with that, but I guess my small-town Canadian upbringing hadn't been completely erased."

Izzy had gone to Harvard and had been granted early acceptance to medical school. In fact, she was supposed to be going into her second year now. But she had decided that wasn't what she wanted. She wanted to do her own thing. A year or so earlier, she had left New York for California, taken an online yoga teachers' course and seemed to be teaching yoga as far as Eliza knew.

"We haven't seen her in over a year," Eliza said, looking more miserable than I'd ever seen her. "Now it seems she's arrived home, and Jake can't cope.'

"Are you going home now?" Phillip said. "Leaving us?"

Eliza looked up from her drink. "No, Phillip, I don't think I am. I think I'm going to stay right here with everyone in my family."

Phillip raised his hand for a high-five. Eliza looked confused for a moment before realizing what he was doing. She gave him an awkward high-five and then said, "On another note, I want to know what you gave Emma for her seasickness. I want some of that."

Phillip's eyes twinkled, and we both laughed as he said, "Later, Eliza. Later."

~

It was time for dinner. We knew this because Gordie came into the bar and herded us all out and into the wood-panelled dining room.

Once we were seated around another round table, Gordie announced, "No menus tonight. Traditional fish and chips all around." He looked at Emma. "And something special for you, love."

Gordie had arranged everything. When he gave the nod, two servers brought out litre-sized carafes of unnamed white wine and put bottles of dark malt vinegar and pitchers of gravy on the table. I wondered what the gravy was for. They went back into the kitchen and returned with plates of fish and chips.

After all of us except Emma had been served, one of the women returned with a small tray. She placed a plate and a glass of something milky in front of Emma. "Gordie here told me about your affliction. I have a daughter who's sickly as well and can't eat so much, so I've prepared your beans just for you. Used a pair of tweezers—clean ones, mind you—to take out the scrunchions, so you can enjoy. And a glass of almond milk should do it." Emma smiled as though she had been offered a feast.

Eliza, drunk or not, was always the cookbook author and had to ask about her fish and chips. "Are those scrunchions on the fries?" she said.

The server smiled brightly. "Specialty of the house, ma'am. And the gravy is to die for on them, too."

Eliza smiled and dug in. I turned to her and said, "Eliza, you *do* know what scrunchions are, don't you?"

She finished chewing before answering. "I'm not a vegan," she said.

"I know, but you are Jewish. They're pure pork fat."

Eliza looked at me, then at her plate, raised another forkful of fries with scrunchions and gravy and shrugged.

THIRTEEN

Eliza

I COULDN'T REMEMBER WHEN I'D HAD a more delicious dinner. Jake and I frequented so many of New York's finest restaurants. We travelled to the cosmopolitan capitals of the world. We dined at Michelin-starred restaurants. But I had never felt as comforted by food as I did that evening, stuffing myself with what at another time and place I would have called a heart-attack-on-a-plate.

Each time I bit into a piece of the golden-coated fish, I could hear the crunch of the perfectly fried batter, and I wondered what they used to make it so delectably crisp. Then, beneath the blanket of crispy delectation, there was the tender, flaky cod, exuding the delicate aroma of the sea. The fries were beyond perfection—flawlessly seasoned with salt, scrunchions and the malt vinegar that I thought I would avoid. I was so glad I didn't. It added just that touch of acidity to counteract the saltiness. I was thinking about finding the cook so that I could pry the recipe from her (or him, perhaps?). When I was down to the last mouthful, I stopped a moment to let the flavours dance on my palate, leaving me longing for an ocean breeze and the smell of fish stalls with seagulls soaring overhead. Then I shook myself and looked around. I was, indeed, still on the Great Northern Peninsula of Newfoundland, not in a Michelin-starred restaurant, and that was suddenly fine with me. Perhaps the rum appetizer had prepped the palate.

~

When dinner was over, Emma and I headed back to our room. Emma was still acting slightly odd, with her constant smiling and air kissing everyone. It was so not her.

I had replenished the ice we had in a plastic ice bucket on a chair in front of the fan because, of course, the ice had long since melted, and I despaired of getting even a breath of air. I lay down on the bed as Emma emerged from the bathroom wearing what appeared to be a new T-shirt—a T-shirt that in no way resembled her usual boho vibe.

"Nice shirt," I said. She was unlikely to perceive the irony. It was large and red and had the words "always high" emblazoned across the chest in large white letters.

Emma smiled as she got into bed. "It's great, isn't it? Phillip bought it for me at the tuck shop in the lobby."

Always high? I turned off the light and lay back on the flat pillow, my hands under my head. Before long, I could hear Emma's slow breathing, as if she might have drifted off already. Suddenly, I heard a sound like a foghorn, except it seemed to be emanating from Emma.

She turned over, and I could feel my nose twitching.

"Emma! What the hell?"

Emma sat up while I fanned my hand in front of my nose. "Geezus, Eliza. Haven't you ever heard a fart? I feel so much better now," she said. "I might have another one, though."

"Emma, that's disgusting," I said.

Emma stared at me. "Disgusting? Eliza, there's nothing disgusting about normal bodily functions. I just farted."

"Stop saying that," I said.

"Fart, fart, fart," she said, giggling harder by the minute. It was a word my mother had strictly forbidden us from saying when we were kids. "Say it with me, Eliza. Fart, fart, fart."

"I give up. Fart. But that smell, Emma. I cannot believe it came from my little sister."

I could see her smiling brightly in the ambient light from outside the building to the rear. "Ah, the beauty of beans for dinner!" she said. Then she slid down and was fast asleep before I knew it.

I got out of bed and walked over to the window where I thought I might be able to catch a breeze. As I stood there, I thought I could see someone—perhaps more than one someone—outside near or on the Adirondack chairs. Was that a flash of a lighter I saw? Was someone smoking? Then I heard voices. Erica and Phillip.

FOURTEEN

Erica

MOM FELL ASLEEP MUCH FASTER THAN I EXPECTED. I, on the other hand, blessed as I was with hot flashes at the best of times, knew it was going to be a long night if I didn't do something about it. I put on a T-shirt, shorts and flip-flops and quietly made my way down the hall. I rapped gently on Phillip and Uncle Fred's door. I was hoping (expecting) that the wine that Uncle Fred had consumed at dinner might have put him to sleep, but I knew Phillip also preferred cool to cold temperatures for sleeping. I had visited his home in Montreal and knew he and Marcus slept with the air conditioning at morgue level, even in the middle of the winter. I hoped he might still be awake.

The door opened a crack. "Hey, sis," he said. He, too, was wearing a T-shirt and shorts.

"Bring your stuff," I said. "We're going out."

Moments later, we were creeping out the back door toward the chairs overlooking the shoreline. They were just visible in the moonlight that danced off the water.

"It's going to be a long night, Phillip," I said.

"Maybe not as long as you think." He opened the small case he was carrying and set it on the arm of the chair. He opened a small plastic bag and retrieved a little white cylinder. "Share?" he said as he lit the end.

Three inhales later, and I heard a voice behind me.

"What in god's name are you two doing out here?" It was Eliza.

Phillip and I looked at one another and started snorting with laughter. "Pull up a chair, cuz," Phillip said. "Drag?"

"Oh, my actual god, you're smoking marijuana." Eliza pronounced it as if she had just learned the word.

I spluttered with laughter. "And if you don't want a drag, Phillip has a stash of gummies. CBD if you want mellow. THC, if you want a trip."

Eliza looked into the case on the arm of the chair. "Dear god, Phillip, what is that? Put that away!"

"Chill, Eliza," Phillip said. "You're in Canada. You're allowed. It's legal here, in case you've forgotten. Geez, you Americans are so uptight." He passed the joint to Eliza, who, much to my surprise, took it from him and took a long, deep drag, holding it in for just a moment and letting it out in a long, smooth exhale. You could have knocked me over with a feather. She'd done this before.

"Welcome home, cuz," Phillip said.

"So, what did you give Emma earlier today?" Eliza said, taking the seat next to Phillip.

"Oh, just a little THC gummy," Phillip said. "Greatest thing for motion sickness."

"How do you know so much about all this?" Eliza said, reaching for the joint.

"Turns out Phillip is part-owner of a popular cannabis boutique in Montreal."

We all started blubbering with laughter. Maybe it wouldn't be such a long night after all.

LISTEN TO THE WIND

Fun Facts About Vikings

- *The Vikings gave us the English words snort, lump, scrawny and berserk.*
- *Vikings preferred blonde hair.*
- *Viking helmets did not have horns.*
- *Vikings were all about hygiene—shaving, plucking, combing.*
- *Vikings ate two meals a day.*
- *Vikings were great sailors, but they also loved to ski.*
- *Viking Leif Erikson set foot on North American soil five centuries before Columbus on the northernmost tip of the Great Northern Peninsula on what is now known as the island of Newfoundland.*

FIFTEEN

Erica

IT WAS A LONG, HOT NIGHT, MADE SLIGHTLY MORE BEARABLE by the pleasant buzz I was feeling as I lay there in my narrow, vaguely lumpy bed in the dark while Mom slept soundly. I could hear a gentle snoring and suspected she'd taken one of those tiny pills she used only under extreme circumstances, and if ever a circumstance qualified as extreme—and bizarre—this was it. I don't precisely know the air temperature in that motel room that night, but it was a far cry from what we'd all been expecting on this Great Northern Peninsula of a province famous for its cool and grey weather. I couldn't help but think, though, that there was something just a bit unusual—possibly even exotic—about the atmosphere here. It just felt different. Or perhaps I felt different.

Under the normal circumstances of my life as I'd created it, if you had told me that I'd spend an hour or two sitting outside in the moonlight smoking up with my brother and cousin, I would have said you were unhinged. To know me is to know that I am ambitious and opinionated, sane and sensible. I am a wife and mother with a responsible job that puts me in the public eye. I have always had to watch my behaviour lest my employers consider me a liability to their image. Smoking dope? Not really ever been on my radar, and I expect not on theirs, either. I had only tried it once or twice before (okay, maybe three times), but I hadn't been very impressed. Phillip's weed, though, was a different story. And no one can argue that this was not a situation begging for a little help to get through. With apologies to the Beatles, I was going to need more than a little help from my friends. As the dear late Nora Ephron, one of those writers that women my age can identify with, once said, "Insane people are always sure that they are fine. It is only the sane people who are willing to admit that they are crazy." I was at that moment willing to admit I was a little crazy—and I hadn't even been aware of that until that moment, lying there, sweating in the dark, wondering what tomorrow would bring. Then I giggled a bit and said quietly into the darkness, "Bring it on."

~

The following morning, after breakfast, we once again piled into the vehicle (that I was now beginning to think of as our bus) and were off. The bus tour people had left at the crack of dawn, so the dining room had been quiet. When we asked about the lack of people, Gordie told us they'd left bright and early so they could catch the ferry to Labrador. I sat back to enjoy my quiet cup of coffee.

As Gordie pressed the button to turn on the ignition, he turned in his seat so he could see Phillip and me. "Okay, boys and girls, you can say it now."

"Seat belts, everyone," we said in unison, although it was beginning to lose its freshness. Phillip and I would have to work on that.

As we pulled out of the parking lot, Eliza, who was behind us as usual, said, "How long is the drive today, Gordie, and where exactly are we going?" I figured she probably had her phone out and was plotting our day on the map.

"Ah, lovely lady, it's not about how long the journey takes, now, is it? And it's even less about the destination." I could almost feel Eliza rolling her eyes behind me, but I didn't bother to turn around. He continued. "I've always thought Chinese philosopher Lao Tzu had the right idea when he wrote, 'A good traveller has no fixed plans and is not intent on arriving.' We will go in the general direction of where we will eventually arrive. But for you, Ms. Eliza, you might want to drop a pin on L'Anse Aux Meadows. It is our ultimate destination."

There was a brief silence from Eliza's direction. I glanced behind and saw she was deeply intent on her phone. Then she looked up and said, "Dear god, people, that's all the way up in the middle of nowhere."

Gordie laughed. Even Mom turned around and smiled in Eliza's direction. Yes, we were headed to that spot on the northernmost tip of the northernmost peninsula on this island where Vikings landed sometime in the eleventh century—discovering North America centuries before Christopher Columbus and John Cabot, making it the earliest evidence of European settlement in what they used to call the New World. I, for one, was actually looking forward to this.

"I suppose it is in the middle of nowhere if you think the middle of somewhere needs skyscrapers and crowds, love, but we think of it as a little slice of heaven, making it somewhere, indeed," Gordie said, effectively putting Eliza in her place. "We're going to enjoy the journey north and just a bit east and, if you must know, if we didn't stop, it would take us almost two hours. But what would be the fun in that, eh?"

I completely agreed.

"We're headed along what you call the Viking Trail here," Gordie said, beginning what I supposed would be his tour guide spiel just as the first raindrops started hitting the windshield. "Although to tell you the truth, it wasn't the trail the Vikings took back in the day. It's our trail to get to where they landed. Well, would you look at that," he said, "just a wee bit of rain to add to the atmosphere. We'll just head down the shore for a little stop, then across to St. Anthony," he said, pulling onto a small road headed directly toward the shore.

When we finally stopped, it was raining hard. "Fishing villages in the rain are the finest kind," he said. "Finest kind." He leaned behind the driver's seat and pulled a plastic bag from under his seat. "These here are rain ponchos," he said. "Only for the bravest among us, mind you!" Then he leaned and picked up his camera with its enormous lens from the centre console, pulled his hat on and opened his door. "Who's coming?"

Phillip and I scrambled to put on ponchos after Mom handed them out and put her own on. We were right behind her as we picked our way down a rocky incline toward where the waves crashed on the shore. Phillip seemed to be revelling in the rain as much as I was, pretending to be a superhero with his cape flapping in the wind behind him. I was impressed with my brother, who I'd often thought had lost his sense of fun as he grew up. The little boy who looked at the world with wonder had been buried under grown-up seriousness and responsibility, and I should know. They say it takes one to know one, and my inner child had been just as deeply buried. Gordie was right. It was the finest kind.

I don't know how long I stood there, rain dripping into my eyes from the poncho's hood while Phillip jumped from rock to rock, and Mom stood with Gordie a bit further down the beach, taking photos. I had planned to take some pictures myself, but all I could do was stand there feeling the rain and breathing in the crisp, briny scent of the North Atlantic—or, to be more precise, I suppose it was the Gulf of St. Lawrence. We were still on the west coast of the peninsula. Either way, I had never felt this way before. I had never stood in the rain before. I had always run for cover. It was like a spell. What was it about this place? I had no idea, but I liked how it felt.

Eliza, Emma, and Uncle Fred had all opted to stay in the bus. When we got back, Eliza complained about the dripping and the dampness, but we didn't care. We had our photos and our experience. Then we were off, heading east toward the village of St. Anthony.

By the time we reached the village, which was definitely on the eastern, North Atlantic coast, the rain had stopped, but the sky remained grey. Gordie herded us out of the truck and into a large, one-story green clapboard building with a larger-than-life statue of someone called Sir Wilfred Grenfell guarding the entrance.

When we were all gathered in the lobby, Gordie started talking. "A trip up north here isn't complete, in my view, without taking a moment to consider the remoteness of the communities here about and a bit of history."

"Remote seems a slight understatement," Eliza said.

Gordie raised his eyebrows. "Consider, Ms. Eliza, what life might have been like for the native communities here and across in Labrador. Think about the long winters, the miserable conditions, the lack of health care. You could say that our Sir Wilfred Grenfell, a medical missionary, was possessed of unwavering empathy, the like we see so rarely these days, don't you think? You know, a bit of kindness goes a long way. When he first visited, he knew he had to do something. So, he came to this desolate place to set up the mission and create a beacon of hope for the communities here and on the mainland. And," Gordie said, looking directly at Eliza, "consider this for a moment. His wife, Lady Grenfell, was a socialite from Chicago who bankrolled the work here. She gave up her cotillions and white gloves and creature comforts to come out here to help her husband and the poor."

I was impressed with Gordie's passion, although Eliza didn't look as impressed. Perhaps it was because she knew whose creature comforts he was really talking about.

"She must have been quite a spouse," Mom said. "Gordie, do they still make those parkas?" she said, changing the subject.

I had no idea what she was talking about.

"Yes, ma'am," he said, winking at Mom. I'm *sure* he winked this time. "Come downstairs to the shop after the tour, and I'll show you the new ones."

Gordie left us with a museum docent, and we took a tour around, viewing artifacts and musing about how difficult life must have been back here in the nineteenth century. I was even thinking about how brutal the winters must be here, even now in the twenty-first century. When we finished our tour, I noticed Mom must have slipped away at some point. We wandered down the open staircase in the middle of the building into the inescapable gift shop. It was there I found Mom and Gordie, deep in conversation, heads together as they stood in front of a rack of winter parkas with fur-trimmed hoods.

Gordie looked up when he saw me. "Erica, darlin', come over and see these. I do believe your mother might be buying one."

I looked at the blue parka with an intricately embroidered scene depicting two Inuit on the ice wearing similar parkas. Mom seemed to be quite taken with it, and I wondered where she'd wear it in Toronto. Everyone there could be counted on to wear black from head to toe from some point in early November until at least mid-April.

Mom was running her hand over the cloth. "I always wanted one of these when I was a little girl in St. John's," she said. "You know, Erica, this is called Grenfell cloth because it was developed specially for Sir Wilfred when he wanted something to wear to keep out the strong winds. Isn't it wonderful?"

I moved closer. "Yes, it's quite extraordinary," I said as I browsed the collection of colourful parkas.

"What are you looking at?" Emma had just come down the stairs and noticed us in the corner beside the rails of coats. "Ooh," she said as she looked at the embroidered design on the parka Mom was holding. "Oh my god, these would be perfect for winter days in the village. I have to have one of these." Then she looked at the price tag. "Oh, maybe not today," she said, then she ran her hand over the fluffy fur trim on the hood. "Is that real fur?"

"I expect it's fox fur," Mom said. "Isn't it divine?"

"Absolutely not," Emma, the vegan, said. "Real fur? Not for me." Then she moved away, heading toward the postcards.

I looked around and saw Eliza across the shop, browsing what appeared to be a shelf of knick-knacks. The items I could see on the shelves seemed to be small stone and wood carvings—not at all the kind of decorative items I would have expected Eliza to covet. She seemed to be caressing what looked like an Inuit soapstone carving of a bear. I watched her as she lifted it and turned it over—like you do—and I wondered if she did that to her hosts' china when she went to dinner parties. God, I could be so snarky when it came to

Eliza, and here, I had been thinking that I'd put my bitchy persona to bed. I guess you can't bury parts of yourself forever. Maybe we're not even supposed to. I must admit, however, I'd been feeling slightly less irritated with her since I'd discovered that her perfect life might not be so perfect. So, sue me. I'm only human.

In the end, Eliza bought the piece she'd been admiring, and Phillip bought a pair of hand-made green suede slippers trimmed with rabbit fur for Marcus. Dear god, I could never imagine perfectly turned-out Marcus wearing such things, but Phillip seemed to think he'd adore them. Mom bought the blue parka trimmed with red fox fur—real fox fur. I bought a pair of what the salesclerk had called hand-knit, thrummed mitts for Maddie. They were red and looked like they had a bird's eye pattern of off-white, but the clerk told me these were actually pieces of sheep's wool woven in every three stitches. Maddie would love them.

Once more back in the bus, and we were on our way to the ends of the earth.

~

Gordie told us to buckle up for a picturesque drive along the coast and a surprise. I wondered what kind of surprise it might be in this remote part of the world.

"Not sure I'll be able to deliver on this today, but I have good intelligence. Sit tight," he said half an hour later as he pulled off the narrow highway and bumped along a dirt road until we came to a stop just where the rocks rose. I presumed there was a drop to the sea below on the other side, which we couldn't see from our vantage point.

Since it had stopped raining, everyone piled out, and we followed Gordie. This time, we really did look like a line of lemmings following our leader to the edge of a cliff, where we would then plunge to our deaths. But Gordie had other plans.

As he reached the top of the hill ahead of us, he opened his arms wide, reminding me of Charlton Heston as Moses parting the Red

Sea in *The Ten Commandments* and said, "Behold!" As we moved closer to him, he said, to no one in particular, "In all things of nature, there is something of the marvellous." Then he turned and said, "Aristotle." In case we thought it was an original Gordie O'Brien, I suppose.

I reached the crest of the hill just as the word "marvellous" slipped from his lips, and I looked beyond. "Magnificent," I said, wishing that the word awesome was still one that really meant what it said. There, just off the shore, was a massive slab of bluish-white ice—an iceberg in all its glory on this July day. It was just there, drifting languidly in the direction I'd heard referred to as "iceberg alley," the route icebergs took in the spring from the glaciers farther north along the coast of Newfoundland. I just hadn't expected to see one in the summer. As I whipped out my phone to try to capture the moment in a photo, I thought about how most of the iceberg was beneath the surface. I'd read somewhere that ninety percent of the iceberg is beneath that water line. I looked at Eliza, who had taken up a position not far from where I was standing, and I wondered if I really knew my cousin at all.

SIXTEEN

Eliza

I HAVE NO IDEA WHAT HAD COME OVER ME. I wasn't the sort of person who bought tchotchkes in gift shops in remote places in the world, or anywhere for that matter. What would Jake say when he saw this little bear carving? I had no idea. I only knew that as I stood there in the gift shop stroking its back, I felt calmer. I knew I'd still have to deal with the Jake and Izzy problem, but for now, I felt slightly more tranquil, and I liked that. I had texted Izzy to see if I could get the story directly from her, but, as expected and as usual, she had not responded. Now, as I stood there on the crest of the hill, gazing out over the North Atlantic at an iceberg of all things, I realized how small I really was.

I glanced over at Erica and caught her eye briefly before she looked away. I wondered what she must be thinking about her perfect cousin who no longer appeared to be so perfect—no longer cloaked in the persona I had tried so hard to create over the years. Then I turned back, breathed in deeply and realized that there was no way I could capture the grandeur of what I was experiencing at that moment, so I put away my camera and just looked. I'd remember.

After we all returned to the truck, Gordie told us we'd reach our northernmost destination in ten or fifteen minutes, depending on traffic. Everyone laughed. We hadn't seen another vehicle in miles.

We finally pulled into a parking lot, at the end of which was a low building with glass doors that seemed to be almost built into the hill. We all went inside the building, which turned out to be the visitor centre for the archaeological site of the Viking settlement Gordie had called L'Anse aux Meadows. Gordie set us up with a small group of people who were already assembled waiting for their tour and an elderly tour guide who looked like even a slight breeze might knock him down. The guide then began droning on about how the Vikings had "discovered" this spot in the eleventh century and had built this settlement that consisted of eight timber-framed, turf-covered huts that they called mounds, which had been buried under the elements for centuries until a Norwegian explorer discovered them in 1960. He then went on to say it was a UNESCO World Heritage Site, and my eyes started to glaze over. I'd never been a history buff.

Finally, as a group, we walked outside the building toward a wooden walkway over what seemed to be a bog leading toward the sea. Just before the shoreline up ahead, I could see the mounds, and I suddenly didn't want to be part of a tour group. I looked up ahead and noticed that Erica and Phillip had the same idea.

I walked slowly away from the group. I gazed out over the bog where the summer grasses undulated in the wind as if the earth were breathing in and out. In and out. Every once in a while, the grasses were punctuated with tiny white and yellow summer flowers. It was mesmerizing. When I'd put enough distance between myself and the group, I stood there alone, looking out at the shoreline, wondering what it must have been like for those first Vikings in their longboats as this shoreline came into focus after what must have been months of travel from Scandinavia. I felt a blanket of desolation and loneliness descend on me, and it made me think about Jake and Jake's family. And Izzy. I shivered.

When I reached the settlement, the only ones there were Erica, Phillip, and two or three reenactors dressed in Viking garb, who were presumably there to answer questions. I was glad there were no other tourists there. The guide was so slow and droning that the rest of the tourists wouldn't arrive at this spot for some time.

I walked toward the first mound and realized there was a wooden door beckoning me inside. I hesitated at the threshold, letting my eyes become accustomed to the gloom inside. *This must be how they lived,* I thought. *What a life.*

The interiors of the mounds had been recreated to resemble what the archaeologists must have thought the settlement had been like, with their wooden carved beds and tables and even a throne presumably for the leader. To the right of the oversized throne-like wooden chair that was raised on a plinth, there was a slightly smaller one. *That must be where the leader's wife sat,* I thought. I surprised myself with my apparent interest in how Vikings had lived.

I looked around to ensure there was no one else about and got up onto the throne—not the one for the wife, but the one for the leader. I could feel the softness of the sheepskins under and behind me. I reached for the heavy metal sword that was leaning on the side of the throne and tried to conjure a picture of life in another time. I was having so much difficulty with life in the present time that perhaps I could glean some inspiration from the past. I closed my eyes.

When I opened them, I was staring at a very large man dressed in a dirty linen tunic that might once upon a time have been ivory or even white, tied at the waist with a rope and well-worn leather boots. A Viking. I blinked in case I was seeing things. He smiled at me.

"I see you've chosen your throne, m'lady," he said, helping me down.

Erica and Phillip walked in through the door just as I reached the floor and handed the sword to my Viking. I don't know how long I'd been alone in the midst of history.

"Hi, Eliza," Erica said. "We're heading to another part of the Viking displays for a bit of axe-throwing and other things, according to Gordie. Coming?"

I nodded and followed them—after thanking my Viking.

By the time the three of us found the rest of our group, Dad and Emma were already trying their hand at axe throwing. When they asked if I'd like to join them, I politely demurred. I looked around for Aunt Maureen and Gordie, but they were once again among the missing. I was beginning to wonder about those two. I decided to take a walk around by myself for a few minutes. By the time I'd made a circuit, I saw Erica and Phillip standing outside a small tent. They seemed to be deep in conversation. I almost felt like I was interrupting them.

Erica noticed me and looked over. "Eliza, Phillip and I were just discussing the topic of runes."

I had no idea what she was talking about.

"You know? The Norse used symbols to communicate—like an alphabet—but they also cast spells and did a bit of fortune-telling. There's a woman in this tent who does them, and we were wondering which of us should have a reading, but now that you're here, we think you should do it."

I shook my head. The last thing I needed was for some quack fortune-teller to tell me about my future. I'm not at all sure I wanted to be able to see beyond this moment—a situation I'd never before experienced. They were very insistent. In the end, just to keep them quiet, I relented. What harm could there be?

~

The tent was small and low, an inverted V-shape of canvas over poles. Inside the small space, the walls rippled in every breeze. The woman—a fortune-teller, perhaps—sat behind a low table on a sheep-skin-covered chair. Across the table, facing her, was a sheep-skin-covered bench for the "client." I paid my five dollars (a donation) and sat down on the bench.

The woman appeared to be near seventy, wearing what I imagined eleventh-century female Viking garb must have looked like—a dull orangey tunic with a brown leather belt wrapped around her ample waist. On her head was a linen cap. I counted three chains around her neck, each one bearing a different pendant, none of whose markings I recognized. I also didn't recognize the symbols on the rings that adorned at least eight of her fingers, but I was sure they had something to do with the "runic reading" I was about to endure.

On the table between us sat a small, slightly grimy suede pouch. As I sat down, she undid the leather thong that kept the bag closed and turned it upside down, spilling its contents onto the table. I counted sixteen flat stones about the size of silver dollars and watched her as she turned each of them over to reveal a different symbol. I had never seen any of the symbols before, but I recognized two of them as markings on pendants around her neck.

The woman ran her hand over the stones, caressing them as one might caress a lover's arm. Then she began to talk. "So, the old Norse would use these symbols when they would write, and as you can see, they were carved into these stones. Now, they were not just for communication, though. They knew the symbols held secrets of the past, present, and future, woven into the fabric of the universe."

She then began turning them over so that the symbols were no longer visible. "As we do the reading, you'll know that these represent messages for you today from three very important ladies called The Norns. Yes, the Norns, who sit at the base of the world tree—an old branching ash tree supporting the universe. They were the three sisters, Norse goddesses, so the secrets held for you come from these goddesses." She then moved her fingers over the stones, moving and rearranging them.

I have no idea why, but I felt a bit more at peace as I sat there, knowing the reading was from goddesses. *Get a grip*, I thought. She continued.

"Now, it is time for you to select *your* stones. You will pick three," she said.

She closed her eyes in deep concentration for a moment as if channelling the ancient energies of the runic symbols. I hesitated a moment, although I'm not sure why. When she opened her eyes, I pointed to one, which she moved away from the group. "And a second," she said. I complied. "Now a third."

As she moved the rest of the stones away, leaving the three I'd picked in the middle of the table, she said, "Now, take heed, these are messages for *you* today from the Norns themselves. Messages from *your* past, present and future." Then she turned over the first stone, revealing a marking that resembled a little roof turned on its side.

"Your first rune here represents the past and is called *Kenaz*," she began, her voice soft yet authoritative. "The torch of knowledge, regeneration and healing. It symbolizes controlled energy, passion, creation & transformation. It guides you toward keeping your inner passions flaming while gaining the strength—regeneration—to heal from all those outside influences you have endured that may have prevented you from pursuing that passion."

I found myself thinking about how I'd controlled so much of my energy over the years, trying to fit into the life I expected to have and wondered if there could be something as simple and powerful as regeneration.

She turned over the second one. This one looked like the letter "p" with a pointy rather than rounded loop. She called it *Wunjo*. "Ah," she said," this is your present moment if you permit it. This symbol represents joy and fulfilment. Hope and partnership. It speaks of harmonious actions in the present moment, but only if you allow the proper alignment."

Hope and partnership? Was there hope for my current partnership? Was I allowing the proper alignment? I had no idea what that meant, but I did know that ever since Jake had called, I felt peace or harmony within myself only in those moments when I stopped thinking about the situation brewing at home and stayed in the moment. I would have to think more about that. *Dear god*, I thought, *am I really buying this?* But it was true that I was sensing a glimmer of something approaching recognition that I could not explain. I was riveted.

Then, she turned over the final stone. "*Naudhiz*. And so, we come full circle," she said. "This symbol tells you that you are facing issues that you continue to ignore. It takes us back to what is blocking you from maintaining your passion. This is your future symbol and reminds you that you must rebalance." She sat back and stared at me. "Remember this, my dear. Your first symbol is your past, from which you must learn. The second rune signifies the present, the here and now, where your path intersects with destiny. And the third rune reveals the future, the unknown yet to unfold."

I found myself listening intently, hardly recognizing as my skepticism gave way to a strange sense of anticipation.

I hadn't even noticed that both Erica and Phillip had been standing silently behind me, listening to the reading as it unfolded. I wondered what they must be thinking. And I didn't care.

I thanked the woman, got up and stepped out of the tent and into the sunshine. I felt strange. If I were a more spiritual person, I probably would have found a new willingness to embrace the mysteries of the universe—and for the first time in my life, I realized that perhaps I was something more than I thought. I was still a skeptic at heart, but I couldn't deny the lingering sense of possibilities. I needed a sense of possibility at this moment, perhaps more than I ever had before.

Neither Erica nor Phillip said a word. It was so unlike them, but perhaps they sensed my contemplation as I silently made my way toward yet another gift shop and sought out my runes. I wasn't leaving without them. The clerk placed them in a tiny faux-suede pouch, and I crammed them into the pocket of my jeans.

~

Half an hour later, Gordie announced it was time for lunch. "Better late than never," he said laughing. "I've got a friend near here with a little café who can fire up a scoff that just might do a wee bit more than fill your hollow tooth."

Fill your hollow tooth? I vaguely remembered the phrase as something Gran said to us so many years ago when she served dinner. And, of course, Gordie had a friend with a café.

He turned off the road in a village so tiny it didn't even warrant a mention on my online map and pulled up in front of a red, clapboard, one-story, unprepossessing building with a peaked roof.

There was a sign outside, blowing in the wind, that said "Partridgeberry Country Lodge and Café." It was definitely in the middle of nowhere, or at least in the middle of a vast wildflower-filled meadow with a sea of yellow flowers waving in the wind. With every gust of wind, the flowers swirled and twirled in a mesmerizing display that reminded me of looking through a kaleidoscope as a child and seeing a phantasmagoria of yellow, white and green. I might have been feeling a bit more mellow back at the Viking settlement, but as I contemplated the unassuming, almost ramshackle building in front of me, I could sense that feeling slowly ebbing away as I envisaged lunch here.

As we crowded into the tiny "lobby" of the lodge, I looked through into the dining room and saw that we were the only guests. Not a good sign, in my view. Then, my breath caught when I saw the view over the rocky headlands out toward the sea. *Is that another iceberg way out there?* I thought, squinting at the vista.

The owner, Donna, a fifty-something woman with bright red hair and a ruddy complexion, was wearing an apron that said, *"I'm not perfect, but I'm from Newfoundland. It's pretty much the same."* She smiled and laughed at everything Gordie said, then led us into the dining room. With the exception of the back wall, which was glass from ceiling to floor, the rest of the room was decorated in rustic, rustic and more rustic with its knotty pine wood walls and ceilings and its kitschy wall hangings that evoked the 1980s in all its macramé brilliance. Once I was settled at our table, my cookbook author persona reinserted itself as I perused the menu.

"Now, everyone," Gordie began, and I was sure he was going to recommend precisely what each of us should have for lunch. I wasn't disappointed. "You see this here on the menu? This is what you call cod au gratin." I heard a small snicker emanate from cousin Phillip, our resident French expert. Even I knew that wasn't how *au gratin* was pronounced anywhere else but here.

"This is the house specialty," Gordie said. "You cannot leave Newfoundland without trying it, and you can't get better cod au gratin than here. Donna's cook is the best there is."

As the words left Gordie's lips and as if choreographed, the cook, who turned out to be Donna's husband, popped his head out of the kitchen and waved to Gordie. "Cod au gratin all around?" he said.

"Got ourselves a vegan over here," Gordie said, pointing to Emma.

I supposed that must have made Emma feel a bit self-conscious when Donna and her husband pulled that startled face that clearly conveyed, "WTF?" But, then again, weren't we all the culmination of our choices in life? This was Emma's.

"That's going to be a head-scratcher, Gordie," Donna said, not making eye contact with Emma. "I'll see what I can find."

"Is it really that hard?" Emma said, sounding more exasperated than I'd heard her up to this point. Perhaps she needed another of Phillip's magic gummies.

"What do you mean?" Aunt Maureen said.

"I mean, I'm a vegan. I don't have a contagious disease."

"I certainly hope not," I heard Phillip say, presumably under his breath. I couldn't help but chuckle slightly.

"Well, darling," Dad said to Emma, "you do have to admit it's a bit challenging in a place where the cuisine is based on historical staples. Fish is among those staples."

"And don't forget the scrunchions," I said. "Emma, if I can eat pork fat, even with a few religious convictions, you can certainly eat a bit of whatever's on offer. After all, it's just an exclusionary dietary choice."

I could see Emma's face reddening from the neck up. It was her childhood tell that she was about to erupt. "You don't get it. None of you!" She was undoubtedly correct in that assertion. "No one seems to understand the seriousness of this. It's not just a choice. It's more of a—"

"Oh, but it is a choice," Phillip said. "Maybe it is time we talked about this."

I could see Erica put her hand on Phillip's arm as if to stop him from continuing. It didn't work.

"Emma, you call yourself a vegan, the same way you might tell someone you're right-handed — or gay. It is not the same thing. It is your choice. And just like any choice, that choice you make can be unmade when it has to be." Phillip was on a roll. "And I have to say that I'm sick to death of your pseudo-science and cherry-picked statistics to defend your plant-powered posturing. I'm tired of people who are vegans thinking everyone else has to fall in line. I'm here to tell you that our line is a lot longer and wider than yours, so just get over it. Try something that tells you something about your roots."

Emma was silent. I was feeling oddly conciliatory. "Emma, you're my little sister, and I love you, but I think Phillip might have a point. You might want to consider what you're doing, cutting out most of what human beings eat from your diet, before he starts telling you how problematic it would be if the pigs and cows and chickens started roaming freely only to become extinct because they can't survive in the wild." Oops, I hadn't intended for my comments to get political.

It didn't seem to matter anyway because Emma just sat there, her arms tightly folded, glaring into the middle distance, not making eye contact with anyone. That was the moment when Donna and her husband emerged from the kitchen with steaming plates holding individual casserole dishes containing our lunch.

As I've mentioned, fish has never been among my favourite foods, but as I looked at the bubbling cheese smothered in golden breadcrumbs over the fish covered in white sauce, I heard my stomach grumbling. I was ready. After one bite, I knew I had to have this recipe. I was getting quite a collection.

That's when Gordie said, "Well, people, I have good news and bad news."

I was sure I couldn't handle any more bad news.

SEVENTEEN

Erica

I TRIED TO GET PHILLIP TO TAKE A BREATH before giving Emma a piece of his mind, which I had known was inevitable. Just the evening before, Phillip had told me about his general distaste for people who made dietary choices and expected others to cater to them—literally. He evidently had a colleague on a board who expected every catered lunch menu to be meat-free, dairy-free, gluten-free and taste-free to hear Phillip tell it. "Kale," he had said, "if I hear him mention kale again, I'm going to puke." So, when he started in on Emma at lunch, I wasn't really surprised. I have to admit I was also getting a bit sick of the sanctimonious way she had stared at me the first evening at dinner as I enjoyed every morsel of my turkey. Live and let live was the way I had conducted my life. I just wished she could do the same.

Phillip's harangue did not, however, hit its mark if he expected Emma to change her mind in an instant and eat the fish on offer. I knew full well that wasn't how things worked. People with convictions like Emma's (I hoped they were deeply held convictions) didn't just cave to a cousin's tirade. Anyway, I was just about to enjoy my first bite of the steaming hot cod au gratin while still thinking about the lemon meringue pie I'd ordered for dessert when Gordie announced yet more news—good and bad. I put my fork down and thought, *Here we go again.*

"Gordie, dear," Mom said, "let's start with the bad news and get that over with. I hope there isn't more bad news about air conditioning."

Gordie beamed at Mom. "Darlin' Maureen, your wish is my command. The bad news first, then. I will be absent from our happy little group for a good twenty-four hours—give or take. I have some business to attend to, but don't worry yourselves. You won't be left high and dry at the motel. There is also good news." He looked around the table. "My son, Peter, will be meeting us at the motel for dinner this evening and will take over driving and guiding responsibilities tomorrow. He's a bit of a rock buff anyway and is the best person to guide you on your hike of the Tablelands."

I had looked up The Tablelands when I saw it on the original schedule because it was a term that was new to me. It seemed we were headed back to the national park, where we'd be going on another boat and hiking the area Gordie was talking about. I'd discovered it was one of the only accessible places where you could walk on the Earth's mantle, that layer between the core and the crust that usually lies deep within the Earth. When I looked at the photos online, I thought I was looking at a moonscape and could hardly wait to experience it. I had also been looking forward to Gordie's wry sense of humour as he guided us through. I wondered if his son shared his traits. I figured we'd soon see. It didn't seem like such bad or good news—only news, and I should know about news after all those years as a journalist.

There was, however, more good news. The lemon meringue pie that Donna served after the main course was as luscious as I had hoped. As she placed it in front of me, my eyes popped at the sight of the mile-high meringue with a pop of creamy yellow just peeking out from under it. With the first forkful of deliciousness, I could taste the tang of the lemons perfectly balanced with the touch of sweetness in the meringue. It was perfection on a plate. During a manic phase of trying to be more domesticated, I had tried my hand at making lemon meringue pie but had never really succeeded, ending up with meringue that didn't quite whip. I wondered how they got that full three inches of fluffy meringue so flawless. Eliza must have been wondering the same thing.

"Donna," Eliza said when our hostess returned to ask us how the first bites had been, "I have never had pie this good. I must have your recipe."

Donna blushed.

Mom said, "Donna, in case you don't know, Eliza writes cookbooks. Maybe she'll put your recipe in her next one."

"Oh, that would be a lovely grand thing. My mum's recipe in a cookbook. That would be something."

Later, as we all once again piled out of the café and back into the truck, I saw Donna slip Eliza a sheet of paper. Maybe Eliza would write a cookbook of Newfoundland cuisine. She could even include a few vegan possibilities. Emma seemed to have enjoyed her pancakes with blueberry sauce. I just wondered if Donna had managed to make them without eggs. I didn't ask—and for once, neither did Emma.

~

As we headed south once again to Ocean Point Motel for our second possibly sweaty night, I had hoped the cooler temperatures of St. Anthony might follow us. No such luck. By the time we were back in the parking lot, emerging from the air-conditioned delights of the truck and retrieving our various bags and purchases from the back, I could feel the sweat beginning to pop out on my forehead already. When I opened the door to our room, Mom said she'd stand back. Wise woman. The wall of heat struck me in the face, and I noticed with some alarm that the cleaner must have closed the window when she was in to make up the room hours earlier. It was stifling.

When I asked her if she wanted to join us in the bar, Mom said she just wanted to rest a while and then take a walk. I splashed some water in my face and didn't even bother with lipstick. I needed a drink.

As I walked into the bar, Phillip, as expected, was already seated there with what appeared to be a rum and coke on the bar in front of him. Surprisingly, he was chatting amiably with Emma. Had he given her another gummy? I hoped so. She was far less sanctimonious when she was mellowed out. I took the empty seat next to Phillip just as Uncle Fred came in.

"Mind if an old man joins you young ones?" he said.

"Uncle Fred," I said, "we're hardly young ones. Can you call someone over half a century old young? No matter. Sit and have a drink with us." Phillip and I both laughed. Emma frowned—she wasn't quite as old as the rest of us.

Fred ordered a double gin and tonic, then spoke across us to his youngest daughter, who was now inhaling her second glass of wine (wine is a vegan dietary option, evidently. Grapes, you know). "Emma, I hope you weren't too insulted by the lunchtime talk about your veganism. Of course, you're an adult and have the right to your own convictions and choices."

"Thank you, Daddy," she said and raised her half-empty glass. We all did the same. "Phillip and I have made up, and I'm going to Facetime Tobias in a few minutes so he can meet everyone."

"Geezus. Tobias," Uncle Fred said. I was sitting next to him and was the only one who heard.

"What about Tobias?" I said softly as Phillip and Emma once again started chattering.

"You know, Erica, he's a bit of what they'd call a sleveen in this part of the country."

"I'm not sure I know what that means."

"It means sneaky and probably untrustworthy. Since the first day I met him almost ten years ago, I have hardly believed a word that came out of that young man's mouth. There was something about him that didn't instill confidence that he was the right fit for my daughter, but what do I know? I'm just her father. When Madelaine is older, you'll understand." I shivered at that thought as Uncle Fred glanced nervously at Emma, who was still fully engaged with Phillip. He continued. "He told us stories about his family that I've never been able to corroborate. He and Emma have been together for ten years, and we've still never met any of them. And this veganism thing? It was Tobias who first influenced Emma. I always got the impression she did it to please him. Before she met him, Emma was a free-spirit in the best sense. I never truly understood her, but she always seemed to be herself. After Tobias entered the picture, she wasn't nearly so free-spirited. She became almost subservient. And he's a bit of a good-for-nothing, too, working at that bar and picking up the odd acting job. Just not the sort I'd like to see Emma end up with."

Just then, Emma stood up at the end of the bar, holding her phone in front of her. "I've got him," she said. Then she looked down at her phone and said, "Toby! Now you can meet the rest of my family."

Emma passed her phone down the row, and we all said hi. When her father returned it to her, she looked at it and said, "Hey, Devon. Are you all there with Toby?" Then Emma turned to us and told us Tobias was evidently having dinner in a pub with a few friends, including a young woman named Devon, which explained the odd surroundings I'd seen on the screen. "Our friend Devon has taken his phone," Emma said, giggling. "She's going to show us the group at the table."

Emma walked down toward her father, and I peeked over his shoulder to see the merriment that seemed to be happening back in Nova Scotia. Then I noticed something.

"Hey, Emma," I said, "could I have a look?" She passed me the phone as Devon panned across the group and seemed to purposely zoom in on Tobias's dinner plate. I was momentarily stunned. I didn't quite know what to say, but I knew I was going to say something.

"Enjoying your hamburger?" I said to Tobias, who was now on camera.

He smiled and gave me a thumbs up, took a bite, then, as if he had realized what was happening, waved Devon off and put his arms over his plate. But it was too late. I know a medium rare beef burger when I see one. It was half-eaten, so the centre was fully visible. To make matters worse (at least in the world of veganism), a slice of melted cheese oozed over the slab of ground meat.

"Hamburger? Did you say hamburger?" Emma said, grabbing the phone away from me. "Tobias, did Erica say hamburger?" There was a moment of silence, then, "Show me your dinner!"

I'm not sure how to describe what happened next. The expression that might come closest would be *shit show*. Emma started screaming. The three people playing pool over on the other side of the bar stopped only for a moment, shrugged, swigged their beers, and then returned to their game as if such behaviour might not be all that unusual here. She was hysterical, throwing curses at Tobias about how he had betrayed her. I may have even heard the words "fucking traitor," but I was so surprised to hear such language emanating from my cousin, who didn't seem to have such a vocabulary, that it is possible I might have misheard. Emma then threw her phone across the room, where it skidded across the linoleum floor before coming to a stop at the feet of the pool player with his baseball cap on backwards. He stooped to pick it up, rubbed it off on his less-than-pristine T-shirt with a Toronto Maple Leafs logo on the front and proceeded to present it back to Emma.

"Sounds like he's not worth the powder to blow him to hell, love," he said as Emma reached for the proffered phone.

Emma stopped in her tracks and started to laugh. "You're right. He's not." She turned to her father, who was now standing up, gripping the bar. "Dad, what was that you used to say when we were kids? That expression from your childhood that meant everything's gone to hell?"

Uncle Fred and the three pool players said in unison, "The arse is gone out of 'er."

"That's the one," Emma said, taking up her place at the bar once again. "The arse certainly is gone out of 'er, and I'll have another drink. This time, I want what he's having," she said to the older woman with the fluffy hair who was behind the bar drying glasses. She was pointing to Phillip's glass. "But leave out the coke."

GREAT BIG SKY

SCREECH: *verb* **UK** /skriːtʃ/ **US** /skriːtʃ/: *to make
an unpleasant, loud, high noise.*

SCREECH: *noun* **Newfoundland**: *a type of rum; native to
Newfoundland with 40% alcohol by volume; traditionally used at the
"screech-in" ceremony for CFAs and liberally consumed at other times.*

EIGHTEEN

Eliza

IT WAS SO HOT IN OUR ROOM WHEN WE GOT BACK to the motel that Emma ran a brush through her hair, splashed some water in her face and announced she was going to the bar. And did I want to join her? I did, but I needed a few moments to myself before I did.

My mind was roiling with that kind of monkey mind Zen gurus talk about. It was the kind of unsettling anxiety that I hated so much. I had spent my life learning to present a calm face to the world, and it was so much harder when my mind did this to me—or maybe I did this to my mind. I didn't know anymore. As I tucked away the recipes for cod au gratin and lemon meringue pie into the folder with the other ones, I wondered why I was collecting them. Then, my mind strayed to the runic reading that I'd scorned at the outset.

I opened the little pouch, and the three stones I'd purchased at the gift shop spilled out onto the ugly orange flowered bedspread. The mattress let out a loud squeak as I sat down beside them and ran my hand over them. I now wished that I'd had the sense to record what the woman had said. I frowned, trying to recall some of the details.

Past. Present. Future. I remembered that she'd talked about regeneration and healing from things in my past so that I could pursue my passion. I remembered that this had puzzled me because I'd always prided myself in the belief that I *had* pursued my passion—writing about cooking and doing it as far away from my family as I could reasonably manage. I suddenly began thinking about New York and Jake—and Izzy. She still hadn't responded to any of my texts. This was my present moment, and everything in my past had brought me to now.

I looked at the second stone. My present. The only thing I remembered the woman saying were the words hope and fulfilment—and partnership. I sighed. Hopeful and fulfilled were not the words I'd use to describe my present moment, even if I had managed to create a career I loved and the family situation I hoped might satisfy me. And as for partnership? My partnership with Jake was anything but fulfilling at this moment. Then I remembered she had said this hopeful fulfillment could only happen in the presence of proper alignment, whatever that meant. I was about to pick the three runes up from the bed and pitch them into the waste basket when I glanced at the last one: the cross with the crosspiece at a slant.

Full circle, she had said. Still facing issues that I continue to ignore, she had said. And my thoughts lingered on Jake once again. How long had I been ignoring *that* issue? Whatever the situation was with Izzy at this moment, I knew I would have to handle it. Whatever the problem was, Jake would not be able to deal with it. He never had been able to deal with Izzy. She was his princess who could do no wrong, of course, until she did, and then he washed his hands of her. On more than one occasion in her teenage years, he had said to me, "She's *your* daughter. *You* deal with her." Then, mere weeks later, Izzy would whine to her father that she needed money for this new purse and that new phone (why did kids need a new phone every year?) or the ski trip she just had to go on with her friend's family. In those moments, she was Daddy's girl— coddled, spoiled, pampered. In a word: princess. It was infuriating. Jake was infuriating.

I met Jacob Adam Cohen more than twenty years ago when I first moved to New York City. It was the day after Labour Day in September 2001 (yes, that September), and I had just landed a new job. My new green card was my ticket to becoming an American and leaving my Canadian roots behind. It was a good plan, or so I thought. I had a degree in English and the arrogance to think I knew what I was doing. I was out celebrating with a group of newly acquired acquaintances from my newly acquired job as an editorial assistant at a food magazine. We were a noisy group of five or six young women, one of whom was our food stylist, Allegra Cohen, enjoying a few cosmos when her brother walked into the bar with a group of swaggering young men wearing expensive suits.

I had never met young men like this before: stockbrokers and business executives from wealthy families, wearing their wealth and success in their custom-made suits, their Hermes ties and their Rolex watches. I'd never been that close to a Rolex watch in my life. My father was a successful, small-city physician—a big fish in a little pond. I had always thought of our family as privileged, but we weren't even close to being in the same league as these people. I was at first put off by the showiness of wealth and success (mainly their family's success, I soon learned). Still, when Allegra introduced me to Jake, a vice president in their family's business (at the time, I had no idea it was Bluestone Pharma), I began to picture myself in that same rarefied circle. And the rest, as they say, is history. Jake and I became a couple. Several years later, we were married, and over the years, I had begun to notice that he would always be Mama's boy, and Esther's wishes would always come ahead of mine. And the money? There was lots of it, but there were always strings. Now, here I was, sitting in a motel in Newfoundland, staring at objects of mystic prophecy (in which I usually didn't believe), feeling that there were things I needed to sort out.

I scooped up the runes and put them back in their pouch. Then I splashed water in my face, texted Jake to say we should talk later this evening and headed to the bar.

When I turned the corner and approached the bar, I could hear a commotion emanating from within. I could not imagine what was going on. Then I heard Emma's voice and something about hamburgers.

"Show me your dinner!" Emma was yelling as I walked into the bar.

I saw her grab a phone away from Erica. I had never before heard a four-letter word escape Emma's lip, but now all I could hear was, "Fucking traitor," and "Well, you can fuck right off, Toby. Did you hear me?" Then, I watched as she pitched her phone across the floor. She then asked Dad something, and I heard Dad and the two people playing pool across the room say, "The arse is gone out of 'er," and I remembered Dad saying that whenever everything had gotten out of hand. And I laughed. *Yes, indeed, Eliza, the arse is undoubtedly gone out of 'er.*

As I sidled up to the bar, I asked the bartender to give me whatever Emma was drinking and found myself looking into a glass of straight rum. I downed it in one and asked for another.

~

All of us, Dad included, were a bit tipsy when we finally got up from our seats at the bar to stagger to the dining room where Gordie and Aunt Maureen had already taken up residence (was there something going on between those two?). They were sitting at the large, round table set up in the middle for our group with a third man I'd never seen before. Even in my half-drunken state, I was able to deduce that the third person was Gordie's son.

"Well, it looks like you lot had a time," Gordie said as he stood up from the table. "Come on then, have a seat, and you can all meet Peter."

I sat down heavily on my seat, as unaccustomed as I was to drinking rum straight. After the first one, though, it tasted better and better. I looked across the table as Emma sat down beside the newcomer to the group and saw her leer as she noticed his blue eyes, tousled blonde hair shot through with grey and his boyish expression. Or maybe I was the one noticing? Anyway, this was Peter, Gordie's son, as he was now telling us all. Peter, our fill-in driver and guide.

Peter was probably in his late forties, maybe a bit younger than I was—or perhaps men really are just better preserved than women as they age—wearing a blue button-down collared shirt. I'm not sure why this surprised me, but it did. I suppose I was expecting a T-shirt and baseball cap, although Gordie himself was always well-turned-out in nouveau hiker style.

I must have had more to drink than I realized because I didn't taste much of my dinner of roast turkey and French fries with, of all things, dressing and gravy—served on top of the fries. And anyway, I was still half-stuffed from lunch. Whenever I looked up and caught Peter's eye, he seemed almost to wink at me, causing me to run my hand over my hair once or twice to see if something was sticking up. Emma, on the other hand, seemed to be basking in his attention. Erica and Phillip had filled me in on Emma's conversation with Tobias and its genesis, so it looked to me like she was flirting with the first man who crossed her path. I suppose Tobias was now a thing of the past? One could only hope. Oh, tomorrow in the car was going to be fun.

~

Emma and Peter were still talking when I excused myself and made my wobbly way back to our room after dinner. I wanted a few minutes alone so I could talk to Jake and, most importantly, Izzy.

Jake picked up after the first ring. "About time you called me back," he said. "I cannot believe you've left me here alone to deal with your daughter."

So, she was my daughter now, and that was his problem. I asked him if he could be more specific about the perceived problem, and all he said was, "You sound drunk. Are you drunk?"

I sighed. "Jake, let me talk to Izzy, and we'll sort this out, whatever it is."

"Whatever it is? When my mother hears about this…" he trailed off and then said, "What a *shande*. You cannot even imagine."

I thought for a moment before I remembered that *shande* was Yiddish for scandal or embarrassment. I hadn't heard the word in some years, and only ever emanating from Esther's lips when she was gossiping about one or another of her friends. I'd often thought that with a friend like Esther, those women didn't need enemies. Anyway, it was not like Jake to invoke the traditional Yiddish. This must be serious.

Finally, I said, "Jake, I refuse to discuss this with you any longer if you're not going to say anything specific about the problem here."

"Izzy needs to tell you herself," he said, sounding like the petulant, spoiled young man he was when I met him. I thought he had changed.

"We're not getting anywhere, and this is not helpful," I said. "Get Izzy on the phone. Right now."

"She's sleeping—or sulking."

"I do not care if she is sulking, sleeping or shitting." That ought to get him going. That last one was not a regular word in my vocabulary, but given the right provocation, I could do much worse. "I want you to put her on the phone this minute."

I heard rustling, and I could picture Jake rousting himself from the depths of his favourite leather chair in his library upstairs and trundling through the hall toward Izzy's room at the front of the house. Then I heard knocking and his voice telling her I was on the phone. Finally, she came on the line.

"Izzy, I texted you several times, and you did not respond." She didn't immediately answer. "Izzy, I'm talking to you."

"I heard you, Mom."

I decided that a more honeyed approach might work better. "Izzy, dear, you seem to have upset your father. And now he has upset me. What in the world is so wrong that you have fled sunny California for New York, a place you said you detested? For months, we haven't heard anything more from you than the odd text, and now you suddenly appear without warning?"

"You know, Mom, not everything is about how you and Dad feel."

I had no idea where she was going with this, but I just hung on for the ride. I was just glad I was sitting down for her bombshell.

"I'm pregnant."

I could feel myself pursing my lips like my mother used to do when she was appalled at one of us. *I'm not my mother. I'm not my mother*, I kept saying to myself. Then, with some horror, I realized I was, in fact, turning into my mother. I was appalled at my daughter—no, it was more than that. I was infuriated. My head started spinning, and I could see stars. And lest you think I was embarrassed by this announcement or concerned about the shame of it with the relatives, be assured that the reasons for my discomfiture were quite different.

I thought I had been meticulous in teaching Izzy a few important life lessons when she was a teenager. Like all teenage girls, she had a mind of her own, but I had felt the lessons about being responsible, taking precautions, and never getting oneself into a situation that was unplanned had hit home. Evidently, I had been mistaken.

"Mom? Are you still there?"

I pulled myself together. "I am still here, Izzy. And I just don't quite know what to say about the abject stupidity of your situation. And since we are a people with little faith in the myth of the Virgin Mary, might I inquire as to the identity of the father?"

"He's nobody."

"I see," I said, trying to keep an even keel. "And nobody was involved in this except you. Am I getting this right?"

I had a creeping sensation that I ought to be more supportive. Clearly, she was going through a difficult time. However, in my view, it was her own fault, and she had been doing these kinds of things since she was thirteen. This time, however, the stakes were so much higher. She was not the only one involved.

I knew I had to say it. "Izzy, have you looked into having an abortion?"

That was the moment she burst into tears and started sobbing. I had never been good with sobbing, but it did stop me in my tracks. I had no idea that the concept of abortion was anathema to her.

"I'm sorry I brought it up, Izzy. I had no idea the idea of an abortion would upset you so much." I realized I had no idea what my daughter thought about any number of subjects, abortion being chief among them at that moment.

"It's not that, Mom." She sniffed and sobbed a bit more before continuing. "It's just that it's too late."

"Too late? How much too late?" A picture was beginning to emerge, and I knew without a shadow of a doubt I wasn't ready to handle it. The picture was of me, Eliza Houlihan Cohen, as a grandmother. "How much, Izzy?"

"The baby's due at the end of October."

I did a quick calculation and knew at once that my life—our lives—were about to change. I felt like one of those birthday balloons that was losing its helium, breath by breath. I was defeated. I would have to be there for my daughter. I just wasn't sure I knew how.

"Mom, are you okay?" It might have been the first time in my daughter's life that she had inquired about the well-being of another person. Maybe we could get through this.

I took a deep breath. "I am, Izzy, and I will be there for you. Your father and I will be there for you." I took another deep breath before continuing. "Do you need me to cut my trip short and come home?"

"No, I don't think so. It's only another week, isn't it?" I told her it was. "I think you should stay there and celebrate Gran's big birthday." Suddenly, Izzy sounded far more grown up than I could ever have expected.

We said good night and promised to talk again tomorrow. I just sat there on the ugly bedspread, noticing a tear that was beginning to form in the corner of my eye.

"Hey, sis." I looked up to see Emma standing in the open door. "What's wrong? Who died?" she said, closing the door behind her.

I gave myself a mental slap up the side of the head and looked up at her. "No one, Emma. I was just talking to Jake. He's just being the asshole he has become."

Emma shrugged. "Oh. I think I'm going to go to sleep."

NINETEEN

Erica

AFTER EMMA'S MELTDOWN IN THE BAR when she saw Tobias and his dinner on Facetime, our group dinner that followed was tame by comparison. When dinner was over, Mom and Gordie were the first to leave, as expected. After all, at their advanced age, it was only appropriate for them to get to bed early. Uncle Fred was right behind them. Emma said she was going to take a walk, and Eliza said she had things to do.

That left only Phillip, Peter and me to return once again to the bar for a nightcap, bearing in mind Gordie's parting words reminding us that we had a jam-packed day ahead of us while he left us in his son's good hands as he put it.

The bar was empty, except for the three men who had been playing pool earlier. As we slid into three stools at the bar under the string of lights that looked like it had once graced a Christmas tree, the three pool players waved their beer bottles at us. I wondered if they'd been drinking non-stop ever since they'd had the experience of bearing witness to my cousin's existentialist vegan crisis.

"I'm taking bets," Phillip said as the bartender poured three glasses of rum on the rocks that Phillip had kindly ordered. "I have a hundred dollars that says Emma won't be a vegan for more than twenty-four more hours."

"I'm not sure you'll find anyone in the family to bet against you, Phillip," I said, sipping my rum as the bartender gave us all the evil eye. We might have outlived our welcome since it was probably nearing closing time.

"Vegan? Your sister is a vegan?" Peter said. I noticed he'd had only a glass of wine with dinner and was nursing his rum. I guess he was concerned about being sober at nine am when we were leaving. After all, he was our new driver.

"Not sister. Emma's our cousin, and yes, she is a vegan," Phillip said, trying to stifle a snort of laughter. "But she's just found out that her boyfriend—and major vegan partner—eats hamburgers when she's away." He was now in full-on mirth mode.

"It's not really funny, Phillip," I said, trying to inject a bit of gravity into a situation that had all the makings of a Phillip/Erica caper. We would definitely have a bit of fun with Emma over this— and, I might add, over the way she had flirted with Peter. It was so outrageous, it was funny. Phillip gave me the stink eye. "Oh, maybe it is funny." I started laughing.

"Tomorrow looks like it will be a bit of fun," Peter said. "You lot seem to be a congenial bunch."

That last remark just set the two of us off on further gales of laughter.

"Congenial is not quite the word I'd use to describe this clan, Peter," Phillip said. "We may be a family on paper, but unless incompatibility is a characteristic of a congenial family these days, we may have to conclude that blood may not be thicker than water."

Peter, being the least drunk among us, stared first at Phillip, then at me. "I suppose we'll see." Then he asked us a few questions about Mom and Uncle Fred and, finally, Eliza. "Eliza didn't want to join us for a drink?" I wasn't sure if he was telling us or asking us.

"Oh, Eliza always has something she has to do. She's a big-time cookbook author in New York," I said without even a trace of the animosity I usually felt toward my cousin.

"She seemed distracted at dinner. Anything I should know about? I don't want to say the wrong thing."

Phillip and I looked at one another. "Not really," I said finally. "I think she might be having a bit of a long-distance argument with her husband, though."

"That's tough. What does Eliza's husband do?" Peter said.

"Big shot at Bluestone Pharma. In fact, it's his family's business. You know that company?"

Peter looked down at his hands for a moment, then shrugged. "I think I might have read something about them on the news a while back."

"I don't think anyone who follows the news could have missed a few of those stories," Phillip said. "They have the ethics of a house of cards. I've often thought they'd collapse if anyone ever took a deeper look."

"I presume Eliza doesn't share her husband's moral mentality," Peter said.

I told him I didn't think so, then said, "Peter, what do you do when you're not guiding your father's guests across the island?"

He shrugged. "At the moment, I'm on a bit of a vacation. That's why I had the time."

I wondered if that meant he was unemployed. I didn't like to ask, though. It seemed rude, and we'd just met him.

"So, do you live near here?"

Peter shook his head. "I live just outside St. John's at the moment."

"Do you have a boat?"

His eyes lit up when I asked. "Yes, as a matter of fact, I do."

My journalistic sensibility kicked in, and I put two and two together. He lived outside the city and owned a boat. He also had time available to pinch-hit for his father as a tour guide. That meant he must be self-employed. Ergo, he must fish for a living. Why didn't I just ask him? Good question.

~

The following morning, once again, we assembled in the "lobby" to await our guide. Since we had completed our two-night stay here at the motel, we had all our luggage with us. Tonight, we would be in a different place. Another motel, perhaps? A few minutes before nine, Peter pulled the truck up to the front door.

"Eliza," Mom said, as she walked toward the vehicle, "why don't you take the seat up front with Peter this morning? I want to sit in the back and chat with Erica and Phillip," she said, looking at Emma who had begun pouting the moment Mom suggested Eliza take the front seat. I knew my mother well enough to know that she could see Emma glomming onto Peter at dinner and wished to avoid the world of awkwardness that would develop if Emma had a chance to move forward with her flirtation. "Emma, you and your father can sit behind them. Erica, Phillip and I will take the third row."

Once we were settled, Peter turned around in his seat, "Everyone ready?"

Phillip and I looked at one another and shouted, "Seatbelts, everyone!"

Peter started laughing. "Fellow fans! Now then, let's take some chances, make some mistakes and generally get messy!"

Phillip and I had found a soulmate.

~

As Peter pulled the truck onto Highway 430 heading south, he said, "We've got about three and a half hours to our main stop this morning. So, settle in, and I'll put on some local music to get you ready for tonight."

"What about tonight?" Mom said. "Will there be music?"

"In fact, there will," Peter said. "But that's all I'll say right now. It's a surprise Dad cooked up for us." Then he clammed up about the music and turned on the radio.

The radio came to life in the middle of a commercial for a company advertising something called jam-jams, and then a song started. It was only a few bars in when Peter cranked up the volume to a near ear-splitting level.

"This one," he said, "is such a great one. Gotta have it loud!!"

I didn't recognize the song, but the group's sound seemed familiar. I had a vague sense I'd heard them before.

"This bit," he said over the music, "everyone knows the words." Then he sang several rounds of "oh-me, oh my" at the start of the chorus before Mom and Uncle Fred got into the spirit, and Phillip and I joined in. Emma was in her own world by this point—either drowning in a sea of remorse about her lost love or, and this was far more likely, leaning into the gummy I'd seen Phillip slip to her in the lobby before we left. We were headed for another boat adventure, after all. Eliza turned to look at all of us with a look that suggested, "WTF?" I would have loved to hear her say it, though.

When the song faded out, Peter said, "Gotta love that Great Big Sea," and I remembered where I'd heard the sound before.

Years ago, when I was a real reporter filing stories from foreign places, I'd had a colleague from another media outlet who hailed from Newfoundland and kept CDs in her room. Whenever we'd get together for a drink before dinner, she'd put them on. Great Big Sea was one of her favourite bands, and she told me that listening to them always brought her spirit home—even when she couldn't be there in her body.

Peter turned the radio down to a level where conversation might once again be possible. "You know, that song's one of those head-scratchers around here. It's called 'Excursion Around the Bay.' Of course, you have to believe they sang it just for us, eh?" He laughed. "It's a grand one for a sing-along and getting everyone going, but you have to admit the words are a bit dark. It takes a cheery Newfoundlander to forget that the song is about the wife dying, after all." I could see him turn slightly toward Eliza for a moment before returning his eyes to the road. "A bit of the old optimism once in a while never hurt, eh?"

Was that the start of a smile I saw as she turned her head toward Peter? *Well, well, well*, I thought. *Maybe there is someone in the world who can make the dour Eliza Cohen smile.*

We drove on, listening to the music on the radio—an array of songs with names like "Let Me Fish off Cape St. Mary" and "The Brier and the Rose." I had heard some of the music during those summers we spent here as children, but I hadn't ever really listened to the words.

At some point, Peter and Eliza seemed to have struck up a quiet conversation. Mom turned to Phillip and me, and I wondered if there really was something she wanted to talk about. "Erica, whatever is wrong with Eliza?"

"You mean other than the fact that she's a condescending bitch with an over-inflated sense of entitlement?"

Mom sighed and looked toward Eliza, who was deep in conversation with Peter, so she was unlikely to hear us speaking as softly as we were. "Erica, I don't know when you and Eliza are going to get over whatever it is that created such animosity between the two of you, but it's high time you did. You're both grown women—past middle age already." Count on Mom to get right to the point. I started to protest, but Mom was right. Eliza and I were both edging past middle age moment by moment. She continued. "And you might consider toning down the rhetoric. There is something wrong in that girl's life." She stopped for a moment and examined her nails. "What do you two think of Gordie?" she said nonchalantly as if she were tossing out an insignificant observation. I knew my mother well enough to know that insignificant observations were not her thing.

Phillip leaned over me. "Perhaps it's more to the point, Mom, if you tell us what *you* think of Gordie."

"Phillip, I asked you your opinion. I am not at the centre of this."

I suspected she was. "Why do you ask, Mom?" I said. So, there *was* something Mom wanted to talk to us about. I was right. I had sensed a spark between them, and we were only a few days into our trip.

"No special reason," she said. "I was just hoping you were both enjoying our vacation, and his presence is part of that experience. Since we're here now, I was hoping we could all have a little fun as a family."

"Is that what this is?" Phillip said. Mom didn't answer.

"Well, Phillip," I said, "as Jerry Seinfeld once said, 'There's no such thing as fun for the whole family.'" He cracked up. I turned to Mom. "So, you and Gordie seem to be getting along well. You seem to be having fun."

She shrugged and waved her hand as if swatting away an annoying housefly. "Why wouldn't we? After all, we're almost the same age."

"I suppose that's it, then," I said, turning away and smiling.

~

Peter eventually dropped us off beside a waterfront restaurant in a picturesque cove on Bonne Bay, back in the National Park, where we were going to get on a boat again.

"I'll just pick up our tickets and be right back," he said, popping on a baseball cap adorned with a gold and blue logo I didn't recognize.

It was a gorgeous day with unexpected sunshine and a comfortable temperature. The heat had moderated, and I even considered a light jacket for the boat, which was tied up at the dock just ahead. It was another one of those two-level tour boats, not unlike the one we'd been on in Western Brook Pond only two days earlier. It had a blue hull and an open top with benches. People ahead of us were already boarding.

"I hope Peter soon gets here with our tickets," Eliza said as she bumped into me to let other tourists pass. "We're not going to get good seats at this rate."

I rolled my eyes. Count on Eliza to pull a black cloud over a beautiful sunny day.

Peter returned momentarily and herded us all onto the boat and up the stairs to the open top. We all managed to find benches to sit on although not all together—as if that mattered. The boat pulled away from the dock and the tiny community of colourful, low houses. I turned in the direction we were heading and noted that the scenery wasn't as spectacular as the fjords of two days ago.

Nonetheless, it was tranquil and a breath of fresh air—literally and figuratively.

I could hear the distinctive seagull calls—squawking, squealing, and even laughing—as they mingled with the sound of the water splashing gently against the hull. There was little wind and almost no wave action. It was nearly as smooth as glass.

As the boat meandered along just out from the shore, I settled in to appreciate the serenity of the rolling hills surrounding the bay and the sight of a bevy of kayakers who seemed to be on tour themselves, their bright red, green and blue boats slicing quietly through the water below us. Everyone on board seemed to have a camera or a smartphone trained on something, and I wondered how much of our lives these days we saw only through a little screen. Perhaps it was time for me to put my phone back in my bag and sit back to watch and listen—and feel the sunshine and the breeze on my face.

Occasionally, one of the crew members would offer insights into the area's rich history and ecological significance, enriching the experience with fascinating tidbits of information. When we reached the middle of the bay, Peter came over and squeezed into the seat beside me.

"We're all headed downstairs for a special treat in a bit."

Eliza, who was sitting directly in front of me, turned her head. "What kind of treat, Peter?"

Peter's eyes twinkled, and he smiled broadly at Eliza. "I always think a treat is best when savoured in the waiting." Eliza gave him the stink eye she was so good at. He continued. "There's a James Joyce quote my grandmother used to invoke from time to time when we kids were impatient. 'The longest way around is the shortest way home,' is how it goes, but I think the longest way around is the sweetest way home. Stick with me." He patted Eliza on the shoulder and went down the steps to the lower deck.

Ten minutes later, Peter returned and herded us all down to the lower deck. When we got there, we found ourselves in an open room with rows of seats and what looked like a small stage at the front. On the stage, there was a table with bottles, tiny glasses and something large wrapped in newsprint. We found seats and waited for the "treat" to begin. A large man wearing a yellow rubber sou'wester—one of those hats with a long peak down the back to keep the rain off the neck and a short peak at the front to keep the rain out of the eyes—stepped up to the centre of the stage. Peter stood at the side, his hands stuffed into his pockets, looking on with a sardonic grin plastered on his handsome face.

"Welcome to The Rock," the emcee began. "All you mainlanders here—what we like to call the CFAs—are you ready to become honourary Newfoundlanders?" There was a smattering of clapping. "This here's the screech we're gonna need," he said, pointing to the bottles on the table. Then he pointed to the large, newsprint-wrapped mound. "And that there, well, that there is a codfish."

I could see Eliza's hand fly to her mouth. We were about to be "screeched in." I looked over at Phillip, and he started clapping. I could hardly believe myself, but I started laughing. In all the years we had come to Newfoundland as kids with our Newfoundland father to visit our Newfoundland granny, we had never become honourary Newfoundlanders. However, Gran had told us about the ceremony. I guess we were never worthy. But now, I was so ready.

The emcee looked around as if sizing up his crowd. His gaze landed on Eliza. I snorted because I could see what was coming. I was sure Peter must have put him up to this. "You there, ducky, you look a bit like you got a stick up your arse, but by god, you'd be a pretty one with a bit more meat on your bones. Up here, love."

I could see Eliza's shoulders stiffen. I knew her well enough, though, to know that to refuse would be to suggest she couldn't cope, and if there was one thing my cousin needed you to know was that she could cope—with anything. She reluctantly put her hand in his and he fairly pulled her toward the stage.

"First, on this boat, we starts with Newfie steak."

Eliza's eyebrows raised. If Eliza were trying to give the impression that she had never heard of this, she would have been lying. It was what Gran used to call bologna when she wasn't referring to it as the unsung hero of processed meats. I had actually liked it as a kid, especially when Gran fried it, and it curled up at the edges, forming little boats. She would then put mashed potatoes in the middle, and we'd smother it with ketchup. Oh my god, just thinking about it made me hungry.

I watched as the man picked up a tiny skewer with a piece of bologna threaded onto it. I suppose in these days of sanitation madness, it would be uncouth to lift it with one's fingers. He offered it to Eliza, who very hesitantly slid it off the skewer, looked at it, cleared her throat and popped it in her mouth to wild applause.

The man turned back to the table, and I knew what was coming. I heard Phillip beside me, trying to suppress a snort of laughter. He, too, knew what was coming. The man lifted the long package from the table and peeled back the newsprint at one end, revealing the large snout of a healthy, but no doubt very dead cod.

"Now, my ducky, comes the ceremonial kissing of the cod. Now, now, don't be scared. It won't bite." He laughed one of those deep belly laughs as if he might have heard the best joke of the decade. He held it close to Eliza's face. "Pucker up, m'lady, and smooch like you've never smooched before."

In that moment, Eliza looked defiant. As he brought it closer to her lips, she puckered up and gave it a loud smack. I was so impressed that I led the applause.

"Now," she said, "where's the screech?"

She was coming around! Human, after all.

TWENTY

Eliza

I HAD KNOWN PETER O'BRIEN FOR FEWER THAN twenty-four hours, and I had already begun to loathe him. *Judas*, I thought as I arose from my folding chair on the lower deck of that boat. *Only someone who doesn't know me at all would have suggested to the emcee that this was even approaching a good idea.*

How is it possible that spending a few amiable hours in a car, chatting agreeably with another person, getting to know him a bit, could turn on a dime? How is it possible that suddenly, a man I had begun to compare to Jake as kinder, gentler, and more intuitive could have gotten me so abjectly wrong? I was not the sort of person who thought these group activities were fun. I took a deep breath and allowed myself to be guided to the front of the audience.

I have been interviewed on *Good Morning America*, done a cooking demonstration on *The View*, kibbitzed with Conan O'Brien and given countless presentations throughout my career. Still, I had never felt my heart racing as it was doing now. Why did getting up in front of an audience of tourists to be the poster child for this highly suspect ritual make me so nervous? I knew enough about it from my childhood vacations with Gran to know they weren't planning on making me a human sacrifice. Then I looked over at Peter.

He was standing there looking like the cat who swallowed the canary, and if there had been any doubt in my mind that he'd put them up to this, it was dashed in a moment. And for what reason, I couldn't possibly imagine other than to make a fool of me. And yet, as I looked at him standing there grinning, I suddenly felt like I had something to prove to him or to the world—I didn't know which, and I didn't have any idea why or perhaps even what it was.

I turned my attention back to the man in the ridiculous yellow rubber hat who looked like he had just stepped off a fishing boat. I then stared at the table, and I knew perfectly well what was wrapped in newsprint. I had done my research. I was readying myself when he said something about Newfie steak and passed me a tiny skewer at the end of which was a pinkish square of something resembling food. I tentatively took the offered skewer from him and automatically sniffed it as I would have done if Jacques Pepin had offered me a taste of one of his French culinary delights. I winced as the familiar aroma assaulted my olfactory senses.

In all my years of recipe testing and cookbook writing, I'd encountered this smell—spices with a hint of vinegar—in only one location previously. I coughed slightly, pretending to clear my throat as images of summer vacations and Gran's kitchen began forming in my head. I felt my nose twitch as my olfactory memory kicked in, and I could almost feel myself sitting at the red Formica-topped kitchen table, squirming in my seat as she placed dinner in front of each of us—Emma, Lucy and me.

On the plate, I could see carrot coins and a boat-shaped piece of meat filled with mashed potatoes, and I remembered. Bologna boats. Fried bologna that curled into a boat shape and then filled with Gran's creamy mashed potatoes. As I closed my eyes and popped the piece of skewered bologna into my mouth, I remembered how much I had hated raw bologna sandwiches—and how much I had adored the fried stuff. I chewed, swallowed and listened to the applause. Then, it was time for the next step.

I stared at the emcee as he proudly uncovered the cod—quite dead, I might add—then lifted it lovingly in his arms, its pursed mouth pointing directly at me. I glanced over the crowd and caught Erica's eye. I knew that someone with her personality would lock lips with that codfish and come up laughing. Then I glanced in Peter's direction and knew I could do no less.

"Pucker up, m'lady, and smooch like you've never smooched before," the emcee said, his yellow sou'wester falling rakishly over his left eye.

And so, I did. Then I looked up defiantly, once again catching Erica's eye as she applauded loudly, and Peter whistled like I'd never heard anyone whistle before. What could I do?

"Now, where's the screech?" I said, and someone appeared out of nowhere with a plastic cup of that Newfoundland nectar—low-grade rum that used to be made in Newfoundland and that I happened to know was now made in Jamaica and bottled here. I grabbed it and gulped. I could feel it burning all the way down from the moment it touched my tongue until it reached my stomach. Then I had another.

The crew passed around tiny plastic cups of screech to all the passengers, and the emcee, who appeared to have already finished his third or fourth drink, said, "Now, all you CFAs lift your glasses and answer me the question."

Just as I noticed they all seemed also to be holding a small piece of paper, someone thrust one into my hands, and I looked down as the emcee said, "Now, do ye all want to be Newfoundlanders?"

On the paper, it said. "Indeed, we do, me old cock, and long may your big jib draw." With much laughter, in unison, the words filled the air. I had no idea what it meant.

"Now, then, consider yourself honourary Newfoundlanders, the lot of you!"

Just then, Peter came over and put his arm around me, leading me away from the front of the crowd. "Now, that was a time, as we like to say here in Newfoundland," he whispered. "And kind of awesome." I have no idea why these words, coming from a complete stranger, filled me with a fuzzy kind of warmth I hadn't felt in years. But I was still mad at him.

~

The day was not over yet. After disembarking the boat, feeling just a bit warmer inside (perhaps it was the screech?), we reassembled in our vehicle, Peter still at the wheel and me still firmly in the front seat. No one would let me sit anywhere else.

"Next up," Peter said as he pulled out of the parking lot, "back to Gros Morne National Park and the Tablelands. Everyone got their hiking boots on?"

I looked down at my tennis shoes and sighed. Hiking boots were not something that had ever resided in my closet. I glanced back at Erica and Phillip who were both sporting what looked like sneakers with soles resembling the Michelin Man. Perhaps that's what they called hiking sneakers. How would I know? I had noticed that both Dad and Aunt Maureen were wearing sneakers and those awful safari-style hats that were so popular among the over-seventy crowd on cruises and Newfoundland bus tours. Emma sported what appeared to be oversized red and green hiking shoes that clashed appallingly with her billowy, gauzy dress.

Just over an hour later, Peter pulled the truck into another parking lot.

"Okay," he said. "We hike from here."

"What exactly are the Tablelands?" Emma said, looking slightly panicked by the idea of a hike. I couldn't blame her. She wasn't exactly dressed for the occasion, except, perhaps, for the footwear. Who was I kidding? Neither was I. And neither of us could ever have been accused of being the slightest bit "outdoorsy."

As Peter rummaged in a big plastic box in the back of the truck, he said. "Well, they say these Tablelands are one of two places on this earth where the earth's mantle lies exposed."

"The earth's mantle?" Emma said as she swatted away the flies that seemed to like her vegan body odour more than they liked the rest of us.

"Oh, I'm sure you studied it in high school science, Emma. The earth is made up of three layers—the outer one we walk on every day, which is relatively thin called the crust; the inner core, which is superheated, molten lava; and the middle one, which is the mantle." He finally seemed to have finished his rummaging and held up something that resembled a ball cap with other benefits. "*Voila*! There you are," Peter said as he placed the peculiar hat with a front peak and a kind of cape all around it on his head for sun protection, no doubt. It was an unusual sartorial choice. Peter was so outdoorsy with his odd hat and his fishing vest covered in multiple pockets. Even his shorts were adorned with pockets, causing me to wonder what he kept in all of them.

"So, you mean we're going to walk on the underneath part of the earth?" Emma said, taking a small notebook from her pocket. Then she looked around. "Where is it?"

"You're kind of looking at it," Peter said, gesturing toward what looked to me like a moonscape of rocks strewn everywhere, utterly devoid of trees or other living features except for a few lines of low-lying greenery in the distance and a few strange flowers emerging from cracks in the rocks. Emma was heading toward one along the path that we'd begun to traverse.

"About two K in and two K out," Peter said, following Emma, who was crouching down in front of the plant, making little marks in her sketchbook. "Emma here's found the Newfoundland provincial flower." He whipped his phone from one of the myriad pockets (I wasn't sure how he even knew where it was) and started to click photos from a variety of angles.

The rest of us caught up to them, maneuvering around for a look at this elusive plant. It was strange, to say the least. I had never been interested in plants unless they had some culinary value, but this one was difficult to ignore. As I stared at its unique appearance, I thought it resembled the Venus fly trap, although it was a distinctly different colour—varying shades of dull green and brick red rather than bright green.

"Is this plant carnivorous?" I said.

Peter beamed. "Eliza gets the prize. It is, indeed. And elegant in its way, don't you think?"

I looked at the ugly little group of flowers and thought, yes, they are elegant in their own way. It seemed odd to me that something I might once have deemed too ugly even to consider might have merits—elegant merits, at that. Its slender, tubular leaves seemed to form upright pitchers, some of which had veins or speckles.

"See the leaves," Peter said. "They're shaped to capture insects." He leaned down and pointed to the parts of the plant, but he didn't pick it from its place beside a large rock that resembled it in colour. "Each leaf forms a hollow pitcher with a flared opening at the top. The shape of the pitcher is adapted to trap insects and prevent their escape. Then, the interior has downward-pointing hairs and a slippery surface. Insects are lured into the pitcher by nectar secreted around the rim. The critters become disoriented and eventually fall into the liquid-filled bottom of the pitcher where the plant's digestive fluids—well, I suppose you know what happens then." He grinned and stood up from where he had been crouching. "As Ms. Frizzle once said, 'Look to Mother Nature for the best of everything.' Let's go."

Mother Nature? The best of everything? Peter and I seemed to be entirely on different wavelengths. I was gagging for a drink of water, followed by a martini or even rum, since my drink of choice—scotch—seemed to be in short supply around here. At least the quality of scotch I was used to seemed scarce. *Well*, I thought, *at least I can avoid having to talk to Jake and Izzy for a while. Maybe this will let me forget my issues for a few hours.*

As the group of us moved along the path, I began to feel disoriented. We seemed to be in the middle of nowhere with only the faraway mountains around and dusty rocks strewn as far as the eye could see. Luckily for me, the path was a wooden walkway that had obviously been created for the less outdoorsy among us. There were even a few stone benches along the way where Dad and Aunt Maureen perched for a few minutes.

I found myself standing alone among the dusty, red-hued rocks, staring into the distance and listening to the wind. For a few minutes, my head was clear, and my mind wasn't racked with thoughts of what I had to do, how I was going to do it, and what my life was going to look like in the end. For the first time in a long time,

I wasn't wondering what I was going to do about Jake and me. Equally, I was not wondering about Izzy's news and what that would mean to me. I was alone with the great big sky, the sun and the wind. And for that one minute, I felt something approaching peace.

When I awakened from my reverie, I turned and saw Peter standing on the other side of the path, looking at me. For a brief moment, our eyes locked, and this time, I didn't see anything but understanding in his eyes. I took a deep breath of the fresh air and walked toward him.

"Thank you, Peter."

"Thank you for what?"

"For this," I said, gesturing around. "For showing me your world." I looked down at my tennis shoes. "And for taking me on a path where I didn't need anything more than what I have."

Peter nodded and smiled enigmatically. I had the feeling he knew what I meant.

When we got to our destination at the centre of the park area, I sat down on a bench and folded my hands in my lap while everyone else ran around taking photos of the earth's mantle. Peter was showing everyone how to use their phones in more creative ways to take pictures that might better capture something of the place. I preferred to use my eyes and my memory of the sights as well as the sounds and the feelings.

As I sat there, my mind began wandering back in time to the earliest days of my relationship with Jake and what happened after. He had been too arrogant for my liking at first, but he had grown on me. By the time I'd fallen in love with him, I had gotten used to his approach to the world. I had even convinced myself that I'd been mistaken about his arrogance. I preferred to think of it as self-confidence. One of my closest friends in my single days had called him a self-important megalomaniac with a god complex. She and I didn't see much of one another in the days after Jake and I married. I wondered where she was now. I had decided he was an assertive self-starter despite the fact that his business opportunities and money came directly from his father. It was during this time that I began to long to be part of his larger community—I wanted to convert to Judaism.

It had been my choice, although Esther, my mother-in-law, was ecstatic when Jake told her I was considering taking this step. To her, it was just something I should do—nothing more than what she might have expected. To me, it had been a profound longing to become a part of something greater than myself. I had met with Jake's rabbi, who I found to be pompous and supercilious, telling me that it would be a long road to becoming a member of god's chosen people.

Jake's sister, Allegra and I had become good friends, first because we'd worked together and later because we were going to become sisters-in-law. After I'd met with the rabbi, I told her how I'd felt in his presence. Her reaction had been to roll her eyes and say, "Then you need to meet Eli."

Eli turned out to be the rabbi at the synagogue that she'd fled to in an effort to avoid seeing her mother more often than every Friday night for dinner. Eli was as different from the first rabbi as chalk is from cheese. When I told him what I'd been considering, he picked up my hand and said, "My dear, Eliza. This choice is a long journey and one that will challenge your beliefs—long-held beliefs from your childhood and the wider world." When I told him I'd lost any faith I'd had, he shook his head. "Your beliefs still live in your mind and soul whether you have faith in them or not. They are still there, and they will continue to inform you as you move along this new path. If it is something you want to pursue, and it is not something you are doing to placate Jacob or his mother, then I will take your hand and guide you as far as I can. The rest will be up to you." I had found my sherpa.

It had always been my choice—no one else's—and I had never wavered in my belief that it had been the right choice for me. I had followed the path, and I was Jewish. But now, as I sat there in the sunshine, feeling the wind on my face, in a place on earth I never expected to be, I could feel a seed of doubt begin to creep into my consciousness. I no longer seemed to be sure of my place in the world.

When Peter finally called us together, and we started back along the walkway to the parking lot, I got up and brought up the rear, still deep in thought. Suddenly, before we were even halfway to the truck, the heavens opened, and rain began pelting down. I could feel each gigantic drop as it splashed on my hair and my shoulders. That moment should have been when I would start to panic about how my hair would look. It should have been the moment when I began to run for cover as fast as I could. But I just walked calmly, feeling the rain soak through my clothes and shoes and drip into my eyes. After all, it was coming from somewhere up above.

TWENTY-ONE

Erica

WE MUST HAVE LOOKED LIKE THE PIED PIPER'S enchanted children as we trekked along behind Peter toward the centre of wherever we were going. As I began to take stock of my surroundings, I began to feel that perhaps I was just a little bit enchanted, and it was this place that was doing its magic. There was something bewitching about the open feeling of the rock-strewn land stretching out in all directions toward the hills in the distance and the sky above. I had never been one to be so drawn to the forces of nature, but knowing that this place had been created over half a billion years ago was truly breathtaking, especially to a city girl like me. I wished that Andrew and Maddie were here to share this with me. But they weren't, so I had to content myself with sharing it with Phillip, my partner in crime.

"What would Marcus think of this?" I said as I caught up to my brother and slipped my arm through his.

"Marcus? Marcus, the quintessential urban businessman party guy?" Phillip whistled. "I suppose he'd think it was a bunch of rocks and wonder when he could get back to a hotel, take a shower and find a bar serving perfectly stirred martinis."

I started to laugh. "You two are such city people."

"Look who's talking, sis. You're not exactly hiking material yourself. And this isn't anything like downtown Toronto where you usually hike from your front door to the liquor store." Then he got serious. "Why do you think Gran really wanted us to take this trip? It seems so odd, *n'est ce pas?*"

"Well, I don't suppose there's much point in trying to figure out the mental musings of a one-hundred-year-old woman. We all just seem to have to go along for the ride and maybe all will be revealed at the end." I wasn't sure what I meant by all would be revealed. What could possibly be revealed? Then again, I hadn't thought the rest of this inexplicable island had anything to reveal, and yet it did. "Anyway," I said, "I, for one, have decided I'm just going to continue to be a child and get as much fun out of this experience as I can." I took my phone from my back pocket. "Let's see who can take the best pictures."

~

An hour after we'd left the Tablelands, we arrived at our destination for the night, a small village called Rocky Harbour. The weather had turned sharply cooler, nudging the sweaters and sweatshirts from our bags. There would be no need for air conditioning tonight, although our accommodation had it anyway, according to Peter. The village snaked along a rocky shoreline — hardly a surprising discovery given its name.

From across the street, the multi-coloured two-story hotel building looked out over the grey waves reflecting the slate-coloured sky that seemed to hang low over the water. It was melancholic and yet strangely peaceful, even with the sharpening wind.

Once Peter had returned from checking us in, pulled all our cases from the back of the SUV-bus and given us room keys, Phillip, who had been checking his text messages, looked up toward the front entrance and said, "This looks like a place with a good bar. Am I right, Pete?"

Before Peter could answer, Eliza said, "I'm just looking forward to a shower and a sleep after I talk to Jake."

Peter grinned. "Yes, there is a great bar here, Phillip, but we don't have time for that." He turned toward Eliza. "Can you make that phone call a quick one? We have places to be. People to see."

Eliza looked at Peter as if she had no clue as to what he might be talking about, so I intervened. "What's on the agenda for this evening, Peter?"

"Yes, Peter," Mom said, "what precisely is on the agenda for this evening if no one has time for the bar? And when is your father rejoining us?" Mom had seemed slightly out of sorts since Gordie had left our little group. I had noticed more than her usual shortness with people.

"What's on the agenda is a kitchen party at old Mrs. McCarthy's." Peter beamed as usual. He always seemed to be pleased.

"Not Mary McCarthy?" Mom said, clutching at her silk scarf as a look of horror passed over her face.

"The very one!" Peter said as he helped Mom with her suitcase. "And we leave in," he looked at his watch, "exactly twenty-five minutes."

"Dear god," Mom muttered, taking the handle of her case firmly away from Peter.

Eliza started shaking her head. "No, no. I'll have to pass on the festivities this evening. As much as a kitchen party sounds," she seemed to be searching for the right word, "amusing, in a quaint sort of way, I'll have to beg off and let the rest of you carry on without me."

Peter was still smiling, and now I seemed to discern that glint his eyes took on whenever he looked at Eliza. "Sorry, Eliza, but I have orders from your grandmother via my father. No one is to be left out of the amusement." Was he mocking her use of the term?

Eliza dropped her carry-on case onto the pavement and seemed to stamp her foot as I'd seen her do so many times when we were children together in the summers. She had never been a child who gave in when she didn't get her way. At least she never gave in without a fight. I expected her to jam her hands onto her hips like she used to, but it seemed that stamping her foot was as far as adult Eliza would go. "I'm sorry, Peter, but Gran does not have control over what I'm doing while I'm here or anywhere else." Peter was still smiling. "I still have a life, and I have things I need to deal with. No one here has any idea."

For the briefest of moments, I thought Eliza might start crying, which seemed odd for her. Even I knew that would not be a good idea.

"Eliza," I said, "it might actually be fun. I mean, it is a real Newfoundland experience. These kitchen parties are legendary." I turned to my mother. "Mom, help me out here."

"Don't look at me. The second last person on earth I want to see at this moment in my life is Mary McCarthy and her spawn."

It was on the tip of my tongue to ask her who the first person was, but Uncle Fred interrupted her. I suspected he knew. He turned toward his daughter. "Eliza, Mary McCarthy is an old friend of the family who used to live next door to us a lifetime ago in St. John's." He looked at Mom, who was rolling her eyes. "She and your grandmother were great friends off and on through the years even after they left the city to come all the way over to this side of the island so her husband could be the town's doctor. Your Aunt Maureen here didn't get along very well with Mary's daughter, Bernadette."

"That's putting it mildly," Mom muttered.

Uncle Fred turned to Peter. "Please tell me Bernadette is still in St. John's, Peter."

Peter nodded. "Yes, sir. I believe that's where she lives, but I can't vouch for where she might be this evening in the middle of the summer when the family all assembles to visit their matriarch."

"Just say it, Peter O'Brien," Mom said. "My mother has instructed your father to guarantee that I revisit every unpleasantness of the first two decades of my life."

Uncle Fred looked puzzled. "Wait a minute, Maureen. This isn't all about you. We're all in this together. None of us asked to be here this summer. Mother has her reasons, and I think we all should be open-minded about following through." Uncle Fred seemed to be warming to the idea of Gran's tour.

"Easy for you to say," Mom muttered as she headed toward the hotel's front door. "You were always her favourite." Before Uncle Fred could answer, she said, "I'll be back in twenty-five minutes, ready to go to this kitchen party." Then, she turned toward Eliza. "And if I can go, you can go." Then, she disappeared through the lobby doors and was swallowed up by the hotel.

"Well, then, that's settled." Peter checked his watch. "Twenty-one minutes and counting."

"That's not enough time. I can't go to a party without showering and dressing," Eliza said, at least acquiescing to the finality of the decision that we would all go.

"Give it up, Eliza," Emma said to her sister. "Slap on that expensive lipstick you seem to like so much and brush your hair." She turned to Peter. "That's all we need, isn't it?"

Peter smiled and nodded. "Not even any need for the lipstick. It's a kitchen party."

~

Twenty minutes later, I'd managed to brush my teeth, throw on a scarf, change my shoes, and return to the parking lot. Mom was still back in our room, sulking. I had never seen Mom like this in all my five decades of being her daughter. She had told me to go ahead and that she would be along in a few minutes. When I arrived in the parking lot, Phillip and Uncle Fred were already there. Peter emerged from the hotel lobby and checked his watch again.

"Peter," I said, "is it always necessary to be so prompt for a party like this?"

"I'm told it won't do your grandmother's relationship with Mary McCarthy and her clan any good if the lot of us are late. Depending on what's on the menu this evening, we might want to be the early birds."

I had no idea what might be on the menu at a kitchen party, but it didn't seem we had time to discuss the matter. I'd find out soon enough.

Finally, everyone had arrived. Once again, Eliza sat in front, and the rest of us just piled in anywhere. Peter said it was only a ten-minute drive to the McCarthy homestead. "By the way," Peter said to no one in particular, "I have taken the great liberty of purchasing some liquor on your behalf to offer to the hostess."

"Dear god, Peter, should we be bringing anything else? I can't believe I've forgotten my manners." Mom always needed to be on top of the etiquette in any situation, regardless of how she might feel about the participants.

"Cut yourself some slack, Mom," Phillip said. "He just sprang this on us. Thanks, Peter. Let me know how much we owe you."

"Don't mention it. It's all included, courtesy of Nora." And with that, he put the truck in gear and pulled back onto the main road through the village.

After ten minutes of wending our way along the shoreline, Peter turned the truck into a long driveway that seemed to be noticeable only to someone who had been there before. It led up a slight incline away from the water, with tall fir trees densely lining it. When we emerged into a clearing at the top of the hill, we were looking at a massive three-story white clapboard house with a porch that spanned the entire front. The top story looked like it had one of those widow's walks—a small deck with a railing where potential widows looked out over the ocean in search of their husbands out at sea.

The gravel driveway that had widened at the top was already lined with too many vehicles to count. There were pick-up trucks, several SUVs, an old grey Toyota that looked like the first car I'd owned in the 1990s, and, oddly, at least to my eye, a bright red Mercedes convertible. *I wonder who owns that one*, I thought as I extricated myself once again from the truck. I could feel my old reporter curiosity coming alive and thought, *This might just turn out to be interesting after all.*

By the time we were all out standing beside the truck, several people had appeared on the front porch.

"Well, if it isn't Peter O'Brien," a voice from the doorway roared. A tall, thick-set man with dark curly hair shot through with grey strands, wearing a plaid shirt rolled up to reveal beefy forearms, smiled broadly as he moved toward the top of the steps. He had a bottle of beer in one hand.

"Everett Malone," Peter called. "I've brought you Nora's family." Peter then turned to the group of us who were standing there stupidly as if we might be facing a firing squad. "Everett is Mary's grandson. He and I go back a long way. Classmates at one time."

At that moment, a woman emerged from behind Everett. She was about Mom's age, with short, spikey red hair, an odd colour for a woman clearly approaching eighty, I thought. Dear god, I was beginning to sound like Eliza. The woman was wearing a tight cream-coloured sweater, leggings and high heels.

My mother, who was standing beside me, grabbed my arm. "It's worse than I even imagined," she whispered.

"Who is that woman?" I said.

"That, my darling daughter, is Bernadette McCarthy—I suppose Bernadette Malone at this stage if she's still married to Harold Malone, whose father owned every car dealership in the city when I was growing up. Everett's mother. Mary's daughter, or should I say evil spawn."

I raised my eyebrows. It was so unlike my mother to talk about people that way. I needed details, but I could see now was not the time.

"I suppose that flashy red car is hers," Mom hissed as she plastered on an artificial smile and moved toward the porch.

I looked at the Mercedes and then at Phillip. "The plot thickens, brother."

"I guess," he said. "Curiouser and curiouser."

"Yes," I said. "It is a bit like Alice in Wonderland."

~

By the time we got inside, we could see the party was in full swing. There were people everywhere.

"I thought this party would be in the kitchen," Emma said, looking around at people milling about the living room.

"It is, too, in the kitchen," Peter said. "But one of Mary's parties is everywhere since there are so many people. But the kitchen is where the musicians will be set up and where the singing and dancing will be."

"How can a kitchen be big enough for singing and dancing?"

"You'll see," he said. "In the meantime, you might want to check out the hors d'oeuvres." He pointed toward the dining room.

I followed Emma into the huge dining room. Eliza and Phillip followed behind. Uncle Fred and Mom seemed to have disappeared. The décor was what I would call country style, with maple wainscoting on the lower part of the walls and floral wallpaper above. The heavy drapes were the same pink and purple floral as the wallpaper. It must have been quite the place in its day, but it had a kind of tiredness about it. It was a tiredness that was in direct contrast to the ebullience of the people. And there were people of all shapes, sizes, and ages, although there were actually few people in the dining room. Perhaps they had already eaten.

The colossal table that looked as if it could seat twelve comfortably for dinner groaned under the weight of the food. If everyone had already eaten, this must have been the second helping. Peter had directed us to hors d'oeuvre platters that held food I'd never seen on a menu before. Eliza just stood there and stared. I wondered how a culinary "expert" would view the food.

"What exactly are those?" she said, pointing to skewers on a large platter.

Emma leaned over to take a better look. "They are certainly not vegan-friendly," she said.

At that precise moment, I heard a snort of laughter from the other side of the table. I looked up to see a woman, possibly sixty or seventy—it was hard to tell—with her hands clasped across her ample mid-section, smiling broadly at Emma—a bit like one might smile at a daft child.

"No, my dear child. No one breathes that word in the presence of Mary McCarthy, mind."

Emma looked over. "What word?"

The woman looked around conspiratorially. "That V-word, child. Trust me. Do not suggest to Mary that anyone in the world would choose to be a V-person."

"V-person? Do you mean vegan? But I am vegan," Emma said.

"Are you still?" I could not help myself. After that little display the other evening at the bar, I wondered.

Emma looked daggers at me. "Why wouldn't I be?"

"Just asking," I said as innocently as I could manage as I picked up one of the skewers. I turned to Eliza. "Eliza, you'll be familiar with these."

Eliza picked up a skewer just as three children ran madly past her in one dining room door and out the other. "Dear god," she said. "Not more bologna."

Someone had spent a lot of time threading bologna cubes, pickled onions and cubes of what appeared to be cheddar cheese onto dozens of skewers. I nibbled the cheese off the end and then the onion. Then, there was a pickle resembling a minuscule cucumber. "Eliza, do you remember these?"

Eliza's nose was twitching, but I knew she remembered. We'd loved them as kids at Gran's summer place on her cold plates, a gourmet delight I hadn't thought about in years. These were tiny gherkin pickles. I popped it in my mouth and savoured the crisp tang of the vinegary flavour. I felt that satisfying crunch as I bit down, and summers at Gran's filled my mind. I hadn't eaten a gherkin pickle since I was about fifteen years old and now, I wondered why. "Eat it, Eliza."

Eliza took a deep breath and ate the bologna and cheddar. Then she bit into the gherkin, and I could see she remembered as vividly as I did.

"Well, what does your gourmet palate think of that?"

180

"Salt, herbal notes of dill and the acidic tang of vinegar," she said, her eyes closed. Was she almost smiling?

Emma, on the other hand, was picking off the bologna and cheese as if touching them might somehow betray her putative veganism while the woman across the table continued to look on, a bemused look on her face.

"You lot are Nora's people, aren't you?" the woman said. We all nodded. "Her grandchildren here on the island for the old bat's birthday, I suppose."

I almost choked. Old bat? Didn't everyone love Nora Houlihan?

"Glad to meet you all. I'm Iris Noseworthy, Mary's niece." We introduced ourselves. "Well, girls," she said while I wondered how three middle-aged women could be referred to as girls, "take my advice. I've known Nora since I was a girl, and I have to say one thing about her. She's as constant as the North Star. Never changes. Never has. Still as bigoted and crotchety as ever." She turned to Emma. "And one more word of advice for you, my ducky, don't mention your affliction to your grandmother and eat whatever she has on offer. You might practice with those," she said, pointing to a plate filled with little sausages on toothpicks that I recognized as another summer delight—the Vienna sausages that Gran used to extract from a little can. Then she turned to the cabinet behind her that held what looked to be a large slow cooker surrounded by bowls. "And Aunt Mary's moose stew."

Emma blanched. I suppose I did as well, but Eliza looked intrigued. Emma swallowed and said, "You don't mean that someone killed a moose and put it in that pot?"

"Well, of course I do, ducky. How else would you make a moose stew?" Iris laughed. "And don't forget to sample the fish cakes." She pointed to another platter in the middle of the table. "Aunt Mary will ask you how you liked them." She stared at Emma. "Anyway, there's drinks in the kitchen, and the music is about to start. That's where everyone'll be."

That explained why there were now so few guests here in the dining room. I absently picked up a Vienna sausage on a toothpick and popped it in my mouth—salty and smoky with that smooth, over-processed texture I'd loved as a child. I needed a drink.

We followed the sound of instruments tuning up into the enormous kitchen. It was more of what I would think of as a combination kitchen-family room with its expansive counters, maple cabinets, an old woodstove in one corner beside a gleaming, stainless-steel stove, two sofas and a rocking chair. In another corner, there was a massive plastic basin filled with dozens of bottles of beer nestled in a bed of crushed ice. On the counter sat an enormous punch bowl where I saw Peter standing, ladling something from it into a plastic cup. He gestured us over.

I picked my way through the crowd, followed by Eliza, while Emma stayed in the doorway. Phillip was with Peter, and I saw Mom and Uncle Fred over by the rocking chair, chatting with the woman sitting in it. I concluded that it was Mary McCarthy herself. Red-haired Bernadette hovered near the musicians—a guitarist, an accordion player and a drummer holding something I recognized as a Bodhrán, an Irish drum played with a short stick. They were getting ready.

When we arrived beside Peter, he handed me the cup and filled another one for Eliza. It looked like one of those slushies that kids like so much in the summer.

"Here's the local version of Newfoundland slush, ladies. Don't drink it too fast."

I took a tentative sip and was startled at how it warmed my throat all the way down despite its icy cold mouth feel. It was no regular slushie. "What's in this?" I said, trying to make myself heard over the noise level that was increasing by the minute. The music began, and three people went to the centre of the floor and started dancing. The style resembled what I imagined step-dancing to be.

"Well, this version seems to be apricot brandy and vodka with a hint of lemonade and orange juice, if I'm not mistaken. I also taste a bit of pineapple. Frozen and served with a splash of lemon-lime soda."

I could see my education was severely lacking. This particular party offering was new to me, and I could see by Eliza's face that it was certainly new to her. "What do you call it?" I said.

"Well, just Newfoundland slush," Peter said, "but I'm driving, so a sip's all I get!"

Peter's friend Everett maneuvered his way toward us and started introducing us to anyone who came near. The names went in one ear and out the other. Then I could see Mom gesturing for us to come over toward her.

Peter saw her and said, "You better go over and meet our hostess herself. Then you can relax and have a good time."

We made our way past the dancers and singers—everyone was singing something about there's going to be a time and fishing off some rocks. It was a catchy tune that we may have heard earlier in the day if I didn't miss my guess.

Mary McCarthy was sitting primly in her rocking chair, wearing a crocheted sweater over a floral dress and a string of pearls. Her thin white hair stood in wisps, and I judged her to be near Gran's age. She peered at us through large plastic glasses with thick lenses. Mom introduced us one at a time, and Mary took each of our hands and said, "Welcome, girls. I want you to know that we all love you here despite you all being CFAs. Nora wasn't as lucky as I was, all her offspring leaving her—although you might say I couldn't blame them." She cackled. Although Peter had suggested Gran and Mary had once been friends, it sounded to me that there was little love lost between them. "But rest assured," she continued, "I'll be at her party with bells on." I was surprised to hear this and wondered how many of the rest of Mary's family might attend Gran's birthday party the following week in St. John's.

After meeting Mary, I wandered around the house for a while, dodging people here and there, introducing myself as necessary. Eliza, Emma and Phillip had all found a second and maybe third drink, and I think I even saw Emma singing. I decided to search for a bathroom. I made my way up the wide staircase with its turned maple balustrade and its carpeting that matched the dining room drapes and wallpaper. I found the bathroom down a corridor on the second floor, and when I'd finished, I wandered a bit further, my reporter's curiosity piqued. At the end of the hall, there was another narrower staircase leading up to a third floor. I walked up, and at the top, there was a third, even narrower set of stairs. *This must lead to that widow's walk*, I thought. *There must be a great view from up there. What harm could there be in going up?*

As I emerged at the top of the staircase, I could see someone leaning on the railing, looking out over the water. It was just past dusk, and I couldn't discern the person's identity. As I took a step, a floorboard creaked, and the person turned. It was Peter.

"Hey, Erica, fancy meeting you here."

"What are you doing up here, Peter?"

"Looking at the view. I used to come up here with Everett to drink beer when our families were visiting. I haven't been up here in years. Things can get so hectic, and sometimes, you know, I just prefer the quiet." I joined him at the rail and looked around as he continued. "What are *you* doing up here? Doing some journalistic snooping?" I was surprised he knew about that. "You the kind of person who looks in other people's medicine cabinets?" He laughed.

"You'd be surprised what you can learn about people from their bathrooms," I said.

"I know you, Erica Flanagan," he said.

I was startled. "What do you mean? I don't think we've ever met before these last few days."

"We actually did, very briefly, one summer decades ago. You wouldn't remember, and that's not what I meant, anyway. I know you from television."

I looked closely at his face. "I would never have taken you for an afternoon television kind of guy, Peter."

"Ah, I suppose I'm a man of many surprises, Erica," he said, laughing. "I have seen you recently on your evening show a few times, but, yes, I first stumbled upon you on afternoon TV. I was also a great fan of your husband's work. Andrew Taylor was the greatest national news anchor this country ever had. I missed him when he retired. I still miss him."

"Then you know more about me than I know about you," I said, realizing that I knew nothing about Peter O'Brien other than what I had surmised—and I had no way of knowing if I had nailed him.

"Tell me about Eliza," he said before I could ask him anything.

"Eliza? Well, my cousin is pretty much a what-you-see-is-what-you-get kind of woman. She's an uptight, bossy, snobby New Yorker."

"I'm not so sure," Peter said, gazing into the darkness over the trees toward where the moon shimmered on the water.

I started to worry about Peter's evident interest in Eliza. "Are you married, Peter?"

"I was. Not anymore."

"Well, Eliza is married, as I mentioned to you at dinner yesterday, so if you have any ideas about an attraction to her, you might as well let them go. Besides, I did mention that she's snobby and a bit elitist, if you ask me."

"Elitist, eh? I suppose you're implying that I might not fit into the rarefied atmosphere of the elite," Peter said without a shred of offence.

"I told you her husband Jake is a member of the Bluestone Pharma family—with more money than brains, as far as I'm concerned. Eliza seems to have developed certain expectations about the people she associates with. Anyway, as I said, she's married, so the discussion is all academic."

"Tell me more about her husband."

"Jake? He's a vain, pretentious mommy's boy. I've never liked him. I remember their wedding. It was at the Plaza Hotel in New York, and it was attended by hundreds of obnoxious friends, relatives, and business acquaintances of Jake's family. As Eliza's family, we were in the minority in a big way. I remember how offended Uncle Fred had been when he'd suggested they be married in Eliza's hometown and that he pay for it as the father of the bride in those days always did. Jake's mother wouldn't even entertain that idea. I always thought that Eliza might actually have given her father that privilege if she'd had any say in the matter. She didn't seem to. It must have cost hundreds of thousands. But that's just a drop in the bucket to her in-laws. And did I mention that her mother-in-law is a nightmare?"

"You told me you thought Eliza and Jake might be having a long-distance argument of some sort. What do you know about that?"

"Nothing. Honestly, Peter, if you're developing a crush on my cousin, I'd recommend that it's in your best interests to step away. Really."

I could see Peter's smile in the semi-darkness. "There's something about her, Erica. I'm convinced there's more to your cousin than meets the eye—yours or mine. And I'm going to find out what it is."

TWENTY-TWO

Eliza

I WAS FEELING TIRED AND DUSTY as I stood there beside the truck in the parking lot in front of our new "hotel" in Rocky Harbour. The drive had been quiet, almost as if everyone else might also have found the landscape as profoundly moving as I did. I had never expected to begin to question decisions I'd made in my life—none whatsoever. But now…well, now I didn't quite know what to think. All I knew at that moment was that after only a few days, I was already tired of Gran seeming to have control over our lives while we were here. Then Dad said that none of us had chosen to be there, and I began to consider why that might be.

Gran—Nora Houlihan—had always been a presence larger than life when we visited her in the summers. We had done what she wanted to do when she wanted us to do it. If Gran had said we were going to spend the day traipsing around Bowring Park, then we would follow her—Mom, Dad, Emma, Lucy, and me. And if our visit overlapped with our cousins, Erica and Phillip, along with their parents also went. My grandfather never seemed to have anything whatsoever to say about it all, and, of course, after he died, it was all Gran anyway.

It seemed that even after a century of living, this planet had done nothing to quell Gran's belief that she always knew best. I realized there was little point in arguing further that I was too tired and uninterested in attending something called a kitchen party, so I held myself back from stamping my foot any longer. I took the handle of my small suitcase, went into the hotel to slap on that expensive lipstick Emma mentioned, slammed into my room and picked up my cell phone to make a call I didn't want to make before returning to the group I didn't want to be with tonight to do something I didn't want to do. Kissing a codfish hadn't improved my attitude — much.

Emma, my roommate, did not immediately follow me, and I was very grateful for that. I needed a bit of privacy, and I suspect she may have recognized this despite her catty comment about my lipstick fetish.

"How are things, Jake?" I said when he finally picked up just before it went to voice mail. I could imagine him sitting there in his den in a massive black leather chair, sipping a glass of expensive scotch (I have to admit I was a tad jealous of that), checking the caller ID and wondering if he would even answer. But I knew he needed me. So, he answered.

"How do you think things are, Eliza? I'm here, and you're not. I'm having to deal with everything."

I had been standing staring out the window at the grey skies. Now, I sat down on the edge of the bed and wondered how I got here. I sighed. "Just tell me what you mean by everything, and then I'll talk to Izzy."

"You won't talk to Izzy now because she isn't here."

"What do you mean she isn't there? Where the hell is she? Don't tell me she's out partying?" Jake was beginning to annoy me even more than he usually did with his whining and preening. In recent years, I'd learned to ignore his more disagreeable traits and focus on the good times. There had been good times. I just couldn't think of any at that moment.

"There you go again, Eliza. Can't you control your temper?"

The only thought in my head at that moment was that if he'd been in the room with me, I might not have been able to control this urge I had to throttle him, although I knew that would get us nowhere. I checked my watch and saw I had only fifteen more minutes before I had to be back outside. I took a deep breath to calm my rising anger and said slowly and deliberately as if I were talking to an obtuse child. "Jake, please just give me an update and tell me where Izzy is so I can talk to her."

I heard Jake slurp something and wondered how much he'd had to drink already. He was famous for his after-work forays into a favourite bar near his office, where he and several of his colleagues liked to gather to review their day. The image of his secretary—what was her name? Eleanor, if memory served—floated across my consciousness. Perhaps she had joined them to take notes.

"I think you should cut that trip short and come home, Eliza. You should be here. Izzy needs you."

"Jake, an update please." I gritted my teeth and clasped my phone so hard I thought for a moment I might crush it.

"She won't talk to me. I tried, Eliza. But you know what she can be like."

I rolled my eyes, thinking of all the times through Izzy's life that I'd told Jake to stop calling her princess. Just as I'd predicted, the more he called her princess, the more she believed she was one. "Jake, what happened?"

"She just packed her bags and told me she was going to stay with a friend. I think she said her name was Astrid."

If Jake had really known his daughter as well as he liked to think he did, he would have known that Astrid Larsson had been Izzy's best friend since high school and that Astrid had gone to Medical School at Columbia when Izzy had deferred her acceptance. I also knew that it would have taken more than a mild argument with her father to propel Izzy back into that tribe that she'd left behind to pursue freedom in California.

"Jake, you didn't happen to mention any of this to your mother, did you?"

"I suppose I did. And why not? Izzy is her granddaughter."

I could picture exactly what had happened. Esther was not known for her diplomacy or her open-mindedness. She would have been furious at Izzy for getting "into trouble," which is what I'd heard her say in the past when gossiping about young women who ended up unmarried and pregnant. Esther was a walking, talking anachronism. She would have wanted to know who the father was, when they would be getting married and how Izzy could have been such an idiot.

"I suppose you let your mother talk to her, didn't you?"

Jake told me that Esther had insisted on talking to Izzy when she heard she was home and the reason for her reappearance and that Izzy had taken a fit and left almost immediately afterward. I would have to do damage control, and it wasn't going to be easy from this distance. I was also grappling with the unsettling thought that Esther Cohen wasn't that far off the mark. It had been a rather careless thing for an otherwise intelligent young woman to let happen. However, that kind of thinking wasn't going to help any of us.

I hung up and quickly dialled Izzy's number. It went immediately to voicemail, so I left her a soothing, motherly message, telling her that I'd talk to her tomorrow but that she could call me whenever she needed me. When I hung up, I tossed my phone into my tote bag, ran a brush through my hair, slapped on that lipstick, lifted the bag onto my shoulder and opened the door to find Emma waiting in the hallway with her suitcase.

"So, have you finished yelling at Jake?" she said, sliding by me. "I thought I'd let you have the room for a few minutes."

I said nothing and made my way directly to the parking lot.

~

I have always loved food. I cannot remember when I first began to notice my interest, but it has been with me since I was a child. Over the past few days, I'd been introduced — or re-introduced — to foods I hadn't thought about since childhood because if Gran had been in charge of what we did and where we went during our summer visits, she had also very much been in charge of what we ate. I didn't like everything she served, but I had always found it interesting. So, half an hour later, as I walked into Mary McCarthy's dining room, a bit leery of what the evening would bring, I was curious about the food on offer so I wandered into the dining room.

I was almost knocked over by children running amok through the house as I reached for a skewer of oddities that passed for hors d'oeuvres as Peter had suggested they were. Why did people think that it was appropriate for children to attend evening parties? I shook my head and returned my attention to the skewer.

First, there was yet more bologna. I ate the cube of pink processed meat once again and then a morsel of what appeared to be ordinary cheddar cheese. Then Erica asked me if I remembered the tiny green pickle that was threaded on the skewer next. I bit into the gherkin pickle and remembered Gran serving them with sandwiches. I had always known how tastes and smells could transport people back to times when they'd first encountered them, but I had never imagined it could be so vivid. It was as if I could reach my hand through space and time to the summer moments before life and family issues intervened and made me leave my younger self behind to create a new life and a new family. As much as I had longed to disconnect—and had done so for a very long time—it felt as if there were bonds that I couldn't break no matter how hard I tried. I looked at Erica and wondered if, in a different life, we might have been friends.

I followed Erica into the kitchen, where we were told the music was about to begin. I had been to countless parties in my life—parties that had become increasingly tedious in recent years—but I had never been to one like this.

Everyone seemed to be happy to be there. For many people, that may be a given at a party. I suppose a party should be something you enjoy. But I can tell you that I'd been to more than my share of parties where everyone, including me, had seemed listless and bored—jaded with the sameness of one cocktail party after another. It seemed to me that parties had become extensions of everyone's working lives, with not a second to be wasted on enjoyment when schmoozing and networking were on the menu. This was different. Based on my quick inventory of the conversations going on around me, where people talked, laughed, and, most of all, listened to one another, this was very different from my experience.

I wondered how long it had been since I'd enjoyed a party. It occurred to me that it might have been sometime before Jake and I were married. That was a lifetime ago.

I followed Erica over to where Peter was ladling something into plastic glasses. He handed me one, and the moment I tasted it, I knew I'd have to find the recipe. It was an alcoholic beverage, but one that I'd never experienced in my life. Peter called it Newfoundland Slush, and it was undoubtedly a slushie for grown-ups. Peter then introduced us to more people than I would ever be able to remember, and once the music started, it was too loud for talking. I turned my attention to the music and was immediately entranced.

I watched the band carefully, realizing it had been too long since I'd seen anyone enjoy making music as much as these people seemed to. I was staring at the drummer, who was lost in the rhythm of a song about an ordinary day—how your day was up to you. I wasn't sure which fascinated me more—the young man or the music. He was probably about Izzy's age—early twenties—with blonde hair that curled out around a blue baseball cap sporting a hockey logo. I seemed to recall that it was for the Montreal Canadians. He wore jeans and a plaid shirt with a T-shirt poking out in front. He held the drum in his left arm and used a short, double-ended drumstick to create a sound that I had probably heard before, but it was only now registering.

I could feel the deep, resonant beats that seemed to ground the melody, providing a heartbeat-like pulse. I could feel each beat driving the music forward. It was as if I could feel it driving my heart forward. As much as I loved attending the New York Symphony performances, I had never felt so moved by music. It seemed to me that Tchaikovsky and Vivaldi had nothing on the richness of the Newfoundland music in which I recognized an Irish provenance.

When the song was finished, the drummer, who had noticed me staring, nodded to me and beckoned me over.

"I don't think I've seen you here before," he said as I peered at the drum.

"Nora Houlihan's granddaughter, Eliza," I said.

He nodded knowingly. "Pleased to meet you, Eliza. I'm Alex." He must have noticed me staring at his drum. "This here's what you call a Bodhrán. It's an Irish drum."

"May I touch it?" Alex nodded, and I felt the smooth, leatherlike softness of the drum head. "How long have you been playing it?"

He thought for a moment. "I suppose I first played one at my grandfather's knee when I was a young lad of about four or five. He taught me all the old Irish and Celtic music. I've never put it down."

Just then, the guitarist nodded to Alex to start the next song.

"Stay here by me," Alex said, "and I'll teach you."

I have no idea why the drum fascinated me so much, but I stood there waiting. As I jammed my hand in the pocket of my jeans, I felt my runes that were still there. I rubbed my fingers over them, remembering their symbolism—my past that needed regeneration and healing, my present that spoke of joy and fulfilment if I'd let it and my future where I'd have to face issues that I'd continued to ignore. At that moment, I decided that the future matters would come soon enough. For now, I would be in the present moment and try to absorb some of the joy I could feel around me. Before I knew what was happening, Alex was putting the drum into my left hand and placing my fingers on the drumstick that he had put in my right hand. Then, he told me how to beat out the rhythm. I was flailing around at it as the next song began, feeling a bit like a fish out of water, but as I looked around, I could see smiling faces. Everyone seemed to be supporting me without judgement, without prejudice. It was exhilarating—and new.

~

After that one attempt at playing the drum, I handed it back to Alex and suddenly found myself pulled into the middle of the small dance floor. I had a moment of panic. To say that I was no dancer would be something of an understatement. But there I was, following along with three women, two men and a couple of children who were step-dancing as far as I could figure out. Someone would do a movement, then stop for me to mimic it. I have no idea where my usual reserve and potential embarrassment were that night. Perhaps I'd left them in the bottom of that plastic cup of slush that I'd emptied twice. But suddenly, I found myself on a different plane, moving to the music and not feeling judged in any way for my awkwardness. It was exhilarating.

When the musicians stopped to take a break, Alex came over and introduced me to his wife, Melody, a petite raven-haired beauty in jeans and bare feet. What mesmerized me the most was the chubby, happy baby, about eight or nine months old, who she was holding lightly on her hip. And I thought about Izzy, her baby, and me. Eliza, the grandmother. I could feel tears pricking at the corners of my eyes. So, I told Melody how lovely it was to meet her and fled to find somewhere to recover myself before searching for Peter and my ride home.

I stumbled into the dining room, which was now filled with people hovering around the table, laden with desserts. I could see Emma deep in conversation with Iris, the woman who had remarked on her veganism "affliction" earlier. They seemed to be discussing the contents of one of the trays. I picked my way past people eating plates of pie and cakes until I stood beside Emma.

"Do you have any idea where Peter is?" I said. "It must be time to leave."

Emma shook her head and went back to her conversation that seemed to be about the merits of lemon meringue pie.

"Girl, you're crazy. You won't eat the most delicious thing you'll ever taste. My lemon pie." Iris shook her head. "I'll never understand these things people get on about. Imagine. Veganism. Mind you, remember what I said. Don't breathe that word to your grandmother, Nora. She'll be right crooked. She'd just as soon slap you up the side of the head as look at you."

Emma rolled her eyes and picked up the plate containing a slice of lemon pie. She proceeded to push the meringue—a mile-high confection of whipped egg whites—off to the side and took a bite of the lemon filling and the crust. Her eyes closed in ecstasy.

"So, Emma," I said. "Enjoying the pie?" She nodded. I turned to Iris. "Did you make this divine-looking dessert?" She nodded proudly. "And that pastry crust. It looks beautiful. What's your secret?" I was asking, but I already knew the answer. I hadn't been a cookbook author for that many years without learning a thing or two about the details of pastry making.

"That, my ducky, is the best pastry you'll ever taste. The taste is in the butter and lard, and the flakiness is in the way I does it. I keeps everything cold and takes a light touch when I works the dough. Perfect every time."

Emma's eyes flew open as she popped a second forkful of pie into her mouth. She chewed, swallowed, and put the plate gingerly down on the table. "What did you say was in this?"

"Well, what do you think, girl?"

"Vegetable shortening?"

The woman laughed, causing a roll of fat at her waistband to jiggle under her T-shirt. "Vegetable shortening? Not in my kitchen," she said.

Emma turned to me. "I just ate lard and butter. Animal products."

What did she expect me to say? I just shrugged. "You won't die. Anyway, sis, I suppose it's a choice you've made to restrict your life to bland, tasteless, and boring experiences. Our life is full of choices." As I listened to my own words, I realized I wasn't talking to Emma at all. I was talking to me.

~

I looked around at the tempting plates of sweets and decided to sample a few. The pie was, as expected, divine. The crust was flaky and perfect, and the lemon filling was just the right balance of sweet and tart. And what could you say about three inches of perfect meringue? Is there something beyond perfect? I don't think so.

Then there was something called blueberry grunt—blobs of sweet dough boiled in a sweet blueberry sauce. It was messy but delicious, and I managed to charm the recipe for it from another of the ladies who were only too happy to share their kitchen secrets. I also loved the jam tarts, especially the ones filled with local partridgeberries, but I thought having that recipe wouldn't do me much good since partridgeberries—with their combination of sweet and tart—were not widely available outside of Newfoundland. I certainly had no idea where I would find them in New York. So, I just enjoyed them. Then I realized that if I ate another thing, I would probably be sick. I looked around at the crowd, and outside of Emma, no one in our little group was to be seen.

I wandered into the living room, where those who were in search of a bit of peace and quiet seemed to have fallen onto sofas and chairs. I sat in a tall wingback chair on one side of the massive fireplace. I figured at least someone from our group would happen by and pick me up before leaving.

Dad and Aunt Maureen were the first to find me. "Eliza, dear," Aunt Maureen said, "let's get going and try to find our driver. Peter must be around here somewhere."

Yes, I thought, *where is Peter, anyway*? I suddenly realized that I'd hoped he might appear during the dancing. He didn't. I put the thought out of my mind.

As the three of us stumbled into the foyer, Erica came down the stairs, followed by Peter. I was hit with a blinding flash of something I had never felt in my life as I wondered what they had been doing upstairs. Then, I chastised myself for where my thoughts seemed to be going. Erica and Peter? After knowing one another for two days? With Andrew, the perfect, stashed in Toronto? Absurd. And yet, I felt almost jealous. It was time to stumble back to the hotel.

STOP THE WORLD & LET ME OFF

Fun Facts About Gander, Newfoundland

- *Gander, Newfoundland, used to be known as the "Crossroads of the World" because it is very close to the Great Circle route between New York and London.*
- *The airport in Gander welcomed its first flight in 1938.*
- *Gander International Airport was once a main refuelling spot for transatlantic flights.*
- *Fewer than 10,000 people live in Gander.*
- *On September 11, 2001, when US airspace was closed following the terrorist attacks on the World Trade Center and the Pentagon, Gander took in 38 international commercial flights and their more than 7000 passengers from all over the world.*
- *A 2019 Washington Post Magazine article referred to Gander as "the capital of kindness" in a piece about how the residents of Gander took international passengers into their homes to await the reopening of US airspace in September 2001.*

TWENTY-THREE

Erica

I MIGHT HAVE BEEN ABLE TO LAUGH at how dismal we all looked the morning after the kitchen party if laughing hadn't hurt my head so much. Mom hadn't drunk as much as I had (perhaps I might be as sensible when I'm her age), so she showered quickly and left me to my own devices in our hotel room, which was oddly and unexpectedly stark, all modern greys, taupes and stainless steel. When I was dressed and prepped, I made my way to the dining room, stopping first at the coffee urn by the door. As I turned to find our table, I was blinded by the sunshine coming in through the vast windows, stabbing at my grainy eyes. *Damn it*, I thought, *why couldn't it be as grey today as it was yesterday? And why, oh why, had I let myself drink three of those slushies, not to mention several beers, something I rarely drank*?

As I sat down beside Mom, who was reading the news on her iPad, while Uncle Fred read an actual newspaper, I saw Phillip come in. He was wearing dark Ray-Ban sunglasses but still had to put a hand over his eyes to keep out the glare. He didn't look any better than I felt.

Finally, Emma and Eliza staggered in, both stopping for coffee before thudding heavily into two of the three empty seats. Eliza looked at Phillip and said, "God, you look awful."

Phillip peeked over the top of his sunglasses. "You might consider looking in a mirror, cuz." Then he returned to perusing the menu. "I think I'll have eggs and bacon. The best cure for a hangover besides chicken soup, which I don't see on the breakfast menu."

"Must be a Montreal thing, is it?" Eliza said. "I thought bananas were the way to go." She then rifled around in her giant satchel, which she had stashed under the table, and emerged with her sunglasses.

Dear god, I thought, *please let us not get into a debate about the best way to handle a hangover.*

I was saved by the server, who just then swung by to tell us it was a continental breakfast buffet this morning, to which Phillip responded, "What? No eggs and bacon?"

She then suggested they could manage to give us all fishcakes with our continental buffet, and I had to stop myself from gagging. Phillip coughed, and Eliza just looked green. The mention of fishcakes always made Emma look green, so that was nothing new. We all declined the server's kind offer and stumbled to the breakfast buffet for dry toast and orange juice.

As I sat down with my plate, Peter walked in through the dining room door wearing sunglasses—which he removed upon entering—and a smile as big as the sunshine seemed. He saw us and immediately came over to the table.

"What a wonderful day," he said. "Everyone ready for a new adventure?" There was a bit of groaning before he continued. "We're off to Gander, leaving behind this wonderful western part of the province, and we have two treats ahead of us today. First, I have all the tickets for us to see "Come From Away" this evening at the Joseph R. Smallwood Arts & Culture Centre, as promised. Second, we'll be picking Dad up in Gander. He's returning to our little tour group."

Eliza seemed to click into life. "Are you leaving us, then?"

"As it turns out, I'm going to hitch a ride with you all back to the city, so you're stuck with both of us for a couple of days."

For some reason, that seemed to brighten Eliza's spirits, and I thought back to my conversation with Peter the evening before. This was dangerous territory.

"Did you say your father is rejoining us?" Mom said, turning off her iPad and putting it back in her purse.

Peter's eyes twinkled at her. "I did, indeed, Dr. Maureen."

Mom smiled sweetly and patted her lips with her napkin. *OMG*, I thought, channelling Maddie, *this is trouble.*

~

"Today's drive is a long one," Peter was saying as he helped us pile our luggage into the back of the SUV-bus once again. "Almost four hours, so I have a nice lunch stop in mind."

Phillip pulled his phone from his pocket and started clicking. "Okay, I see our route here on the map. Where will we be stopping?" Phillip was almost as obsessed as Eliza was with knowing where we were every minute of the trip.

"We'll swing off the Trans-Canada Highway to King's Point for lunch. It'll only take us a half hour longer, and we can have lunch on the waterfront there. Sun's out, so it should be gorgeous."

Once again, Eliza sat in front with Peter while the rest of us piled in the back. Mom and Fred sat directly behind them this time while Phillip, Emma and I took up the rear seats.

"What do we have here?" Mom said, leaning into the front seat between Eliza and Peter.

Turning around to look at Mom, Peter smiled, the corners of his mouth crinkling and his eyes shining. "Oh, just a little treat."

I craned my neck to see what Mom was talking about. I saw a huge, family-sized bag of honey Dijon potato chips on the console between Peter and Eliza. "Who's the potato chip fan?" I said. Then I remembered that when we were kids, Eliza had been an absolute potato chip fanatic. "Eliza, I seem to remember you loved the things back when we used to visit Gran in the summers."

Eliza didn't move. She kept her eyes firmly focused on the road ahead and stayed silent as Peter swung the truck onto the highway.

~

Two hours or so later, we arrived in a tiny village on the water where fishing boats clogged the wharves and tourists seemed to be sparse. The noon hour sun was warm, and a walk along the docks taking in the unmistakable scent of the salt sea air was welcome after a few hours of driving. I breathed deeply. The scent was briny and slightly fishy, although it wasn't at all unpleasant. I followed behind the rest of the family along the wharf toward where Peter had stopped to show us what the locals were fishing.

I could see what appeared to be millions of small fish writhing and sparkling just under the surface of the water beside the dock. Peter called them capelin. This area seemed to have a vast store of them. The next moment, he was reaching for one, scooping it out of the water and placing the writhing little creature in Eliza's hands. She looked shocked. I guess she was used to dead fish in her kitchen, but this little one wriggled and squirmed while Peter laughingly took her photo and a few seconds of video.

"Your grandmother will love this one, Eliza," he said, laughing.

Eliza let it go back into the water, and after we'd all had a chance to take our own photos, Peter led us to a café on the waterfront as promised, where we settled into two tables for lunch. It was like being inside a knotty pine box. The walls, ceilings and the floor were all knotty pine boards.

I ordered fishcakes that came served with mustard pickles and a slice of homemade bread. If there was one thing I loved to eat, it was bread that hadn't seen the inside of a bread factory. As I bit into the lavishly buttered slice, I vowed to learn to make my own bread. I wondered what Andrew would think if I took another foray into domestic life. You couldn't get any more domestic than making bread, as far as I was concerned.

I noticed that almost everyone else was having soup and a sandwich, but Eliza had opted for the cod au gratin that Gordie had introduced us to only a few days ago.

After lunch, we had another couple of hours in the truck, during which, at Peter's urging, Eliza reluctantly opened the bag of chips and passed them around. Eliza grudgingly admitted that she might have mentioned to Peter that these were her favourite guilty pleasure. I suppose I shouldn't have been surprised that Peter had done this for Eliza, but I was worried, even though it was really none of my business. It was just that Eliza seemed odd the past couple of days—odder than usual, I should say. I supposed that if I'd been a better cousin, I might have taken her aside and asked her what was wrong. But knowing Eliza (and our history), she would probably clam up. In any case, Peter seemed to have a crush on her, and I didn't want to see him get hurt. Eliza had a well-deserved reputation for steamrolling over people. Peter seemed to be a nice, uncomplicated man with an uncomplicated Newfoundland life. I suppose I was beginning to feel slightly protective. But then, there was Mom and Gordie.

What the hell was going on *there*? They had known one another for less than a week, and Mom seemed to take on the persona of a schoolgirl whenever he was around. Were she and Eliza falling under the spell of this island—or perhaps the O'Brien men?

We finally arrived at our destination for the night. It was a hotel on the outskirts of the town of Gander called Aladin's. It was in a kind of strip mall area surrounded by parking lots. The lobby was dark and dreary, with brown carpets and brown leather furniture. It did, however, have a bar where Phillip and I met to have a drink before having dinner and heading off to the theatre.

The bar was small, with only four tables. I was sitting at the bar that accommodated five stools. "Vodka tonic?" I said to Phillip as he approached and sat down. He nodded, and I asked the bartender for two vodka tonics, our drink of choice on hot summer days.

"Sorry, ma'am," he said. "No tonic."

"No tonic?" Phillip said. "I've never been in a bar that didn't have tonic. Are you sure?"

The young bartender looked at Phillip and sighed as if he'd heard this a million times before. "Sorry, sir. No tonic. What can I get you?"

I shrugged and said, "Vodka on the rocks, maybe?" Phillip shrugged and nodded. "What kind of vodka do you have?" I was hoping for a shot of Grey Goose or another premium vodka that was good for sipping.

"Iceberg," the bartender said, pulling the bottle from the shelf behind him and placing it on the bar.

"Iceberg?" Phillip said. "I've never heard of it. Where's it from?"

"Right here on the island," the bartender said proudly. "Made from the purest water on the planet. Comes from the icebergs. Worth a try, don't you think?"

We agreed. How bad could it be? We watched as the young man poured generous shots over the ice. "Sorry I can't say the ice is from an iceberg, but it's good anyway," he said, pushing the glasses toward us.

Phillip and I toasted to Gran's good health and sipped. What a surprise.

"Wow," Phillip said. "That has to be one of the smoothest vodkas I've ever tasted, and I've tasted plenty, especially when Marcus and I visited Moscow back in the day."

I agreed and added that to my growing list of surprises hidden on this enigmatic island.

~

After a quick dinner in the large dining room overlooking an outdoor pool, Peter gave us a ten-minute warning that we would be leaving for the theatre. "And look who I found in the lobby," he said.

Gordie walked out from behind Peter. I looked over at Mom, who was beaming.

"Good to see you all again," Gordie said. "I hope Peter here hasn't been giving you too much grief." He looked at Mom and smiled. "Doing all right, Maureen, darlin'?"

Mom nodded. "Finest kind!"

Gordie laughed and clapped his hands as if applauding her mastery of the Newfoundland language. Then he turned to Emma. "Anyone get you to try a fishcake yet?"

We all laughed. Even Emma.

TWENTY-FOUR

Eliza

WHEN I CLIMBED INTO THE FRONT SEAT of the truck that morning in Rocky Harbour, it was impossible to miss the bag of chips that sat on the console separating Peter from me. *Why did I even mention that I loved those things?* I thought, remembering our brief chat about snacking, a habit I abhorred in principle but occasionally succumbed to in reality. How could I have known he was a person who did these things? Why was he doing these nice things for me? I certainly didn't deserve anyone's kindness at this point and had never needed it. Not once in my life. And I was feeling like the worst kind of wife and mother—the selfish kind who persisted in remaining here on this island with a bunch of people with whom she had little in common (or so she thought) when she could have defied her grandmother and left at any moment to be by the side of her needy husband and daughter. I was sure Izzy needed me. I just wasn't so sure I needed Izzy at that point. That, more than anything, made me a bad mother in my own eyes. Still, here I sat.

That afternoon, when Peter nudged me to open the bag of chips and share them around the truck, I pretended to demur, not wanting to share. Still, before long, I gave in, and everyone was soon munching and laughing and comparing their preferences for potato chip varieties. It seemed that I was the only one hooked on honey Dijon, but Erica and Phillip both had to admit they were pretty delicious. Dad and Aunt Maureen were firmly in the plain potato chip category, while Emma held fast to her love of salt and vinegar.

When we arrived at the hotel later that afternoon, Emma decided to take a walk, and I decided it was high time I spoke with my daughter. Finally, she answered when I rang.

"Mom, hi," she said. "How's your trip going?" Izzy sounded listless, but what could I expect?

I gave her a quick rundown to try to lubricate the mechanism of mother-daughter interaction, and then I said, "Tell me what's happening with you. Your father tells me you've gone to stay with Astrid. Are things with him that bad?"

That was when she started to cry, and the words began spilling out. Her father had been useless. Her grandmother had actually come to the house to reprimand her for being pregnant and unmarried, even going so far as to suggest a matchmaker she knew who probably had someone who was desperate enough for a wife that he might marry her. A matchmaker? What kind of lunatic suggests such an antediluvian practice in the twenty-first century? Were there even such oddities still around? The moment that thought crossed my mind, I remembered that, indeed, there were. Esther had mentioned a friend whose daughter had been set up with a matchmaker only a year or so earlier. Dear god! That was the straw that broke the proverbial camel's back as far as Izzy was concerned. And the moment she told me about it, all I wanted to do was get on a plane, fly home and get in my mother-in-law's face to tell her she had finally lost the plot entirely.

I told Izzy I would talk to her father about how she was feeling and ensure that she wasn't subjected to her grandmother again. That's when I started to consider what it meant to be a grandmother.

My own grandmother, Nora, was best viewed from a distance—a long distance. It seemed that Esther, Izzy's grandmother, was the same. What about me? Would I be one of those grandmothers that children liked only from a distance? I shivered when I considered this. And the more I thought about it, the more convinced I was that this was going to be fine. Izzy was going to be fine. The baby was going to be fine. And I was going to be fine. At that moment, I didn't care one way or another whether Jake or his mother would be fine.

Izzy said Astrid was being very supportive and that she thought she'd just stay put until I returned. I found this mildly surprising since I had the impression Astrid had thought Izzy was bonkers when she gave up her medical school acceptance to teach yoga. I told her I'd make an appointment for her with my family doctor, and we promised to talk every day. When I hung up, I felt different. I had always felt strong as an individual, but this situation had thrown me for a loop. I realized it had been a long time coming, and now I felt I was at least beginning to sense where I stood. Jake and I would have to have a long and no doubt vitriolic discussion when I got home. I knew how much he hated talking about relationships and feelings, and when I thought about that, I almost smiled.

I joined the rest of the family in the truck later to make our way to the local arts and culture centre, where the annual run of "Come From Away" was playing. As we had determined a few days earlier, Erica and Aunt Maureen had both seen it in Toronto—its birthplace—while Phillip had seen it on Broadway. I had heard about it—it was impossible not to, living in Manhattan—but Jake hadn't been interested in anything related to 9/11, and knowing it was about Newfoundland *and* that fateful day in 2001, I thought it probably wasn't for me. That's how it came to pass that I was among those who had yet to experience this musical that portrayed what happened in Gander on September 11, 2001, when thirty-eight transatlantic commercial flights with over seven thousand passengers landed in this small town (I knew this because Gordie told us), not knowing when they would be able to leave. However, I wasn't the only one who would be experiencing this musical for the first time. Neither Emma nor Dad had seen it yet.

Gordie had taken over the driving responsibilities, and Aunt Maureen had taken my seat next to the driver. That put me in the back, stuffed between Emma and Peter.

"I know you're going to love it," Peter said.

"So, you've seen it?" How could I have even considered the possibility that he had not?

Peter nodded. "Couple of times. Couldn't have kept me away," he said.

~

It wasn't a big theatre. As we filed into our seats in the middle of the auditorium, Gordie, taking back his tour guide responsibilities along with the driving, informed us that it sat four hundred people, and the building also housed a swimming pool. It looked like it did. The building resembled a large high school. But the theatre itself didn't look much like I remembered high school auditoriums looking.

It was a proscenium theatre—one of those theatres with an archway framing the stage—with only an orchestra section. No balconies were hanging above where we sat, and no overhang.

As I settled into my dark, vinyl-covered seat, I looked around at the crowd. I'd been to Broadway shows more times than I can count. I'd seen lively musicals with bright lights, elaborate sets, peppy dancers and music so uninspiring and forgettable that you could depart the theatre humming the sets, as a theatre friend of ours used to say. I'd seen mind-numbingly tedious plays that tried so hard to make a point that they bored their audiences to death. There had been times when the only way I could get through to the end of a play was to guzzle a glass or two of champagne at the interval. Eventually, I managed to pry Jake from his seat at intermission, never to return. Even if he hated a show, what he hated even more was the thought of having paid for a ticket and not "getting his money's worth." As far as I was concerned, the only reason we went to some of these plays was that someone in our social circle had made a point of mentioning he or she had gone, and we *must* go. I also believed that returning to a show after intermission only to sit there seething about how much I hated it was beyond pointless and certainly not getting my money's worth. If Jake and I stayed to the end of a show, it meant the show was, in a word, incredible. But even for those shows, rarely was an audience as enthusiastic as this one before the show even began.

In all situations, the only time I had noted such enthusiasm before a show even started was when we'd taken Izzy to see "The Lion King" all those years ago, and there were more over-sugared kids than there were adults. The crowd here to see "Come From Away" was positively quivering.

So many people in the audience seemed to know one another. There was much waving and chatting across the aisles. This behaviour surprised me because I thought everyone in the vicinity would already have seen the show. Then I remembered that when I asked Peter if he'd seen it yet, he said, "Several times." I'd never seen a show more than once and had never imagined why anyone would do so. Surely, if you've seen it once, that would be enough.

Imagine my surprise when I turned around to scan the audience to see if the auditorium was filled (it was) and actually recognized the man sitting behind me one seat over.

"Eliza! What a treat to see you here!"

I didn't immediately click in. How could I possibly know someone in Gander, Newfoundland? Then, suddenly, it came to me. It was Brian—from my New York to Halifax flight. We had gotten drunk together.

"Brian, how lovely to see you again," I said.

Brian then rose from his seat, clearly expecting me to do the same. "Bring it in," he said as I turned and rose slightly as he lunged in for a hug. Then he turned to the people next to him. "It's her. That lady from New York, I told you about it." Then he turned back to me as I sat back in my seat, feeling a tad awkward. "Jeez, you never know who you'll run into. In Gander for long?"

"Just overnight," I said. "We've been touring the island."

"Well, good for you," Brian said, smiling broadly under the peak of his baseball cap. "You know what they say. 'The longest way round is the shortest way home.' Enjoy the show, Eliza. It's the finest kind."

The longest way round is the shortest way home. Where had I heard that before? Peter, who was sitting next to me, turned and said, "I didn't know you knew anyone in Gander, Eliza."

I explained where Brian and I had met and under what circumstances, then Peter said, "And someone else who quotes James Joyce—or perhaps CS Lewis, depending on who you believe said it first."

That's when I remembered where I'd heard it before. Peter had said it to me. Perhaps I needed to pay attention.

I then turned my attention to my program and looked at the stage that was set up for the first act with no curtain covering the scenery. It was a very simple set that seemed to be constructed of plain wood and included lots of old-looking wooden chairs and tables scattered around. It reminded me of another Broadway musical that Jake and I had attended on the recommendation of a ladies-who-lunch wife of one of his racquetball friends. I was trying to remember the name of the show, but it had been so absolutely off-putting that I'd blotted it out. What was it? What was it? Then, the name popped into my mind. It had been called "Once," a putatively poignant love story set in Ireland that had bafflingly won a Tony award. There was, indeed, no accounting for taste, I suppose. It had been beyond awful. Since this scenery evoked in me the same unspeakably dismal feeling I'd had while attending "Once," I didn't hold out much hope for this one. (Jake and I had left that one at intermission.)

I was sitting between Erica and Peter. Erica was chatting with Phillip, and Peter was now sitting quietly with his hands on his lap. As the lights began to dim, he turned to me and whispered, "Well, then, here we go. Hold on tight." And he squeezed my hand briefly.

The music began. "Bum-bum-bum-bum…bum-bum-bum-bum…" It was the sound of the Irish drum thrumming through the airwaves. I felt the hairs on the back of my neck rise, and as the opening lines began, and when the cast began singing "Welcome to The Rock," I began to find it difficult to breathe. I was one of those come-from-aways they were talking about. I was someone who didn't understand what it was to be an islander. But when they began to tell us where each of them had been the moment they heard the 9/11 news, I was with them. I was not here in Newfoundland, but I was with them, as I remembered.

It had been a beautiful September morning, and I was still so new to my job. I'd met Jacob Cohen only a few days earlier at that bar where I'd been having a drink with my new friend, Allegra, who had turned out to be Jake's sister, and several colleagues from the magazine where we all worked. It was a Tuesday, so we were all gathering in the conference room for our weekly story pitch session. The meeting was scheduled to begin at eight-thirty, but it was usually a few minutes late starting because everyone had to select one or more muffins from those on offer from our favourite bakery down the street.

I remembered looking at the clock as I always did, just as our editor called the meeting to order. It was 8:36. Ten minutes later, we heard the first thunderous crash just as we were about to start the first pitch. It was a terrifying, deep roar that sounded like nothing I'd ever heard. It wasn't thunder, and it wasn't gunshots. To say it was unsettling would be an understatement. And yet, we moved on with our agenda. We weren't ten minutes into the first pitch when our editor's secretary came rushing into the room, apologizing for interrupting. Behind her were three of our media people pushing a television on a high stand. It was the one we used to review videotapes.

They quickly plugged it in and turned it to the news. No one knew what was going on, but the live feed on the screen showed smoke as it billowed from the north tower of the World Trade Center. One of my colleagues ran to the window and screamed that she could see the smoke. In horror, we then watched the small screen as a plane, seemingly out of nowhere, came into the frame and plunged into the south tower. The wall clock ticking up front said it was 9:03. All I could think about was that something had gone terribly wrong on those flights.

Our editor stood there, a mask of horror distorting her usually calm, pretty features, her hand over her mouth. "Luke, Luke…" was all I could hear as the tears began pouring down her face. Her husband Luke had been in the restaurant at the top of one of the buildings having a breakfast meeting. Hers was only the first horror story of many we would hear over the following weeks. It was when the world changed. When my world changed. It was the event outside ourselves that brought Jake and me closer together—for better or for worse.

I tried to shake the feeling and return my attention to the stage as the rest of the story unfolded so far away from where I was, and yet I felt so close to them in our shared experiences of disbelief and anguish. It was as if we all grew to adulthood in that one moment—together and yet so far away from one another.

By the time the chorus began singing about being on the edge, I was right there with them, tears streaming down my face, Peter gripping my arm. I was on the edge of my world, trying to understand exactly where I was and where I would be if I took that one step off into the unknown. Over the edge. That's what it felt like. I was going to fall over the edge. The question on my mind was this: could you ever come back from the edge?

Then, the chorus began the finale. All I could hear was a song about what was lost but what was gained. Losses and gains. I couldn't get the thought out of my head. Did you always have to lose something to gain something else? What was I prepared to lose? What could I possibly gain from a loss at this point in my life?

As the applause rang in my ears, the lights came up, and I tried to dab at my face to be sure no one would ever know I'd been crying. But I knew Peter knew. I glanced over at him, and I could tell that he was pointedly keeping himself from looking at me as he stood on his feet, still applauding. I had known him mere days—no, mere hours, I suppose—and yet I think that was the moment I began to love him just a little.

TWENTY-FIVE

Erica

I REMEMBERED THE FIRST TIME I'D SEEN "Come From Away." At that time, Andrew and I rarely had time to attend the theatre despite living in a city where there was much on offer. However, Andrew's producer had two tickets (Andrew was still a well-known, highly recognizable national news anchor at the time, and I was a familiar afternoon television personality). The show had been conceived and developed in Toronto and had played to rave reviews in smaller theatres like The La Jolla Playhouse in California and the Seattle Repertory Theatre. It was coming home for its debut in a large theatre in a major theatre city with hopes it might make it to Broadway. Of course, all the rest is history, but that evening at the Royal Alexandra Theatre in downtown Toronto, we were among the audience members who were quite simply, blown away. The music, the performances and above all, the story. It was all about the story. And what a story it had been.

I was thinking about this as I sat there listening as the final strains of music died away. The lights came up, with the audience still on its feet, applauding madly. I remember taking a screenwriting course as an elective when I was in journalism school decades ago. We had to study the work of screenwriting teacher Robert McKee, who once wrote, "Storytelling is the most powerful way to put ideas into the world." And I considered how the ideas in this musical—the capacity for human kindness in a world where there is so much divisiveness—were powerfully portrayed to audiences who I hoped were listening. I couldn't imagine how anyone could see this theatre piece and not be moved. Just as that thought crossed my mind, I glanced at Eliza, who seemed to be madly dabbing what looked like tears from her eyes. If a theatre piece could move my implacable cousin, it could move anyone. So, the imperious Eliza Cohen had a heart, after all.

I looked over at Mom, who had an odd expression on her face. I wondered what someone like her—someone who'd grown up in this place but had left—felt when she considered what we'd just seen or, for that matter, what we'd been experiencing over the past week. I had often wondered why Mom really left Newfoundland. She had always maintained that it was so that she could go to graduate school in Toronto, which I understood, but I'd never been entirely convinced that was the whole story. Whenever I asked her about her original home, she always fluffed me off with a quip about higher education and changed the subject. Now, she was back, and Newfoundland was all up in our business, as I'd overheard someone say in conversation over the past few days. Judging from her odd expression now, this bit of theatre entertainment must have moved her in some way.

Her brow furrowed slightly as if she might be perplexed or puzzled about what she just saw. Her gaze, firmly focused on the stage, was thoughtful. I wondered what she was thinking about. Before I had a chance to lean over and ask, Gordie said something to her, and she turned her head toward him. I couldn't hear what they were saying.

I was thinking about the show and Mom while I brushed my teeth later. Mom told me she was going to have a drink with Gordie, so I had gone ahead back to our room alone and hoped she knew what she was doing with this complete stranger. I had never known Mom to get quite so comfortable with anyone so quickly—or perhaps at all.

I had just hung up the phone from talking to Andrew and Maddie and was sitting in bed just starting to read the news on my iPad when Mom returned to our room later. She looked startled when she saw me sitting up with the lights on.

"Erica, darling, I thought you'd be asleep by now." She placed her handbag on her bed and took off the cashmere wrap she'd been wearing.

I put my tablet down on my bed beside me and said, "Just catching up with Andrew, Maddie and the news. Did you have a nice drink with Gordie?" I hoped my voice didn't sound suspicious.

Mom sat down on the edge of her bed and kicked off her shoes. "As a matter of fact, I did."

I sat up straighter. "Mom, I was wondering how you liked the show."

"I liked it well enough, Erica, but...I don't know." I didn't say anything, hoping she might continue. Mom had never been a touchy-feely kind of parent. That had been my father's domain, always with a hug. Mom was more stand-offish and formal around her children. She then sat back and grabbed one of the pillows off the bed, hugging it to herself closely. "You know, Erica, I saw the show a few years back with Douglas." Years after Dad died, Mom had married Douglas. Douglas had been her husband for only three years before dying of a heart attack on a cruise in the Caribbean. "He loved it, but I didn't, and I couldn't quite put my finger on why. The music was quite good, and the storyline was interesting, possibly even compelling in its way."

That's an understatement, I thought, but did not say out loud.

"You know, Erica, all these messages that your grandmother seems to be sending are giving me cognitive dissonance." I had no idea where she was going with this, but I thought if I just listened, Mom might actually shed some light on her relationship with Newfoundland and perhaps, even her mother. That relationship was as much or more baffling to me. She continued. "On the one hand, I realize that the musical we saw this evening wants us to see the unparalleled humanity that the local people showed to others. The message is so clear and a bit in-your-face if you ask me. These people from a small town in a small province of Canada welcomed unknown individuals into their town and their homes, providing support when the visitors most needed it." Mom stopped as if trying to figure out where she was going with her rumination.

"If that's on the one hand, Mom, what's on the other hand?" I said, trying to nudge her to talk more.

"Yes, yes," she said, seemingly coming back to attention to the topic at hand. "Yes, that's on one hand—all that empathy and kindness. But on the other hand, in my experience, there's no such thing as an honourary Newfoundlander; everyone is welcome as long as they don't stay, and if you're a Newfoundlander who leaves and doesn't return to live, you're at best pitied, at worst, vilified."

"Have you felt vilified, Mom?" I said quietly, not wanting to interrupt her train of thought and yet needing to know more.

Mom looked straight ahead at a painting of a puffin on the wall opposite her bed. "You know, Erica, I never like to talk about this, but I think you should know that your grandmother has spent her life criticizing me and making me feel like I was never enough. I didn't do the things she wanted me to do, and she was clear in her disapproval of everything I did. I didn't hang off her every word like Frederick and her friends did. And make no mistake, this little display of Nora's will that we're experiencing this week is precisely what I would have expected from her. Nora Houlihan has never been wrong and she will never be wrong as long as she lives, to hear her tell it." Mom closed her eyes.

I sat up on the side of my bed and faced my mother. She looked like she might cry. Despite Mom never being the hugging kind of mother, I slipped off my bed and over beside her on her bed. I put my arm around her and could feel her shaking as if she might be trying not to cry. We sat there in silence for a few minutes.

"Mom," I said, not sure I should even continue with this line of discussion, "I've known you for over five decades, and I've never known you to spend much psychic energy blaming others for things that happened in your life. I mean," I was choosing my words carefully, "I've heard you criticize other adults who seem to blame their parents for everything."

Mom waited a beat before answering. "Erica, it's not about the criticism. Not entirely, anyway. I wish I could tell you the rest of the story, but I can't, and let's leave it at that."

Now, I was even more curious about Mom and Gran's relationship, but it was clear Mom wasn't going to enlighten me—yet. We were again silent for a few moments.

Finally, Mom broke the silence. "Erica, darling, I'm not sure I can do it."

"Do what, Mom?"

"See my mother the day after tomorrow. I told Gordie how I feel, and he's encouraging me to see it through."

I frowned. What in the world could this person we'd all just met have to say about Mom and Gran? I realized that Gordie had some kind of prior relationship with Gran, but this seemed like none of his business. "Is that what you and Gordie were talking about?"

"Among other things," she said, getting up. "I'm going to brush my teeth." She disappeared into the bathroom, leaving me to consider this strange turn of events.

When she returned a few minutes later in her bathrobe, I said, "I understand Gordie is a friend of Gran's, but how good a friend is he? How well does he know her?"

Mom huffed a bit. "Friends might be stretching it a bit, but they have known one another for many years."

I felt a lightbulb go off in my head. "*You* knew Gordie long before he picked us up in Deer Lake, didn't you?"

Mom sat on her bed and shrugged. "Perhaps."

"Mom! I want details."

"Erica, I'm tired. Yes, I knew Gordie from years ago—many years ago. It's ancient history. We haven't seen one another in decades. We went to school together if you must know. Now, that's all I'm going to say for now."

I knew when to stop badgering my mother. "So, Mom, you *are* coming with us to St. John's, and you will be seeing your mother. Right?"

Mom sighed as she got into bed. "It seems Nora Houlihan always gets her way."

~

The following morning, we all met for a planned breakfast at seven-thirty. Eliza and Phillip had both complained about the early hour, but Gordie had told us he wanted to be on the road before nine so that we could enjoy our long and jam-packed day. He said he and Peter would give us all the details at breakfast.

"Okay, Gordie," Phillip said. "I'm on vacation and hate to be up this early when I'm on holiday. There better be a good reason for this."

Gordie smiled. "You better suppose there is, Phillip, my boy." He looked around just as Peter came into the dining room carrying a large cardboard box. "There he is now. Hard to get good help these days," he said, smiling.

Peter walked toward the table and placed the box on the floor beside it. He then leaned down, opened it and began lifting out what looked like pieces of clothing in individual plastic bags. One by one, he passed them to Gordie, who proceeded to hand them out, one to each of us. We all just stared.

"Well, don't just sit there," Gordie said. "Open up your newest gift from Nora."

I started to slowly open the plastic bag and pull out what seemed to be a black sweatshirt.

"What in god's name is this?" Eliza said as she held her "gift" up in front of her.

We were all equally dumbfounded. Suddenly, Phillip stood up and started laughing. "She's got us now," he said, holding up an oversized black hoodie with a gold logo on the left front. The logo seemed familiar. Then he turned it around and started snorting with laughter. In large blue and gold letters on the back, it said, "I am an Islander." The logo on the front was, indeed, familiar. It was "Come From Away."

"Now, once we get ourselves to Elliston this afternoon, you're all to put your hoodies on, and Nora wants a family photo."

Eliza started groaning.

"Now, listen here, missy," Gordie said, staring intently at Eliza, "you'll find you're going to need to wear this today anyway." Then he cracked a smile. "We're heading into the Bonavista peninsula for a history lesson," now *I* groaned, "and a wee bit of puffin watching. How's that sound?"

Did we have a choice? Not at all, and puffin-watching sounded interesting. I pulled my hoodie over my head and turned to Mom. "How do I look?"

Mom smiled. "Well, Erica, darling, as Coco Chanel once said, 'When I find a colour darker than black, I'll wear it. But until then, I'm wearing black.' Who are we to argue with Chanel? Black seems to be our colour." She stood up and pulled her hoodie over her head. "Nora strikes again."

I thought I was the only one who heard that, but Gordie looked in her direction and shook his head. What in the world was going on?

THE LONG WAY HOME

"Everybody that went away suffered a broken heart. "I'm coming back someday," they all wrote. But never did. The old life was too small to fit anymore."

~ Annie Proulx, *The Shipping News*

TWENTY-SIX

Eliza

I DO NOT DO LOGOS. I especially do not do hoodies. Where I come from, anyone who wears a hoodie, especially with the hood up, is suspect and to be avoided at all costs. In addition, I do not do sweatshirts, especially baggy ones that make me look like a massive lump of coal. And only nitwits and rednecks pose for family photos wearing identical sweatshirts. I am not that person.

This was the nightmare that I could not awaken from. As Aunt Maureen pointed out, the only redeeming feature of this obnoxious piece of clothing was that it was black. That there were only three more days to go was the only thought in my head as I tucked the plastic-covered bundle under my arm and once again boarded the truck for a day of jollity and adventure. Dream on.

Gordie and Aunt Maureen, of course, were in the front seat. Again, I was in the back between Peter and Emma as we set off from Gander along the Trans-Canada Highway toward the Bonavista Peninsula. According to Gordie's tour guide monologue, our first stop would be the town of Bonavista.

"Now, I promised a touch of history today," Gordie said as we sped along past kilometre after kilometre of coniferous trees and dense shrubbery. It would be some time before we saw the ocean again, but Gordie promised us we would not be disappointed. "We're headed to the spot where John Cabot, that famous Italian-by-way-of-England explorer, first set foot on the island back in 1497."

"He must have thought it was a good view, then, did he?" Phillip said, no doubt referring to the name.

Gordie laughed. "Yes, indeed, sir. He is reputed to have said, *O Buon Vista*. I suppose it was a sight for sore eyes for those who travelled all the way from England in his ship, the Matthew. And, of course, Bonavista became an important part of the fishing and sealing industry because of its nearness to the richness that lay off our island's coast at the time."

"Sealing?" Emma said, coming to attention. "Do they kill seals here?"

Peter turned to Emma. "It's a history lesson, Emma."

He sounded almost annoyed, an emotion I didn't think Peter O'Brien even possessed. Perhaps there was more to him than met the eye. *Dear god*, I thought, *why am I even thinking about him? He'll be gone and out of my life in a few days. I just need to hold it together until I can fly home.*

"I know that," Emma said peevishly. "But there's always a connection between history and the present day, isn't there?"

"Yes, my dear Emma, there is," Gordie said from up front. "And yes, there is still a sealing industry today, although it's regulated to the hilt and humane practices are mandated by law."

Emma huffed. "Everyone would like to think that it's humane to use animals. But it never is."

"Emma," I said quietly, "perhaps this isn't the time to climb up onto the moral high ground that you seem to like so much. Just let it go, and all of this will soon be over. Besides, perhaps it's time you opened your mind a bit to the realities of life." I suppose I was talking as much to myself as to my little sister.

About an hour into the drive, Gordie pulled off the highway and down a hill into what appeared to be a fishing village. He seemed to be looking for something. Before we knew what was happening, Gordie had pulled the truck into a clearing by a wharf where half a dozen or more people were standing around a large, makeshift wooden table with buckets of fish all around. They all appeared to be working diligently at something on the table in front of them. I couldn't quite make out what they were doing.

"Now, here's where you start to see the real Bonavista history coming to life in the twenty-first century," Gordie said as he got out of the truck, followed by Aunt Maureen and the rest of us.

The moment I set foot outside the truck, I realized that there might, after all, be a benefit to having a sweatshirt ready. Everyone began pulling theirs over their heads until I was the only one left shivering as I wrapped my arms around myself, clad only in a lightweight cashmere T-shirt.

Peter leaned back into the truck and pulled my sweatshirt out from under my seat where I'd stashed it. "Eliza, you might find this handy right about now," he said, handing the package to me. His eyes held that smile I'd come to know in the past few days, and I figured even if he was mocking me, he had good reason to do so.

I shrugged and pulled it over my head. That was the moment Peter, Gordie and Erica all pulled their phones from their pockets and began taking my picture. "This is one for posterity," Erica said, laughing.

As I looked around at the people on the wharf and the fishing boats tied up alongside, I breathed deeply of the salty air, taking as much of it as I could into my lungs. It was grey and a bit damp, but I wasn't bothered by it at all. It was almost as if taking in that breath of air was like taking a hit of anti-depressant. I had a sense of lightness in my body (despite the bulky sweatshirt), but not only in my body. I started to think that my soul felt lighter, but that made no sense to me. I had never thought much about my soul, even at the height of my religious studies. At that moment, I suddenly wondered why I hadn't. I felt an unexpected sensation of clarity and optimism, and for the first time since I'd learned Izzy's news, I felt like I had this. I could handle whatever was ahead—as I always could.

Was there something in the sea air here? Or was seeing people delightedly working together doing nothing more than gutting fish enough to make me see my world more clearly? Contrary to what Gordie might have thought, this was not the first time I'd watched people gut fish. I was, after all, something of a foodie, and my research had taken me to more than one fisherman's market. I moved toward the group at the table.

"Mind if I join you?" I said.

The large man with the grey beard at the end of the table seemed to be in charge. He looked skeptical. "Fill yer boots, my love," he said, handing me his own knife.

I pushed back the bulky sleeves of my sweatshirt and took the knife from him. I tapped my finger on it. It was, indeed, sharp. The man with the beard leaned over and picked a codfish from the metal bucket beside him, slapping it on the table in front of me. I took hold of the head and the tail, setting it up firmly in front of me, then, keeping my hand securely on the head, I took the knife and started.

I first made a shallow cut along the belly from the anus (located near the tail) up towards the head, taking care not to go too deep so as to puncture any internal organs. That would be nasty. When I had the incision on the fish's underside complete, I used the tip of my knife and then my fingers to open up the incision. I did it slowly and carefully, and once I had the internal organs exposed, I carefully removed them, dropping them into the bucket between me and a woman who'd stopped her work to watch me. Then I reached for the hose that was lying in the middle of the table and rinsed my fish. I checked inside to be sure I'd removed everything, rinsed again and put down the hose.

The applause began from Peter, who was standing behind the man with the beard. Then, all the people standing around the table started clapping.

"Well done, miss," the man with the beard said. "That's not the first time you've done that, now, is it?"

I smiled as I rinsed my hands with the hose and gratefully accepted the towel the woman beside me was now offering. "It is not, sir. But perhaps this has been the most fun, and I thank you for that."

As I turned from the table and breathed in again, I realized how much I liked the smell of fresh fish and ocean air. I looked around and saw amazement on the faces of my so-called family. "Well, what's everyone staring at?" I said, trying to keep a straight face.

Erica came over and unexpectedly threw her arm around my shoulder. "Dear god, Eliza, that was fantastic! Maybe I will have you on my show after all!"

I was shocked to hear Erica say that. In all the years she'd been on that afternoon talk show, she had not once shown the slightest bit of interest in my career as a burgeoning cookbook author with a growing international reputation despite that being a very appropriate topic. Now that she was doing a prime-time, women-focused news-type show, I hadn't expected any interest at all. I just might have to take her up on that, but now was not the moment to discuss it.

As we all walked back to the truck, the clouds began to clear. I could see a bit of blue sky ahead.

"Well, now," Gordie said as he helped Aunt Maureen back into the truck while she tried to protest that she needed no help. "Will you look at that sky? Almost enough blue to make a pair of sailor's trousers." We all looked at him and burst out laughing. He said, "It means the weather is about to clear." More laughing from the bunch of us. "Onward, kids," Gordie said, shaking his head and smiling. "Next stop: Bonavista."

"I thought we *were* in Bonavista," Phillip said, whipping out the map on his phone once again.

"Technically, we're on the peninsula," Peter said. "But Dad's talking about the town. I think he has lunch plans there."

Lunch. Now, that was something I was ready for, and I hoped there would be fish and chips on the menu. I was feeling close to cod right about then.

~

As the truck climbed over the final hill, the postcard-perfect town of Bonavista came into view. With its array of brightly coloured, clapboard-covered houses arranged over the small hills and valleys, the town looked like a much-loved antique patchwork quilt. The sun bounced over the bright reds and blues and yellows of the houses and made diamonds on the water of the little harbour. When Gordie asked us if anyone would like him to stop so that they could take a photo, I surprised even myself by being the first one to say yes. I had to capture this view. It was not lost on me that this scene was as far removed from my life—a big, expensive townhouse on a leafy street in the Upper West Side of Manhattan surrounded by Michelin-starred restaurants and boutiques—as anything could be. I could be at the North Pole, and it wouldn't be any more dissimilar. But it wasn't just about how it looked. I could imagine the kind of simple life that the residents must have with no traffic, no noise, no annoyances. Although I do have to admit, I was reasonably sure obnoxious mothers-in-law were not only an urban affliction. There were probably a few of them in this idyllic setting, too. In any case, I had to be able to remember it, so there would be photos, indeed.

Finally, we pulled into a small parking lot beside a red, two-story wooden building sitting directly on a wharf at the marina. All along the front, facing the boats moored in the harbour, was a string of brightly coloured Adirondack chairs. They looked like a string of baubles on a necklace—lime green, orange, turquoise, blue, yellow. Was there anything here that was not picture-perfect?

The restaurant did not disappoint. Once inside, we found ourselves surrounded once again by a sea of wood—tables, chairs, ceilings, walls, and floors. It was like being inside a hollowed-out log. And there it was on the menu: my fish and chips. The diet would wait until the next week. I was eating fried food this week.

"That smells delicious," Emma said, eyeing my plate of crispy, golden fish and home-cut fries.

"Sorry, Emma dear. Not vegan or even vegetarian."

"I suppose it might not hurt for me to at least have a taste."

My head snapped to attention, and I almost choked on the delicious fry I'd just popped into my mouth after drizzling malt vinegar over it—another Newfoundland taste that had captivated me. I looked at Emma and then noticed that I wasn't the only one whose head had snapped to attention at that remark. "What did you say, Emma?" I said quietly.

"A taste, please," Emma said. Then she looked around at everyone who was now pretending not to notice. "And the rest of you can just shut up." And so, they did.

I put a forkful of fish on Emma's plate, and she gingerly took up her fork and started to poke at it. "It's just fish," she breathed as she lifted a tiny morsel to her mouth.

I watched her as she slowly placed it on her tongue, closing her eyes as her lips closed around the fork. It was pathetic how much I felt like I was on pins and needles. After all, it was just a piece of fish, but a piece of fish could be so much more, couldn't it?

Everyone went back to their lunches or at least made an effort to look like they weren't keenly interested in Emma's reaction. I waited. Emma chewed and swallowed, then opened her eyes and looked at the salad in front of her. I distinctly saw her nose twitch, a family trait and a dead giveaway.

That was the moment when our server happened by to ask how everything was. She looked at Emma's untouched salad. "Honey, everything okay with that salad there?"

Emma looked up. "Oh, it's just fine," she said, "but I think I'm going to need a bit of protein. I'll have what she's having." She pointed to my plate, and the server smiled broadly before practically skipping off to the kitchen. She had not entirely understood when Emma ordered only a salad in the first place. She had kept asking her if she was sure she didn't want chicken on it—or shrimp or lobster. I could imagine the server telling the cook that they'd managed to convert another one.

~

After lunch and a short drive, we arrived on the edge of the world, or so it seemed. Up two flights of steps, standing proudly in the sunshine, was the imposing figure of the explorer John Cabot in all his glory. The vivid blue of the now clear sky gave him an almost artificial-looking backdrop as if someone had digitally removed the background from a photo and replaced it with solid blue. Yet this was real—authentic, or at least as authentic as a representation of someone dead for centuries could be. I sighed, thinking how often these days we could rarely tell the difference between the real and the counterfeit. Today, I was looking at something genuine.

TWENTY-SEVEN

Erica

WHEN ELIZA STEPPED TOWARD THE GROUP of fishers gutting codfish on that dock, I thought I'd seen everything. As I watched her adeptly wield that knife, slitting that fish open as if she'd done it a hundred times, I realized there must be more to writing a cookbook than simply acquiring recipes from others. Perhaps Eliza *would* be a good subject for a feature spot on our show, after all. I whipped out my phone and madly recorded it. I'd send it to Sam later, and maybe we could use it for B-roll material (background stuff, in case you don't know). She'd be delighted since she had been so annoyed that I'd never mentioned that Eliza Cohen was my cousin.

Phillip and I stood on the dock side by side in our matching hoodies. Phillip was staring at Eliza. "I never thought I'd see the day when the fastidious Eliza, who never liked to get her hands dirty when we were kids on summer vacation, seemed happy to be up to her wrists in fish guts. It's actually quite disarming, you know."

Phillip was right. It *was* disarming—and I never thought I'd enjoy being disarmed in the presence of my cousin. And I mean that in the most literal way possible. I was always armed and ready to do battle with Eliza—at least, I had been since I was about thirteen. Before that, we were actually friends. Then later, as we neared the town of Bonavista, and Eliza was the first one to say she wanted to stop to take a photo, I whispered to Phillip, who was beside me in the very back of the truck at this point, "Where is Eliza Cohen and what have they done with my cousin?"

"You've got to admit, sis, that she does seem to be connecting with the bizarre Newfoundland atmosphere. Hang in there, and we might see her decide to move here and shack up with Peter."

I rolled my eyes. "In case you've forgotten, Phillip dear, Eliza is married, and I doubt if Jake and his nutcase of a mother would go down without a fight."

Phillip lowered his voice as he gestured toward Eliza and Peter, who were sitting in the second row behind Gordie and Mom this time. "Just look at them."

I did look at them. Eliza nodded and smiled as Peter pointed out various landmarks. "Oh, Phillip. I hope Eliza knows what she's doing. Peter is so not her type."

"Maybe her type is changing," Phillip said, grabbing his phone and getting ready to hop out to take a photo.

I thought about what Phillip had said about Eliza being disarming, and I started to wonder if, perhaps, it was time to lay down our arms. We would be in St. John's the following evening, the place where our differences of opinion had truly taken root. Perhaps it would be just the setting we both needed to embrace one another as family members once again. As I stood there on that wharf under a blanket of grey skies, breathing in the salt air and listening to the cawing of the seagulls overhead, I was hopeful. And I would make it a point to have a chat with her.

~

After the shocking turn of events at lunch—Emma eating a morsel or more of fish—we were back on the road. Our first stop was a history lesson with John Cabot. I remembered having to study John back in elementary school history classes. At the time, I, along with the rest of my contemporaries, considered Canadian history to be a true snoozefest. The history was short by European standards, and the stories were fairly unremarkable. Unlike the Americans who had George Washington and the American Revolution, we had

Sir John A. MacDonald and the War of 1812. Hardly a fair comparison of iconic figures and drama.

As I stood there in the sunshine gazing up at the statue of Cabot, I realized I'd always thought he was British since his excursion to "the new world" had set sail from England. It was only years later that I realized he had, in fact, been Italian—Giovanni Caboto had been his name, to be exact. If I had known that name back in my history classes, perhaps I would have recognized his origins, but our history seemed to have been anglicized. Anyway, Gordie seemed to be more than conversant in everything about John Cabot, especially since he was thought to be the only European to reach the shores of North America since those Vikings who landed in L'Anse Aux Meadows. Perhaps the history of our dear country wasn't so dull after all.

Once the photos had been taken and everyone had spent enough time basking in the newfound greatness of such a historical figure, we were off to the stop I'd been waiting for all day. We were going to see the puffins.

A short drive took us to a village called Elliston, whose claim to fame that was announced on all its signage was, "The Root Cellar Capital of the World." Really? Could a place be famous for its root cellars? Evidently, the answer is a resounding yes.

Gordie parked the truck in a small parking lot across the road from where I could see cliffs that fell off into the sea. At the edge of the parking lot was the first of many root cellars he would point out.

Standing beside this first one, which looked like a door carved into a grass-covered hillock, Gordie began to tell us about them. "This is a root cellar, kids. Historically, they were used for—"

"I know, teacher," Phillip said, waving his hand in the air, causing me to roll my eyes and Gordie to grimace at being interrupted. I guess he wasn't used to guests interrupting him. "I know," Phillip repeated. "They were used to store roots!"

"Very funny, sir," Gordie said as he continued his lesson. "As I was saying, they were used to store," he gave Phillip the stink eye, "root vegetables like potatoes and carrots. They'd keep well over the long winter months. As we head on toward the cliffs, you'll see the landscape is dotted with these root cellars, often built into the hillsides or cliffs."

Eliza caught up to Gordie and said, "They seem so well-preserved, Gordie. Are root vegetables still an important part of the local cuisine?"

Gordie looked at her carefully. "You could say that, Eliza. But mind you, root vegetables have always been a part of the cuisine of any place that has long winters where nothing can grow. It's a good cook who can find a million ways to cook a potato." He looked over at Peter, who was standing behind Eliza. "How about it, son? How many ways did your late mother have to cook potatoes?"

Peter furrowed his brow as his eyes fluttered up to the left as if he might be trying to evoke a visual memory. I had learned how to decipher people's facial and body movements when I learned how to do on-air interviews. "Well, I remember riced potatoes, Mom's version of mashed. Then there were her scalloped potatoes, boiled potatoes with Jiggs Dinner and potato salad in the summer on a cold plate. I remember home fries and baked potatoes stuffed with lobster. I also loved her Shipwreck Casserole with layered potatoes and hamburger. That was my favourite."

He winked at Eliza, who had taken out a small notebook and was furiously jotting notes. Once a cookbook author, always a cookbook author. Now I was sure there would be a Newfoundland cookbook with a come-from-away twist in the offing.

When the litany of potato recipes came to an end, Gordie led us across the road and on a short hike atop the cliffs until we came to the edge of the world — or so it seemed. As I looked up from having picked my way carefully over the granite rocks, I gasped as my breath was taken away by the sight in front of me. The magnificent rock formations that had clearly been carved by millennia of crashing waves were awe-inspiring. But I didn't see any puffins.

Gordie assured me we would see them. "Patience, Erica, darlin'. Patience." Then, he distributed several sets of binoculars and pointed toward the huge rock-faced island that arose from the sea just offshore. I took a pair from him, and it wasn't long before it was clear that I was looking directly into a puffin colony.

I could feel a frisson of excitement. Imagine being excited by the sight of a flock of small birds. I know this sounds strange, but that's how it was. Spotting a puffin is like finding a real-life cartoon character. No other bird looks like a puffin with its vibrant orange beak that seems almost too big for its round body. The moment I spotted my first puffin, I couldn't stop myself from giggling, and Erica Flanagan could never be described as a giggler. But I couldn't help myself. It was as if nature's version of an eccentric comedian had come to life.

As I watched the colony in action, I realized that the show was just beginning. When they weren't just standing taking in the sea air, they waddled around on the cliff until one or more clumsily took flight, seeming to defy the laws of aerodynamics with their rapid wing flaps.

I surrendered my set of binoculars to Emma, who'd come up behind me, and took out the camera Andrew had insisted I bring. I had become one of those people who only take photos with a phone, but Andrew had insisted that, as a former journalist, I would appreciate the zoom lens on this one. He had been so right. I don't know how long I stayed there on the cliff, crouched in a most unladylike position, snapping photos of these amazing birds. It was decided. I would definitely be bringing Andrew and Maddie to this very place sometime in the not-too-distant future. As I looked up from my camera, I could see Phillip crouched not far from me. He seemed to be enjoying the experience as much as I was. And we were both children again. I wished adulthood had more of these moments.

I was almost disappointed when Gordie said we'd have to get going. Then I stood up—with some difficulty—and realized my fifty-something knees were not the same as my twenty-something knees. It felt good to get going.

Our last stop for the day was also in Elliston. We piled into the bus, and Gordie drove us along a small road that snaked along the cliff edge and into the village of two-story wooden houses clinging to the landscape. He parked, and we walked toward an open area overlooking the sea far below. In the middle of a small paver-stone-covered area stood a forlorn, windswept sculpture. It was a life-size rendering of two men frozen in time—one cradling the other in his lap.

Gordie explained that the sculpture was called "Home from the Sea," but it had a story that was so much more important than the magnificent bronze sculpture itself. Gordie wanted us to appreciate the hardship and heartbreak of life for those who chose to make their living from the sea. The sculpture memorialized the loss of some two hundred and fifty-one lives on a dark night in 1914 when two sealing ships went down in bad weather.

As I stood there staring at the sculpture, I could hear Gordie talking about the men whose likenesses were depicted. They were Reuben Crewe and his son Albert John, who was just sixteen at the time. Reuben was cradling Albert in his lap. They had been found together in this exact position, frozen. I could feel a tear escape my eye as I thought about how lives could be changed in an instant. There couldn't have been a family for miles who such a disaster wouldn't have touched. And this was how they lived. And died.

TWENTY-EIGHT

Eliza

I STOOD STARING AT THE SCULPTURE of the two men, frozen in time, both literally and figuratively. I felt a tear prickle at the corner of my eye, and I had to really consider why it seemed this place—this entire island—had moved me in directions that were new and not exactly welcome. Peter stood close to me in silence, and I was sure I felt his fingers brush mine. I had to stop thinking about him, or anyone else, in that way. I was going to be a grandmother. That much was clear.

We all piled back into the truck for the one-and-a-half-hour drive to our final hotel on the road trip in a town called Clarenville. After the past week's experiences, I had managed (read: lowered) my expectations *vis a vis* accommodation. At one point during the week, I'd asked Gordie why we weren't staying at the Fogo Island Inn. He practically laughed in my face.

"Eliza, my darlin', no one stays in that monstrosity except dimwitted celebrities and those who have more money than brains. You know the cheapest room'll cost you almost two thousand dollars, my dear, and what do you get for that money? A hand-made quilt and a view of the ocean. You can get that at Mary McCarthy's."

"Have you ever been there?" I had to know if he was just demonstrating disdain for people with money or if he based his conclusions on personal experience.

"Well, as it happens, I have graced their premises. So, I've seen it with my own eyes, and I know what it's about there."

He may have been to Fogo Island, but I doubted that he'd ever stayed at the inn, which served only to provide him with a distorted view, but I decided not to pursue the matter any further. We weren't going.

I'd read about Fogo Island, a tiny island off the coast of this bigger island. I'd first heard about it when I read that Gwyneth Paltrow called it "heaven" in an interview she gave after staying at the now-famous inn. And although I consider Ms. Paltrow to be the epitome of absurdity for her questionable choices of products to promote on her substantial public platform and sell on her "lifestyle" website, I had always admired her business acumen. Then, of course, there was the time Barack Obama stayed there. I had thought perhaps it would be a part of Newfoundland I'd enjoy. Perhaps.

I was thinking about this as we pulled into the parking lot for our overnight stay in Clarenville. As usual, the hotel was small by city standards, likely fewer than seventy-five rooms all in three stories, with an outdoor pool, a dining room and the tiniest bar I'd ever seen. As we disembarked for the second to last time—tomorrow in St. John's would be our last disembarkation—I considered the next part of this "adventure." I was looking forward to St. John's since I'd gone out of bounds with Gran's directions, told Emma she could have the room Gran had reserved to herself, and booked my own suite at the hotel. At least St. John's was enough of a city to have several nice hotels. As I unfolded myself from the truck, Gordie began telling us about the dinner that he had planned. He told us he had the private area attached to the dining room booked for us that evening.

"We'll be having a preordered dinner with a pre-selected menu," Gordie said.

"I suppose that means my mother selected the menu, doesn't it?" Aunt Maureen said as she took her case from Peter, who was unloading them from the back of the truck.

"Maureen, if Mother has selected the menu, it is bound to be something that everyone will like." Dad seemed to be trying very hard to enjoy this forced family time.

"Fred, you have always been and will always be a bit of a suck-up when it comes to Mom."

I was shocked to hear Aunt Maureen talk about my father, her brother, that way. In fact, I noted several times over the past week when she'd been less than complimentary about her mother as well. I could hardly blame her, though. I wasn't Gran's biggest fan either.

After checking into our rooms, we assembled back in the private dining room Gordie had arranged. Decorated in yet more wood — more knotty pine, if I am not mistaken — it was just off the main public dining room. There was a single large round table set with a white tablecloth and lots of wine glasses surrounded by multi-coloured wooden chairs. I chose the one closest to the door, hoping that Peter might sit next to me. He was, at least, a good conversationalist. That and a few good glasses of wine should get me through.

Once we were all seated, Gordie nodded to the server who was waiting at the door to the kitchen, and the dinner service began.

The dinner started with what is called a cold plate. It consisted of a mound of potato salad, several slices of questionable processed meat (bologna among them), the ubiquitous mustard pickles and a light purple lump of some mysterious vegetable that turned out to be beet salad made from roasted beets and mayonnaise. It was — interesting. There was also a deviled egg (one of the few foods that I loathed) and something that resembled jellied beets. All in all, an odd collection of tastes. I ate about one-third of mine.

The next course was something called "Jiggs Dinner." The short description of it is corned beef and cabbage with boiled potatoes. I knew this one because I'd had it at Gran's in the summers, and my mother made it far more often than my young child's developing palate could cope with boiled cabbage. As long as it was smothered in the mustard from the (you guessed it) mustard pickles, I could get it down. As I contemplated my plate, I thought, *Why not? I'm all grown up. Perhaps I can appreciate it more now that I've been exposed to so much more in the culinary world.* So, I lifted my fork and took up a mouthful of boiled cabbage *sans* mustard.

My tastebuds, which were usually so accommodating to new experiences these days, revolted immediately. As I started to chew, I began to contemplate how to spit it into my napkin without attracting attention, but Erica, Phillip and Peter were watching me. Each chew of the slimy, bitter, disgusting vegetable felt like an eternity as I tried to get it down. Finally, I was able to swallow it.

"Liking the cabbage, Eliza?" Phillip said, smiling in that naughty way I'd remembered from our childhoods and that he seemed to have maintained.

I patted my lips with my napkin. "I believe it's an acquired taste."

"And one I assume you have yet to acquire?" he said.

I just nodded and took a bite of corned beef. Just as I remembered, it was incredibly tender, easily teased apart with a fork. And the taste was another olfactory memory—savoury and slightly salty without a hint of mushiness one might expect of something that had been boiled half to death. It was delicious. Yes, I realized that it was highly likely that a piece of salt pork had made its way into the preparation, adding to the salty flavour, but I wasn't as fastidious about my food choices as Jake's mother would have hoped.

Before I'd come down to dinner, I had made up my mind that I was going to tell everyone my news. I knew sooner or later, I'd have to share the news that Izzy was going to have a baby. After all, these people were the closest thing she or I had to a family, if you didn't count Jake's lot, who had already weighed in and made their displeasure perfectly clear. Now, as I sat there finishing my main course, I nodded to Peter to indicate that I would like a bit more wine. I had decided that the moment had come.

As much as I hated the practice, I clinked a spoon against my water glass to get their attention. At least it wasn't a wedding, so we were not likely to be treated to an awkward public display of affection.

Aunt Maureen was the first to notice. "Everyone! It seems that Eliza is trying to get our attention." As people started to quiet down and turn in my direction, Aunt Maureen said, "Eliza, the floor is all yours."

I cleared my throat and took another sip of wine. Why I decided to stand up for this announcement, I have no idea, but there I was, hovering over the table and steadying myself on the edge after more than one glass of wine. "Well, everyone, since this is our last dinner—"

"Last Supper is more like it," Aunt Maureen muttered. "Tomorrow, the trial and crucifixion."

I had no idea where that was coming from, other than it seemed more of the same sentiment from her, and I wasn't going to take the time to find out, or I would lose my nerve. "As I was saying, it is our last meal on the road together. I have to admit that I had not been looking forward to this trip at all, but now that I've been here, I find I have mixed feelings. What I mean to say is…" dear god, why was this so hard? *Was* I drunk? I carried on. "What I mean to say is that this trip has been eye-opening in more ways than I could ever have imagined. I don't know what it is, but I do feel closer to you all as a family." Did I see Erica roll her eyes? I ignored her and continued. "That's why I wanted to share some news with you. Good news." I choked a little on that one, then hesitated.

"Go on, Eliza," Aunt Maureen said encouragingly. "We're all listening." She pointedly looked at Erica and Phillip, who had begun their usual childish kibbitzing. I suppose they were wondering what kind of good news I could possibly have that would interest them in the slightest.

"Well, the truth is that I'm going to be a grandmother." There was dead silence. I could suddenly hear the sound of actual crickets outside the window.

"How is that even possible?" Emma, who was sitting directly across from me, looked at me wide-eyed. "You're too young to be a grandmother, and surely Izzy isn't having a baby." She stopped for a beat. "Is she?"

"She is." I shakily raised my glass in the air. "To Izzy and her baby."

Erica stood up with her glass. "And to Eliza, a soon-to-be grandmother."

Everyone gave a little cheer and clinked glasses. I glanced at Peter, who didn't seem to be paying attention as he stared down at his phone. I suppose someone like him would think it odd that someone like me would have a daughter who would be a mother at such a young age.

~

The following morning, I was awoken early by the drumming of rain on the window. I'd never seen anything like it. Emma was already up, sitting in the chair by the window, watching the rain, which looked like a sheet, as it flowed down to the sill.

"Hey, Eliza, you're up."

"I suppose I am. What's happening outside other than rain?"

"I think I saw some lightning." She turned to look at me. "How do you really feel about Izzy's news? It must have come as quite a shock to you. I mean, she's not even twenty-two yet, is she?"

I sat up in bed and hugged my legs. "She's not, but soon. I must say I was startled by the news and even more startled that she didn't tell us until now." I had mentioned to everyone the evening before that the baby was due in October.

"You a grandmother, Eliza. I just cannot picture it."

"I'm having a hard time picturing it myself. But what can I do? I have to support her in this."

"Where's the father?"

"You know, Emma, I wondered the same thing. All she'll say is that he's in California, and if I were to take a wild guess, I'd suspect he's married."

Emma's hand flew to her mouth. "Oh, no, Eliza. Are you sure?"

"I'm not, but I'm hoping Izzy will let us in on a few more details as time passes. I need to get home to talk to her in person, so these next few days are going to be a bit of a trial." I looked at the clock on the bedside table between the twin beds. "Look at the time! We better get going."

By the time we all huddled under the portico out front, waiting for Gordie and Peter to pull up in the truck, it was still raining, although the wind seemed to have died down a bit. There's something about a dull, rainy day that dampens even the brightest, most enthusiastic person. We all stood there dully, staring out at the rain.

"Well, I suppose this is par for the course," Aunt Maureen finally said. "Rain is inevitable around here, and it seems only too appropriate for it to usher us to our final destination. At least it might extinguish the fires of the eighth circle of hell." She turned to Dad. "Fred, you do know who's in Dante's eighth circle, don't you?"

"I don't," Emma said.

She looked at Emma. "It's the place for seducers, flatterers, hypocrites, thieves, sowers of discord, and liars." Then she turned back to Dad. "Sounds about right, doesn't it, Fred?"

Dad looked at her and sighed. "Give it a rest, Maureen. Can't you and Mother just bury the hatchet over the next couple of days? She's turning a hundred."

"You say that as if it's some kind of personal achievement, Fred," Aunt Maureen said. "It's not. Lifespan is a lottery, and she won the longevity award. End of story." She crossed her arms and gazed out across the parking lot where the black truck was coming into view.

To say that everyone was sullen for the first part of the morning would be an understatement. Even Peter seemed a bit out of sorts, spending more time texting than interacting. After almost two hours of slow slogging, driving through the rain, we pulled into a village just off the road. The rain had lightened up, and the sky, although still steel grey, seemed slightly brighter.

I looked out the window and saw we were in another fishing village. Off in the distance, up on a hill, looking for all the world like the famous Hollywood sign, was a sign proclaiming our location.

"Does that say Dildo?" Erica said as everyone looked in the same direction.

Gordie smiled. "I knew that'd get you all smiling. It does, indeed. Welcome to Dildo!"

Phillip started laughing before pulling out his phone and getting out in the rain. "I have to take photos of this. Marcus isn't going to frigging believe there's a place called Dildo. Have they ever thought of changing their name?"

"Don't suppose anyone wants to change it since it always gets this kind of reaction from the tourists."

Gordie had planned a stop that would include a bit of Dildo souvenir shopping. I didn't have much interest in shot glasses or T-shirts that said, "There's a little Dildo in everyone," beside a cartoon of a fisherman in a yellow sou'wester rain hat like the one the emcee had worn when I was screeched in. I did, however, think that my PA, Mary-Lou, who often seemed like she had a stick up her ass, might enjoy a tea towel with that sentiment. So, I bought it for her. Later, as I climbed back into the truck and stashed the bag under my seat, I realized that I was probably going to keep it for myself. How about that?

Our soggy tour that day took us through places with names like Heart's Content, Heart's Delight and Harbour Grace. We stopped for lunch and waited out another downpour before setting out again. The afternoon dragged on as we drove in and out of small villages making our way to the city of St. John's, the capital city of Newfoundland and Labrador. Although sunset wasn't supposed to set until around 8:30 that evening, an hour later, it was so dark that I thought we had been driving for much longer than we had.

Everyone seemed so lost in their own thoughts (and phones, it has to be said) that we were all surprised when Peter said, "Well, this is me," as Gordie pulled into what appeared to be a driveway in the middle of nowhere.

I wasn't sure where we were, but I knew we had not yet reached the city. Peter seemed to be leaving us abruptly and without any warning. I felt like I'd been punched in the gut, and I didn't know why. He did, however, seem to be climbing out. As he did, he took my hand briefly and said, "It's been so nice to meet you, Eliza. I'm going to try to be at your grandmother's birthday party, so I hope we might be able to raise another glass together." I nodded stupidly.

Erica looked out the window and said, "Where are we? This place looks vaguely familiar, but I can't quite make it out."

I looked out through the raindrops on the window and could barely make out a small, one-story house surrounded by a picket fence with a huge SUV in the driveway. The SUV was almost as big as the house.

As we pulled away, leaving Peter standing in the rain waving at us, Erica said, "Gordie? Are we in Topsail?"

Topsail was the village where Gran's cottage was located and where we'd spent much of our summer vacation time when we were kids. She had two tiny cottages, side-by-side (or side by each, as I remembered her saying), perched on a bluff overlooking Conception Bay.

"We are, indeed, Erica," Gordie said.

"That was Mom's cottage," Aunt Maureen said, seeming suddenly to realize where we were.

"Indeed, it was."

"Is Peter staying there?" Aunt Maureen said.

Gordie didn't answer right away. Then he said, "I thought you all knew. Nora sold it to him last year. He's working on the property."

I could tell that both Aunt Maureen and Dad were surprised by the news. I must admit it didn't make any difference to me who Gran sold her cottage to or why, but I wondered why Peter hadn't mentioned it.

I thought about this for the next half hour that we had left to reach our hotel. Peter was living in Gran's old cottage, and he had never once mentioned this connection to me—or any of us, it seemed. It felt odd to me, but then Peter did seem like the type to want to fix up an old house. Perhaps a tiny cottage was all he could afford. I'd probably never know.

~

The suite was divine. With a vast king-sized bed and a large living area, not to mention piles of fluffy white towels, I thought I'd died and gone to heaven. I felt I was being rewarded for having put up with the recent accommodation. I didn't even care that I was paying for this myself. The *pièce de resistance*, though, was the enormous, jetted tub in the corner. For the briefest of moments, I had an image of Peter being here with me to share it. I swatted the thought away like the annoying insect that it was and proceeded to order room service and get the tub ready. Then, I don't quite know what happened.

I must have tripped on the belt of the fluffy hotel bathrobe I'd left on the side of the tub. The next thing I knew, I was splayed out on the floor with my arm twisted under me in the nastiest position possible. I could barely move, and when I did, I discovered that I had also knocked the wine glass I'd placed on the side of the tub to enjoy during my soak onto the floor, where it smashed into hundreds of shards, at least one of which appeared to be stabbed into my thigh. There was suddenly blood everywhere. My hip was sore, and when I tried to move my arm, I was sure it was broken. What to do?

I pulled myself up on the edge of the tub, trailing blood over the pristine white tiles surrounding it, and managed to reach my cell phone that I'd left there. I clicked on Erica's phone number. Erica had demonstrated in her career as a front-line war correspondent that she was good in a crisis, so I was counting on her. There was no one else in this motley group who could be trusted to be sensible, and I certainly wasn't going to call my father for help. Erica would have to do.

She answered after three rings. I told her of my predicament. As expected, Erica jumped to attention and arrived quickly at my door, toward which I was barely able to pull myself to let her in. She looked around at the mess, and a look of horror crossed her face.

"Dear god, Eliza. What happened? You're bleeding."

I was indeed bleeding. Erica quickly wrapped the belt of the bathrobe around my thigh, snugly wrapped a towel around my indescribably painful wrist and asked me if I had a pair of yoga pants and a sweatshirt I could throw on (since I was wearing only the bathrobe she had flung across me). Yes, to the yoga pants, but the only sweatshirt I had was the horrendous black hoodie. She quickly helped me with these items and called the front desk to get us a taxi right away. I stumbled to the elevator and through the lobby, hoping no one would notice us—at least no one we knew. Thankfully, by the time we got to the lobby, the taxi had just pulled up, so we clambered into the back seat and sped off to the emergency room.

As one might have expected, the emergency department waiting room was crowded that evening. As I looked around, I knew that it would be a painful wait. Erica told me to sit tight, and she'd see what she could do. A few minutes later, she returned.

"Seems I've found an Erica Flanagan fan." She nodded toward the nurse who was approaching with a wheelchair.

Before long, I was lying on a stretcher in a cubicle surrounded by curtains with an IV drip containing something for the pain. A young man who introduced himself as an emergency room nurse practitioner (I had never heard of one) came by and cleaned up my thigh gash.

"Oh, that's a nasty one," he said. "I'll just whip in a few stitches."

He did so expertly, and I was just starting to feel a bit mellow from the pain medication in the IV when I was whisked off for an X-ray. When I returned, Erica was waiting in the cubicle.

"I explained to them that you don't have any kind of Canadian medical coverage, but I managed to convince them that you were good for it."

Indeed, I was. A few minutes later, a young woman with her dark blonde hair in a messy bun at the back of her head pulled back the curtain and stepped inside. She was wearing green operating room scrubs topped by a wrinkled white lab coat. She introduced herself as the orthopedic surgery resident. I'd forgotten that this hospital was part of the university's medical school.

"I'm just going to take a look, Mrs. Cohen." As she lifted my arm from the temporary splint a nurse had put on it before I went to the X-ray department, I cried out in pain. "Sorry about that. The X-ray should be ready in a few minutes, and I'll just pop it up on that computer screen to see what we're dealing with."

"Ellen, you in there?" came a male voice from outside the curtains.

The resident, who was still painfully manipulating my wrist, said, "In here."

The curtain opened, and the man said, "There's an MVA on the way in…"

The familiar voice trailed off as I looked up. Erica, who was sitting on the other side of the stretcher, looked up at the same time. It was clear to me that the painkillers they were giving me were more potent than I thought. I seemed to be hallucinating.

"Dear god, Peter?" Erica was saying. "Whatever are you doing here?"

I looked up, and I was not hallucinating. It *was* Peter. "Peter?" I said, looking at his scrubs. "Are you some kind of orderly?"

The young resident snorted as Peter said, "Ellen, I'll take over here. You go ahead."

"Sure thing, Dr. O'Brien."

"You're a doctor," Erica and I both said simultaneously.

"Guilty as charged," Peter said as he sat down and began manipulating my wrist. Just then, the computer pinged. Peter clicked on something, and my X-ray appeared on the screen.

"You work here in this emergency department?" I said when I finally found my tongue.

"It's worse than that," Peter said as he looked at the X-rays. "I'm the head of Emergency Medicine."

"Why didn't you tell us?" Erica and I both said.

His eyes twinkled once again. "Because no one asked."

THERE'S GONNA BE A TIME

Donna's Cod au Gratin Supreme (for 2)

- 1 cup whole milk
- 1 ½ tbsps butter
- 1 ½ tbsps flour
- 1 heaping tbsp Dijon mustard
- ½ tsp summer savoury (or more if you like)
- ½ - 1 tsp finely grated lemon zest
- Salt and pepper
- ¼ cup shredded Parmesan cheese
- ½ lbs fresh cod fillets
- ¾ cup shredded cheddar cheese
- 1 cup fresh breadcrumbs preferably made from 2 slices Tramezzini Italian crustless bread
- 1 tbsp olive oil
- 1 tbsp preserved lemon, diced (or to taste; optional but omit it at your peril!)

1. Prepare two individual cod au grain dishes by buttering well
2. Pre-heat oven to 350F (180 C).
3. Scald milk in microwave on high for 1 ½ - 2 minutes or until it reaches 83o C. (180 F).
4. Make a white sauce by melting butter in a high-sided saucepan and whisking in flour until smooth. Slowly add the scalded milk, whisking continuously until smooth.
5. When your white sauce is thickened, stir in summer savoury, lemon zest, mustard, salt & pepper.
6. Stir in the Parmesan cheese just before you're ready to pour it over the fish.
7. Arrange cod fillets in the bottom of the prepared dishes in one layer. Pour sauce over fish.
8. Divide cheddar cheese evenly and sprinkle over the sauce.
9. Toss breadcrumbs with the olive oil and divide evenly on to of the gratin dishes.
10. Bake in a pre-heated oven for 35-40 minutes depending on the thickness of the fish fillets.
11. Remove from oven and top with preserved lemon. Serve immediately.

TWENTY-NINE

Erica

IF I HAD THOUGHT THE SIGHT BEFORE ME WHEN Eliza opened her hotel room door was the only shock I was going to experience that evening, I would have been sorely mistaken.

The voice sounded familiar and yet out of place in this sterile hospital environment. And I have to say it didn't have quite as strong a Newfoundland accent as I remembered. But when the young orthopedic surgery resident said, "Sure thing, Dr. O'Brien," I looked at Peter, unexpectedly dressed in scrubs and a lab coat emblazoned with the logo I'd seen but not recognized on his baseball cap a few days earlier, with a stethoscope hanging around his neck, there was only one conclusion to be drawn. Peter was a doctor.

I was surprised that Eliza was conscious enough to blurt out in unison with me, "You're a doctor!"

Then, when Peter said that no one had asked, I realized that he was right. And I wondered what else we had failed to ask because we had all been so focused on our own family situation. What a bunch of navel-gazers we turned out to be.

"Your father must be so proud of you," Eliza said, slurring her words.

"I suppose you could say that," he said. "Maybe a little."

It was time for the only one of the two of us who was competent to intervene. "Peter, I'm so sorry."

He laughed. "Don't be. I was actually under strict instructions from Nora via Dad to play along and keep myself out of the limelight. And it was fun."

Peter checked Eliza's X-rays and told her she probably had a chip fracture in her wrist. There was no line fracture that he could see on the X-ray at this time, but she'd have to wear a padded splint for three or four weeks. He said he'd get a nurse to apply the splint and provide her with an instruction sheet. Once the medical issue was taken care of, there were so many questions I wanted to ask Peter about this whole situation and how he and his father had gotten involved.

"I only have a few minutes," he said, "but I promise to raise a glass with you to the whole story if I can get away from here to get to your grandmother's party tomorrow evening. I didn't expect to have to work tonight, but when I got that series of texts earlier today, I knew it would be pretty hard for me to find anyone else to fill in for my colleague who's sick and will likely be off for a week. Sometimes the boss has to get his hands dirty," he said ruefully.

Peter explained that at least part of his story had been true. He *was* on vacation and had filled in for his father as a tour guide on a lark. "I'm supposed to be taking a four-week holiday, but it's difficult when you have staff issues."

Peter had bought Gran's cottage only a few months earlier and was living in it while he built a new house on the property directly behind the cottage.

"I apologize for not mentioning it earlier, but again, your grandmother was adamant that Dad and I should blend into the background. Anyway, you both have to come out to see it while you're here," he said. "It's kind of a unique design, closer to the water than your Gran's cottage with a dynamite view of Bell Island."

"What's unique about the design?" I said, always interested in houses.

"It's round." We both looked puzzled. "Just come out the day after tomorrow," he said. "You'll get the whole picture by then."

"So, you're going to be living out there in Topsail," Eliza said, having a lucid moment.

"I'm not exactly sure how many weeks or months a year I'll be there. I'm actually weighing two job offers. I might be relocating and keeping this as my summer house."

"Job offers?" Eliza said.

"Look, ladies, I'll tell you all about them tomorrow, but I have to go." And he was off to save a life or two.

Eliza and I both stared after him as if we had seen an apparition that might or might not reappear at any moment.

"What the actual fuck was that all about?" Eliza said. "Peter is a doctor? Oh my god, I feel like such a fool."

"Why? We all just made assumptions about him. He never said a word that would have led us to believe he was anything other than Gordie, the tour guide's son."

"I thought he was a person who fished for a living or something like that. I'm so embarrassed."

I looked at Eliza thoughtfully. "I don't think there's really anything to be embarrassed about. We all just took Peter at face value. And fishing for a living isn't embarrassing either." I stopped for a moment, thinking about the broader implications of what I'd just said. "You know, Eliza, I'm thinking we've all made a lot of assumptions about a lot of things in the past week. We all had preconceived ideas, and I don't know about you, but I feel a lot different about this island—and maybe even some people in my family—than I did a few weeks ago. It seems to have cast some kind of a spell over me."

Eliza pulled herself up on the pillow behind her. "You know how much I hate to admit it when you're right," she said, with an expression that I could almost have interpreted to be a smile, "but I do have to agree. There's something odd about this place. You know, Erica, you and I used to be the greatest of friends when we were young, spending summer vacations here with Gran."

"I know. But you know as well as I do why we fell out." I sighed.

"Maybe it's time we shared our secret with the rest of the family. It could explain a lot."

I shook my head. "Eliza, all those years ago, I wanted to tell immediately, but you disagreed, and that's where our feud started."

"And that's when I stopped trusting you."

That was the entire reason we'd barely spoken in years. Now, it seemed so childish, but we couldn't change what happened. "Now, it's too late anyway, Eliza. Airing the family's dirty laundry in public wouldn't benefit anyone. Anyway, why the sudden interest in honesty?"

Eliza shrugged and slid back down on her pillow. "I suppose I'm at a point in my life when I might be able to identify with Gran."

My eyes widened. "With Gran? I hope not, Eliza. I hope not."

~

It was after midnight when Eliza was finally discharged from the emergency room. As I helped her into the back seat of the taxi, I told the driver where we were going and asked him if he could take a slight detour along Circular Road before dropping us off at the hotel.

"Why do you want to go that way?" Eliza said as she settled her splinted arm in her lap and clutched her pain prescription.

"I just wanted a quiet drive by Gran's old house."

"Does she still own it?" Eliza said. "I have to say I haven't kept up with the news on that front over the past few years and after the news she sold the cottage to Peter, nothing would surprise me."

"Mom told me Gran still lived in the house until a year ago when she moved to the Lodge." The Lodge was Bonaventure Lodge, the swankiest assisted living facility in the province, or so Mom had told me. "But she never mentioned anything about Gran selling it, and I think Gran would have mentioned it to Mom and your father."

"At age ninety-nine, Gran still lived in that big drafty old house with all those stairs?"

"Evidently, she moved her bedroom to the main floor in the den at the back of the house and had a full-time housekeeper to help."

"Where did she get all the money?" Eliza said as the cab pulled away and into the dark street. "I thought that old house was her nest egg, and if she still owns it…"

"I don't know the details," I said as I gazed out into the quiet, dark, wet streets. The rain had stopped, but the damp pavement still glistened. "I know Gran sold Grandad's business a year or so after he died, but that was back in the middle of the 1980s. There had to have been money from that sale." My grandfather, Thomas Houlihan, had been a swaggering St. John's businessman who was thirty-one years old when he married nineteen-year-old Nora Callaghan in the early 1940s. That was about as much of the family history as I knew.

"Yes, Grandad's business," Eliza said, staring out the window. "We did spend some time in his store back then, didn't we?"

I sat back, thinking about Grandad's clothing store on Water Street. He sold men's and women's clothing to the most affluent of St. John's society back in those days. "I think he was trying to get us to appreciate the benefits of making a good impression."

"By making us dust and vacuum his store while we were on summer holidays?"

I laughed when I remembered how Eliza, most of all, had balked at that. Emma had been too young, and Lucy was always Gran's favourite, so she spent her time in Gran's kitchen learning to cook Newfoundland dishes like Gran's famous fishcakes. I often wondered if that experience had played a part in Lucy's decision to move to St. John's from Halifax, where she had been born and raised. Uncle Fred had left Newfoundland to go to medical school in Halifax and never returned except for the odd visit. So, Eliza, Lucy and Emma had all been born and raised in Nova Scotia. I couldn't imagine why, but Lucy had decided to go to university here in Newfoundland rather than in her hometown as her sisters both did. After her first two years at Memorial University, where she met her husband, she dropped out and settled in a house not far from Gran. Ah, Lucy. I couldn't honestly admit I was looking forward to seeing her. It had always made me cringe at how obsequious she was around Gran. I wondered if that had changed.

"Slow down, would you please?" I said to the driver as we neared the corner where Gran's house stood. As he approached the house, I said, "Would you mind stopping for just a moment?"

The taxi rolled to a slow stop right in front of the house. It was just as I had remembered it. Although it had been only five years since Andrew and I brought Maddie to visit her great-grandmother, I saw the house as frozen in time in the summers of the 1970s and 1980s. In the dark, I could just make out the contours of the three-story Victorian with two chimneys and bow windows flanking its massive front steps. Then I noticed the car in the driveway and a light in an upstairs window. Eliza must have noticed, too.

"If she hasn't sold it, who's living there now, Erica? Someone must be."

I shook my head. "I have no idea, Eliza."

Eliza seemed to snap to attention. "You don't suppose that toadying sister of mine is living there?"

I sighed. "What difference would it make if Lucy lived there now, Eliza? Neither you nor I need a house in St. John's, Newfoundland, do we?"

"I suppose not," Eliza said. "But Emma might have a different view."

"Anyway, we have no idea who's there. All of this is sheer speculation. Maybe Gran is renting it out." That seemed to satisfy Eliza, so I told the driver to continue, and we finally arrived at the hotel.

The lobby was deadly quiet as we made our way to the elevators and our respective rooms.

"I'm going to take a walk up to Signal Hill in the morning, Eliza," I said. "Interested in coming with me?" I had no idea where my sudden interest in spending time with Eliza had come from, but I felt we'd made some progress.

"Thanks, Erica. Normally, I would. It might shake out the cobwebs before that family meeting tomorrow afternoon—

whatever that's all about—but it's been a long night. My stitches will probably impede my walking anyway, and I'm likely to be a bit zonked from the pain medications. Maybe we could take Peter up on his offer to go out to Topsail and see his house the day after tomorrow."

"Sounds good."

As we got into the elevator together, Eliza said, "So, you really have no idea what this mysterious family meeting is supposed to accomplish?"

"You know as much about it as I do," I said as I exited the elevator on my floor. "Should be fun. 'Night."

~

The following morning, I left the hotel early after a quick cup of coffee. As I headed toward Battery Road leading up Signal Hill, I was glad Eliza had begged off. It was one of my first opportunities to be by myself. And I had the damp, early morning mist embracing me, adding to the ambience and quiet. The tourists would arrive at the top of the hill on buses much later.

Signal Hill is one of those special, iconic places in a city—a sight like the CN Tower in Toronto or the Eiffel Tower in Paris. When you see it, you know immediately where you are. Located near the entrance to the harbour—on the east side of the narrows—the bluff rises steeply from the surrounding landscape, offering commanding views of the harbour, the city and the surrounding rocky coastline from the top. I remembered visiting St. John's on business years ago when Andrew was covering an event in the city. At the time, while he was otherwise occupied, I had actually done the touristy thing and visited the "Geo" Centre on the hill. I remembered how surprised I'd been to learn that I was walking on volcanic and sedimentary rocks that had been there for somewhere in the vicinity of 3,800 million years (imagine that!) and were a part of the Appalachian Mountain range.

I reached the top of the hill just as the mist seemed to evaporate and took a moment to gaze at Cabot Tower, a Gothic-Revival-style stone building—not very big—that was built in the nineteenth century to commemorate the four-hundredth anniversary of John Cabot's landing on the island. I walked around the tower to the side that overlooked the city. There were lots of commercial vessels in the harbour—mainly ships that serviced the offshore oil platforms and large fishing trawlers. There were also a couple of yachts, but the biggest surprise was seeing a cruise ship as it made its majestic way through the narrows and into the harbour to dock in downtown St. John's.

I shifted my gaze to the downtown streets area. I was thinking about Grandad's shop on Water Street and what it had meant to us as kids visiting in the summer. I suppose I should thank him for putting me to work down there. It was where I had the experience of my first paycheque—or at least my first five-dollar bill that served as payment for a few domestic chores. I laughed as I remembered his employees.

There was Derrick, his tailor, who was a bit of an oddball character with his suspenders and measuring tape that always hung around his neck. I also remembered Dolores, who was what Grandad called his "shop girl." Those were the days when women didn't seem to be bothered much by bosses who were slightly inappropriate with their daily comments about how lovely they looked. That was Grandad's style. Then I remembered Valerie, another shop girl, but only part-time.

Eliza and I had been in total agreement about how much we disliked Valerie. Valerie was always mean to us—or at least that's how we viewed it. She treated us like we were the hired help rather than her employer's granddaughters. And she constantly criticized us. You would think we would have been used to that given our overly critical grandmother (and both our mothers weren't far behind—Eliza's was worse, though). She also seemed unaccountably interested in everything Grandad did—always offering to help with things and telling him she'd be happy to work late to help him with the accounts—part-time indeed. And Grandad seemed to lap up the attention.

She was at least thirty years younger than Grandad—perhaps more. At that age, I could never tell how old someone was. She just seemed a lot younger than he was. I remembered she had straight dark hair that fell to her waist and the shortest skirts I'd ever seen. I remembered Eliza remarking that her mother would never let her wear anything that short. Although, I do remember that Eliza's mother was an extraordinary prude. What I disliked most about Valerie was the way she touched Grandad's arm when she spoke to him and laughed at every tone-deaf joke he told. Even at the ages of eleven and thirteen, Eliza and I recognized an off-colour joke when we heard one.

Anyway, I hadn't thought about Valerie in years. I wondered what might have become of her. I only hoped she wasn't going to reappear in our lives at Gran's birthday party. The thought made me shiver.

~

When I arrived back at the hotel an hour and a half later, Mom was in the lobby chatting with Uncle Fred.

"Good morning, Erica, dear. I see you got an early start." I told them I'd been walking up Signal Hill, enjoying the quiet of the morning. "You're just in time, then," Mom said. "It seems that your grandmother has invited us all for brunch before the family meeting. Fred and I are just waiting for our taxi."

"Is it at the house?" I said. Mom nodded, then asked me if I'd like to come along with them. I told her I'd prefer to change and freshen up before a family gathering but that I'd be along as soon as I was ready. "What about everyone else?"

"Phillip and Emma said they'd walk, and I haven't seen Eliza this morning."

It seemed that Eliza hadn't yet emerged to tell everyone about our hospital escapade and the new information we had about Peter.

I wondered if Mom knew, and I suspected that she'd known all along, but it wasn't the time to ask.

"So, I guess it's show time, then, eh?" I said. Mom looked puzzled. "Nora Houlihan is one hundred today, Mom."

Mom breathed out loudly. "Well, I guess that's true. 'Once more unto the breach,' as Shakespeare once wrote."

THIRTY

Eliza

I SAT ON THE SIDE OF MY BED, still groggy from the late night and the pain medication I knew I would have to take for a few days. Getting dressed was awkward, and taming my hair was even more difficult. I got up and stood in front of the full-length mirror hanging on the wall by the door.

"Who the hell are you, anyway?" I said to my reflection. Who, indeed?

My hair was wild, my eyes sported bags large enough for a two-week vacation, and my skin looked blotchy. I could not appear in public like this. I sat myself down at the desk, took out my huge lighted mirror, which I never left home without and went to work—a one-handed makeup session it would be.

Half an hour later, I looked, if not great, at least better. My only consolation was that Peter would not be there until at least this evening at the party—if at all. As I sat staring at my reflection in the lighted makeup mirror, I realized it was probably time to ask myself why that mattered. Just then, my phone buzzed. It was Erica.

"Eliza, you did get the memo this morning that Gran expects us at her house for brunch in half an hour, didn't you? You want to walk or share a cab?"

"I'm not sure I want to walk with this splint. Let's share a cab if that works for you."

Twenty minutes later, Erica and I were getting into a taxi in front of the hotel for the short drive to Gran's old house that we'd gazed at less than twelve hours earlier.

By the time we made our way into the house, everyone else was already there. The old house hadn't changed much over the years with its heavy Victorian décor, antique wooden tables and settees. The centre hall plan meant that the living room was on one side of the foyer and the dining room on the other, with a massive staircase directly in front leading to the second-floor landing.

The large dining table that usually sat twelve people was covered in white Irish linen and set up as a buffet. I could see a caterer moving back and forth between the kitchen and the dining table to finish setting out the dishes. I looked into the living room, and there she sat. My grandmother, Nora Houlihan.

She was sitting at one end of the room in an enormous chair upholstered in a faded floral print surrounded by enough flowers to suggest her well-wishers thought she might have already died. If it hadn't been for the giant, helium-filled balloon that was affixed to one of them proclaiming "Happy 100th Birthday!" I would have been ready for a funeral. But then I looked at Gran and realized she was very much alive.

She was nodding and talking. I could see Lucy fluttering around her like a little bird, no doubt ensuring that Gran had everything just the way she wanted it to be. Lucy looked every bit the middle-aged matron with her thick middle, her cotton dress and what appeared to be—dear god, it wasn't possible—a perm in her hair. Then, I gave myself a mental shake and told myself that I was being judgmental. What else was new?

My grandmother was someone who never seemed to stop talking. I knew that she'd have something to say about my splint, but that wasn't what worried me. I could not imagine what kind of tongue-lashing I could expect for giving birth to a daughter who would get herself pregnant "without benefit of marriage." That was Nora's way—quick to judge. I had to admit the irony was that I was probably like her in that way—the only way, I hoped. I remembered I'd had a brief Wayne Dyer affliction some years ago when I thought his writing might help me build my business. He had once written, "When you judge another, you do not define them; you define yourself." There was little doubt about the veracity of that in Gran's case. She certainly did define herself by her judgments, although it occurred to me it might never be too late to redefine yourself. And I knew I was about to be judged. I hoped no one had mentioned Izzy to her yet (I have to admit that I harboured a tiny hope that she might die before the birth. How awful was that?). Too late.

"Well, well, well, if it isn't my hoity-toity granddaughter who has deigned to lower herself to come home from that den of iniquity some people call New York City."

You had to give her credit. Nora Houlihan might have been one hundred years old as of today, but she still had all her marbles — for better or for worse.

"Gran," I said, approaching the throne where she was clearly holding court, Dad, Aunt Maureen and Lucy, her loyal minion, beside her. "It's so nice to see you. It's been too long."

"Don't give me that horse shit, Eliza Houlihan. It's not at all nice to see me, now is it? And it's all on you besides. Let me look at you." Her eyes immediately fixated on my splint, which Aunt Maureen and Dad were also seeing for the first time.

"What happened?" Dad said, getting up. "Let me look at that." Once a doctor, always a doctor.

I quickly told them I'd simply fallen and that I had a small break in my wrist.

"I suppose you were soused, now, weren't you?" Gran had a way of getting to the point.

"No, I wasn't drunk, Gran. Anyway, how are you?"

"How do you suppose I am? I'm a hundred years old." There is really no appropriate response to that. "So, Eliza, I hear I'm going to be a great-great-grandmother."

Oh my god, I thought. *Here it comes.* I stood rigidly waiting for the onslaught from the Irish Catholic contingent that I supposed wouldn't be very different than the opinion of Izzy's Jewish grandmother.

"It wasn't enough that you had to leave the Catholic church. Now, you have to add to the Jewish population when you could have been bringing a new little Catholic into the world. How is dear Izzy?"

Dear Izzy? When had Gran ever thought of her great-granddaughter as dear Izzy? Wasn't she going to tell me how it was so immoral for this to have happened?

"So, Gran, you don't have any words of reprimand for my daughter having a child on her own?"

Gran shrugged. "What odds, Eliza? These things happen."

These things happen? I never thought I'd hear my narrow-minded, intolerant grandmother say anything like that. I guessed that Phillip hadn't yet had his initial audience. I remembered the summer he'd told her he was gay. Her response had been, "I take a dim view of that."

Just then, Erica stepped into the room. Gran looked over at her. "Well, if it isn't the highfalutin Erica Flanagan come to wish her granny happy birthday. How did you find time in your busy schedule, my dear? I don't have much time for that television stuff myself, but my friends tell me you're still there. Come over here. You look a bit like death warmed over with that hair colour, you know. Don't they have hair dye in that wicked place you live?"

To tell you the truth, I liked Erica's salt-and-pepper hair. It suited her complexion and had actually made me wonder if it might be time for me to eschew the hair dye. Izzy had even suggested it, but Jake had been dead set against it. Perhaps he thought he'd feel older if he looked at his wife with silver strands. That might be the best argument yet in favour of going *au natural*.

"You lot go ahead to the dining room and get a plate of food," Gran said. "I've eaten—at a table. Can't stand eating with a plate on my lap. It's uncivilized—a savage mug-up if ever there was one."

We slunk out and across the hall to pick at the buffet. "Are we having fun yet?" Erica whispered as we left.

After everyone had eaten, under Gran's critical eye, sitting awkwardly in the living room with our plates balancing on our knees, I could see the caterer clearing the dining room table. When the platters and tablecloth had disappeared, a chicly dressed young woman followed along, setting up the dining room as if for a meeting.

At precisely one pm, Gran grabbed her walker, stood up to her full five feet and two inches and proclaimed it was time to begin. She then shuffled her way across the hall and into the dining room, taking the chair at the head of the table. Once we were all seated and ready to listen, Gran looked at her watch. "Can't start yet. A few more people to arrive."

We looked at one another and couldn't imagine who else was supposed to be here. A few minutes later, the front door opened and in walked Gordie. Gordie O'Brien? What the hell was he doing here? He was followed by a woman I'd never seen before.

She looked like she was more or less around my age, with shoulder-length blondish hair, wearing a pair of tight white jeans and a light blazer-style jacket and carrying a large tote bag. There was something about her that looked familiar, but I didn't think I'd ever met her before. But Gordie O'Brien, our tour guide? I couldn't even imagine why he might be joining us.

"Now we can begin," Gran said. "I realize I may have perpetrated a bit of a prank on you by letting you think Gordie was a tour guide."

"Wait just a minute now," Gordie said as he sat beside her, removing a raft of papers from the well-worn, expensive-looking, brown leather briefcase he had carried in and placed on the table. "You wait just one minute, Nora Houlihan. I *am* a tour guide and a damn good one at that." He put the pile of legal-looking documents on the table in front of him and sat beside Nora. Then he took what looked like a gold fountain pen from his inner breast pocket.

That was the moment I clicked on the briefcase and Gordie's current wardrobe: a white button-down dress shirt with no tie, khakis, and a well-cut beige jacket that looked like expensive summer-weight wool. I knew expensive fabric when I saw it. What in the world was going on?

Gran huffed a bit. "If you say so." She turned to us. "As most of you may not know," she looked at Aunt Maureen, who assiduously kept from meeting her mother's eyes, "Gordie O'Brien is my solicitor."

What?

"Betsy, could you please pass out the cards?" Gordie said. Betsy was the young woman who had set up the dining room for a meeting and appeared to be his (or someone's) assistant.

I looked at the cream-coloured card she placed on the table in front of me. It said, "G. Terrance O'Brien, QC." QC, as in Queen's Counsel? I hadn't been outside Canada long enough to have forgotten that lawyers are given this designation for distinguished service and leadership. Then, I looked at the tiny letters on the lower right-hand corner of the card. "Chief Justice, Retired. So, it appeared that G. (presumably for Gordon) Terrence O'Brien was not only a lawyer but a retired judge, as well.

Erica must have clicked in at the exact moment that I did. "You're a retired judge?" she said, holding the business card out in front of her. She then looked across the table to where Aunt Maureen was sitting. "Did you know this, Mom?"

"Erica," Aunt Maureen said quietly, "can we talk about this later?"

Erica sat back as Gran weighed in. "Of course, your mother knew. She's known Gordie for her whole life." Gran turned to Aunt Maureen. "I see I may not be the only one with a skeleton or two in the closet, Maureen. Nothing better than to rattle a few family skeletons, now is there?"

I wasn't sure I was ready to rattle family skeletons.

"Come on now, Gordie," Gran said, "let's get on with it. Some of us have less time left than others, you know."

Gordie smiled and put on a pair of half-moon reading glasses. "Well, everyone, welcome. Nora has asked me to be here to help her run this family meeting." He looked at Gran. "First, Nora, we should take a moment to acknowledge this special day. Happy birthday to you, my friend."

Gran nodded. "Thank you, Gordie. Now move along."

"Indeed," he said, picking up a legal-sized document. "I believe it's important to begin by establishing my position here."

Where had Gordie's Newfoundland accent gone? All that seemed to be left of it was a bit of an Irish lilt.

My eyes wandered to the unknown woman, and for a moment, I wondered if she might not work for Gordie. Otherwise, what business would she have at our family meeting? Then I looked at Betsy in her chic black skirt and crisp white blouse and at Gordie's expensive jacket and realized it was unlikely that she worked for this lawyer—retired or not.

"I have had the pleasure of being Nora's solicitor for some twenty-five years before ascending the bench. And my father was privileged to do all the legal work for Nora and your late grandfather—or father, as the case may be—Thomas since he embarked on his business enterprise in the city. I retired from the bench earlier this year, but over the years, I have kept Nora as one of my few clients." He looked down at the paper in front of him. "What I have before me is Nora's last will and testament."

I heard a collective intake of breath around me. What was going on? Were we here for a reading of a will with the not-yet-deceased sitting next to us? I rolled my eyes. Only Nora Houlihan would think that this was in good taste.

"This is an odd situation," Gordie said. "But knowing your grandmother as I do, it didn't come as a complete surprise when she called me six months or more ago and asked me if I'd do this."

"Is this even legal?" Phillip said.

Gran shook her head. "Another country heard from. Just button it for the moment, Phillip. You're not in Montreal, you know."

Phillip seemed to shrink back in his chair. But I had wondered the same thing. Gran nodded to Gordie once again, but before he could open his mouth and utter a word, Aunt Maureen butted in.

"Really, Mom? Is this little display necessary? Do you have to do this?"

"Put a cork in it, Maureen. You and your I'm-so-much-smarter-than-everyone-else attitude and your PhD in that philosophical nonsense can be as stunned as me arse. Just sit back and pay attention."

Gordie turned to Phillip. "Phillip, let me just say that this situation may be unusual, but there is nothing in the law that would stop Nora from doing this." He then went back to his notes and documents. "Now, ladies and gentlemen, we are going to read out Nora's will at this time. She has informed me that her reason for doing this now is so there will be no misunderstandings." He looked at Gran and then back to what presumably was her will. "Before I begin, I just want to acknowledge for you all that wills generally contain this and that about who gets what. But many times, families don't realize that a will also tells a story. In their various clauses, wills tell stories about how a person lived, who a person loved and why a person behaved the way they have over the course of their life. Nora has had a longer time to create her story than most people. And I know from first-hand knowledge that she's changed her story more than once or twice. But today, that story is encapsulated in the clauses of a legal document."

"Jesus, Mary and Joseph, Gordie. You always could spin a yarn longer than anyone I ever knew."

Gordie smiled indulgently at Gran. "You are always right, Nora. I do get carried away. And yet, I'm going to continue." He turned back to his document. "As I was saying, a last will and testament is a story, and as such, learning that story after someone is laid out in a coffin seems a bit of a lost moment. So, when Nora asked me to do this, I thought I wouldn't miss the chance to see the faces of her beneficiaries as they learned about their grandmother—or mother as the case may be."

"Do the gifts in the will come to people before she dies or after?"

Everyone looked at Lucy, who was sitting on Gran's left across from Gordie. Was she hoping to get her part of Gran's estate today?

Gran patted Lucy's hand. "That's not how it's going to work, my dear. Rest assured, everyone will get what they deserve. Eventually."

Then Gordie began reading. *"This is the last will and testament of Nora Callahan Houlihan... I hereby revoke all former Wills and other Testamentary dispositions by me at any time heretofore made and declare this to be and contain my Last Will and Testament."*

THIRTY-ONE

Erica

AS I SAT THERE IN THE DINING ROOM on that uncomfortable, high-backed dining chair, I wasn't sure which of the scenarios I was witnessing piqued my journalistic sensibility more—the fact that we were at the reading of a will with the nearly-deceased (one has to think that Gran isn't going to last much longer, after all), or the fact that my mother had a history with Gordie O'Brien, the details of which I knew little about—not to mention the dressing down she had been taking from my grandmother. Is it true that we never really know our parents? I was beginning to think that we are all so caught up in our own lives and seeing our parents in only that one role that we forget they are people who lived for many years before we were part of their lives. I had spent the past decade as a television personality, but for a decade or more before that, I was a serious journalist, and I knew a story when I smelled one. Mom would, indeed, be telling me the entire story after this—whatever it was— was over. Mom had told me only that she and Gordie had gone to school together decades ago, but I had to believe there was more to the story and that she had known he was a retired judge.

Gordie had finished telling us that a will is a story—something that had never before occurred to me—and was now reading Gran's will.

There was the usual stuff about who would be the executor— a trust company, as it turned out—and other legalese. Then, he got to the heart of the matter. He began the litany of Gran's assets—and it was long.

Much to my surprise—and judging from Mom and Uncle Fred's reactions, I was not the only one surprised—Gran still owned the building and the property downtown where Grandad's store used to be. She had been leasing it out for four decades. She also owned the property next door to it, which currently housed a restaurant. Then, although she had sold one of her cottages and its property to Peter, she had kept the second one next door. She also seemed to own another large parcel of land in the same area of Conception Bay that was currently being developed into high-end subdivisions. According to Gordie's aside on that topic, she had already sold off much of the property to a developer, and the one remaining parcel would be sold when she died, adding to the considerable cash assets that she, quite shockingly, still held. There had not yet been any mention of the house.

All the listed assets were to be put into a trust that would be divided into one hundred portions. Each of her family members was then to receive a share.

"But," Gordie said, "before we get to that, there are a few details you'll all need to know about so that you can further understand Nora's story." He turned to Nora, who gestured for him to continue. Gordie pulled out another piece of paper from beneath the will. "Nora has asked me to introduce Melissa Dawn Burke." He looked in the direction of the woman no one seemed to otherwise know.

Gran lifted her arm and gestured to Betsy, who brought over a chair that she put next to Gran at the head of the table as if this might have been choreographed in advance. Melissa stood, picked up her handbag and made her way to the chair beside Gran. She sat down and wordlessly folded her hands on the table in front of her. Gran put her hand on Melissa's arm.

"You may think I have been remiss over the years," Gran began, "in failing to introduce you to Melissa. But I can't take the full blame because I didn't know where she was." Were those tears forming in Gran's century-old eyes? "Melissa is my granddaughter."

You could have heard a pin drop. All eyes around the table widened in disbelief, mine included. There was no way this woman could be her granddaughter. I was her granddaughter. Eliza, Emma and Lucy were her granddaughters. Phillip was her grandson. Gran had no other children to have grandchildren for her. It was impossible. Lucy was the first to say something.

"That can't be, Gran. There is no way you could have another granddaughter. She must be trying to scam you. Please, Gran. We can help." Lucy sounded more and more desperate, and I realized that Eliza had probably been correct in her assertion that Lucy expected to be amply rewarded for being there for Gran when the rest of the family revelled in their CFA status.

"Lucy, dear, rest assured I have not been scammed in any way. Melissa is, indeed, my granddaughter, and if you'll all hold your tongues and listen to me—and to Gordie—in due course, you'll get the whole story." She looked at Gordie. "A will is a story, eh? Well, it leaves out a lot of detail." Gran turned back to the rest of us. "I'm going to tell you a story. Just sit there, clap your mouths shut and listen." She coughed a little, then spat into a tissue she held in her hand.

Then, she started, slowly at first, until she warmed up, her eyes shining at the memories. The story began in January of 1941 when eighteen-year-old Nora Callahan stood on top of Signal Hill with her best friend Mary, watching the *Edmund B. Alexander* steam in through the narrows and dock in St. John's Harbour.

"Oh, it was a grand sight for the two of us girls who had never been anywhere but the island and no farther afield than Conception Bay. We had heard about the American military fellows arriving. The Americans took a shine to our little island and its strategic location, so they sent the boys to build an army base."

I'd heard about a place in St. John's called Fort Pepperell that the Americans had used for years, starting during the Second World War.

"Once the boys were settled, they started in with the weekly dances. Mary and I had to sneak around in those days, what with our parents constantly watching over our virginity so that we could have that big church wedding with the priest and all the trimmings.

I remember that one night so clearly; it's like it happened yesterday. I may sometimes forget what I had for breakfast this morning, but I'll never forget that night."

Mary, who, much to my surprise, had grown up to be old Mrs. Mary McCarthy, and Nora told their parents they were going to the picture show and would probably have a soda at the soda fountain on Water Street. But instead, they snuck over to the base, slipped into the ladies' cloakroom and rearranged their clothes. Gran told us that she removed her blouse and put her red cashmere cardigan that her parents had given her for Christmas on backwards with the buttons now on the back. She wore it with a black pencil skirt, pearls and high heels she had secreted in her handbag. She also swiped on bright red lipstick to match the sweater, something her parents forbade. Then they were ready.

They hadn't been at the dance more than half an hour when Harold, looking smart in his American army uniform, asked her to dance. One thing led to another, and Gran found herself going back to the dances Saturday night after Saturday night. Mary, who was two years younger than Nora, soon became bored of them, always having to follow Nora around, so after that, Nora went on her own. She could never tell her parents, but she'd fallen in love with Harold.

"It was like magic," Gran said as she told her story. Her old eyes, normally almost glassed over, came alive as she spoke, clearly remembering every detail. "Being in love is like someone has cast a spell over you. It's like having a wizard of sorts whispering in your ear and making you think and do things that you wouldn't normally do. It consumed me, and I ignored my parents' counsel and everything I'd been taught. The next thing I knew, I was in the family way—and in big trouble. Harold was shipped off to Argentia to work on building the new base there before I could even tell him. He may still have been here on the island, but Argentia was a long way away in those days, the roads being what they were. He might as well have been in France."

I looked over at Eliza, who had taken a loud breath. No doubt, she was thinking about how much had changed and yet how little. I was sure Izzy must be on her mind.

Gran's story got very grim from there on. Her parents sent her away for a year to Boston to a Catholic home for unwed mothers to have her baby. When she had done as her parents commanded her, she returned to St. John's, where her parents had managed to find her a suitable husband. Thomas Houlihan was willing to take her on as his wife despite her serious transgression—as long as no one ever knew about it. Her parents had told their friends they had sent her to Boston to finishing school. Finishing, indeed.

It took Gran a while, but she finally cut to the chase. She had given birth to a son she had never even been permitted to hold, a situation that was common in those days. The nuns took the baby immediately, telling her they had a good Irish Catholic Boston family who would adopt him and raise him. He would never know where he had come from. Melissa was that baby's daughter. Gran did, indeed, have another granddaughter.

"Melissa grew up in Boston and then moved to Maine when she got married. I wasn't there for her father—god rest his soul—who did not have the benefit of my wisdom over the years as Maureen and Frederick had. He was the little lost soul whose memory should be kept close."

As I listened to Gran's story, I remembered Mom saying that Uncle Fred had always been Gran's favourite. Perhaps it was because he reminded her of the son she'd been forced to give up.

Gran continued. "Melissa hasn't had the benefit of her extended family as you all have had over the years, so I believe it's only fair that I make it up to her. She will inherit the house, and that's that."

I heard a strangled gasp from Lucy. Mom's hand flew to her mouth, although I'm not sure what she was thinking. I knew, for a fact, that she didn't want the house. Everyone else seemed stunned. I know I was still back on the fact that Gran had given birth to a child before she had even met Grandad. No wonder she didn't take a strip off Eliza about Izzy's situation. People in glass houses came immediately to my mind.

"Is she living in it now?" Lucy said, her voice choking.

Gordie said, "She is not. In fact, I am currently living in the house, but I plan to vacate within the next few months. Your grandmother has been kind enough to let me stay there since my wife died and I sold our house last year. My new condo on the waterfront will be ready soon. Then, the house will be empty."

"Will Melissa be moving to St. John's?" Lucy almost spat out her name.

"That will be up to Melissa. She will get to know the family home, and then she can decide what she wants to do." Gran nodded to Gordie. "Now get on with finishing your story."

Gordie proceeded to detail how the 100 parcels of Gran's considerable estate would be divided when she died.

"Nora has ten beneficiaries." Then he proceeded to name them— all of us around the table, plus Peter O'Brien and the Newfoundland Symphony Orchestra.

"Now, before you all get your knickers in a twist," Gran said, "Peter is getting a gift because he treated me three times in the emergency department when I fell." She looked around. "None of you knew I'd taken a spill or two, did you? That's the way I wanted it. In any event, Peter gets a gift. As for the symphony, I've taken a shine to the symphony recently. They need money. I'm giving them some."

Phillip turned to me, his face full of confusion and alarm, and I was pretty sure it had nothing to do with finding out that Gran had fallen once or twice. He whispered, "Erica, what the hell is she talking about? Peter *treated* her?"

I tried to be as quiet as I could. "It turns out Gordie isn't the only one with a secret identity. Peter's a doctor." I could see Phillip's jaw drop. "I'll tell you the details later." He just shook his head as if trying to understand the surprises that just seemed to keep coming. We both turned back to Gordie, who was talking about the division of Gran's estate.

There were ten beneficiaries and she was bequeathing an equal ten portions to each. I thought Lucy was about to faint. Even I was surprised. Gran had said her beneficiaries would all get what they deserved. I wasn't sure how each of us around the table deserved the same amount, given our different levels of engagement with Gran. Then I thought about it for a moment. The best gift-giving didn't come with strings. I remembered a quote I'd underlined and added to my list of favourite quotes a few years earlier when I'd read it in Spanish author Carlos Ruiz Zafón's book, *The Shadow of the Wind*. He said, "Presents are made for the pleasure of who gives them, not the merits of who receives them." I didn't understand this sentiment at the time. Now, I did.

Throughout all of this, Melissa Dawn Burke said nothing. It was going to be uber awkward later at the party. I could tell already.

~

The party was scheduled to begin at seven on the dot, according to Gran. After the shock of the afternoon's "family meeting," Phillip and I decided we needed at least one drink before we made our way to the event space in a building on Signal Hill that used to be the Battery Hotel. The university now owned it, but Gordie mentioned having pulled a few strings to be able to use the space for Gran's party because Gran had insisted she wanted her party to be in the Battery Hotel—despite having been told it was no longer the hotel she remembered.

I'd been in the event space years earlier when it had still been a hotel. At the time, the room had been painted bubble-gum pink, which was offset only by the spectacular views of the harbour and the city. I hoped they'd redecorated. Before I could meet Phillip in the hotel bar, though, I needed to sit down and speak to my mother. I had so many questions.

After the meeting, I sat for a while, thinking about what had just happened. I don't know how long I was there, but when I returned to the present moment, everyone else had left the room. Phillip had said he and Emma were going to walk back to the hotel together—I suspected he would tell her about Peter since she was the only other one present who hadn't heard the news of Peter's real job. Eliza had left with her father the moment the meeting concluded. I got up and walked out into the foyer, wondering if I should walk back to the hotel to clear my head. I saw Mom and Gordie with their heads together in the foyer, but I couldn't hear what they were saying. I watched as Mom kissed him lightly on the cheek the moment she saw a taxi pull up in front of the house. She walked out onto the porch and down the front steps, and I followed behind quickly, jumping into the cab beside her.

"Mom," I said as I pulled the door closed, "we need to talk."

Mom looked at me and smiled, but her smile looked tired. "Yes, I suppose we do, but I think we should include your brother. To tell you the truth, I'm too weary to have to tell the story twice." Mom was no fool. She knew what I wanted.

I immediately texted Phillip and told him to meet us both in the bar sooner than later. By the time Mom and I walked into the hotel bar ten minutes later, Phillip was already there. He was sitting at a table in the back corner. There was an open bottle of wine in an ice bucket beside him and two wine glasses on the table. He had his hand around what appeared to be a glass of scotch. The look on his face suggested he was feeling as untethered as I was.

Once we were settled and both Mom and I had taken a first sip, I started the ball rolling. "The three of us can get to a discussion about Gran's bombshell in a bit, but Mom, Phillip and I are going to have to know what the hell is going on with you and Gordie. Why didn't you tell us you knew him years ago?"

Mom took another sip and placed her glass on the table. "It's a story that predated my life with you two and your father by many years and didn't seem like a story that anyone else needed to know. It's one of those things one keeps locked inside one's heart, I suppose."

"And now Gran has outed you?" Phillip did know a thing or two about coming out.

"Okay, I suppose I can tell you a few things about my history with Gordie."

"We want the total story, not a few strategically selected things, Mom," I said.

"Let me preface my story by telling you that you two and your father were the most important things to me for all my life in Toronto. Whatever happened before then was done and gone. Do you understand?"

"What I understand, Mom, is that you had a life before you married Dad. And that's okay. We all had lives before we met our partners for life." I turned to Phillip. "Except for Phillip, of course, who's had Marcus forever." Phillip laughed.

"Fine. You win. Yes, as your grandmother so succinctly put it, we have a few family skeletons. Let me take you back to my childhood."

I knew some pieces of Mom's story from listening to her and seeing her interact with her mother over the years. But that kind of outside observation never really illuminates the whole story.

"I was an A student, but that was never good enough for my mother. I also had to play the piano well, act like a lady, and sit quietly and primly at Mass every week, where I was told how I should think. From an early age, I knew I wasn't prepared to take what others told me strictly at face value. I suppose that's why I chose to study philosophy when I went to university."

"Gran must have been pleased when you started at MUN," Phillip said. He was referring, of course, to the local university — Memorial University of Newfoundland.

"Pleased? Not when she heard what I planned to study. It was a good thing I had scholarships to pay the way. It was the 1960s, and the only thing your grandmother wanted me to acquire at university was my MRS. And she expected that husband I would take on would be Gordie."

It turned out that Mom and Gordie had known one another since early childhood, but Gordie was two years older than Mom, so they were never in the same class. When Mom started her first year at

MUN, Gordie was finishing his undergraduate degree in preparation for going off to law school at McGill University in Montreal. That last overlapping year in university was the year they realized they were more than friends. They both recognized they'd been madly in love with one another from afar since they were young teenagers, their paths crossing only once in a while. According to Mom, her first year in undergrad was one of the best years of her life.

She aced all her courses, winning awards and accolades from seemingly everyone except her parents—her mother in particular, who continued to criticize and berate her for every tiny infraction. She was able, for the most part, to ignore her mother's castigations because she was in love and was now able to spend time with Gordie. And she did. Lots of it, to hear her tell it. But at the end of the year, when Gordie was graduating, Mom didn't quite know how to handle it. He told her they'd see one another whenever they could. He hoped she'd visit him in Montreal. Most of all, he hoped she'd marry him when he finished law school in three years and settle with him in St. John's, where it was preordained that he would join his father's law firm. From Mom's perspective, life in St. John's would mean a prolongation of everything she'd had to deal with about her mother for two decades already. However, she was young and told him that she would study hard, try not to miss him too much and wait for him to return.

The final two years of Mom's undergraduate degree culminated in her having the highest aggregate average of all the graduating students that year and three scholarship offers for graduate school. Gordie came home for her graduation.

"I was so in love with him," Mom said, clearly overcome by emotion, her eyes moist and her lip quivering. "He stood there beside me as my parents proudly took photos, and Mom kept saying how nice it would be to have us set up a home near hers. She even had the audacity to tell us would let us know when the right house came on the market. She was intolerable." Mom paused for a moment before continuing. "Gordie made it official after my graduation dinner that evening. He presented me with a tiny silver domed box. I knew it couldn't be anything but an engagement ring, and I couldn't even bring myself to open the box. I realized that the last thing in the world I wanted was to live in St. John's near my mother for the rest of my life. And there was nothing else he wanted to do but stay in St. John's and practice law. It had been the only thing he ever wanted to do."

"Did Gordie consider moving away with you?"

Mom shook her head. "When I told him I wanted to take up the University of Toronto's offer to do my master's degree and suggested he could practice law in Toronto, he was distraught. He would be doing his articling with his father's firm regardless." Mom lifted her wine glass to her lips but hesitated as if she had just thought of something. "You know, kids, I was going to say that I gave him an ultimatum—either with me in Toronto or in Newfoundland by himself. But it was the other way around. He told me I could stay in Newfoundland and marry him or leave to go to graduate school in Toronto by myself. And the conversations we've been having over the past week suggest to me that he had wagered that I'd stay with him and lost." Mom cleared her throat. "Your grandmother never forgave me for turning down Gordie's proposal and leaving the island."

Phillip and I both remained silent, taking in the story we'd just heard. I was thinking once again about how little kids know about their parents. It was probably the same with Maddie. She could never really know who Andrew and I had been before we were her parents.

"About the past week, Mom," I said. "We all got the emails that said Gordie O'Brien was going to be our tour guide, so you knew about it in advance."

"I did."

"And you recognized him at the airport after all these years?" Phillip said. "Or have you seen him when you've been home to visit Gran over the years?"

"I had not seen him since 1967, but yes, there was no mistaking him even after more than fifty years."

"And he knew you were coming, didn't he?" Phillip said.

"Yes, of course. Your grandmother planned it that way. I don't know what she thought she was playing at, but it was a bit distressing, particularly when he asked me if I would play along and not tell the rest of you about the connection. For some reason, your grandmother thought it would be fun for you to believe that Gordie was a simple tour guide and not the retired Chief Justice of the Supreme Court of Newfoundland and Labrador."

"Yes," Phillip said, gesturing to the server for another scotch, "that was quite the surprise."

I sat back and thought about the situation for a moment and what my mother had decided all those years ago that set her life off in a particular direction. "Have you ever regretted your decision to turn down his proposal, Mom?"

"You know what they say. 'Of all the words of mice and men, the saddest are, It might have been.' Sad indeed."

"Kurt Vonnegut? *Cat's Cradle*, if I remember my Vonnegut phase," Phillip said. Mom nodded.

"Over the years, whenever I had the occasion to think back about my life, I felt sad and perhaps even imagined what might have been. But the truth is that I have *never* regretted my decision. It was the right one then, and it remains the right one. I think that at the moment I die, I'll be able to concur with Edith Piaf. *Je ne regrette rien.*"

"And if you'd made a different decision, Mom, Erica and I would never have been," Phillip said.

Mom smiled and extended both hands, placing one on each of our arms. "And that could never have been a good thing for the world—or for me."

As I sat there listening to Mom's story, I realized that every decision I had made in my life led me to where I was at that very moment. And I must admit, I hoped that I, too, would be able to continue to say, *Je ne regrette rien*. I regret nothing.

Phillip jolted me out of my reverie and immediately back to the present moment. "So, what now, Mom? Are you and Gordie going to pick up where you left off?"

Mom laughed. "Hardly. Neither of us is the same person we were back then. But he does still cut quite a dashing figure, don't you think?"

Phillip and I both laughed. He certainly did.

"And now, Mom, I'm concerned about you after the news that you have a half-sister," I said. We needed to talk about the Melissa situation.

"Yes, I suppose I do, don't I?" She finished her wine and offered her glass to Phillip, who refilled it for her. "I must admit to being completely taken unawares by Mom's announcement. Your Uncle Fred and I are going to have to have a bit of a heart-to-heart. But I do have to say that Mom's experience does seem to explain some of her behaviour over the years. She doted on Fred—the replacement for the son she lost, I suppose—and was so hard on me. I now realize she was trying to keep me from making the same mistake she did. I wonder if she might not have been happier if she had not lived under Dad's thumb. After he died, she seemed to have become more of an individual—just as obstinate, perhaps even more so, but independent."

I hesitated even to ask Mom this question, but it had been on my mind all afternoon. "Do you suppose Grandad ever had affairs?"

Mom laughed. "My father? I suppose if you were in need of a regular ego boost and were married to Nora Houlihan, you might well have looked elsewhere for a bit of adulation."

Our parents—and grandparents—were far more complicated than we ever gave them credit for.

~

Mom told us she was meeting Gordie before the party, so she left to get ready. We didn't ask any questions. Phillip and I stayed in the bar for one more drink before we both considered ourselves to be prepared to party with Nora and company. We were talking about Melissa—and how we had all not known how to approach her after the family summit, so didn't—and what that news meant for a family like ours that wasn't really all that close anyway when we heard a familiar voice.

"Phillip! I'm here!"

Phillip and I both looked over toward the lobby as a familiar figure made its way toward us. He was dressed in a chic pair of knife-pleated khakis, a dark navy blazer and dove grey suede driving shoes that are so impractical for anything but sitting at the wheel of a BMW convertible and tooling around Montreal. It was Marcus. I looked at Phillip. "What the hell?"

Phillip shrugged, smiled and got up, throwing his arms around Marcus. "Man, this is a surprise."

"And I do hope a very welcome one at that," Marcus said brightly. Then he looked over at me. "*Ma chère Erica, tu es ravissante, comme toujours.*" Ravishing as always? I doubted that. Then he raised my hand to his lips and kissed it. Marcus was nothing if not the most charming man I'd ever had the good luck to have known for almost thirty years. He had been a member of our family now for even longer than Andrew.

"I had no idea you were coming," I said.

"Neither did I," Phillip said.

Marcus pursed his lips as he picked up Phillip's glass and sipped it, making a face as he did so. Scotch was not his tipple. He was more of a martini kind of guy. "Well, I do hope you are both happy with the surprise. I am here to crash the party."

~

What does one wear to one's grandmother's one-hundredth birthday party when said grandmother is likely to have a less-than-complimentary remark to say about any piece of clothing? I had thought about this for some time before embarking on this family adventure, packing two potential outfits. Even now, as I left Phillip and Marcus to head upstairs to dress, I was still considering this. I was also still thinking about everything that had transpired so far today and wondered what was yet to come. As I'd heard someone local say, there was going to be a time.

Since Mom had already left with Gordie, I was alone in our shared hotel room contemplating party attire, family skeletons and the meaning of life, I suppose. I sat on the side of the bed, kicked off my shoes and pondered Mom's story.

She had made a choice back then that was so significant that it had reverberated through the years with consequences for many people's lives, not least of which was mine—and Phillip's, and my father's. My parents had always seemed happy, but I do have to say that my mother tended toward the contemplative while my father was, if not the life of the party, at least more extroverted, enjoying a party and the companionship of others much more than Mom ever did. I suppose it would be easy to conclude now that she was, if not mourning, at least contemplating the loss of the love of her life, but that would be putting too fine a point on her decision. As she said, she regretted nothing. But now what?

Now that she was here with Gordie all these decades later and both were widowed, was this going to be one of those romantic stories where the lovers reunite? Could octogenarians (Mom was not quite there yet, but soon) do long-distance relationships? Because I could not, in any reality, see my mother moving back here. But Gordie? Well, I didn't know him well enough to be able even to speculate about what he might or might not want to do.

I checked my watch and realized that I'd better decide on my ensemble soon. I groaned and thought about all the years on afternoon television when someone else chose my attire. I needed one of those stylists here now. I had brought along two choices: one red and one black. I finally settled on my black sheath dress with a draped front. It was simple yet sophisticated. As I zipped it up, I wondered for a moment what the usual local party attire would be. I guessed it was something a notch up from the kitchen party apparel. I sighed. I knew that whatever I chose would be wrong from Gran's perspective. But since it was suitable from my perspective, I was ready.

I shared a taxi with Phillip and Marcus, who were already several drinks in (I suppose I was, too) and jolly in their well-cut suits. They were both wearing impeccably subdued summer suits—Phillip in taupe and Marcus in light blue linen—but they had opted for more colourful shirts and no ties. I knew they had always had a vibrant social life in Montreal—openings at Phillip's gallery as well as other galleries, ribbon-cuttings for Marcus's new builds, charity galas, private dinners—so they possessed more than an ample supply of party clothes. And we were going to a party.

"Marcus," I said as the taxi pulled away from the hotel, "what possessed you to come? It's lovely to see you, but I'm sure Phillip told you Gran specifically mentioned that no spouses or partners were invited. She's sure to have something graceless to say about your presence."

"I know," Marcus said, smiling the cheeky smile that I recognized whenever he had a plan. "The truth is that I've been planning this ever since Phillip told me about it. I sure wasn't going to miss his grandmother's one-hundredth birthday. I've never met anyone that old, and it's my goal in life to win her over before she dies. This could be my last chance."

I rolled my eyes. As charming and lovable as Marcus was, Gran had maintained her aversion to things she didn't understand, and she most assuredly had never understood her grandson being gay. It just didn't compute in her world, no matter how much Mom had tried over the years to make her understand that Phillip being gay was no different than him being right-handed. Maybe turning a hundred changed one's perspective. I guessed we'd see.

We soon arrived at the party venue. Just as I had hoped, the room had been redecorated—no more bubble-gum pink walls—but the spectacular view of the city and the harbour was still just as breathtaking. The room was set up with round tables for dinner around the periphery, with a space left in the centre. The table in the centre of the window held a three-tier birthday cake with a giant candle proclaiming "100!" on the top. When we walked in, the corridor leading to the party venue and the room itself were already buzzing with people. Gran was holding court from a chair directly in front of the table with the cake, and there was a receiving line. She was flanked by Mom and Uncle Fred, with Lucy standing to the side, her arms folded.

The three of us made our way to the bar. I took my glass of chardonnay and wandered over to peek into the adjacent room, where an extensive buffet was set up. I could see Eliza standing at the end of the large table, talking animatedly with a woman who looked vaguely familiar. Where had I seen her before? I nudged Phillip and asked him if he knew who she was.

He peeked in. "Oh, I saw her at that kitchen party we went to a few days ago." Then he turned back to Marcus, took him by the arm and headed toward the receiving line.

Phillip was right. It was the woman—I recalled her name was Iris—who had been in precisely the same place at Mary McCarthy's kitchen party: standing beside the food. I supposed she and Eliza were talking about food. Just then, Emma came up beside me. "Where's Phillip?" she said. "I was hoping to talk with him."

Before I could say a word, I heard Gran's voice booming across the crowd. "Well, would you look here? What has the cat dragged in today?"

Then, there was some shuffling, and as I turned into the room, I could see that Phillip and Marcus were standing in front of her. I saw Marcus pick up Gran's old hand and kiss it.

"Get on with you," she said. "You look like a fart in a mitten here about."

I snorted, and a bit of wine came out of my nose. Emma looked sharply at me. "I haven't heard that one in a long time," I said.

As I walked farther into the room, I could see Marcus and Phillip saying something, and Gran started laughing. She was laughing! *Well done, Marcus,* I thought. *Well done.*

Eliza had just come out of the buffet room. "What's going on? Who is that? Is it Phillip's Marcus?" Eliza had met Marcus over the years, but it had been a while. I told her it was. "What's he doing here? We weren't supposed to bring spouses or anything like that. Why was Phillip allowed?"

I turned to her. "Did you want to bring Jake?"

"You've got to be joking," she said with more vehemence than I had expected. "At this point in time, I'd prefer not to have to go around the corner with Jacob Cohen, if you must know." After she said it, she seemed to be surprised at her own words.

"Eliza," I said carefully. "Are you and Jake having problems?" Based on my journalistic observations over the past week, I was confident I already knew the answer, but we hadn't really addressed the issue. And why should she share anything personal with me, anyway?

Eliza leaned against the wall. "To tell you the truth, Erica, and I suppose telling the truth is the theme of the day, I'm not sure I can stay married to him."

"Oh, Eliza, that's serious. How long have you thought that?"

"I'm not exactly sure when it started, but for the past year, it's been on my mind so much I'm even having trouble meeting a deadline for a new book proposal for my agent and editor." Then she brightened up. "But I think I'm on to a new idea."

Eliza pointed to the woman I'd seen her with beside the buffet table. I looked over.

"You see Iris over there? Iris Noseworthy isn't just Mary McCarthy's niece. She's a professional cook. Well, she's actually a trained chef, but when I called her that, she corrected me. And she owns a diner here in St. John's. They did the catering for this party. It's authentic Newfoundland cuisine all the way. I've just asked her if she might be interested in coauthoring a cookbook with me."

"You're going to write a cookbook about Newfoundland food?" As if I hadn't seen this coming.

She smiled. "I've been fascinated with the food we've been sampling this past week and have already accumulated a raft of recipes that I've sent on to my assistant in New York to get the supplies we'll need for recipe testing. I think we'll call it *The CFA Guide to Authentic Newfoundland Food*. What do you think?"

I thought it was brilliant.

THIRTY-TWO

Eliza

"YOU'RE THAT COOKBOOK AUTHOR FROM NEW YORK, aren't you?"

I looked up from where I was standing, examining the platters of food laid out on the buffet table. I saw Iris, the woman we'd met at the kitchen party—the one who'd known so much about the food. I had been hoping to keep a very low profile as the party progressed, and being recognized was not on my agenda. I also had yet to recover from the family meeting and all the truth-telling that was going on. But I couldn't ignore her.

"I *am* a cookbook author. How do you know?" It had been my experience that the average person rarely notices the name of the author of the cookbook she's using. Of course, I'd been in the media quite a lot over the past ten years, but it had never occurred to me that anyone here would have noticed.

"Wasn't sure about who you were when we met at Aunt Mary's, but I looked you up since. Got more than a passing interest in food myself. I own that book of yours, *A Schmear on a Bagel*, you know. Funny as hell, you are in that book with the way you write your tips and tricks. I must say I was surprised to hear you were Nora's granddaughter, not being a Catholic and all. But that's none of my business." She looked at one of the platters on the table and rearranged it so that it looked better from her angle. "Anyway, I love a bit of Jewish food. In fact, I've taken a few of those recipes of yours and given them a bit of a Newfie twist, if you know what I mean."

I wasn't sure I did. "Anything in particular?

"Oh, let me see. My customers love my Cod Gefilte Tagine. Oh, and my Jiggs Brisket is a real showstopper."

"Your customers?"

"Down to the Holloway Diner, my place on Water Street." She pulled a business card from the breast pocket of the floral shirt dress she was wearing and handed it to me.

I looked down at the card. "Iris Noseworthy, Cook and Proprietress, Holloway Diner."

"So, you're a chef."

"Not a chef," Iris said, correcting me. "Cook. I've always been a cook and will always be a cook."

"So you're self-taught?"

Iris shook her head. "Not self-taught. Learned from my grandmother and then my mother. Then, they packed me off to George Brown College in Toronto for a few years. Came back and opened the diner."

"So, you *are* trained as a chef."

"That's what it says on my George Brown diploma and the one I got myself from the American Culinary Institute in your fair city, but I've always been a cook and will always be a cook."

I was astonished. Had I not yet learned that underestimating the people around here would get me into trouble? Was I still such a snob? And her perspective was interestingly refreshing—a cook was her preferred title. An idea was beginning to take shape in my mind. "What time does your diner open tomorrow?"

"We'll be getting the breakfast ready at eight. Planning to stop by?"

"I think I will." I hesitated before blurting out a half-baked, semi-conceived idea, but what the hell? Life was taking a series of odd turns these days, or so it seemed. "Have you ever thought about writing a cookbook?"

"Just every day of my life," Iris said. "No idea how to go about it."

"You and I need to talk tomorrow, Iris. I'll be there at eight when you open."

I was about to return to the main party room when I heard Gran's voice loud and clear. Both Iris and I turned in that direction, and she followed me into the room where Erica had just snorted wine out of her nose, no doubt in response to whatever Gran was saying. Then I noticed Phillip and Marcus. Of course, Gran would be loud when she saw Phillip with his boyfriend. It was so like her. I asked Erica what Marcus was doing there, and apparently, he had arrived out of nowhere. I then told Erica more than I intended about my situation with Jake, but as far as I was concerned at that moment, secrets were not all they were cracked up to be. I looked at Iris and thought, *There's the future. Right there.*

I pushed my way through the crowd to pay my respects to Gran and her one hundred years. As I neared the line that had formed to greet her, I looked around to see if there were any familiar faces and saw Lucy standing by herself. She had her arms folded tightly across her chest, and there was a dark, haunted look on her face. There was little doubt that she had the fine art of martyrdom down to a science—all the more so since today's astounding news. In any case, I wasn't up for discussing it with her, or anyone else for that matter, and looked around to see if there was someone I could hide behind. I almost ran smack into Peter, who was standing behind me, grinning.

"I finally got away from the hospital." He looked down at my arm. "How's the arm feeling?"

"The pain pills, along with the copious amount of wine I'm planning to drink to get through this three-ring circus of a family event, should make me as mellow as I need to be. Pain will be a distant memory."

Peter gently took my other arm and pulled me out of the line. "You might want to reconsider the drinking, Eliza. Those pain meds are pretty potent."

I laughed. "I was only joking, Peter."

"Anyway, I wanted to restate my invitation to you—and Erica, of course—to come out to Topsail tomorrow afternoon to see the new house on your grandmother's old property."

I suddenly realized that my flight to New York was scheduled to leave just after noon. If I wanted time to talk to Iris in the morning—and see the house in the afternoon—I was going to have to change that. The minute I could sit down, I'd text Mary-Lou to change my flight to the following day. Texting with one bum arm was not easy and almost impossible while standing up. I knew because I'd already tried.

"Peter, I need to apologize to you for my behaviour last evening—and for making assumptions and thinking you were…"

He laughed. "An orderly? A fisherman? Anyway, I won't accept your apology, Eliza. You cannot imagine how long it's been since I've had such a good laugh. I should be thanking you." He turned toward the head table where Mary McCarthy, of all people, was helping Gran to her seat. "I see Dad was right. Nora and Mary have buried the hatchet again."

"About that," I said as he led me to a table where, oddly, my name card was beside his, "what's their story anyway?"

"Did Nora tell you the details of the story behind Melissa Burke being here?" he said. I nodded, although I was a bit surprised he knew about Melissa. "Then you know she and Mary used to go to the dances at the American military base back in the '40s during the Second World War. When Nora left town for a year," he stopped and looked at my face, "don't look at me like that. Dad filled me in. Anyway, Nora left town for a year and didn't tell Mary she was going or why. They've been having an official feud ever since. There was no one more surprised than Dad when Nora told him to take you all to Mary's kitchen party."

I shook my head. I didn't think I would ever understand the culture here.

We took our seats, and the official festivities began. I looked at the head table and saw that Melissa was seated there with Gran, Aunt Maureen and Dad. A special spot, indeed, but one I certainly didn't envy.

We began by saying grace. I held my breath as a white-haired priest, who was also at the head table, got up and introduced himself as Father John Fitzgerald. He folded his hands in prayer and closed his eyes. I did not. Then he began.

Dear lord in heaven, we are gathered here today in your name to rejoice in celebrating the remarkable life of Nora Houlihan [he was beginning to sound as if he might be practicing for her funeral], *who has reached the splendid milestone of one hundred years. You have given Nora countless blessings throughout her life, and she has blessed all those around her with her wit, wisdom and virtue.* [Virtue? Clearly, he had yet to get the memo about her early years.] *As she embarks on this bright new year, we ask for your continued inspiration and grace. We can all feel the love surrounding our dear Nora on this day of days and hope that she can continue to rely on the support and affection of both family and friends. May she continue to enjoy good health and the beauty of your earth in the days ahead. Bless this gathering, bless this woman, and bless all those who are here to celebrate with her. Amen."* [I think I gagged a little at the memory of so many Sunday mornings beside my mother in a hard pew of St. Catherine's Church in Halifax and wondered if we'd be treated to a re-run of this speech at Nora's funeral at some point in the future.]

Then, we were instructed to go to the buffet table by table. It was interminable (I cannot tell you how much I hate a buffet), but the food, as it turned out, was outstanding. My cookbook idea was beginning to look less bone-headed by the moment.

By the time we reached dessert, people began taking to the microphone and talking about Nora in terms that didn't seem to evoke the grandmother I'd known. The Nora Houlihan that I and all my cousins—and my Aunt Maureen, as it turned out—had always known and, as far as I could see, has continued to be, wasn't anything like the saint they were now describing. Gran had always been tactless, obnoxious and condescending. You could never argue with her, regardless of the topic. She was always right. The things they were saying about her being wise and full of love were the sorts of things one said about someone who has died. It had always seemed to me that when someone died, regardless of how insufferable they had been when they were alive, now laid out in a coffin or sitting as ashes in an urn, somehow turned their whole lives into something no one ever saw. I sighed and poked the delicious orange pudding that Iris had told me was a specialty of her diner by way of her mother-in-law, Marge. I would simply have to include this recipe.

The interminable speeches finally finished, so I excused myself to go to the ladies' room. As I stood in front of the mirror trying to tame my hair, a woman I thought I'd seen staring at me from a table across the room opened the door and came in. She stopped directly behind me so I could see her in the mirror. I'd noticed her earlier because she looked a bit out of place—somewhat upmarket, if you know what I mean—with her cream-coloured dress and matching jacket, her cream-coloured shoes and her cream-coloured Chanel handbag. Now, I also noticed she was wearing a heavy, expensive-looking gold necklace with a matching bracelet, and I could see a Rolex Lady-Datejust Oyster in rose gold poking out from her sleeve. How did I know what it was with such detail? Because Jake had given me one a few years earlier in a bid to get me to stop berating him for always being out at one business-related social event or another with—well, with whomever.

"Well, hello there," she said with only the faintest touch of a Newfoundland accent. Coming from her, it sounded a bit earthy and perhaps even sexy. She was a bit of a bombshell with her blonde hair and lips that might have been enhanced. It was subtle, so it was difficult to be sure.

"Hello," I said as I continued to fluff my unruly hair.

"I saw you sitting and chatting with Peter O'Brien," she said. "You two seem very chummy. May I inquire as to your interest in him?"

I put down my comb and turned to her, puzzled by her question. "My interest?"

"Yes," she said. "Your interest. Your intentions. You look like the sort of woman who would have designs on that sort of man."

Designs on that sort of man? Who said things like that? "Now, just a minute. I have no idea who you are, and to tell you the truth,

I really don't care. You don't know anything about me. And more to the point, I, and my interests, as you put them, are none of your business."

"No, you don't know who I am," she said coolly, sticking out a hand, presumably so I could shake it. "I'm Dr. Claire Barrett."

Was that supposed to mean something to me? "Am I supposed to know who you are?" I said, reaching limply for her hand, which she then gripped before letting it go. Is it possible to dislike someone mere moments after crossing her path?

"Honey, if you don't know who I am yet, I assure you that if you continue to cavort with Peter O'Brien, you soon will."

Cavort? I wasn't cavorting with anyone. If this was one of Peter's girlfriends, I wanted out of here this minute. I was reminded of that old movie *Fatal Attraction,* which conjured images of bunnies being boiled. You had to see it to believe it.

I managed to extricate myself from the bathroom and rejoin Peter, although I had second thoughts about that. I could have just left to find a seat at another table, I suppose, but that was not my style. I was more confrontational.

"Well, Peter O'Brien, I just had a close encounter in the bathroom with a crazy woman."

"That woman wouldn't happen to be clothed head to toe in cream-coloured clothing, now, would she?" I told him she was. "You have just had the unpleasant experience of meeting my ex-wife, the mother of my two grown children and an all-around bitch. And I apologize."

Peter had just begun to tell me about the nationally famous Dr. Claire Barrett, pediatric surgeon extraordinaire, whom he had married in medical school, when a commotion seemed to be breaking out in front of the head table.

Phillip and Marcus were standing in front of the birthday cake behind which Gran sat. Marcus began clinking a knife on his champagne glass. Champagne? Where was the champagne? I didn't see any at the bar.

"Ladies and gentlemen, *mesdames and messieurs*," Marcus said. "May we have your attention, please."

The rowdy guests finally seemed to notice, and the room went quiet. Marcus had taken the floor. He began by waxing poetic about how wonderful Gran was (what the hell?) before coming in for the kill. "And Phillip, her one and only grandson, and I would like to take this momentous time to make a little announcement of our own. After thirty years together, Phillip and I are getting married."

For a split second, you could have heard a pin drop. Then, the clapping started with a single pair of hands. Gran was standing behind her cake, clapping as if there were no tomorrow. "About time you made it legal, boys."

You could have knocked me over with a feather. *The arse is well out of her now, what?*

THIRTY-THREE

Erica

WHEN GRAN STOOD UP TO LEAD THE APPLAUSE, I thought the apocalypse must be nigh. My grandmother, the most narrow-minded woman I'd ever met in my entire life—and perhaps the most vocally homophobic—was applauding. Her grandson and his long-time boyfriend were getting married. Could this party get any weirder? I had no idea.

Gran shuffled out from behind the table with her walker and stood beside Phillip and Marcus, gazing around the room as if she were looking for someone in particular. She spied Gordie over by the bar and waved him over. Then she turned back to where Father Fitzgerald was sitting, having what looked like a glass of rum, and said, "You, there, Father John, you might want to make yourself scarce unless the Catholic church has come to its senses." Father John looked confused.

Gordie approached her cautiously. He knew Gran well enough to know that anything could happen.

Gran continued. "Well, everyone, I want to thank you all for doing this for me today. And now I'm going to do something for someone else." She took Gordie's arm. "I happen to know this retired judge has a notary or two working for him at that fancy law practice." Gordie nodded. "Well, get on that expensive toy you have there in your pocket and call one of them. Tell them to bring the paperwork. I'm a hundred years old and not getting any younger. I'm not going to die before I see my grandson married." She then looked around again. "Gerald? Gerald Mills?"

Hearing his name, a middle-aged man wearing what looked like the world's worst toupée hesitantly lifted his hand. Gran smiled at him.

"Come on up here, Gerald. We're going to need a marriage commissioner." She looked around once more. "Iris?"

Iris Noseworthy stepped forward, smiling. "What can I do for you, Nora, dear?"

"You can get rid of that unfortunate one-hundred sign thing on top of that cake and find me a topper that says something about these two boys." She looked at Phillip and Marcus with a look of love such as I'd never seen before in her eyes.

My god, I thought, *if Nora Houlihan can change, there's hope for all of us.*

"Now, someone, bring me a chair over here, find me a glass of that champagne, and let's listen to some music while we wait. We're going to have ourselves a wedding!"

Mom was now standing beside Gordie, looking happily confused. I wondered if she was thinking what I was thinking. Phillip and Marcus had managed to steal the limelight without stealing the show.

Just as Gran had commanded, four musicians materialized as if out of nowhere with an Irish drum, a fiddle, a guitar and an accordion. They started counting in, the drummer began the beat, and they started singing, "There's gonna be a time tonight."

Half an hour later, everything was ready. And so, with Mom and Gordie as witnesses and the rest of us cheering them on, Phillip and Marcus were married. I don't know who was happier—the grooms or their grandmother.

Oscar Wilde once wrote, "After a good dinner, one can forgive anybody, even one's own relations." After that dinner, everyone was forgiven.

WHO SAYS YOU CAN'T GO HOME?

Marge's Orange Pudding

- *1 cup flour*
- *3 tsps baking powder*
- *1/3 cup milk*
- *Pinch of salt*
- *3 tbsps shortening*
- *1 orange*
- *1 cup sugar*
- *1 ½ cups boiling water*
- *½ tbsp. of butter*

1. *Preheat oven to 325 F (160 C).*
2. *Grate the orange rind and set it aside.*
3. *Juice the orange, saving both juice and pulp. Set aside.*
4. *Sift flour, baking powder and salt together. Rub in shortening with the back of a soup spoon. Add orange juice and pulp. Mix in milk.*
5. *Place the mixture in the centre of a buttered baking dish (a square Corningware dish works well).*
6. *Add the sugar and orange rind to the boiling water. Stir until dissolved. Pour over the cake. Dot butter over.*
7. *Bake for about 35 minutes.*

THIRTY-FOUR

Eliza

As Gran stood cheering the nuptials of the two handsome grooms standing at the centre of all the attention, I thought the sky must be falling. I was, quite literally, slack-jawed. Nora Houlihan, the grandmother who told me I was going to hell when I told her I was converting to Judaism, the grandmother who I'd once overheard telling Aunt Maureen that she must have done something wrong to have given birth to "one of those kinds of boys," the grandmother who had perfected the art of the zinging insult—this was the Nora Houlihan I'd known. And here she was, not only telling me that Izzy can be forgiven, and everyone makes mistakes but applauding her grandson's marriage to the love of his life—no, leading the applause after organizing everything. All of this was a bit difficult to fathom after the shock waves she'd sent undulating through her family only hours earlier. Added onto all these astonishing events was how I felt as I sat there in my seat surrounded by all these people, looking at two people who so obviously still loved one another deeply after thirty years already spent together.

"A penny for your thoughts." Peter leaned over and whispered in my ear.

How could I tell him that instead of rejoicing for my cousin's profound joy in his relationship, I was grieving for the slow death of mine? How could I tell him that I was jealous of what they so clearly had? How could I tell him that I didn't remember feeling a deep connection to Jake, even as I said those marriage vows so many years ago, but that I thought I loved him? And how could I tell this man I'd known less than a week that despite my almost unforgivable pre-judgments, I felt more of a connection to him than I did my husband of twenty-five years? I could tell him none of this, so I said, "Just thinking about how happy they seem together."

"They do, don't they? I wish I could say I felt the same the day I married Claire."

I turned to look straight at him. "What do you mean?"

"I don't know. It seemed like the right thing to do at the time, I guess. Do you know what I mean?"

I realized I knew precisely what he meant. Perhaps we did have more in common than I thought.

~

It was almost one am before I finally crawled into bed. But before I did, I called Jake. Maybe I was feeling guilty about the way I was thinking about us. Maybe I thought if I heard his voice, I'd remember why I'd married him and spent a quarter of a century of my life with him. Maybe I'd stop doubting my reasons for my conversion. There was nothing quite like a wedding to help you wax nostalgic about your own relationship and the decisions related to it.

I called the house phone because Jake often forgot where he dropped his cell phone, and I didn't want him to have to do any more than reach for an extension in his den where he could be expected to be sucking on a drink of one sort or another. The phone rang twice, then three times, then just before the answering machine cut, it picked up.

"Jake?" I said, not hearing anyone on the other end.

"Mom?" The voice sounded slightly breathless and a bit sleepy.

"Izzy? What are you doing there? Where's your father?" She must have run to answer the phone when she heard it.

"Hi, Mom. I decided to come back before you got home. Dad hasn't been here much anyway, so we haven't been arguing, and I've managed to avoid Grandma Esther."

"Where's your father? Why didn't he pick up the phone?"

"He's not here," Izzy said bluntly.

I checked my watch. It was 11:30 in New York, and I expected him to be at home on a Sunday evening. And now that I knew Izzy was there, it seemed even more important for him to be there, although his presence clearly didn't matter to my daughter.

"Are you calling to tell us you're going to be away an extra day? Mary-Lou already told us, so Dad said he was going on an overnight business trip and would be back before you got home the day after tomorrow."

"A business trip? At the last minute—with you home alone?" I could feel the slow burn of my anger moving up the back of my neck. "Did he happen to say where he was going or for how long?"

"He was a bit vague. Boston maybe? To tell you the truth, Mom, I didn't really pay much attention or even care."

"Did he go by himself?" I knew I shouldn't have asked the question, but I couldn't help myself.

"Um, I'm not sure. I think his secretary—I think her name is Ellen or Eleanor, maybe—was in the car that came to pick him up. He mentioned calling her so that she could get his files ready. That's all he said before packing an overnight bag and leaving."

"Okay, honey. I'll see you when I get there in a few days. Text me if you need anything. Go back to bed and look after yourself." Izzy said she would since she seemed to be tired all the time and that she was looking forward to seeing me—something she had not said in a very long time. I smiled in spite of it all, then put the phone down and slid into bed and down under the covers.

I took a deep breath, and a fragile sense of eerie calm descended on me. The raw truth of what was left of Jake and me as a couple cut through the noise in my head and left a void—a nothingness. I knew I had a choice as to how I would react to the realization that I'd been right all along and that it hadn't been all me. I lay there in bed, teetering on the precipice between a knee-jerk reaction like calling his phone that very moment or biding my time so that I could prepare my response and confront him in person in a few days.

After I finally decided to let it go for now, I don't know how long I lay there in the dark, trying to see how I—we—had gotten to this point. What became of that feeling of being in love when the years have gone by, and you find that what you thought were fundamental similarities in values and goals were nothing but sandcastles now worn away by time and the pounding of the truth? Was being in love in the moment somehow different than the kind of deep, abiding love that Phillip and Marcus had? They, more than any of the rest of us, had been forced to deal with so many more obstacles to their love, and yet it survived and even flourished. That was the kind of love I wanted. That was the moment when I realized I would never be able to find it with Jake. I was only fifty and had many good years ahead of me. *Middle age be damned*, I thought, *I still have a future*. I thought of Izzy and the new role I'd be taking on. I thought of Iris and our project. And I thought of Peter—whatever that might mean.

~

The following morning, I arrived at The Holloway Diner on Water Street just as Iris was unlocking the door. To my surprise, I wasn't the first one there. Three local people who Iris clearly knew well and a couple of American tourists (I knew they were Americans because they were dressed like they were headed for an Amazonian rainforest hike and kept talking about how quaint everything was) were already forming a short line when I arrived.

Iris let us all in, and a young woman who looked like she'd just stepped out of a 1950s diner with her pale blue dress, white apron and tiny white cap approached and led me to a booth. Of course, as I looked around, I realized she didn't have to step out of anywhere or any time. She looked right at home. I was the one who looked out of place in this authentically decorated diner. Steeped in nostalgia, the space boasted a black and white checkerboard tiled floor, red vinyl banquettes, Formica countertops and a neon lighting strip that ran over the bar where red-topped stools just waited for someone to sit and order a root beer float. It somehow connected me viscerally to a bygone era when, to hear our parents tell it, things were so much simpler.

Iris's staff must have arrived early because I could already smell the inviting aroma of freshly brewed coffee. I could see the coffee pots under the drip spouts—no espresso machines here. As I sat down and ordered myself a coffee, I perused the menu Iris herself provided after telling me she'd join me once the breakfasts were well underway.

The menu was fascinating. It had an "Oceansea Omelet" made from three eggs, lobster and summer savoury. There was also something called "Aunt Mary's Toutons," which were described as Newfoundland traditional pan-fried bread dough served with molasses as well as butter and Canadian maple syrup, if you preferred that to molasses, and an optional side of homemade baked beans. I'd seen that on a couple of menus over the past week but had hesitated to try it—the idea of pan-fried bread dough seemed to clash with my New York sensibilities. But this morning, it sounded too good to pass up. I'd have that. Then I noticed the Holloway French toast—homemade bread soaked in eggs and cream, rolled in panko breadcrumbs and topped with blueberry sauce made from local blueberries. Dear god. How could I ever decide? I wondered if there was such a thing as a breakfast tasting menu. I needn't have worried, though. Iris had me covered.

After I'd savoured my first cup of coffee and perused the menus for breakfast, lunch, and dinner, which Iris thought I might enjoy, she arrived with her own mug of coffee and slid into the booth across from me. Just as she did so, one of her servers arrived carrying a tray covered with small plates. Iris had decided I should sample her wares. So, I did.

Before I knew what had happened, two hours had passed. Iris and I had bonded over our love of food, but it was more than simply loving to eat. We both loved the process of testing recipes, tweaking them and finding what worked without making them complicated. That was what struck me most. I had tried in the past to work with chefs, but I had discovered that most of them wanted to make their food seem as if it would be too out of reach for the average cook to master. That wasn't going to sell cookbooks or help anyone to enlarge their home cooking repertoire, both of which were objectives of mine. Iris and I were on the same wavelength on these matters. And then there was Iris herself.

Her Newfoundland charm and wit were contagious. She interspersed our discussion of the food and recipes with hilarious stories from her kitchen and her mother's kitchen. I knew we'd have to include them as part of the book. It was going to be brilliant.

Then, before I left, Iris said, "I hear tell the Houlihan clan has a new member." For a moment, I thought she was talking about Izzy's not-yet-born baby and wondered how she could have known. But I quickly clicked in. She was referring to Melissa. "Must have been quite a shock."

I told her that it had come as quite a surprise for everyone, most of all for Aunt Maureen and my father.

"Families are funny things," Iris said, sipping the last of her coffee. "I suppose mostly we think family is about blood, but I think you count as family the people who accept you for who you are and love you anyway. Sometimes, that blood stuff is bogus. You know what I mean?"

I did know, or I was beginning to understand. I smiled as I conjured up a mental image of Iris and my mother-in-law Esther in the same room. Iris could give that woman a run for her money.

~

I arrived back at the hotel at the exact moment Erica returned from what appeared to be a walk, judging from her walking shoes and flushed cheeks.

"I've just been for a walk around town," Erica said. "You should take an hour to see Jellybean Row." I must have looked confused.

Erica laughed. "It wasn't quite like this when we were here as kids in the summer, but St. John's is famous for its rows upon rows of houses, each painted a distinct colour of the rainbow." She whipped out her phone from a back pocket and started scrolling through photos. There they were—the famous row houses where each house was painted a different colour from the one attached to it on both sides. There were red ones next to bright yellow ones, orange ones next to bright blue ones. It was incredible.

"Why do they do that?" I said.

"Why not?"

Why not, indeed?

"Oh, by the way, Erica, I'm going to text Peter to let him know we'll be out to Topsail just after lunch. Does that work for you?"

She shook her head and told me she had a four pm flight and would be leaving for the airport at about two.

"Is everyone leaving?" Would I be left here all alone? To tell you the truth, it wasn't the worst idea I'd heard in a while.

"No, not everyone," Erica said. "I think Phillip and Marcus are staying for a few days longer to do some sightseeing in this part of the island, and Mom has decided to stay an extra week. She says it's so she can spend some time with her mother, but that is highly unlikely with Gordie here." We both laughed at that. "You go out to Topsail, Eliza. Look, in case we don't get a chance to talk before I leave, I want you to know that I've enjoyed getting to know you again on this trip. Maybe Gran had the right idea about how this would work out."

Erica and I seemed to have overcome our childhood differences. It felt good.

Erica continued. "Eliza, I want to know when Izzy has her baby. I know Maddy would love to see her. Maybe we can plan a trip to New York before the end of the year."

"I'd like that," I said as Erica, quite unexpectedly, leaned over and hugged me. I had no choice. I hugged her back. I hadn't realized until that moment how much I needed a hug.

~

When I texted Peter to tell him it would be just me, he offered to come into town to pick me up, but I told him I'd take a cab. The drive from the city to Topsail had changed dramatically since we'd spent summer holidays here. It used to be a place where city people had cottages. Now, it was connected to the city by urban sprawl, and the people who lived there commuted to the city to work—not that the commute was long as compared with cities like New York and Toronto. The taxi ride took half an hour.

As the taxi tires crunched onto the gravel driveway between Gran's main cottage (the one Peter now owned) and her second one next to it on the adjacent property, Peter emerged from the side door. I remembered it led into a small entryway—where there might have been one of those chest freezers—and then the kitchen. I got out of the taxi and looked around. The place was so much smaller than I remembered it. I guess that's what happens when you grow up.

"Hey, Eliza! Welcome to Bayswater Bungalow!" He walked across the driveway to meet me.

"So that's what you're calling it," I said as he approached. I was taken entirely by surprise when he threw his arms around me and gave me a warm hug. *Two unexpected hugs in one day*, I thought. *I wonder what I've done to deserve this.*

Peter then led me into the tiny cottage, which, like its exterior, was smaller than I remembered. Had I become so used to vast open spaces in expensive homes that I didn't remember people lived in such small spaces? The old cottage had a kitchen with a large Formica table for eating, a small living room with a stone fireplace and a bedroom that opened off the living room. There was sort of a second bedroom, but it was so small that it could hardly have been called a bedroom. It was the alcove where my parents slept on a double bed that was pushed up against a wall. Whenever we visited, Emma slept with Mom and Dad while Lucy and I slept on two bunks my grandfather had built into the alcove's closet. As I stood there remembering those summers, I couldn't recall ever thinking it was as claustrophobic as I did now, looking at it from my adult vantage point.

"Gosh, Peter," I said as I placed my large handbag on the kitchen table, "it hasn't changed much. Even most of the old furniture is still here."

"I know, right?" he said as he opened the old white refrigerator that must have been more than fifty years old and pulled out two beers. He opened them and passed me one. I must have looked at it oddly. "Glass?" I shook my head. "Let's go out onto the back deck, and I can tell you how I came to own this wonderful piece of property. Then, we can look at the construction project out back."

Since there was only one small window on the back wall of the old cottage—a design feature meant to keep out the brisk, northeasterly winds— I couldn't see what was going on outside. I took a sip of my beer. It felt wonderfully free to be drinking a beer (which I seldom drank) from a bottle (which I never did) with a man I hardly knew (something I was beginning to realize I should do more often). I followed him out the side door, and as we rounded the house into the backyard, I gasped. Where there had been nothing but an expanse of lawn reaching toward the bluff on the shore of the bay was an immense structure of wood frames and stone chimneys. I could hear some hammering, but I couldn't see anyone working. Peter told me he was doing a lot of the work himself but that he had hired a couple of local students to help him. We sat down in the two new Adirondack chairs painted bubblegum pink, and he started talking.

He began by apologizing for the colour of the chairs. "My daughter, Fiona, had a Barbie moment, and I caved." Then he told me that he had always loved this property and had told Gran that if she ever considered selling it, would she give him first refusal? Last year, she finally decided to sell it, so Peter bought it and began planning.

"It was originally supposed to be my retirement home. Actually, it was supposed to be *our* retirement home—mine and Claire's. But

Claire had other plans." He picked at the label on the beer bottle as he talked. "Claire had what she referred to as an 'indiscretion.' I called it an affair. Anyway, it was a bit of a wake-up call, and I realized how far apart we'd grown and how she didn't need or want me anymore, so I asked for a divorce."

Peter and Claire had two grown children, Fiona, who was a twenty-four-year-old ballet dancer in Toronto and Liam, his son, a twenty-two-year-old law student in Halifax.

"No aspiring doctors?" I said.

Peter shook his head. "No—much to the chagrin of their mother. It was especially hard for Fiona. Her mother thought that ballet was just something little girls did so they could wear pink tutus and get some exercise while pursuing more important things to hear her tell it. If it hadn't been for me, Fiona might never have gone to the National Ballet School after her teachers here told us she had potential. Fiona would never have been happy in any other kind of job. You should see her dance!" I could see a father's pride shining in his eyes. I had never seen that in Jake's eyes when he looked at Izzy, who *had* been headed for medical school, and it broke my heart a little.

I thought about how we all wanted certain things for our children, and despite our best efforts, they were individuals who had to do what they were supposed to do with their lives. I wondered what Izzy would ultimately do because I knew that becoming a mother wasn't going to be enough for her—at least, knowing her as I thought I did, I hoped so.

As Peter had mentioned when he had been unexpectedly called in to work at the hospital, he was supposed to be on a four-week vacation, working on his house. "Here, let's go see the house."

He took my hand as we picked our way across the construction debris and up several steps onto the main floor. As he had mentioned before, the house was inexplicably round.

"Did you know that a round house is more economical? The outside walls of a house are the most expensive part —they protect us from the elements and all—and a round house has less outside wall per inside square footage." I did not know that. "For example, a nine-hundred-square-foot round house has one hundred and six feet of exterior wall while a rectangular house the same interior size has one hundred and twenty feet of exterior walls." He walked toward the front overlooking the bay. "And the views and the acoustics—well, you can't beat a round house."

As I looked out at where the glass would soon be covering the vast curved window space, I was sold. It was breathtaking. I was familiar with the expansive view that took in the bluffs surrounding Conception Bay with Bell Island in the distance, but I had never seen it showcased quite like this.

Peter continued to tell me about where the kitchen would be, the stone fireplace in the middle of the building, the living room, dining room, three bedrooms, three bathrooms. It was so much more than a cottage. And for a fleeting moment, I could picture myself standing here in the window with a cup of coffee on a Saturday morning. As quickly as it came, it faded, and I was back in the present moment.

"You said you intended it to be your retirement home," I said. "Will you move into it now?" I meant now that he and Claire were apart.

Peter stood for a moment, looking out to the view beyond. Then he turned toward me as if he were about to say something, but he was hesitating. "Eliza, there's something I've never told you."

I could feel the hairs on the back of my neck stand on end. I wasn't sure I could handle another secret.

"Eliza, do you remember when you told me your husband was one of the Bluestone Pharma family members?" I nodded, and he continued. "Of course, as I said, I'd heard of them, but there's a lot more to the story."

I was well aware that Bluestone Pharma had been involved in several lawsuits over the past decade. One of the most recent—and most egregious offences, in my view—was related to a physician who had blown the whistle on a clinical drug study where the product they were testing turned out to have seriously harmful side effects that the company wanted to downplay. The physician had stopped the drug trial, and now Jake's company was trying to sue him for breaching his non-disclosure agreement. Peter was that physician. I was stunned.

"Peter, that must have been so difficult for you," I said when he'd finished.

"Not so much," he said. "It was the right thing to do, and now I'm the one being vilified. I just thought you should know how we're connected."

I shrugged. "I'm not connected to Jake's company, so you have nothing to worry about from me. I hope you win." He smiled. I remembered something he'd mentioned in passing. "What about those job offers you said you're mulling over? Will they play a part in your decision to live in this house?"

"They will," he said. "At least one of them will."

It was probably none of my business, but I was going to ask him anyway. "What are those offers? I presume they're not here on the island."

"You presume correctly." He took a deep breath. "One of them is in Toronto, and one is in New York."

I was the one who took a deep breath. I waited for him to tell me more—presuming he would.

"The one in New York is at Columbia University's medical school. They've offered me a teaching position in emergency medicine and head of the resident training program."

"Wow, Peter. That sounds wonderful. What about the one in Toronto?"

"I've been offered the position as head of Emergency Medicine at St. Michael's Hospital which comes with a teaching position at the University of Toronto."

It seemed like a no-brainer to me. Of course, he'd select the one in New York. "Have you made up your mind which one you'll accept?"

"You know, I think I have." He stopped and looked at me. "The New York position is enticing in so many ways, but St. Mike's in

Toronto is where my heart is. It's a big, inner-city trauma centre—world-renowned—and it would be like coming home for me. It's where I did my residency. It's my mentor who's retiring."

I felt oddly disappointed, although I had no right to be. "That will be nice for Fiona."

"Do you ever get to Toronto?" Peter asked suddenly.

I hadn't much in the past.

THIRTY-FIVE

Erica

I HADN'T HAD A CHANCE TO SEE AS MUCH OF ST. JOHN'S as I had hoped. That last morning, I was determined to take a walk up and down the hilly landscape, taking photos of the houses on what had come to be called Jellybean Row. The myriad colours of the row houses lining the streets should have been jarring, but they weren't. The colours spoke of a culture that didn't take itself too seriously, and god knows, we could all use a bit more of that in my neck of the woods. My own neighbourhood in Toronto was a collection of stately, red-brick houses. They were all different and yet the same, and together, they created a sense of earnestness and solemnity as if they were all too important to have a sense of humour. I liked the St. John's approach a lot.

I was happy to run into Eliza as I returned to the hotel so I could tell her I couldn't go to Peter's that afternoon. My flight had initially been scheduled for later in the evening, but I wanted to get home earlier to see Andrew and Maddie and try to sort out all the ideas I had for feature pieces for the show. I knew I would be returning to Newfoundland for some of them. I also wanted to have the chance to say goodbye to her.

As much as I had never been attached to the notion of extended families, I realized that Eliza and I were more alike than we had wanted to admit, and now that we'd decided to be adults about our issue, we might actually be able to be friends. And I thought she might need a friend over the next little while as her life changed. I also thought it wouldn't hurt for her to spend a bit of time alone with Peter. It had been not quite a week since they'd met, but I sensed something between them, and perhaps they deserved a chance to see where it might go—depending on what she decided to do about that obnoxious husband of hers. Not my problem.

I grabbed coffee and a muffin in the lobby and was happily jamming dirty laundry into my suitcase a bit later when Mom returned from her morning visiting with Gran and Melissa. She was oddly all smiles about her new-found relative.

"Melissa is really a lovely woman, you know, Erica. She teaches second grade and has no children of her own. She was as shocked as the rest of us when Gran told her about the house. She isn't sure what she'll do, and, in any case, she doesn't get it until your grandmother dies, which at the rate she's going could be years."

Mom then told me that she and Gordie were planning a late lunch, and she'd be checking out of the hotel, too.

"Planning to stay with Gordie? Or should I say Terrance?" I said wickedly.

Mom made a face at me. "I think it's only sensible I stay in my mother's old house over the next week. Remember, I used to live there, too. Gordie just happens to be living there while his condo is being renovated, as you know."

"So innocent, Mom," I said, folding another pair of jeans and trying to jam it into a packing cube. "Anyway, I'm meeting Phillip and Marcus for a quick lunch before I leave for the airport. You planning to drop by and say goodbye?"

Mom said she would.

Phillip and Marcus were already in the dining room when I arrived a bit later. They had ordered champagne and were toasting themselves—no surprise there. After all, the day after a wedding is as good a time for celebration as any.

"I see you two are still celebrating," I said as I nudged one of two empty glasses that were set out on the table toward the ice bucket. I wondered who the remaining glass was for.

"So much to celebrate, don't you think?" Marcus said as he filled my glass.

"After all, sis, we have a new relative. You and Eliza seem to have buried whatever hatchet you had. Mom and Gran are on speaking terms. We just got married, and I have a new artist whose work will be my New Year's gallery opening."

I raised my glass. "New artist?"

Just then, Emma sat down in the remaining chair, smiling from ear to ear. And all the tète-a-tètes I'd seen between Phillip and Emma clicked into place. Emma was an artist whose work, I seemed to recall, was reminiscent of that other oddly well-known Maritime folk artist, Maude Lewis, with a bit of Bernard Bowles sprinkled in for good measure. It was kitschy, if nothing else. Phillip was a gallery owner, always on the lookout for new talent, and it seemed that this kind of whimsical artwork had a market. It was a match made in heaven—or at least, Newfoundland. Perhaps the same thing.

We ordered lunch and another bottle of champagne, although I had to keep an eye on the time. A few glasses of champagne could result in a missed flight if I weren't careful. We talked about the trip and how odd all of this had been. Then we started on the subject of our grandmother.

"How much longer do you suppose she'll live?" Emma said. "I mean, after all, she is over a hundred now."

"I've read that anyone who reaches a hundred is likely to die within four years," I said. Of course, being a journalist meant I had a habit of researching things to death. I also read somewhere that each year a person lives pushes their life expectancy even further.

"I'm not sure I want to live to be a hundred," Emma said, sipping on her second glass of champagne.

"Maybe you should eat a bit of animal fat, then." Phillip couldn't help himself. "Or at least some more fish!"

Emma made a face at him. "Not funny, Phillip. A slip. That's all. Being vegan isn't about eating or not eating animal fat or living longer. It's about values."

"My ass," Phillip said. "Anyway, even if you don't live longer, it will seem longer—a lot longer. Just think of all the wonderful taste experiences you're missing. Just remember that fish and chips, Emma."

Emma sighed again. "I know my diet's restrictive," she said. "And if I thought I was really doing something for the planet..."

I patted her on the back. "You do you, Emma. But you might want to reconsider that boyfriend of yours."

Phillip looked at Emma. "Sorry to rag you about it, Emma. But remember what Ms. Frizzle said."

"*The Magic School Bus*, again, Phillip?" she said.

He nodded. "'Looks can be deceiving, Emma. Oftentimes, what is isn't, and what isn't is.'"

"A good one, Phillip," I said. "I have another one. 'If you don't look, you'll never see. And what you don't see can be very hard to find.'" Advice I needed to take myself.

~

When I stepped off the plane at Pearson International Airport in Toronto later that afternoon, I gained back the hour and a half I'd lost heading to the one place in the world whose time zone is a half-hour off from everywhere else, and I felt different than when I'd left. Was that just over a week ago? It seemed like it had been so much longer—and there was so much I wanted to discuss with Andrew. After Andrew, there was a lot I had to discuss with Sam, my producer. I had so many new story ideas—women and families, women and cooking, women and their gay brothers, women and their mothers and grandmothers. The list was endless for a show dedicated to finding the pulse of women in society in the twenty-first century.

I took a limo into the city (no one in their right mind asks family members to brave the traffic on the Gardiner Expressway just to do an airport pickup). When I alighted on the edge of the sidewalk in front of our house, I felt like I'd been gone for months. Everything seemed to look just slightly different. But I suspected it was me. I was different. I'd been to the edge of the world—this coming from a woman who had reported from war zones halfway across the globe. And yet, Newfoundland seemed to have affected me so much more profoundly. I just didn't know how yet.

Andrew and Maddie were full of questions and all ears when I filled them in on the details of Gran's news, her party and Phillip's wedding. I didn't quite know what to say about the tour itself, where Phillip and I had devolved into our childhood selves, renewed our bickering, and enjoyed ourselves immensely. The only thing different now seemed to be the amount of liquor the two of us could consume. Maddie, however, was fixated on two things.

"Is that what someone a hundred years old looks like?" She said when I turned on the television and played my photos on it. She got up from her seat on the sofa in the family room to stand so close she could probably see the hairs in the noses of everyone in the picture. "I mean, Mom, she looks old, but she doesn't look that much older than Grama." She, of course, was referring to my mother. "Or even you."

"Me? I'm half her age." Well, I was just a bit more than half her age. That last comment was a low blow coming from a loving daughter, but it appeared that kids her age had absolutely no idea what "old" looked like. I moved on.

The second thing Maddie was fixated on was the photos of her uncle Phillip's wedding. "Mom, I cannot believe I missed it. Why did it have to be there? Why couldn't they have gotten married in Montreal so I could be there?"

I explained to her that it was Nora's doing, it happened spontaneously and that no one even tried to dissuade her from hosting the nuptials. "I'm sure your Uncle Phillip will make it up to you by inviting you to a gallery opening soon." I was hoping for invitations for the three of us to go to Montreal for Emma's opening later in the year, and I fully intended to make my wishes known to my brother.

~

After a week or so, things at home settled down, and I was back at work preparing for our fall season on *The Pulse*. Sam, my best friend, wanted to hear all the gory family details. Sam, my producer, was intrigued by my story ideas. It was a good thing those two items meshed. Still, she wanted to send one of our researchers on a tour of Newfoundland before we decided which stories to feature and whether we'd do a special series. I was gunning for a special series.

A few weeks later, Sam told me that based on my recommendation, she'd called Eliza and had invited her to be on the show as a special guest.

"She says she'll have a new book out next year and that it's inspired by the East Coast idea she came up with on this trip you were both on," Sam said when we talked about it. "Doesn't it take longer than that to work out recipes and produce a cookbook?"

"Sam, you really have to know my cousin. No matter what else is going on in her life—and believe me, there are lots of other things—she is driven, focused and more than a little ambitious. If she says her publisher can get it out next year, then she'll have the material to them by the deadline."

"Anyway," Sam said, "Eliza suggested we wait until later next spring when the new book is closer to publication. She said she'd be delighted to come to Toronto to be on the show."

I would look forward to that, but I hoped we might continue to renew our relationship before that time. I'd had a couple of brief text conversations with Eliza since we'd been home. I especially wanted to know how things went with Peter during her visit to Topsail. She told me he was planning on taking a new job here in Toronto (I was delighted at the news since I really liked him), so it was no surprise Eliza was only too happy to come to the centre of the universe where Peter would be by then. Of course, Izzy was now only a month or more away from giving birth, so there was going to be a new grandchild to consider in the short term. She hadn't said much about Jake—and I didn't feel comfortable asking about such a serious personal matter—but I figured that when she got that particular situation sorted out, she'd be in touch. The bottom line was that I was delighted she was going to be on the show in due course, and I rolled my eyes when I thought of how many years I'd resisted any suggestion that Eliza Houlihan Cohen, cookbook author extraordinaire, be a guest on my current or previous show. Perhaps it would have been too soon. Maybe the time was finally right.

Late on a Saturday afternoon in the middle of October, Eliza called. I was pleasantly surprised to see her come up on the caller ID screen.

"It's a girl, Erica. I have a granddaughter!"

Can you hear tears of joy? Do they make a sound? I think so, and I'm sure I heard them. Eliza was a grandmother. Izzy was fine, and the arguments about what to name the little one had already begun.

"It seems that my mother-in-law has had a change of heart on the morality front. She has embraced her great-granddaughter far more than Izzy would like." I suspected it was far more than Eliza wanted, too, but I didn't say anything while she continued to tell me the story. "Esther wants Izzy to name the baby Ruth, but Izzy is having none of that. Too outmoded. Too plain. Too icky, I believe she said. But most surprising to me was that she told her grandmother that the name was too Jewish. I thought Esther was going to faint dead on the floor."

"Were you hoping for that just a little?" I couldn't resist it. I knew how Eliza felt about her mother-in-law. I'd met the woman, and I couldn't blame Eliza for feeling that way.

Eliza laughed. "Maybe a little. The issue now is that Izzy is talking about changing her last name to Houlihan and naming the baby Mary-Catherine. It seems I might have oversold the Newfoundland thing. Izzy is dying to visit her great-grandmother and take the baby to meet her great-great-grandmother before she dies. She came up with the name by researching the most common names in Newfoundland cemeteries. Bizarre, isn't it?"

"What did Esther say when she heard the name Mary-Catherine?"

"The less said about that, the better, I think," Eliza said dryly.

"And the Houlihan thing. I don't quite understand."

"Izzy has a notion she wants to convert to Catholicism. To tell you the truth, Erica, I'm not even sure that's possible. And the Houlihan thing, as you put it—I don't know how she came to think about her Jewish heritage this way, but I'm going to send her to Rabbi Eli, the one I liked so much, to see if he can help her. He helped me recently to the point where I'm now peaceful with my chosen path even if I'm not so much at peace with all aspects of my life."

Eliza then took a deep breath and told me that she could now focus her non-cookbook-writing time on the Jake situation, as she put it. She waited until little Mary-Catherine had made her appearance. "Time to bite the biscuit, as it were."

~

I got back to work, and before I knew it, the calendar told me it was December. It was time to begin planning for the family Christmas. Mom had asked Gordie to come to Toronto for Christmas, so we could count on them for Christmas dinner, at least. I had begged Phillip and Marcus to give up their traditional Christmas Caribbean cruise and join us. They had reluctantly agreed, but I detected a tone of jollity as they did so.

Since his father was coming and his daughter, Fiona, was stuck in Toronto with the National Ballet for the "Nutcracker" season, I also invited Peter, who would not be relocating to the city until March. He said he'd love to but would have to take a raincheck. He had volunteered to work over the holidays, and he'd be just "grand," as he put it. His house was now almost finished, and his son, Liam, was home for the holidays. I felt strongly that Fiona might want to have a family-type Christmas, so I asked Peter to tell her about us. When I called to invite her, she was delighted to accept an invitation to a family Christmas dinner, even if the family wasn't hers. The company had only one day off from performances, so there was no way she could travel to be with her Newfoundland family.

I had also invited Eliza, who had finally told Jake that he wasn't a part of her future, as well as Izzy and little Mary-Catherine. However, Uncle Fred had invited them all to visit him in Halifax. They were having a kind of mini family reunion over the holidays. Then, for New Year's, we were all going to Montreal for Emma's gallery opening. Andrew, Maddie and I were so excited.

On December 21 at two o'clock in the afternoon, Maddie and I were in the kitchen with the Christmas music blasting from the speakers, singing "I'll be Home for Christmas." I had just rolled out the shortbread for cookies—a very un-Erica-like activity—using one of Eliza's recipes, and Maddie was standing at the ready with the cookie cutters. Andrew came into the kitchen, waving his arms as he tried to get our attention over the music and the baking.

"Erica! It's your mother."

"What about my mother? Is she here?"

"She's on the phone. I think you had better talk to her."

I stopped the rolling and wiped the flour on my hands on the apron I was uncharacteristically wearing. "Is it bad news?"

"Maybe," he said. "Maybe not."

THIRTY-SIX

Eliza

I HAD DITCHED GRAN'S ECONOMY RETURN TICKET home from Newfoundland and booked myself a business class ticket to LaGuardia. I was perturbed that I'd have an hour and a half layover in Montreal, but it was the only way to do it. There were no non-stop flights between the two destinations. The whole thing took me six hours, including a half-hour delay in Montreal, so when the taxi dropped me off at home around six-thirty that evening, I was bone tired. I suspected that the tiredness was at least partly in anticipation of what I would face.

As I was about to put my key in the lock, the door opened, and Izzy threw herself into my arms. I was stunned. This behaviour was so unlike what I might have expected of my recalcitrant daughter — or at least the one I'd known pre-California and pre-pregnancy. We spent the next hour just sitting on the sofa in the living room, catching up. Jake still wasn't home from work. Hardly surprising.

Izzy and I were in the kitchen sitting on the banquette, finishing the dinner our housekeeper Marina had left in the oven for us when Jake walked in.

"Well," he said. "Look what the cat dragged in."

I was incensed. How could he possibly be the one saying that? "A nice welcome home might be in order," I said evenly, trying mightily to keep my temper. This was not Izzy's fight. And it seemed she knew it wasn't. She excused herself and said she'd be upstairs doing some online baby shopping.

It had only been a few hours, but it seemed like days since I'd landed back in New York, and I'd felt peculiar ever since. I seemed to have a nagging feeling that I was missing something—that I had left something behind. Was it that damned Newfoundland with its inexplicable pull? Or something else? A piece of me, perhaps? Whatever it was, I wasn't sure I had it in me to have it out with Jake that evening. And yet, it seemed that if I didn't confront what I knew to be true and what I knew he would lie about right at that moment, we might well fall into the trap of silent détente. That was not what I wanted.

"I understand you went on a business trip this week. I thought you might have mentioned it, given that our daughter is here and needs us."

"Marina was here," he said as he casually opened the fridge to look inside. "Izzy's a big girl now. Just look at her." He seemed to find this funny.

"Yes, she certainly has grown up, Jake. Can we say the same about her father?"

He turned abruptly and slammed the fridge door closed. "What's that supposed to mean?"

"Did you and Eleanor have a good time in Boston?"

"Boston? What? Yes, I had a good time, but what makes you think Eleanor was with me?" At least he didn't deny it outright.

"Just stop it, Jake. I know you went somewhere with her, and at some point, I'm going to want to know how long this has been going on. And how many there might have been before her." I held up my hand to stop him from interrupting me. "But right now, I'm tired and want to unpack and take a bath. Then I'm going to have a glass of scotch. I hope you'll find the guest room to your liking."

It was several weeks later, after letting him stew for a while (I knew he wouldn't bring up the subject on his own), while Izzy was visiting her friend, Astrid, that I told Jake it was over. We were over. He had the gall to tell me that it was impossible. We could never be over—the house, the business, the family, Izzy. I told him that he could consider his options until our grandchild was born. Then we'd talk again. For the next six weeks, we were polite housemates.

Izzy went into labour in the middle of the night. Jake was away on another "business trip," and I was just as happy about that. I was good in a crisis. I stayed with Izzy for the next twelve hours until my wee granddaughter emerged into the world—a cherub with masses of dark hair. As I sat beside Izzy who was falling asleep, holding this tiny new life in my arms, I looked down at her and said, "Hello, little one. I'm your grandmother." There, I'd said the word out loud, and the sky didn't fall. It felt, if not exactly comfortable yet, it felt right. And I thought about new beginnings.

~

The first battle on the family front was what to name her. As far as I was concerned, it was Izzy's right and her right alone to decide what to call her daughter. But the day Esther had insisted on visiting, Izzy announced the child would be called Mary-Catherine. Not Ruth, as Esther had suggested. I really thought Esther was going to have a heart attack as she clutched dramatically at the three strands of pearls that lay on the yellow cashmere of the twin set she was wearing. But that was only the beginning.

When Izzy further announced she was questioning her Jewish identity and was considering changing her last name to Houlihan, even I thought she might be making rash choices.

"Mom," Izzy said one evening after making this ludicrous announcement, "I'm not joking about the name change thing."

"I never thought you were joking, Izzy, but I did think perhaps you hadn't thought this through." I was saying this as much for my own benefit as hers. I, too, had been harbouring thoughts about my identity, but I felt I had a stronger foundation for wavering since I'd already made a change. I had a lunch meeting with Eli, my rabbi, the following day. He had helped me before and I hoped he could help me again.

"And another thing, Mom. I hope you'll back me on this because I'm going to need all the help I can get." She seemed to be gathering her courage. "I want to go to medical school. I think I can make it happen—I only deferred my acceptance. But I know it's going to be hard with a baby. I'm going to need you."

On the one hand, I was stunned because this seemed to come out of nowhere. On the other hand, it seemed like a natural progression. I'd always known my daughter wasn't born to make motherhood the only thing in her life. I only hoped Jake would be as supportive as I intended to be.

Ah, yes, Jake. After the six-week cooling-off period, we finally did have that knock-down-drag-out session that had been bubbling to the surface since my return from Newfoundland. The upshot of it had been that he moved out and back into his parents' enormous house. To say he was furious would be an understatement. And I did have to endure a tongue-lashing from Esther—at least, I endured part of it. I hung up after she called me a gold-digging harlot. Then, I hired a nanny for little Mary-Catherine as Izzy began preparing to return to school (I wasn't sure how that was going to happen, but we'd get there eventually), and I worked on the new recipes. Jake and I were still miles from a final divorce, but I, at least, was working on it.

Mary-Lou helped me hire two new interns to help with the recipe testing, so when Iris arrived from Newfoundland in late November, we were in full swing. Iris's eyes nearly popped out of her head when she saw the kitchen—swaths of gleaming stone countertops, masses of hanging copper pots, both an induction and a gas cooktop and four wall ovens, not to mention two industrial-sized refrigerators. But she didn't spend much time gasping over it. Instead, she rolled up her sleeves, pulled four new recipes from her handbag and asked where she could be of the most help. After kitchen hours, the two of us holed up in my office with a bottle of wine and pored over the writing.

Iris stayed in my guest room in New York for three weeks, and by the time she was getting ready to leave a few days before

Christmas, she and I were fast friends. On top of that, we'd managed to find a way to work together, which was a new thing for me since I have never played well with others.

Iris was scheduled to fly home on December 21, just in time to get ready for her own family's Christmas celebration. She'd told me all about the Newfoundland traditions like Tibb's Eve Tipples that she was hosting on December 23, a festivity I'd never heard of before. Then she told me she'd bring me a bottle of Purity syrup when she came back in March, and I remembered Gran having that syrupy stuff around even in the summer.

"Wouldn't be Christmas without it, love," she said. "And my daughter's made the Christmas fruit cakes this year while I was here in the Big Apple." She rolled her eyes. "We'll probably be able to play street hockey with the pieces of her cake, so like a hockey puck they are."

I laughed. In fact, I'd laughed more since Iris had arrived than I had in a very long time. All this talk about Christmas made me wonder how Peter was. We'd had a few texts back and forth, but that was about all. It had all been like a brief dream. I tried to remember what Izzy's favourite Dr. Seuss book said about that. Then, I remembered. "Don't cry because it's over. Smile because it happened." I smiled.

Izzy was packing for our flight to Halifax. We were leaving the following day to spend Christmas with Dad and my sisters. Iris was getting ready to go to the airport an hour later when the house phone rang. Marina came out of the kitchen.

"Mrs. Cohen," she said. "It's your father on the phone. He needs to speak with you."

~

When I hung up the phone, I thudded heavily into one of the chairs in the foyer where Marina had picked up the phone. Izzy was coming down the stairs with little Mary-Catherine on her hip.

"Mom? What's the matter? You look like you've seen a ghost. Your face is so white."

Before I said anything, I wanted to be sure I'd heard Dad correctly.

"Eliza," he had begun. "It's about Mother—your grandmother, Nora. She's dead."

I suppose that call had to come sooner or later, so I'd been ready for it. But it was what Dad said next that I was stuck on.

"I'm sorry about this, Eliza. But there's been a slight change of pre-Christmas plans. The funeral is the day after tomorrow." Then, the zinger. "We're all expected to attend."

I couldn't understand who would be expecting us to go to Newfoundland two days before Christmas—and Hanukkah, which happened to begin on the same day as Christmas this year—for a funeral. According to Dad, Nora had made something she called her "death list." Other people had bucket lists, but I suppose that doesn't make sense when you're a hundred years old. On her "death list" were four things: funeral, flowers, food, and family. I asked him if the funeral couldn't be delayed until the week after Christmas, and he said the arrangements were already complete. He had booked himself a ticket to the island for early the next day and suggested we do the same. He told me he knew it would be inconvenient, but if we could work it out, we could all fly to Halifax from St. John's on Christmas Eve and still salvage the family Christmas—and Hanukkah.

Now that I had my conversation sorted in my mind, I looked up at Izzy. "Pack a warmer coat. We're making a detour to Newfoundland."

THIRTY-SEVEN

Erica

"YOUR GRANDMOTHER IS DEAD," Mom said bluntly. She must have told Andrew why she was calling if he'd deemed the news possibly good, possibly bad. I had to agree with him.

So, I said what people always say when someone dies. "What happened?" And the moment the words left my lips, I realized how utterly stupid they were.

"What happened? Don't be daft, Erica. What happened is that your grandmother was over a hundred, and she died. Is there any need for anything else to have happened?"

Mom sounded testier than I thought she'd be at the prospect of Nora Houlihan's demise. Then I realized that our trip this past summer had reconnected her to her roots in a way I'd never thought possible. She had even reconnected with Gordie, who had held such a place in her heart for six decades. Then she told me the rest of the story, and her testiness took on a whole new meaning.

"Even in death, the woman still wants to control everything, Erica. Our Christmas plans are all a bit upended. We're expected to fly to Newfoundland for a funeral that's scheduled for the day after tomorrow."

"What?" I was horrified at the thought. Yes, we could all fly back on Christmas Eve, but that would mean I'd have to cancel our Christmas Eve wassail party for the neighbours, and the turkey might never get thawed for Christmas dinner. It was impossible.

"We can't go, Mom. We can have the funeral next week." Then I remembered that we were all going to Montreal, and the annoyance continued to build.

"We have to go, Erica. It's all arranged. I'll book tickets for both Gordie and myself as soon as I get off the phone with you, and I recommend you do the same. God, I cannot believe he just got here and has to turn around and go back. Anyway, I'm going to try to get seats on the first flight in the morning. If I remember correctly, it's at eight. Can you all get up early enough to meet us there? I know all this is a bit of a nightmare, and as if that's not enough, there is one other thing." I was all ears. "It turns out there was one element of your grandmother's will that even Gordie didn't know about. It was a codicil that she had prepared by one of Gordie's junior lawyers to be opened in the event of her death. Anyone on the beneficiary list who doesn't show up for her funeral forfeits their inheritance."

Dear god, I thought. *Does this all have to come down to money?* As I considered all the elements, I realized how sad it truly was that Nora believed she had to blackmail her family into coming to her funeral. We would all have gone, but two days before Christmas? It was a bit too much to expect. Then, the more I thought about it, the more I realized I was being unreasonable. It was only a couple of days, and we could be home on December 24. And it was only a Christmas celebration we could have on Boxing Day if we had to—everyone except Peter's daughter, Fiona, who would be performing that day.

So, Andrew, Maddie and I booked our tickets and were at the airport at six am the following morning for an eight am flight to St. John's. When we arrived at the departure gate, Mom and Gordie were already there, complaining about the chaos of pre-Christmas travel. You just had to look around at the morass of humanity, dragging every manner of box and bag onto planes along with crabby, bleary-eyed children to make a fervent promise to yourself never to travel at Christmas again. Then, of course, the flight was late. And there was de-icing. We finally straggled into the airport in

St. John's at two-thirty that afternoon. Gordie had called ahead, and Peter was waiting to drive us into the city.

"We'll never all fit into your car," I said to Peter as our boots crunched along in the thin layer of newly fallen snow on the sidewalks as we headed toward the parking lot.

His eyes twinkled in that way he had. "Oh, I think we can manage it." And he led us directly to the SUV—the bus—we'd used last summer.

Maddie was beyond excited, although she had noted several times that it felt strange to be so excited about going to a funeral. Of course, it was the whirlwind trip to Newfoundland that had captivated her. She clambered up into the vehicle. "Is this what you guys used to drive around in last summer?" When we told her that, yes, it was, she was even more excited.

Andrew was his usual calm, sensible self. He had taken the hasty trip planning in stride, booking tickets, arranging the limo to the airport, and packing for two nights in wintery St. John's. I have always loved his clear-headed approach to getting things done. In fact, it was only one of the things I loved about my husband of twenty-one years. But that would have to wait. We had other things begging for our immediate attention. One of them was Mom.

Mom had seemed remarkably subdued sitting in the airport departure lounge earlier with Gordie, who had only arrived three days earlier. Now, he was turning around and unexpectedly heading home. Then, since we hadn't been sitting near her on the plane, I couldn't tell how she had been feeling. Now, as we all trundled into the bus (I still thought of it as our magic school bus), she seemed especially morose. As Gordie slipped into the seat beside Peter, who was driving, Maddie took up the seat directly behind him with Andrew next to her. That left Mom and me together at the back.

"Mom," I said, squeezing her gloved hand as Peter maneuvered our bus from its parking space, out of the lot and onto the highway heading for the city. "How are you doing?"

I suppose that since Mom and Gran hadn't always seen eye to eye, to put it mildly, I think I had expected Mom to be somewhat more pragmatic about the death of her centenarian mother. Perhaps I was being too glib about it. After all, Nora Houlihan had still been Maureen Houlihan Flanagan's mother for almost eighty years.

"You know, Erica, I didn't expect Mom's death to hit me quite the way it did, and if you ask me to explain it, I'm not sure I can."

I kept holding her hand—leather glove to leather glove. I wondered if, in the midst of grieving the loss of her mother, she might also be experiencing a sense of relief or freedom from a relationship that wasn't wholly fulfilling.

"I suppose I'm thinking about my relationship with my mother as it developed over the years—both before and after I left home. I have memories spinning around in my head like a blender gone wild, and I can't seem to get them to stop." Mom hesitated for a moment. "It might also have something to do with one other thing Mom's codicil decreed." She squeezed my hand. "I'm expected to deliver the eulogy."

I took a sharp intake of breath. It hadn't occurred to me that Mom would be the one eulogizing Nora. I had fully expected that task to fall to Uncle Fred. After all, he seemed to have had a much less complicated relationship with their mother. But I suppose Nora had other ideas.

"It's just like her, you know," Mom said. "She always did like to put me on the spot. She even wanted to make sure she had the last word. It's infuriating."

"But you'll do it, won't you?"

Mom sighed. "I can do no less for my mother," she said. "I remember reading something in a John Steinbeck novel years ago. I think it was in the book *East of Eden*. It said, 'Perhaps it takes courage to raise children.' At least Mom had the courage."

~

Peter dropped Andrew, Maddie, and me off at the Hotel Newfoundland, where we'd stayed last summer and where most of the rest of the family would be staying. Then he took Mom and Gordie back to Gran's old house, where Gordie was still living. Geez, it seemed to be taking a long time for that condo to be renovated, but what did I know about condo renovations in St. John's?

The funeral was scheduled for one-thirty the following afternoon, but we were expected to attend the funeral home that evening for what Mom had called "visitation." It sounded medieval to me, but at least Gran had already been cremated, so we'd only have her urn and some photos to visit instead of the ghastly spectre of the open casket showcasing the waxed, primped and buffed remains of a previously animated body.

When I said that to Mom, she assured me that the people who were likely to attend would be there to "visit" with us and would not be expecting to examine the remains. However, we would have to endure several hours of people saying inane things like, "Sorry for your loss," "She's gone to a better place," and "At least she made it to a hundred." Well, that last one was at least true.

Maddie was a bit disappointed to hear that Gran had already been cremated because, as she said, "I've never seen a dead body." And I hoped she could keep it that way for a long time.

After a quick dinner in the hotel dining room—Phillip and Marcus had arrived just in time for a quick bite—we met Eliza, Emma and Uncle Fred in the lobby and called a couple of taxis. Maddie was disappointed not to have met little Mary-Catherine yet, but Eliza said she and Izzy had agreed that a funeral home was no place to take a baby. I think Izzy was the lucky one in that round.

As the taxis pulled up in front of the hotel under its awning, Phillip took my hand and pressed something into it. "Just a little something to get us through the event." Marcus looked over conspiratorially.

Then he moved on and pressed something into Eliza's gloved hand. We both looked down at our hands at the same time, then looked up with inappropriate, goofy smiles. He had given each of us a tiny plastic bag containing two gummies. Mine were red. Things were looking up.

It was snowing very lightly as the taxi maneuvered through the streets toward the funeral home. There were few cars on the roads, and I didn't blame them. There wasn't a lot of snow on the ground, but the hilly terrain of the city made for slick driving conditions. I felt the tires slip a few times before we alighted in front of the funeral home.

The building looked like it had been recently refurbished, with its modern glass entrance flanked by stonework and rich wood panels. The only word I could think of as I walked inside was that the place looked solemn. Funeral homes seemed to have their own specific décor type. Interior designers seemed to put it up there with art deco, contemporary, art nouveau and modern country, except this style would be called "elegant mourning."

The furniture was a tribute to the durability of polyester, with brown couches and enormous armchairs that had clearly been upholstered with a view to weathering many future tears and, more likely, awkward family moments. A superbly earnest and formal young woman with dark blonde hair scraped back into a bun at the nape of her neck, befittingly attired in black from head to toe, showed us to the "visitation" room. As we walked by the entrance to the room next door, she gestured to the tables laden with plates of food and told us our visitors could obtain some sustenance there.

"I hope there's liquor," Phillip whispered as we walked by.

Marcus leaned over and said, "I'd kill for a martini about now."

I slid my hand into my handbag where I'd secreted the tiny plastic bag and maneuvered it open. As my finger touched the jelly-like candies, I looked at Maddie and thought, *What kind of mother pops a CBD gummy—at least I thought it was only CBD—with her daughter present?* Then I looked at Andrew, who was the picture of the perfect, sensible husband and father and thought, *Frig it. Maddie has one sensible parent this evening.* I surreptitiously popped a gummy into my mouth.

Once inside the "visitation" room, I looked around and saw that Gran's blue ceramic urn was set up on a table at the end, flanked by two photos of her. One seemed to have been taken about twenty years earlier, making her about eighty at the time. The other one was of her with my grandfather on her wedding day in 1943. She looked so young. Then there were the flowers, another of the elements on Gran's "death list."

Towering sprays of lilies and roses, free-standing wreaths covered with masses of white roses and assorted other "funeral arrangements" all seemed a bit overpowering in such a small space. And I have to admit that the smell of lilies has always made me gag just a little. I cleared my throat and the black-clad mortician (yes, she did look a bit like Morticia of *Addams Family* fame) directed us to where we would stand to form a receiving line. Receiving line? Could this get any worse? Mom was rolling her eyes already, while Maddie suggested she was still hungry and went off with Marcus in search of food. And then they began arriving.

For the next few hours, streams of mourners arrived, saying all of the inane things I'd hoped might not emanate from anyone's lips and a few more. It seemed that people were constitutionally unable to say the word "died." She went to a better place, or, even better, she's gone to the angels. (That one reminded me of once when I was visiting, and Gran had a friend over. The friend happened to mention that someone had "gone to the angels." Gran snorted and said, "Her? Gone to the angels? The Angel Gabriel will have his work cut out for him, what? He'll have to blow a lot louder for that one to hear from where she'll be settling.") Then there were the ones who said, "Now that Nora has passed…" It was all I could do to stop myself from saying, "Passed what? Gas? A kidney stone?" But I just smiled, perhaps stifling a giggle or two since I was feeling rather mellow by that point, and nodded and thanked them for their kind wishes.

After the first hour, I was beginning to regret my footwear selection. I had first considered wearing flat-soled riding-style boots with my black dress, but I had succumbed to the thought that I'd look so much more sophisticated if I wore heels, so I dragged along the only pair of boots I had with a three-inch heel—a mistake for sure. I must have been wincing because Mom leaned over and said, "I think you've done your duty, Erica. Why don't you go find Maddie and have a bite to eat?" I leaned over and kissed her cheek, then fled.

I found Maddie and Andrew in the "reception lounge," as Morticia had called it, sitting at a table munching on nachos and dip. The place was packed.

Andrew looked up, brushing crumbs away with a paper napkin. "You seem a lot more chill than I thought you'd be."

"Remember, I'm a professional, darling husband. I can chill with the best of them." He just shrugged and went back to his conversation with our daughter.

I looked around and saw Marcus across the room, deep in conversation with a middle-aged man who was wearing a black puffer jacket and a black baseball cap—no doubt his funeral home cap—and waved. I could see that he was holding, of all things, a beer.

"Where did Marcus get the beer?" I asked, looking around. I didn't see anything that remotely resembled a bar.

"Oh," Andrew said, "it's quite an education here. One of the boys over there has a makeshift bar in the back of his pick-up truck in the parking lot." Andrew nodded back toward the door where Phillip also now stood, beer in hand. So, Phillip had managed to find a drink, too.

It seemed that Nora's friends from out along the bay (who knew she had so many "friends"?) were used to this kind of thing. The visitation evening was sure to be dry at the funeral home, so they brought along their own libations. It seemed to me like a supremely good idea for an event that seemed supremely asinine, in my view. But then, after my years of reporting from conflict zones, my personal opinion of what death means to us as humans seemed to be different from the way others saw it. It was a good thing that Andrew and I shared that experience. Of course, how we view cultural activities is all related to the culture from where we see it. I was just thinking that when Eliza materialized.

"Well, this is good," she said.

"Good?" I said. "How can this be good?"

Eliza stifled a snort, and I concluded that she, too, had succumbed to Phillip's little gift. "Just be grateful you're not Jewish," she said. Maddie looked up at her with a confused look on her face. Eliza continued. "Then we'd all be holed up sitting Shiva for seven days in Gran's house." Eliza laughed, and Maddie's eyes nearly popped out of her head. "Oh, by the way," Eliza said. "I know that Gran wanted something resembling an Irish wake after her funeral, so Iris has invited us all to her diner tomorrow evening to celebrate something called Tibb's Eve Tipples. She says it's a Newfoundland Christmas tradition for the day before Christmas Eve, and she thinks it will be the best way to celebrate Nora."

Sounded like a good idea to me.

~

The funeral was at The Basilica Cathedral of St. John the Baptist, a massive limestone and granite, two-towered structure that had graced its imposing location on Military Road in St. John's since the middle of the 1800s. I had attended mass there under duress on more occasions than I care to remember during those summer vacations with Gran when we weren't staying out in Topsail at the cottage. But it had been decades since I'd been inside. It hadn't changed at all. It was still a big Catholic church—something I hadn't been inside since the last Catholic wedding I'd been forced to endure. I was, after all, a recovering Catholic. As I took my seat in the front pew nearest the altar with the rest of the family, I wondered how Eliza was feeling (I still had my second gummy and was considering a little chew. Perhaps she'd been smart and had already eaten both of hers). After all, she'd had an even more dramatic split from her church of origin than I had. I had simply drifted away.

Once we were all settled in, the funeral mass began. I had often wondered if religious funeral rites had been developed for the sole purpose of making everyone present feel as morbid as possible. There was nothing in my experience that made me feel melancholy as much as the sombre strains of a pipe organ with a chorus of mournful singers belting out funeral music. The organ started, and then the soprano voice roared from the choir loft. I was so startled that I began to snort, resulting in the need for me to clap my hand over my mouth to stifle the laughter just bubbling under the surface. Mom looked turned and looked daggers at me. The voice *was* a bit of a shocking sound. I looked down at the program on my lap. The music was by Gabriel Fauré: "Pie Jesu" from his "Requiem," a piece of music written, no doubt, for a voice of a more refined nature than the one currently assailing our eardrums. I closed my eyes and remembered that Gran had chosen everything for her funeral, right down to the masses of white lilies adorning the altar, so there was little doubt about her intention with the music choice.

Father John, of Gran's birthday party fame, led the funeral mass. When it came time for his reading from the bible, he said Gran had chosen Matthew 5:1-12a. When he got to the part that said, "Rejoice and be glad, for your reward will be great in heaven…" I started to giggle.

Andrew, who was sitting on the other side of Maddie, who was next to me, looked over and frowned. Phillip, on my other side, dug me in the ribs, which nudged me to stifle the giggle. Then, he leaned over and whispered in my ear, "In heaven?" and we both snorted, a sound that I hoped might resemble grief to any onlookers. Then it was time for the eulogy and we both sobered up.

Mom looked small and all of her seventy-nine years as she climbed to the altar and took her place at the podium. Then, as if she had suddenly been filled with intention, she grasped the podium and began.

"You may not be familiar with the psychological phenomenon called 'childhood amnesia.' As a result of this peculiarity, it's not that we can't remember people, events, or places we experienced as very young children; rather, we begin to forget those early experiences at about age seven. Whenever I think about my early memories of my mother, Nora, they do seem to date from that age. I don't remember evening hugs and kisses or bedtime stories. And the truth is that my most vivid memories are probably not what other grown children reminisce about when they think about their mothers." I braced myself for what I expected to come. Phillip grabbed my arm and hung on.

"I have no memory of loud, happy dinner tables stuffed with friends and relatives. My mother was not the sort of mother to say, 'Why don't you ask your friend to stay for dinner?' Ever. Our house was well-ordered and well-run. Our house was quiet. Except when I was in a teenage flap, angry because there was one more thing that Mom likely did not wish me to do. My habit was to run upstairs, thudding heavily on the carpeted steps. The sound of that slamming bedroom door that followed was always caused by me—never my brother—as I ran into my room, trying to dislodge as large a piece of plaster as I could on the way. But I got over it quickly.

"No, my most vivid memory of Mom is captured in an old photo of her at a mid-winter Hawaiian-themed party she and Dad attended together at the yacht club. Mom is all smiles in her off-the-shoulder, flowery peasant blouse and flower lei. She is holding a drink in one hand and a cigarette in the other. Nails done—probably bright red if memory serves. The photo is in black and white.

"And I remember all those New Year's Eve's when she and Dad posed for photos before heading off to a New Year's Eve ball at the old Hotel Newfoundland, Mom in a succession of brocade or chiffon gowns. She never looked better—always smiling.

"Mom was a hard taskmaster. She and Dad were sticklers for good manners and elegant behaviour. Thank god for that. I can't tell you how many times in my life I've truly appreciated knowing precisely what fork to use.

"It seemed that over the years, I rarely did what Mom wanted me to do—and god knows she had lots of opinions on everything from the length of my hair to the length of my skirts. I suppose I didn't do much of what she wanted in those smaller ways, but I'd like to think that in the more significant matters—in matters that actually meant something—I did her proud. Mom's problem was that her life mantra was this: 'I might not always be right, but I'm never wrong.' And she lived her life that way, for better or for worse.

"Nora loved hats, ginger chocolates, Dean Martin, the Mills Brothers and my father as far as I knew. I remember her saying that she wished she was as sure of heaven—as she was of Dad. A bit strange when I think about it now, I must admit."

As I tried to picture Mom and Nora through the years, I winced at her description of Gran and Grandad. She continued.

"Nora loved her children in her way, although," Mom looked at Uncle Fred, "I do still think she loved you most." She smiled, glanced at her notes and continued. "I don't ever remember her telling me she loved me as a child, and god knows, we were never a family who hugged, but somehow I knew. I never doubted that I was loved. I just never really thought much about it.

"Mom did love her grandchildren and, much to my surprise, accepted each one of them for themselves while at the same time 'taking a dim view' of many of their choices." Mom looked at Phillip and Marcus. "She was able to get over herself, which is more than many of us ever accomplish." Mom stopped for a moment as if conjuring a memory. "I remember Mom's oatmeal chocolate cake, her lemon meringue pie and Jiggs Dinner. She made the best roast beef and Christmas mincemeat tarts.

"I could make her laugh and didn't put up with too much from her. I knew she liked it—even as she expressed disdain. Her best motherly advice to us? Stand up straight and hold in your stomach.

"Oh, and please don't say you're sorry we've lost Nora. She's not lost. We all know exactly where she is."

Mom stared into the silent crowd and stepped down.

THIRTY-EIGHT

Eliza

I FELT TEARS PRICK AT THE EDGES OF MY EYES as Aunt Maureen spoke. There was little doubt that Gran had been a difficult woman, and after Father John had painted her as the saint we all knew she wasn't, Aunt Maureen told it like it was, although I winced at her mention of Gran's love for Grandad. I just didn't buy it. Nora Houlihan had been a disagreeable woman in so many ways. And finally, relenting and accepting your gay grandson and his partner probably didn't make up for all the years she criticized all of us and reacted with disdain to most of our life decisions. Then I sighed, thinking about how some of my own choices might have benefited from someone verbally shaking some sense into me before I made them. At least considering Gran's life and legacy kept me from focusing on the hard church pew and the whole Catholic thing that I thought I'd left behind.

It was finally over. The family filed out of the church in a procession before the rest of the congregation was permitted to leave. When we walked out the door, it was right into a blast of cold wind that showered us with snowflakes and ice pellets. It was only mid-afternoon, but the sky was slate grey, and the snow was coming down as fast as the two young men who were wielding shovels could clear a path to the waiting vehicles. The cars were hired to take us to the cemetery where Gran's urn would be placed in an alcove. I hated that part of any funeral.

The cars slid and slipped as they made their way through the snow-deadened streets of the city. When we arrived at the top of the hill where the urn was to be placed, we were a much smaller group—the family and a few cars carrying people who I supposed were close acquaintances of Nora's. Melissa, of course, had also arrived, and I wondered what she was thinking about the whole production. Of course, we all knew she would have to be here if she wanted her inheritance, so it was hardly surprising. Whether we liked it or not, Nora was her grandmother, too.

As we stood there in the cold, I noticed a well-dressed man who looked to be in his early forties standing by himself. He didn't seem to know anyone or at least didn't seem to be interacting with anyone. He seemed familiar, though. It was out of character for me, but I thought I would go over after the short ceremony to see who he was. Then, when everything was over, he had gone.

We were finally finished with the aspects of the death and funeral festivities that were designed to make the survivors—if I can use that phrase—feel as depressed as they can possibly be. Erica and I commiserated on this subject as we stood together in the cold of the columbarium, staring at the hundreds of niches that had been created by leaving bricks out of the grey limestone wall. As we picked our way carefully over the snow-covered swath of cemetery in the middle of which stood the columbarium, I had a momentary thought about trying to get on a flight this evening. Then I remembered Iris. She and I were now partners and friends, and since she was hosting the party for Nora in combination with her Tibb's Eve celebration, which Phillip had suggested might be better called Tipsy Eve, I knew I couldn't leave.

As we left the cemetery for the hotel, the snow seemed to have stopped. I sat in the back seat of the car with Dad and Emma while Lucy and her family were in the car ahead. The rest of the family was dispersed among a line of big black cars with big black snow tires.

"The snow seems to have let up," Dad said as he gazed out the window at the piles of snow that had now been pushed to the sides of the streets by snowplows. "Reminds me of winters when I was a kid. You forget how things used to be, you know." He sounded wistful, and I wondered how the funeral had affected him, but I didn't quite know how to ask him, so I left him to his thoughts.

When we arrived back at the hotel, Dad told us he wasn't feeling very well and might not attend the party that evening.

"You know," he said. "I can babysit Mary-Catherine so you and Izzy can have a good time. I haven't quite gotten used to being a great-grandfather yet."

Izzy was ecstatic since she'd been in a quandary about taking Mary-Catherine or, worse, missing a party. She was really in need of a party, as far as I could tell. I told him I'd give Iris his regrets and went off to get ready for the party. As I stepped out of the shower, my phone pinged. I wrapped a towel around me and went to look at it.

"Looking forward to seeing you at the party." It was from Peter.

~

The party was in full swing when Erica, Izzy and I arrived at fifteen minutes after six. Phillip and Marcus were already there, as were Aunt Maureen and Gordie. In truth, there was only one person I wanted to see.

I headed toward the long neon-lit counter where Iris had several good-looking young men tending the bar. Izzy trailed along behind me.

"Hey, can I get you a drink?" the young man with the blonde hair and dancing blue eyes said to me while fixing his gaze on Izzy. He was wearing a plaid shirt that looked less islander and more ironic on him. He had a slight Newfoundland accent that seemed tempered with mainland.

He poured Izzy a glass of wine and was pouring gin into a cocktail shaker to make me a martini when I heard a voice in my ear. "Watch out for that one. His martinis are potent." I turned and couldn't help the smile that I could feel overtaking my face. It was Peter.

"I hope so," I said. "Funerals always make me thirsty."

Peter slid onto a red-vinyl-covered stool beside me and watched for a moment as the bartender chatted to Izzy, who looked happier than I'd seen her in years.

I turned to Peter. "That's my daughter. I'll introduce you to her when she can pull herself away from that adorable young man."

"I'll introduce you to my son Liam when he can pull himself away from that extraordinarily pretty young woman."

~

Peter wasn't drinking because he had to be at the hospital at midnight. We were sitting in a booth later—I sipped the martini Liam had made for me since the scotch selection was less than stellar, while he had a non-alcoholic beer—when I spotted the same young man I'd seen at the columbarium earlier. I still thought he looked familiar.

"Peter," I said, "do you happen to know who that young man is?"

Peter looked. "I don't exactly know him, but I know who he is." I poked Peter's arm so he'd continue. "His name is Tom Pittman. He's a violinist with the Newfoundland Symphony. There was an article about him in the news a few months back. It seems he won a national music award. He must have been a friend of your grandmother's or at least the son of one of her friends."

I stared at Tom Pittman. Where had I seen him before? I had to find out. I told Peter I'd be right back and went in search of Iris, who I found at the buffet table talking to Erica.

"Iris," I said, "do you happen to know anything about that young man over there?" Iris and Erica both looked in the direction I was pointing.

Iris screwed up her face, but Erica's face showed confusion. "He looks really familiar, Eliza," Erica said. "Where do we know him from?"

Iris took a deep breath. "That there's Thomas Pittman. Some kind of musician, I'm told." Iris seemed to be having a cagey moment. I'd gotten to know her well enough to know when she wasn't telling the whole story.

"I know his name," I said. "Peter already told me that much. But who is he?"

"Why do you want to know?" Iris said.

"Because he seems so familiar." I looked at Erica's face. It had gone completely white. "Erica, what's wrong?"

"I know who he is. I know him. Look at that face, Eliza. You've seen it before. You saw it in the photo last evening at the visitation."

I looked again, and I knew. "We were right, Erica. All those years ago, when we were just kids. We thought we knew the truth about Grandad, and now the truth is right in front of us."

Thomas Pittman was the spitting image of our grandfather, Thomas Houlihan. I didn't quite know how to proceed. Just then, Erica's phone pinged with a text. Then mine did.

"My flight's been cancelled for tomorrow," Erica said.

I looked at my text. My flight had also been cancelled. We both looked outside the window and realized that the snow must have started again with a vengeance since we'd been at the party. Aunt Maureen came over.

"The news says the airport's closed, girls."

Gordie was right behind her. "Guess we're about to have a Newfoundland Christmas whether we want to or not." He was beaming.

THIRTY-NINE

Erica

I WASN'T SURE WHAT I WAS MOST DISTRESSED ABOUT. It was either our cancelled flight without any idea of when we could get off the island or the fact that Eliza and I had been right all those years ago. And no one seemed to have done anything about it. We had been only near Maddie's age at the time—that summer we worked for Grandad, sweeping and dusting his shop.

As I stood there in the middle of a festive party, the day before Christmas Eve, with revellers singing and dancing around me, rum flowing, and Christmas lights twinkling from the huge Christmas tree Iris and her staff had set up in the window of the diner, my mind transported me to that summer. To that day. I could see it as if it were a movie playing right before my eyes.

We were supposed to be in the front of the shop, dusting the window display. But we were quickly bored by the tasks Grandad assigned to us and had decided to sneak into the back of the shop where Derrick, Grandad's tailor, was leaning over his sewing machine as he motored along seams. We were fascinated by the fact that he could fix things, make clothes fit the customers and even create custom jackets when asked to do so. The little office where he worked was just beyond Grandad's office door. As we tiptoed past, being as quiet as we could, we were both startled by voices. The door to the office wasn't completely closed, so we did what any curious teeny bopper might do. We peeked inside.

We couldn't see much. Valerie was standing with her back to the desk and Grandad was in front of her. Their heads were very close together.

Suddenly, Valerie put her arms around Grandad's neck, and they seemed to be kissing. Then she put her head beside his and looked directly at where we were, peeking into the office. Her eyes were cold and hard as if daring us to make our presence known. That was all we needed to see to send us scurrying back into the shop and out the glass door to the sidewalk, where we caught our breath and looked at one another.

"Erica! Did you see her eyes? She was looking right at me." Eliza was almost crying. "She's evil, Erica."

"We have to tell Gran, Eliza," I said. I was just as frightened as Eliza seemed to be, but I was thirteen years old to Eliza's eleven years and was expected to be the sensible one. At least in my eyes.

Eliza grabbed my arm. "No, Erica, no, no, no. We can't tell anyone."

I had seen Valerie's cold, hard stare, as well. And I also knew Valerie to be vindictive and vicious when she didn't get her way. She had often taken it out on us in small ways, like making us clean the bathroom with a toothbrush or picking lint from the floor of Derrick's office with our fingers. I couldn't even imagine what she'd do if we told. But I knew what they were doing was wrong, and someone had to know. I suppose even then, I wanted to get her back for how she'd treated us.

Eliza's fingers cut into my arm. "Erica, promise me you won't tell Gran. Promise me!"

I was abruptly brought back to the present moment when Eliza smacked my arm. "Erica! Oh my god, Erica. He has to be Grandad's son. Good lord. Just look at him. He's the spitting image of Grandad in his wedding photo. Valerie. It has to be Valerie. She must be his mother. Do you remember? Poor Gran."

It was the first time I'd ever heard Eliza refer to our grandmother with anything other than some level of disapproval. Anyway, I wasn't sure that Valerie could be fingered as the culprit since I had no idea if Grandad was in the habit of having flings even in his late sixties.

"You were right back then, Erica," Eliza said, continuing. "You were older and more sensible. You wanted to tell Gran or at least your mother about what we saw, but I was frightened. I should never have made you promise not to tell. I was frightened of Grandad, but I was even more frightened of Valerie. She was such a bitch. Then, when you broke your promise to me, I thought I could never trust you again. All those lost years when you and I could have been such good friends. How stupid I was."

"I never promised," I said quietly.

"What? What do you mean you never promised?"

"I never promised you I wouldn't tell anyone, Eliza."

"Promise me, Erica!"

Before I could say a word, Grandad's head appeared in the shop door, and he saw us cowering on the sidewalk out front.

"What are you two doing out here?" he said, his voice booming. His eyes looked more frightened than angry at that moment, but that soon changed. "Well, get on home with you, then. And don't be sneaking around in places where children aren't welcome!" Valerie must have told him we saw what they were doing. "Things aren't always what they seem."

Unless they are.

Eliza and I turned and fled. The next day, I told Eliza that I'd told my mother what we'd seen. She turned on her heel and didn't speak another word to me for the rest of our holiday.

Eliza stared at me. She seemed suddenly to have deflated. "Oh my god, Erica."

"Eliza, it's all in the past. We were both just kids, but you do need to know that if I had promised, I would have kept my promise. But now, we have a more imminent issue to deal with."

"Yes, of course. So, I know you told your mother. Do you think she told anyone else? Gran, maybe?"

"No, I'm sure she didn't tell anyone. She told me it wasn't really any of our business, but I knew it bothered her. But I wonder now if she knows about this Pittman guy."

"What should we do?" Eliza said.

That was the question at the top of my mind when I spotted Mom across the room laughing at something Gordie had just said to her—her eyes shining with affection for him.

Peter leaned over. "What's going on with you two?"

Peter seemed like a very sensible man with a good head on his shoulders. And there was little use in keeping any more secrets, so I suggested we find a quieter place to chat. Eliza knew that Iris had a small office in the back and suggested we go there.

When we got to the office, we closed the door and told Peter the story.

He whistled. "Wow. That's quite a revelation, especially after finding out about Melissa. Although, you don't really know for sure that he's your grandfather's son, do you? He could just be a relative with the family genes." We both looked at Peter as if he were daft.

"Now I wonder if Gran knew about this situation," I said.

Eliza shook her head. "How could she? Do you remember the date that Grandad died, Erica?"

I thought about it for a moment, doing some mental calculations. "You know, Eliza, I think he died about six months after that summer."

"So, he never knew he had a son."

Peter interjected. "You do realize that until this is all confirmed, it's all conjecture. There's no hard evidence."

Eliza looked at him. "Maybe you missed your calling. Maybe you should have been a lawyer like your father. Just look at him. There can be no doubt." Eliza stopped for a moment, then said, "What does that make him? A half-cousin or something?"

"Well, it certainly does make him *your* father and *my* mother's half-brother," I said.

"Good god," Eliza said, "the family just keeps getting bigger and bigger.

It was time to go in search of Mom. We had family matters—both big and small to discuss.

~

Peter looked at his watch and was shocked to see that he was going to be late for his midnight shift if he didn't get going.

"Driving is going to be slow, so I'm off. See you both tomorrow?" he said, staring at Eliza.

We said we would see him, although we had no idea where.

"You'll work it out," he said as he pulled on his toque. "Let me know."

We returned to the party to find Andrew and Maddie deep in conversation with Iris. At the same time, Phillip, Marcus and Emma (who had ditched Tobias at the end of the summer) were chatting with Peter's son and Izzy. In contrast, the party swirled around them as madly as the snowflakes in the streetlights outside the windows. Neither Mom nor Gordie was anywhere to be seen. I madly searched the crowd for any evidence of Thomas Pittman, but he seemed to have vanished.

I made my way through the crowd toward Andrew and Maddie, who seemed to be having a conversation about turkeys. When I asked Andrew if I could speak with him for a moment, he told me with great gusto that he and Maddie were arranging our Newfoundland Christmas.

"Do you have any idea where Mom and Gordie have gone? Have they left?" I said to Andrew.

"Gordie came over a few minutes ago to tell me he and your mom were going to go to your grandmother's house. I presumed it was so they could start to make some arrangements for Christmas Eve and Christmas Day. I doubt if any of us will be flying anywhere for a few days. Iris has an extra turkey here and told us she'd make sure there was enough food on our table for all of us. Maddie is trying to figure out how we're going to have a Christmas tree. So, just relax. Everything is going to be perfect." He kissed my forehead.

No, I thought, *not everything is perfect.*

Half an hour later, both Maddie and Izzy were yawning. Emma offered to walk back to the hotel with them. There would be no taxis in this weather, and it was only a ten-minute walk. Although the wind wasn't howling quite as much as it had been earlier, I was worried about them going on their own, so I said it was probably time for me to leave as well. The next thing I knew, we were all donning our winter gear and heading to the Hotel Newfoundland.

It took longer than the expected ten minutes as we tried to walk over and around mounds of snow that had built up along the streets. The sidewalks were so piled with snow that we had to walk in the middle of the road. It was a good thing there were no cars.

By the time we got back to the hotel, and everyone had said their goodnights, I looked at my phone to see that I'd missed a text from Mom.

"Erica, dear. Tomorrow is Christmas Eve. Could you all please come to the house in the morning and plan to stay overnight? Hope the day wasn't too difficult. Funerals can be draining. Mom."

I had almost forgotten we'd had Gran's funeral earlier. Maddie was already asleep on the pull-out couch in our room when I told Andrew about Mom's plans.

"Sounds like a plan, honey." He turned off the light. "We'll make the next few days great for Maddie. See you in the morning."

Indeed.

~

By the time we were ready to leave for Gran's house the following morning, the snow had stopped, but they were predicting what they called a wrap-around to hit around dinnertime that evening. So, there was still no hope for an airport opening any time soon. We were snowed in.

Mom came out of the living room holding a mug of steaming coffee when the rest of us arrived, bag and baggage. She directed us to various bedrooms to dump our overnight bags and told Izzy she could take Mary-Catherine and Maddie to the kitchen, where Gordie's housekeeper was baking cookies. She then asked the rest of us to join her and Uncle Fred in the living room, where she had coffee set out.

Andrew and I took our small bags to the guest room at the front of the house. I remembered it as the room where Mom and Dad slept whenever we visited. With its four-poster bed and antique dressers, it seemed little had changed. The drapes and duvet cover looked new, although their old-fashioned floral print was in keeping with the Victorian décor.

We walked back down the stairs and into the living room. Uncle Fred and Gordie were sitting in the two wingback chairs flanking the enormous fireplace where a fire crackled, and Melissa was sitting with Mom on one of the long sofas. Across from her on the other long sofa was a lone figure. I did a double-take. It was Thomas Pittman. I heard Eliza behind me catch her breath.

"Come in, everyone," Gordie said. "I suppose it's time for another family meeting." We all sat down, and Gordie began. "I suppose by now you're all wondering just what it is we islanders are up to, what with all the new family members popping up." He smiled at Melissa. "As your grandmother's solicitor, there have been certain things I have been bound to do and one of them was to keep her confidences." He looked at Mom. "There were even a few things I was bound not to tell Maureen and Frederick over there. And I hope they will find it in their hearts to forgive me, but I had a professional obligation." Then he turned to Thomas Pittman. "I would like to introduce you all to Mr. Thomas Pittman."

Thomas looked uncomfortable. "Please call me Tom."

"Tom, it is," Gordie said, smiling. "By now, I'm sure the more astute among you have figured out just by looking at Tom here that he's a Houlihan by blood. And if you have, you'd be correct, although even Tom didn't know this until recently."

I don't know why this startled me, but it did. I immediately began wondering about this Tom, who, by my calculations and his appearance, must have been about forty-three years old.

"My mother told me my father had died just before I was born and that he would have loved me very much," Tom said. "I never had a reason to doubt that. Then, last summer, the local paper ran a story about your grandmother just before her one hundredth birthday with a photo of her with your grandfather when they were young. I was looking at my face. Your grandfather and I were identical."

I couldn't argue with that. As Tom spoke, my eyes wandered to the family photos that were still on the fireplace mantel above the crackling flames. Yes, there was Grandad—and Tom's face.

"My mother worked in a dress shop for years but always seemed to have money for a nice house, a car and my university education. I'm a musician with the symphony orchestra. Anyway, Mom died a couple of years ago with money in the bank, and when I saw the picture in the paper, I was stunned, but I knew I wanted to talk to Nora. When I called, it was as if she'd been waiting for me for years."

When Tom went to see Gran, she told him that she'd always known that Tom was her husband's son. Valerie had come to see Nora when Grandad died and told her that she was about to give birth to Grandad's child. Nora made arrangements for Valerie to have a monthly stipend for the duration, and that never stopped. Compassion had never been one of my grandmother's strong suits, but this time, she showed it in spades. Now, it all fit together. No doubt, all she could think about was how she had been in Valerie's shoes so many years earlier. The difference was that she'd been forced to give up her child. She wanted Valerie to have a chance to know hers.

"Nora told me she'd known what her husband was like, but she always knew he'd return to her. And he did." Tom wiped at a tear that escaped his eye. "I didn't really have time to get to know her, and I know she wasn't my grandmother, but it felt like she was. My other grandparents were long dead, and I have never married, so she invited me over for tea every week, and I played my violin for her."

"And what I wasn't able to tell anyone until now—after Nora's death," Gordie said, "was that the money in her will for the symphony is actually for a specific member of the symphony—Tom. He didn't know anything about it until a couple of days ago. Nora instructed me to get in touch with him when she died."

Tom looked over at me. "So that's why you saw me yesterday lurking around. And I'm sorry if I upset anyone. It was the last thing I would have wanted to do."

I believed him.

"Well, I don't know about anyone else," Phillip, who had stayed uncharacteristically quiet for the duration, said, "but I need a drink." He checked his watch. "I'm sure it's after noon somewhere."

And so, it came to pass that we were an even bigger family celebrating Christmas on "The Rock."

FORTY

Eliza

THE NEWS ABOUT YET ANOTHER HOULIHAN CLAN MEMBER was almost more than I could take. After all, I was supposed to have emerged from a long line of devout Catholics, and here I was faced with the indisputable evidence that there may well have been hypocrisy coating the veneer. And now, here I was on the first day of Hanukkah, celebrating Christmas with the clan.

Maddie and Izzy had practically ransacked the house to find anything Christmas-related. I had no idea that Izzy was so interested in Christmas. When I asked her about this, she said, "You know, Mom, all those years when Astrid and her family celebrated Christmas, I used to go over to enjoy their Christmas tree. It was so different from Hanukkah. I really wanted to be a part of all the Christmas decorations and the presents and the food and the Christmas carols. But I didn't dare mention anything about it to you or Dad—and especially not Grandma Esther." I realized how little I really knew about my daughter—perhaps as little as she really knew about me.

Izzy and Maddie found an old artificial tree in the attic. It must have been there since the 1960s or '70s, as far as I could tell, because it spoke of the era. When they dragged the box containing it into the living room before dinner on Christmas Eve and started to pull it out in all its glittery, tinselly glory, Aunt Maureen burst into laughter.

She walked over to where it lay on the floor in a shambles of silvery, glittery sticks. "I remember laughing at Mom when she bought that tree," she said. "I came home for Christmas that year to find we no longer had a real Christmas tree. Instead, Mom had thought an aluminum tree would do the trick." Then Aunt Maureen showed the girls how to assemble it by poking the straight silver branches into the holes in the broomstick-like tree trunk. Then they stood back to look at it, and Aunt Maureen said, "Well, you have to admit it obviates the need for tinsel."

"Obviates?" Maddie said.

"Write that one down. New vocabulary, honey."

When they had finished, they put it next to the fireplace and rummaged through tatty cardboard boxes to find lights and ornaments. When they discovered two boxes of shiny blue ornaments, Aunt Maureen laughed once again and showed them how to put one on each of the branches. Then she rummaged a bit more.

"What're you looking for, Grandma?" Maddie said.

"Give me a minute," Aunt Maureen said.

"I think we need lights," Izzy said, her eyes twinkling with anticipation. That young Jewish mother there was really in love with Christmas.

"Here it is," Aunt Maureen said, pulling another tatty, yellowed and yet intact box from inside the larger one.

We all gathered around her to see what it was. The box said, "Harmony House Colortone Electric Roto-Wheel Complete with Bulb."

"What in the world is that?" I said, then I took a closer look at the picture on the box. It resembled a small desk-top rotary fan, except where you might expect the fan part to be was what looked like coloured filters—red, green, blue and orange. It was a rotating light that was intended to shine on an aluminum Christmas tree, changing colours as it turned. Before we knew it, Aunt Maureen had it plugged in and trained on the tree. The effect was almost mesmerizing. We all clapped as we saw the light change from red to blue to green, all the while reflecting off the dancing pieces of slivery aluminum that took the place of pine needles.

Just then, Erica walked in, holding a glass of eggnog. "Well, look at that. You know, girls, those are retro-chic these days and sell for something like $600. We did a piece on them a few years ago."

They found old strings of Christmas lights that they used to festoon the staircase and every nook and cranny. It was only when they were finished, and several strings did not light up, that Dad explained to them the drawbacks of the old lights. When one went out, they all went out. The problem was finding out which one had to be replaced. They decided that LEDs were, indeed, an improvement.

Christmas Eve dinner was courtesy of Iris and her diner. It was a good thing she had a four-wheel drive with massive tires, or we might have had to go hungry. There was precious little food in the house. It seemed that Gordie wasn't much of a cook, and Melissa hadn't yet taken possession and moved in, so we couldn't blame her.

Iris had told me that eating salted cod was their Christmas Eve tradition, so she'd made up multiple batches of fish and brewis—salt cod, hard tack bread and scrunchions, those tiny pieces of delicious fried pork fat that even a woman of my faith had a hard time resisting. She told me her version wasn't strictly kosher (yes, she actually said that to me, and I laughed) because she also put fried onions, savoury and a bit of mashed potato in it.

She also brought plates of cookies—ginger and molasses, shortbread, and those ubiquitous Newfoundland Purity Company jam-jams. These were the epitome of a manufactured cookie delight—small jam-filled cookies. If Gran had still been alive, she would have complained about the savage-mug-up nature of eating such dishes on a plate in one's lap, but she would probably have enjoyed it just the same. We certainly did. I tried to see if Emma was eating anything, but she was busy chatting with Phillip and Marcus and madly consulting her phone.

We had no Christmas presents, and I thought that might be an issue for the youngest among us. Still, when we made hot chocolate, brought out more cookies, and turned out all the lights so that we were lit only by Christmas lights and the fireplace, Maddie started singing "Silent Night." For a moment, I forgot that I didn't believe in the virgin birth. What did it matter, anyway? This, I believe, is what family is all about.

~

The sun didn't come up in this part of the world until almost eight am. When we finally all straggled into the kitchen for coffee, and something called toutons that Aunt Maureen was frying up from raw bread dough Iris had also brought the day before, the sun was peeking out from behind the fluffy clouds, and the snow had stopped. Christmas Day was upon us.

What was Christmas without presents—because there were none. I remembered that as children, we'd opened presents, then instead of taking time to enjoy our new toys, we'd been hurried into the kitchen for cereal, followed by hurried dressing so we could all pile into the car and go to Mass. I had always longed for the day when Mass would be a thing of the past. And now it was. So, instead of presents, we ate Aunt Maureen's delicious toutons with butter and molasses and a side of scrambled eggs and then took turns with the snow shovels and the snow blower so that the driveway would be clear enough for Peter and Liam when they arrived later. I felt a frisson of excitement when I thought about it.

They finally arrived later in the afternoon, and we all got ready for dinner. It was a sight to see. I took it upon myself to orchestrate our Christmas culinary masterpiece. With Erica and Izzy helping (I didn't even have a feminist moment to consider why it was the women in the kitchen. I knew why. We knew what we were doing), we bustled around with trays of steaming dishes. The stovetop was covered with pots that soon bubbled with savoury aromas—yes, lots of Newfoundland savoury for the dressing. All afternoon, the air was filled with the scent of roasting turkey, glazed ham, and all the trimmings that Iris supplied when she came by before lunch. She had more than enough for her family and ours, she said.

Finally, we delivered platters of golden roasted potatoes, buttery green beans, creamy mashed potatoes, and stuffing to the table. We served it up family style with all the food in the middle of Gran's long dining table that we'd dressed in her Christmas linens—the white Irish linen tablecloth with red poinsettias embroidered around the edges.

As I looked around at everyone enjoying their turkey, I remembered Christmas dinners past. Like the events earlier in the day, I remembered dinner as being somewhat rushed. We never had platters of food on the table. Mom thought that was déclassé, but I had no idea why. Instead, she served up the dinner for each of us. We were then required to wait until everyone's dinner had been served and she had sat down. Only then were we permitted to eat, at which time, inevitably, Mom would pronounce everything cold and tell us to eat up quickly so that it wouldn't get any colder. I sighed at the remembrance as this time around, we sat for several hours, eating, talking, and laughing, interrupted only when I enlisted Erica to help me bring in the dessert. It was Iris's steamed molasses raisin pudding with a generous ladle of butterscotch sauce for everyone. By the time we'd finished, it was a miracle anyone could get up from the table. But Aunt Maureen declared it was time for some Christmas music.

We moved, en masse, into the living room where Gran's old mahogany baby grand piano stood where it had stood for decades in the front window.

"May I?" Tom said shyly. "Piano was my first instrument, and I can play a little."

Of course, no one objected. He sat down and opened the top. I could see dust motes shimmering in the reflected light of the Christmas tree, but that didn't matter to Tom. He stretched his fingers and began with "Hark the Herald Angels Sing," and I'd never heard a version quite like it. I had expected Tom, a classical musician, to play it straight. But no, he added a bit of swing, and it turned into a magical jazz version. I can't remember ever tapping my foot to that particular melody! Then Aunt Maureen whispered into his ear, and he laughed before setting his fingers back on the keyboard.

Aunt Maureen took her place beside the piano and cleared her throat. Then she belted out the funniest version of "Grandma Got Run Over by a Reindeer" that I'd ever heard. Erica came over beside me and said, "Dear god. I haven't heard Mom sing that for decades."

I was surprised that the calm, restrained, erudite Dr. Maureen Flanagan had it in her. But then, I remembered I'd been so wrong about so many people for some time now. I was thinking about the three runes I'd been gifted with at L'Anse aux Meadows last summer. In fact, I had the three stones in my purse. I remembered looking at one of them that same morning. It was the one with the pointy "p" symbol. "Hope and partnership," the woman had told me it symbolized. "Harmonious action if you allow proper alignment." I thought about that for a moment and realized I might be getting to the point of allowing proper alignment. Harmony was sure to follow, right?

I leaned down to pick up my champagne glass, which was almost empty. Before I knew it, Peter had leaned over and was refilling it for me. As I watched the bubbles froth in my glass, I stood for a moment, my back to the fireplace feeling odd. Despite the warmth I'd been feeling just a moment ago, I had the sensation of someone blowing a cold breath on my neck. It certainly wasn't Peter. For the briefest second, I felt a ghost in the room. Again, I felt a tiny hiss of cold air on my neck.

Peter looked at my face and said, "What's wrong? You look like you've seen a ghost."

"Did you feel that draft?" I said. He shook his head, and I laughed, but it was more of an uneasy laugh. "Must be Gran's ghost," I said, clinking my glass on his.

Peter's eyes twinkled. "Maybe you're right. What do you suppose she'd think of us?"

"Us? By 'us' you mean you and me?" I said, puzzled by the conversation.

"Yes, us," he said.

"Well, I didn't know if there was an *us* for her to have an opinion about."

His eyes sparkled in the candlelight. He put his glass down and leaned to whisper in my ear. "Let's find out, shall we?" That sounded interesting. He continued. "I've always wanted to go to the Amazon."

"The Amazon? As in the river?"

He nodded, and I thought about that for a moment. Then he said, "Come with me."

And I heard the voice as clear as a bell in my head. "Just say yes." It sounded a lot like Gran.

…want to know what happens next for Eliza and Peter? Be sure to read the sequel *Meet Me in Miami*.

…and if you weren't up to date on how Erica got here in the first place, be sure to read the prequel *Good Housekeeping: My Unexpected Adventures in Domesticity.*

AUTHOR'S ACKNOWLEDGEMENTS

THIS BOOK WAS NOTHING SHORT OF A LABOUR OF LOVE. For almost four decades, I've been married to a Newfoundlander who left the island when he was seventeen years old to go to university and never moved back, returning over the years only to visit his parents. Last year, something magical happened.

My husband and I took a ten-day trip back to Newfoundland to do a cross-island tour, something he had never experienced. Being a city boy from St. John's on the east coast of the island, he had never travelled the Viking Trail or hiked in Gros Morne National Park on the Great Northern Peninsula. He had never been to see the Viking settlement at L'Anse aux Meadows or sailed a land-locked fjord. So, we landed in Deer Lake and met our guide with a fancy SUV, just as Erica, Eliza and the rest of the characters populating this book did.

That trip and my mother's one-hundredth birthday last year inspired this story.

Thanks first to Carl Hutton, our cross-island tour guide, who took us to the nooks and crannies of his Newfoundland, places we'd never have seen without a guide. He is also a storyteller in his own right, the author of the children's book *Muddy Makes Music: A Story About Newfoundland's Beautiful Ugly Stick* (Moonlight Press, Toronto). Many thanks to him for giving me permission to use his character, Muddy, the Beautiful Ugly Stick, in the musical collage that graces the section in this book called "Stop the World and Let Me Off." Can you find that beautiful ugly stick?

During our tour, I was captivated by so many things, and the food was one of those memorable things. I'd been exposed to some of it through my husband and his mother, my late mother-in-law, Marge Parsons, whose Orange Pudding recipe is one of the best desserts ever. But when Eliza emerged as a cookbook author, I knew

I would need help. I got that help in considerable measure from a Facebook group called *Newfoundland Dishes and Recipes*, whose members have been supportive and generous in sharing their tried and true Newfoundland recipes and have patiently answered all my questions as I did my research by cooking up a few Newfoundland scoffs.

My biggest thank you goes to Dr. Art Parsons, my husband, partner, media director, lover, friend, alpha reader, beta reader, editor and in-house Newfoundland consultant. I could not have written this book without his help, nor would I have even wanted to write it. I love you more than you will ever know. Thank you from the bottom of my heart. ~ *PJ*

ABOUT THE AUTHOR

PATRICIA J. PARSONS has written more than twenty books, including health and business books, a memoir, two historical novels, and women's fiction. Sometimes her writing is humorous; sometimes it's mysterious. She's an inveterate traveller who lives with her husband, a native Newfoundlander, in Toronto. They love to cook.

Connect with her on Instagram @patriciajparsons

Visit her website at www.patriciajparsons.com

SOME OTHER BOOKS BY PATRICIA J. PARSONS

The "almost-but-not-quite-true" stories

The Year I Made Twelve Dresses (Book 1)

Kat's Kosmic Blues (Book 2)

The Inscrutable Life of Frannie Phillips (Book 3)

Something I'm Supposed to Do (Book 4)

This is the Way the Story Ends (Book 5)

It All Begins With Goodbye (Book 6)

Good Housekeeping: My Unexpected Adventures in Domesticity

Plan B